DREAMING OF ABUNDANCE

THE ABUNDANCE SERIES
BOOK SIX

SHANNA SWENSON

Dreaming of Abundance
Shanna Swenson

Dreaming of Abundance is an original work of fiction. Names, characters, places, organizations and incidents either are the product of the author's imagination or are used fictitiously. Any resemblance to actual persons, living or dead, events, businesses, companies, or locales is entirely coincidental.

Copyright © 2021 by Shanna Swenson

Paperback ISBN: 978-1-955278-03-4

ALL RIGHTS RESERVED

No part of this book may be reproduced, distributed, or transmitted in any form or by any means, including photocopying, recording, information storage and retrieval systems or other electronic or mechanical means, without written permission from the author, except for the use of brief quotations in a book review.

Designations used by companies to distinguish their products are often claimed as trademarks. All brand names and product names used within this book are trade names, service marks, trademarks and registered trademarks of their respective owners. The publisher nor the book are associated with any products or vendors mentioned in this book. None of the companies referenced within have endorsed this book.

www.shannaswenson.com

Cover by: OliviaProDesign
Formatting by: Shanna Swenson

❀ Created with Vellum

DEDICATION

For Jamie,
For even dreams have an end

FOREWORD

The ideas for this book began shortly after I published book 5: *Legacy*.

I knew right away that Stella and Elias had more to tell the world, as well as Jax and Cassidy.

This book can be read as a standalone, but I would highly recommend reading *Abundance Legacy* first, if you haven't already, as it introduces you to the characters and their backstories. (Plus, this book continues where that one left off.)

What started innocently enough as the final *Abundance* book has now grown into a spin-off series, entitled *Kinsen Rodeo Company Cowboys*, with four books and more hot, alpha cowboys than your Kindle can yield, let me tell you.

Stay tuned after this book for a sneak peek at book one in my new cowboy romance series ;-)

PROLOGUE

*E*lias Kinsen took a deep breath and, mumbling aloud, practiced how to start the proposal speech he'd had in his head for weeks now.

"Hey gorgeous, you know how c-crazy I am about ya. How about we, uh..." He huffed. "No, stupid." He exhaled and tried again. "Stella, my shining star, you are my one, my only. I want you to have my name like you have my..." He groaned and buried his face in his hands.

He and Stella Rose Jenkins had been an exclusive couple for over three years. She was still fairly young, hovering at twenty-two years old, but Eli, at twenty-seven years old, had irrevocably selected the woman he wanted to spend his life with. His heart had chosen long ago, beneath the aftermath of a shooting star one amazing Texas night. Today, he was finally going to take the plunge and ask that star to be his wife.

These last few years had been all he'd dreamt they could be, following the embarrassing jilting his cousin had dealt Stella at Jared's party that night. Jax and Stella's abrupt "breakup" had turned in Eli's favor; Stella's humiliation had become Elias's victory. He'd

1

become her heroic knight in shining armor and taken her home, not leaving before letting her know his own feelings on the matter.

Sure, as a rodeo champion, he'd had his fair share of girls over the years, but he'd never been star-struck until Stella. Something about the budding young actress shone as bright as a star in the night sky, the true meaning of her namesake. Be it that sexy blonde hair, a combination of corn silk and flaxen, her erotic hazel eyes–green with equal blasts of gray and amber–full lips that begged to be kissed, and a personality as fun and unpredictable as a meteor shower.

Stella had been crushing hard on Jax Kinsen that night, Eli's younger cousin, and she'd finally gotten her chance to date him when he and longtime girlfriend, Cassidy Boyd temporarily broke it off following a heavy argument. Problem was, Jax had always only had eyes for Cass, and Eli knew in his heart it would've only been a matter of time before Stella was dumped like a hot potato so Jax could have his girl back in his arms. Hell, they'd only been broken up for a month or two before Jax had taken chase and won his child-hood love over again. One of the shortest breakups Eli had ever heard of. Stella hadn't stood a chance from the get-go, but that hadn't erased the pain and embarrassment she'd experienced that night when Jax had gone after a fuming Cassidy–he'd not expected to see her at the party–and left poor Stella among the wolves. As a chivalrous gesture, Eli had moved in to rescue her–and had succeeded in sweeping her right off her feet.

They'd been together ever since.

Stella and Eli currently resided in an apartment in Austin where Stella's acting career had taken flight. Eli had been modeling as well, but, aside from commercials, he didn't particularly see his life heading into stardom–unlike his girlfriend, who'd literally been born into the spotlight. Heck, with a name like Stella, she was virtu-ally written in the stars. Being the only daughter of a starlet like Vivian Alexander and retired pro-football player Buck Jenkins, she'd been destined for stardom from day one. Stella had basked in that

2

stardom, with roles alongside big movie stars, numerous block-busters, even a Golden Globe nominee. She was shining; the world was truly her stage.

Eli calmed his fretting thoughts by raising the bouquet of calla lilies and inhaling their fragrant scent. He smiled, recalling how much he and Stella adored one another. He knew it didn't matter how he started his proposal speech. The right words would come, as they were meant to. Conversing with his soulmate, his best friend, had always been seamless—effortless. They could talk about anything and everything, nothing, and it was the most amazing thing.

He approached their apartment door from the elevator, then unlocked and opened it. He easily assumed Stella was still out, as she'd told him she wouldn't be in until later, and began prepping the flowers for a vase. He trimmed the stems, filled a vase with water, and arranged the lilies. He then set it on the coffee table and looked in the hall mirror, checking his appearance. He wanted everything to be perfect. He couldn't believe he was nervous about this. She would say yes to marrying him, wouldn't she? She loved him just as much as he loved her, and wanted the same things he did, right?

He turned as he heard the door open, unable to see who was entering, but stilled his nerves by fiddling with the box in his jeans pocket. He didn't want to come off awkward.

Stella's sweet voice sounded frantic, and he immediately held his breath, wondering why on earth she could be so upset. *It better not be that asshole of a director giving her shit again*, he thought. He was gonna have to put his foot down where the old coot was concerned.

Elias then heard Tony's high-pitched tone and rolled his eyes in frustration. Dammit, Tony was always here when he needed Stella to himself. Talk about a *downpour* on the parade today, though.

He moved into the hallway as they came around the other side so he could hear their conversation without either of them seeing him, hoping Tony would leave soon so he could have some privacy with his girl.

"God, what am I gonna do?" Stella whined.

3

"Oh, don't worry, Stell Bell. It's still early. We have plenty of time."

"Well, what about the bikini scenes? I'll be all ballooned out by then."

Eli wrinkled his nose in confusion. What the hell was she talking about?

"I don't know how you personally feel about it..." Eli heard the couch sink in as Tony plopped down, "but you could go to Plan B."

"Plan B? Don't you think it's a little late for that?"

Plan B? What was Plan B?

"A-*bor*-tion," Tony stated in a sing-song voice. Elias felt his stomach drop to the floor.

"What? *No*, I couldn't possibly," Stella croaked in protest.

Tony's snort was derisive. "Girl, do you know what a baby is gonna do to that tight little figure of yours?"

Baby? Eli's heart soared on euphoric wings as he envisioned a gorgeous Stella, belly round with pregnancy. *Holy shit!* Stella was pregnant! With Eli's child!

Just as joy blossomed, he heard Stella sigh. "Yeah, you're right."

With a vicious impact, Eli's life flashed before him, sending him into a freefall. Visions of his time with Stella, their love-making and laughs, their joy and heartache...only for crushing pain to consume him. Stella wanted to terminate her pregnancy? Abort their baby? The baby they'd made. In love. Together? God, no... *Why?*

His head reeled, and he felt as if he might puke up his guts. He had to get out of there. Couldn't hear another word of this unspeakable horror. The sickening betrayal. That the woman he loved with all his soul, the woman he wanted to spend his life with, have children with...the one he had been prepared to propose to in coming moments didn't want his child. She wanted to keep this amazing blessing a secret, extinguishing the life they'd created together...without even bothering to give him a choice on the matter? How could she be so cruel, so conniving. No, not Stella...not the woman he adored... Withholding the knowledge, lying to him, and to what end?

Fame! Of course. That's all that mattered to her. All that had *ever* mattered to her, apparently. Elias. His love. His hopes for their future didn't matter. Had never mattered. His dreams, his wants, his plans weren't hers.

The sudden realization broke his heart into a million pieces. All this time he'd been living someone else's life, a life not his own. A life he wasn't meant for. Now he knew he'd only been playing a temporary part in the tragic play of a Hollywood starlet.

Had anything in their relationship ever been important? Had *he* ever been important? Had she ever even loved him at all?

Part of him wanted to interrupt the two co-conspirators, show her he'd overheard everything. Part of him wanted to fight for the unborn child she wanted so badly to dispose of, but his entire being had gone numb. He'd always dismissed the small insecurities that came from dating someone of celebrity status, always fearing he might never be good enough.

Now he had his answer. He hadn't been enough–and neither was their child.

He stumbled down the hallway, despair threatening to pull him under. Tears stung his eyes and his ears began to ring. Any second he might fade to black. The overwhelming pang of regret, sadness, and failure suffocated him. He'd loved Stella Rose Jenkins as fully as he'd ever loved anyone, anything. He'd given up so much for her, to be with her. Now, to have it all thrown back in his face was destroying him.

He wasn't aware of how he got down to his truck. With shaky hands, he pulled the door handle and got in, taking deep breaths to keep from passing out.

Part of him considered he might be wrong, wanting to defend her as he always had, but he knew–he *feared* with everything inside of him–she would go through with it. Stella had always listened to Tony and would do whatever he said, if it meant furthering her career. It didn't matter that the child was also Eli's, that he should have some say in its potential lifespan.

Eli covered his face with his hands and rocked, afraid he might be dying. His soul felt like it was being ripped from his body. He couldn't go back in there, couldn't face her knowing what she planned to do to her body, to his baby...behind his back, without even having the decency to discuss it with him first.

His phone rang from his back pocket, and he robotically pulled it to his ear and pressed the accept button.

"Hey, my beautiful cowboy!" Stella's sweet voice called to him, as if she wasn't hiding a nefarious plot behind his back. His heart burst into a thousand shards. "Where are you? I thought you were coming home for dinner?"

Eli gulped, trying to form words, but none came.

"Oh! Did you bring me these lilies? They're stunning."

He closed his eyes and felt a tear run down his cheek.

"I-I, uh...h-had them delivered," he finally croaked out.

"Thank you, baby. I love them. Are you coming home soon?"

He gulped again, trying to swallow the lump stuck in his throat.

"Elias! Are you ok? Is something wrong? You sound like you're getting sick. Are...are you crying?"

He couldn't say her name, couldn't think straight, couldn't get past the ache of her deception. "I-I'm stuck in Laredo," he lied. "Sorry, I couldn't get away. I..." he trailed off, hating that he was lying. He was sitting outside their condo, but he might as well have been in Egypt as far away as his spirit felt from his body.

"But you said—"

"I know. I'm sorry I— I have to go now. I'll... I'll talk to you later."

"Eli, are you ok? What's wrong, baby? Talk to me, please?" The sorrow in her voice had tears running down his face. He'd never felt pain this agonizing before. Never felt his heart so torn open. She was killing him. Literally killing him.

"We'll talk later, Stella. I— I have to go now."

The silence was shattering as he ended the call and looked at the home screen of his phone. A picture of the two of them, happy, in love...in a BS fairytale world that no longer existed now that darkness, thick as molasses, covered it.

He dropped the phone to the seat and peeled out, heading anywhere–and nowhere–at the same time.

CHAPTER 1

Five days. It had been five whole agonizing days since Stella had seen Eli.

So when the doorbell rang and she opened it to see him standing at their entryway, she immediately threw herself into his arms.

"Oh, Elias. It's felt like an eternity." She leaned up to kiss his scruffy jaw, noting that his arms didn't come around her in exuberance like they normally did every time they saw one another. She tensed and looked into his eyes. "What is it? What's wrong?"

She'd never seen his green eyes so hard, his handsome face so tight.

"We need to talk, Stella."

She gulped. Those words promised impending doom, even if she had no idea what they would "need" to talk about–aside from his obvious avoidance of her.

She'd been calling him, leaving voicemails, text messages, wondering what the hell was happening. If he'd been kidnapped, or jumped off the side of a cliff, or had suddenly fallen out of love with her.

He'd gone to Laredo to film a commercial but had been expected

9

home days ago. Yet he'd given her no clear explanation for his absence. He'd claimed he'd gotten "stuck" there and hadn't really said why. When asked, he'd said he "had to go" or "couldn't talk." Well, now it looked like she was about to find out why.

What could have happened in that small span of time that would alter their amazing relationship so much? They adored each other, had mind-blowing sex, shared everything. They were best friends, lovers, and dreamers. They had big plans for the future. After three years together, Stella had anticipated an engagement at any moment, not the lifeless fingers that she attempted to pull into her own.

Oh, no! Could it be that– Had he met someone?

She recoiled from his indifference but stepped back to let him in, even as her heart threatened to burst with alarm.

He brushed past her, and the delicious smell of his masculine cologne burned her nostrils–both a nostalgic delight and a painful realization all at once.

She'd missed him like crazy, wanted to hold him, kiss his lips, touch his sexy, muscular body. She wanted to feel him against her, inside her. She wanted to share the joy that they were pregnant and tell him she couldn't wait to see their baby in his capable arms.

She looked him over. Aside from dark circles under his eyes, he looked exactly like the same man she'd originally fallen in love with. Tall, broad...clad in his Wranglers, wearing a blue checkered button-down and a tan Stetson. It'd been too long since she'd seen him in his cowboy hat, bringing back a dozen fun, sweet, and steamy memories.

"I stopped by earlier, but... Tony said you'd gone to the–the clinic," his voice was as grave as she'd ever heard it. Again, she wondered what had caused the 360 in him.

She nodded and lowered her head, hating that he'd chosen to sit across from her instead of next to her. Had he cheated? Did he no longer love her? Had he found out that she was pregnant and didn't want to be with her anymore? Was he simply not ready to be a father?

"Dammit, Stella, you could have talked to me about it first!" Elias slammed his fist down onto the couch arm. She looked up, shocked by his angry tone.

She knew she was gaping but couldn't close her mouth as he continued. "I can't *believe* you would actually go through with it! I can't understand how you could do this...to me, to *us*."

What the hell was he talking about?

"And don't you dare even attempt to deny it." He pointed a finger at her, his eyes burning into hers, as if she were one of the women accused of witchcraft in Salem all those years ago. "I overheard your conversation with Tony last week. I was here. I know what you said."

She looked at him as if he'd lost his mind. He'd been *there*? In their apartment? He'd heard the discussion between herself and Tony? But why hadn't he–?

Then it hit her like a ton of bricks. He thought she'd gotten an abortion. He didn't know.

"Elias." Her tone softened, and she stood.

"Don't say my name. Don't ever say my name again." He stood too and moved closer, towering over her. The disgust on his face was palpable. "I can't believe I actually thought that you would change. You're the most selfish person I've ever known, Stella Rose Jenkins."

Stella flinched, as if he'd slapped her. He pressed on, slowly backing her into the island that separated their living space from the kitchen, his finger in her face.

"I've never loved *anything* as much as I loved you. I put you on a pedestal so high that I thought nothing, no one, could ever compare. I wanted you with a hunger that I'd never felt. I've given up *everything* to be with you... But it's all been one-sided."

Stella was speechless, shaking her head as tears began to run down her face in streams of blinding pain. She couldn't believe the words coming from the love of her life's lips.

"I see it now. It's so clear... You can't love anyone aside from yourself. I was too blinded before. I thought..." His deep voice quaked, the hurt so evident in his tone. "God, I was so stupid to think..." Elias turned, hands coming up to cover his face. Was he crying?

Just as Stella's hand came up to comfort him, he turned on her again. A mighty growl ripped from his throat, frightening her. She gasped when he said, "Don't touch me!"

"Eli, please. I–"

"No, you've done enough talking. You're gonna listen for a change, *little star*." Her nickname had never sounded so vile before, never so full of venom. "I've given you everything, Stella. *Everything*! All of me! All I have or was... And you can't even bother to give me the decency of..." Tears fell then, distorting his beautiful face. "I would have done *anything* for you."

She cried too, reaching out and begging him to give her a chance to explain.

"But God forbid you have to 'alter' your body with the life that we created together. Is the love we shared not worth a few stretch marks? Not worth more than your stunning appearance? You have it all: money, clothes, gadgets, trinkets, houses, cars, fame, fortune... Hell, far more than a person could want in one lifetime. You have enough for a dozen. And yet you couldn't even give me this *one* tiny thing, could you? How can you be so self-absorbed?"

His words ripped her heart in two, and she sobbed. "Eli, no, I–"

"No, you couldn't! Because you don't care! Not about me. Not about our baby. You just discarded it, my gift to you, as if it's merely another worldly possession. Nothing ranks higher than your stupid trophies or what you have to do to get them." He motioned to the shelves housing the film awards she'd earned over the years. "And that's the problem here. *Nothing* will ever be enough for you because shooting for the stars is always going to come first. Over me, over our baby. You're always going to put yourself first. To hell with anything or anyone in your way.

"Well, Stella, my love is no longer yours to toy with and sabotage wherever you see fit. You destroyed it when you made it clear what I–and our baby–meant to you."

Stella was dumbfounded as he backed up, fists clenched at his side. He adjusted his Stetson and looked her over one last time. In disgust or regret, she couldn't tell.

As he turned on his booted heel and headed into the hallway, Stella's weak legs followed. A panic attack was coming on. Her entire body quaked with mourning. Her chest burned like a hot poker had pierced her heart. Her world was being sucked away, all she loved was being pulled from her very being as Eli walked out of her life.

"Eli, please," she croaked out and grabbed for his shirt, her fingers gripping him even as he shrugged her off. "No! I didn't–"

"You can have one of your many assistants pack up my things. Just have them sent to my parents. Don't try to contact me."

With that, he was gone...and with him, her soul. She fell to the floor and sobbed.

CHAPTER 2

SIX MONTHS LATER

*B*uck Jenkins looked across the dinner table at his only daughter's pale face. His jaw ticked and his patience waned. When she began toying with the meatball on her plate, her typical aversion to eating, he slammed his knife down onto the table, causing the entire oak piece to shake.

Stella and Vivian gasped in response.

"How much longer is this gonna go on?" he asked because he simply couldn't abide her gloominess any longer. He had to say something or die.

"Buck!" Viv snapped.

"No, I can't continue to sit here and walk on eggshells about this anymore. Stella, princess, you look awful."

Stella's hazel eyes bore into his, then she gulped and looked down at her plate.

"Buck!" Vivian hissed and frowned over at him.

His gorgeous wife of over two decades was just as stunning as ever, her regal gown flowing as she bounded up from her chair beside him and moved to embrace their child.

"He didn't mean it, baby."

"Dammit, yes I did, Viv!"

Both sets of eyes held his, one pair filled with scorn, the other with reproach.

"Stella, baby girl, I love you more than life itself, but you got to cheer up. If you don't, this baby's gonna be born with a list of ailments as long as my injury list."

"Bobby Joe Jenkins, if you—"

"Viv, I gotta say my piece, darlin'." His brows rose defiantly at his wife.

Her blonde head angled, warning him, but when had Buck Jenkins ever heeded a warning? His old warrior mentality was aimed on battle. He couldn't help it. Matters weren't helped by the fact that no one in the entire Kinsen family had seen nor heard from Elias in six months while his daughter wasted away from his absence—and unsolicited words.

"If I ever see that bastard again, so help me God, I'll…"

"Buck," Viv warned again. Buck stood and walked over to where his only child sat, tears running down her face.

"Stella. You have to eat and take care of yourself…and go on living."

Big doe eyes tore into his heart as she looked up at him. God, how could the pain be so intense? Why did it seem to hurt more when his daughter was hurting than himself?

"The things he said were unforgivable, my sweet little star, but—"

"But he was right, Daddy."

Buck frowned in response and squatted beside Stella.

"Everything he said was spot on."

"Stella, surely you don't mean—" Vivian interceded.

"No, Momma, Elias was right. About it all! I *was* selfish. I think I even warned him in the beginning… I put everything before our relationship: my stardom, my career, everything. But I would never have chosen *not* to have his baby. I love him so much."

Sobs racked her small frame, and Buck pulled her into his arms.

15

He cradled her blonde head to his chest and soothed her for the thousandth time.

His hate for Elias Kinsen grew by the day, it would seem. Where was the asshole? Why had he left without giving Stella a chance to talk? Why was he being such a class A jerk? As a father, all Buck wanted was to taste the blood of his enemy, but as a man of sound mind and body, he simply wanted answers. Answers to why his daughter's life had been so forcefully uprooted, answers to why Eli had up and jilted her out of nowhere.

Vivian Alexander Jenkins gazed at her husband with tears of understanding. He took her hand while continuing to comfort their child.

They, too, had once been split up by her demanding career–and a surprise pregnancy, to boot–but it hadn't taken Buck long to realize what he was losing. He'd run after her and *demanded* she take him back. It had only been weeks, not months.

If Elias loved Stella a fraction of how Buck loved Vivian, then how could Eli go on living without his heart? Buck had his own thoughts on the matter but knew neither his wife nor his daughter would want to hear them, so he didn't voice them aloud.

He only sighed and kissed Stella's hot forehead, cupped her cheeks, and swiped at her tears.

"Stella, I promise you that life will go on. Sweetheart, I know right now it feels like it won't. One day, you will be tough enough to face it again, and when you do, you'll be even better for it. But right now, you have to keep your strength for that grandbaby of mine, you hear?"

Stella's beautiful eyes held his, and he gave her a weak grin.

"I'm sorry, Daddy."

"There's nothing for you to be sorry for. I just want what's best for my daughter and grandson, that's all."

His gaze fell to Stella's growing baby bump, and he placed his big palm against the distended mound.

"I just hate that Eli's missing out on all this," Stella said and actually smiled when Buck felt a little toe kick him, as if answering their comments.

Buck laughed then grew serious, brows drawn. "He is. And he has no idea. But that's his cross to bear, little star, not yours."

As angry as Buck was with Elias, he knew some of that animosity was geared at the fact that Elias *was* missing so much. Buck had been hurt too in the past, and understood why Eli would seek solitude after believing Stella had terminated her pregnancy and thrown his love back in his face. She'd done neither of those things, though, and Buck ached for her–for them both.

As a loving father, he hated that their story had taken such an ugly twist, but it wasn't over yet. Not in Buck Jenkins book–not until his baby girl got some sense of closure.

He had Jack Kinsen searching high and low for his nephew's whereabouts. So far, he could be lost to the Bermuda triangle for all the digging that they'd done. Money didn't account for much when someone had appeared to drop off the planet. Although, if Buck knew Eli, he knew he'd be flying under the radar at all costs. Hopefully, he hadn't gone so far as to change his damn name or move overseas.

"Stella, honey, let's eat, alright?" Viv coaxed. Worry etched across her face as Stella's face crumpled once more. Vivian dried Stella's tears, wiping her own cheeks in the process, and assisted Stella back to her seat at the table.

It took a few moments for Stella to gather herself, but she nodded encouragingly at her mother. She took her fork and sliced into her meatball.

Once everyone had calmed down and Buck took his seat again, he gave his wife a reassuring grin. God, how much he loved this woman. She'd stolen his heart years ago on a ballroom floor in Dallas. He could still see her gorgeous frame clad in that sexy dress, the tango they'd danced to together, how much he needed to feel her pressed against him while also impressing their onlookers. She grinned back, seeming to know where his thoughts were.

Buck then tried to put his personal feelings aside and ponder Eli's state of mind. If he'd believed Viv had aborted his child and didn't love him as much as he loved her, where would he be and what would he be doing?

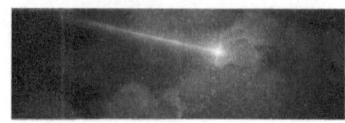

"HEY. YOU OK?" Jax Kinsen asked as Stella moved into the cab of his truck later that night.

She'd met him in the back pasture of his property. The same spot where they'd once made out and she'd bled all over him. That humiliating incident felt like eons ago; she'd been a different person then than she was now.

"I'm hanging in there." Stella brushed one hand through her hair, resting the other on her growing belly.

"Not far to go now." Jackson smiled down at her pregnant belly. "Have you thought of a name for him?"

Stella nodded. She hadn't told anyone, but she'd tell Jax anything. He was the closest friend she had right now, aside from Savannah, who listened when Stella needed to vent, even if she was engrossed in her paintings as she did so. Cassidy was busy at her new nursing job. She and Stella talked when they could, but it wasn't the same with her being so far away, working nights, and unable to answer when Stella called to chat.

When Jax's brow rose in question, she answered, "Tobias."

Jax gulped but smiled, albeit a weak one.

She knew the name was very similar to Elias, didn't need anyone telling her just how similar it was or reprimanding her as to the implications of her practically naming her baby after his estranged father, because she didn't care. It was her choice, as the child's mother and former lover of said estranged father. She needed this.

"Tobias Edward Kinsen." Edward was Elias's middle name. It also happened to be the middle name of his uncle Jack who, in turn, had been named after his father, Edward–the original patriarch of the Kinsen legacy.

Jax sat quietly for a long time before responding with, "It's a good solid name, Stella."

She nodded and stared out the open truck window, listening as the sounds of the spring night held her captive. It was April. Her baby would be born next month, a Taurus, like her Elias and his uncle Jack. A protector. A bull. With a heart of gold.

"Have you– have you heard anything?" she asked cautiously. She always hoped for the best, but anticipated the worst, knowing her heart would bleed out when he let her down once again. It had been six months of no news. Why would tonight be any different?

But as Jax hesitantly nodded, hope began to make Stella's heart hammer in her chest. She took Jax's hand, pleading, "Please? Tell me. Good or bad, I have to know."

"He's in Mexico," he answered and waited for a response. She said nothing as her gaze held his emerald green eyes, awaiting news of the man she loved more than her own self, the man who favored the one seated beside her, so much so that it physically hurt to look at him. "He's been performing in *charreadas* and rodeos south of the border."

So he'd gone back to his cowboy roots; go figure. She could only nod, her head spinning. If there was more, she wanted to know. She nudged him on.

"Looks like he's traveling with the IRCA, the International Rodeo Cowboys Association, with Lovington Rodeo Company. They'll be heading into Texas by August. Their competition starts in June."

Her mouth opened in excited surprise. "That gives me time."

"Time to *what?*" Jax frowned.

"Time to get my shit together."

Jax tilted his head. "What are you talking about?"

"I'm going to win him back."

Jax scoffed. "And the fact that he abandoned you, without even

19

giving you a chance to get a word in edgewise while he handed you your ass, makes no never mind?"

"He was hurt, Jax." She sighed. "He deserves to know the truth. You know Elias. I have to get on his level, play the game."

Jackson looked at her as if she had lost her mind. Maybe she had, but she hadn't spent the last six months with a bleeding heart not to learn from her mistakes.

"Stella…" Jax's tone softened, as if he were trying to negotiate with a hostage taker. "What is it you think you're gonna do?

"I'm going to compete."

Jackson snorted. "*Compete?* You can't even ride a horse right now, let alone qualify for a rodeo about to give birth!"

"Right now I can't. But come late June, early July, I could be ready."

"Ready to do what, exactly?" Jax was as beautiful as Elias was when she stumped him with her tenacity. "You don't mean to–to actually *compete* in a rodeo, do ya?"

She laughed, for the first time in a long time, and rubbed at her baby boy, Toby. She smirked at Jax and tapped his nose.

"I may not be a rodeo cowgirl, *yet*, but put me in a dress and tiara and I can be the next best thing."

CHAPTER 3

FOUR MONTHS LATER

*E*lias rose with the rooster crowing to him that morning and the faint beam of sunlight piercing the small Streamline's dusty window.

He'd dreamt of her again. Of Stella...and Abundance. It was all he did lately. As if he were being haunted by a ghost. A ghost of a past his heart simply couldn't let go of.

HER USUAL SIGH *of contentment as he entered her never failed to steal his breath.*

"Oh God, Stella," Eli groaned as he filled her completely. "You always take me in so easily, my little star."

"That's because my body loves you as much as my heart does." She kissed his shoulder as he withdrew and pulled his chest from hers, just enough so he could look into her unique hazel-gray eyes.

"Have I told you how gorgeous you are, Stell Bell?" he asked.

She gave him a smile then moaned as he thrust deep.

They lost themselves to one another's touches, the connection of their bodies, so tightly entangled one couldn't distinguish her from him. Their

21

lips met, tongues tangled, pleasure accelerating as their need to please and be pleased superseded all else.

"Shit baby, I'm gonna–" He didn't finish as he was rendered helpless in her intimate embrace, his climax hitting him violently as his hips pistoned in and out of her. He unburdened himself as he shot his seed within her clenching walls, her cries echoing in his ears.

"Eli... Yes, baby, yes," she whimpered. He kissed her as he continued to rock into her until they were both spent.

He shivered as her womanhood squeezed the last ounces from his deflating cock, and he grinned down at her. "God, I love you, Stella Rose. You know how much, right?"

She nodded, the ribbons of blonde curls framing her perfect face and making her appear angelic in the moonlight that marked her naked skin. "More than all the stars in the sky?"

"Even more." He kissed her again, his passions returning as he stayed inside her. It never failed to fascinate him how his cock never wanted to part from her enticing silken channel.

"Again?" she teased, knowing one time was never enough for him.

He laughed, getting one out of her.

"I'll have to oblige you won't I, sir?" she stated in a British accent, tapping into her artistic talents.

"Yes, m'lady. You know your cowboy is never satisfied. See what you do to him?"

"Mmm... Why, yes I do." She moved, pulling him from within her and taking him in her small fist.

"Stella... Mmmm," he groaned in equal parts torture and desire, watching her love his flesh with a skilled hand. His eyes moved to hers, reflecting his love.

She worked him until he was begging to be inside her again. When she guided him back within, it was she who held the reins this time. She flipped them over and moved atop him, pulling him into a haven of bliss, where she was the seductress and he was at her mercy. He kneaded her perfect breasts before his palms gripped her bottom while she rode him.

Soon, he was catapulted over a wall of ecstasy where nothing and no one existed but the two of them. Elias and his sweet little star.

THE MEMORY SEEMED SO LONG AGO, in a past far far away. On another planet even. It didn't exist. Not anymore and hadn't for a year now.

Elias had let Stella go in his mind, but his heart hadn't been as quick to follow.

When he'd left her, heart broken and head reeling, rodeo seemed the best place to lose himself. It was where he'd felt most at home, in the life of circuits, competition, and calf-roping. He'd been so good at it in his younger years and didn't realize how much he'd missed it until he was back in the literal saddle again.

Following multiple failed attempts, he aced it once more. Now, he was quickly rising in the rankings of the IRCA and was earning a steady living as a championship calf-roper. He was also the header of a team now too. Luckily enough, his buddy from high school, Gabriel Halloran, had joined in on the fun.

Eli groaned and sat up, head throbbing from the hangover he'd brought on himself following their celebration last night. They'd arrived late to El Paso and began carousing with some of the barrel racers–drinking, of course, as per usual. Next thing he knew, he was blasted and falling into bed with the striking brunette now laying naked next to him.

He glanced at her curvy feminine form beneath the covers, indifferent to her even if his cock wasn't quite on board. His heart yearned for the love he'd left a year ago.

He'd taken many women to bed since Stella, but none had filled the gaping void within–and possibly never would. He'd known almost right away that he'd had the one and only love he'd been gifted. Now, it would seem, his heart had hardened to stone. No woman, no matter how beautiful, passionate, or adventurous, could shatter the ice surrounding it.

"Mornin', stud," came a sultry voice. Eli felt a soft hand crawl up his abs and across his pec. "That rooster ain't the only cock to rise this morning, I see," she purred, and the sound annoyed the ever-living shit out of him. It wasn't that the sound itself was annoying, it wasn't. It was erotic, actually, but he hated that her words stirred his sex. Not to mention, there was a confidence behind the statement he didn't appreciate. This was a woman who got what she wanted and knew exactly what she was doing.

Before she could grab said cock, he was standing, pulling on his jeans, and zipping them.

"Why don't you head on out?" he suggested, and, with a cough, walked to the coffee pot.

She hummed as she began to dress, seemingly undeterred by his dismissal. Or she was just a damn good actress.

What could he say? He was about as interested in sober sex as he was in bull-riding; he didn't want it, not even with a fox like this one. Copulation, for Eli, had simply become a means to an end, a way for his body to have its routine natural release. Getting that needed release was fairly foolproof when he was shit-faced drunk, when he could barely remember his own name, let alone theirs! If it were up to him, he'd never perform the act again. Never open himself up to another human being who might wreck his heart like Stella had. But his cock was greedy and needed the fix. He continued to oblige it, but only when he knew their faces would blur enough so he wouldn't see hers. It was always quick. He'd close his eyes, getting it over as fast as humanly possible. He also didn't kiss them on the lips. That was far too personal.

Girls usually preferred Gabe to Eli as a lover. One had told him that one night, not long ago in fact, sitting around a fire and smoking joints while listening to one of the cowboys play guitar.

"CAREFUL, CLAIRE," *Holly snorted, her arm around Gabriel. "Don't get so excited with this one."*

24

"Why?" Claire looked up at Elias and ran a hand over his thigh. "He looks harmless enough." She cackled, the tequila making her more amorous than usual.

"Well, he's fine and all, but we don't call him the five-minute stud for no good reason."

The laughter followed them into her camper, and, true to form, Elias was done in five minutes. Claire glared at him as if he were the most disappointing person in the world. He simply shrugged and left her to right her clothes, leaving without a word or backward glance.

HE DIDN'T CARE what they thought. It didn't matter to him. He wasn't out to win a lover of the year award. All he was focused on was his form in the arena and winning that championship paycheck. Although, he'd always been damn sure to use condoms. The last thing he wanted was a bastard child—*a bastard child for another woman to abort.*

He cringed at that dark thought, and spun around, attempting to calm his suddenly pounding heart. Instead he froze as he saw—*what was her name?*—standing there.

Camilla? Carina? Catrina? *Cassia!* That was it!

"You aren't as big a bad-ass as you make out to everyone, you know, Kinsen?" she smarted, puckering her lips as she crossed her arms over her chest.

If she wanted a fight, she wouldn't get one from him. He didn't have the time or patience for that shit.

"Look, uh… What was your name again?" He deliberately acted like he'd forgotten. For in all sincerity, he originally had.

The athletic and curvaceous brunette with long legs, tan skin, and brown eyes approached and Elias's fists clenched at his sides. His jaw ticked. Why couldn't she just leave with her tail tucked firmly between her legs like all the rest did? Why did she have to make him be meaner than he wanted to be?

Cassia was a highly attractive woman. Any man would be proud

25

to have her in his bed, still stunning with her hair all askew and mascara smudged beneath her eyes. But Elias wasn't her cowboy and never would be. Why couldn't she see that?

"I know who you are, Elias Kinsen. I know about your past. I know about…"

Oh, Lord… Was six o'clock in the morning too early for bourbon?

Eli raised his chin and crossed his arms, shielding his aching heart as Cassia said the name he'd come to lament, even in his dreams.

"Stella Jenkins. The Hollywood starlet who broke your heart. I heard she went MIA too. Seems you're just as good at breakin' hearts, cowboy." Cassia smirked and leaned forward, separating the distance between them. "What did she do to you? You can tell me."

Her pout would have been sultry to most men, but it grated on that last nerve of Elias's, even as his defiant cock jerked in his pants when her hand cupped him and squeezed. He couldn't stop the growl in the back of his throat and realized it sounded inviting as opposed to threatening, giving her more fuel for the fire.

"Mmm, I know exactly what a man like you needs. Let me show you." The whisper at his ear made him shiver as her tongue licked his lobe. Just as he was grabbing for her shoulders to stop her from going further, she was hitting her knees and unzipping his jeans.

He grunted in protest, only for it to die in his larynx when her full lips enclosed the head of him.

"Shit!" he swore as much from the regret of surrender as from the immediate pleasure that coursed through him. Damn his insolent dick! Damn his rebellious body! Damn his need for human contact that went beyond sexual desire.

He closed his eyes as the mouth on him took all thoughts from his mind. He absorbed himself in the moment of selfish bliss, the surrender of himself to another. He hadn't let anyone do that since…

"Yeah, baby." Cassia cooed. "Fuck my mouth. Fuck it hard. I know you want to." One skillful fist stroked him into submission, the other grabbed his own hand, pulling it into her hair, where he held tight.

He was all too aware that he was falling into the successful trap she'd set. She held him captive, a slave to her torment as a knowing grin hit the lips that encompassed him once again.

He whimpered, aware that he was letting some part of himself go that he didn't want to. But he couldn't stop as his hips rocked into her face.

"That's it. Come for me, cowboy." She pulled her mouth back only long enough to encourage him on before taking him down again.

Elias closed his eyes as he roared and renounced his hold on reality.

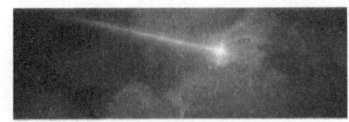

"DARLIN', are you ready?"

"UJ, I'm as ready as I've ever been in my life," Stella replied, feeling butterflies erupt in her belly.

Her handsome Uncle Jack–or UJ, the nickname she'd recently given him–grinned up at her and squeezed her booted calf, giving her the reassurance she needed. He tipped his cowboy hat and signaled her forward, patting the flank of her nine-year old buckskin mare, Salvation.

Stella lifted her chin and straightened her spine as she entered the spotlight, waving with one hand as she gripped the reins with the other. She was confident, proud, and clad in the finest rodeo queen gear money could buy. Decked out rhinestone pleated jeans, a flashy pink button-down, and a diamond-studded cowboy hat, her outfit cost more than a BMW.

"And now we'd like to welcome the stunning and spectacular winner of our rodeo pageant. Ladies and gentlemen, put your hands together, for your presence has just been graced by none other than Stella Rose Jenkins, the famous actress, Golden Globe nominee, and winner of this years' IRCA's Rodeo *Queen*." Cheers erupted, and Stella's smile deepened. "Ms. Jenkins here is new to the sport of rodeo, and if you haven't seen her race yet...well, you're in for a treat tonight."

Stella basked in the feeling of triumph the announcement provided. She realized once more that she'd come a long way in four months. It had been quite the plunge, getting back into the saddle just three weeks postpartum. She couldn't have done so without the help of yoga and meditation, numerous vitamins, and wise advice via FaceTime from a doula she'd found in Bangladesh. And, of course, hats off to her incredible support team.

When she'd informed the Kinsens of her intent to compete, Jack—the man she'd always called uncle—took it upon himself to train her in the art of barrel-racing. But it had been his wife, Natalie, who'd prepared her for competition. Natalie herself had been a championship barrel racer as a teenager. Although she didn't ride as hard as she had back in her youth, Natalie coached Stella in technique and grace.

Stella wasn't great, nowhere near perfect, but she was better than she could've ever anticipated, given the time crunch. Her persistence—and, no doubt, her fame—had gotten her a few local awards, some rankings in prestigious rodeos, and a spot in the IRCA Miss Rodeo pageant, where she'd made it her ultimate goal to win.

Her heart hammered in her chest as she scanned the parade of cowboys, seeking one face in particular. Eli wasn't among the ranks and Stella tried hard to hide her disappointment behind her thousand watt smile, putting on a show for the cheering audience.

They all made several laps as the national anthem was played, then headed back out of the arena.

Stella rode over to the paddock and gate where Jack was, huffing when she got off her horse and landed with an "Umph."

"What?" Jack asked and looked around, brows drawn.

"He's not here." She even pouted, feeling like a deflating balloon.

"The roster tonight clearly states his name, and tomorrow night too."

"Well, I didn't see him."

"He might still be practicin'. Just because he didn't make the parade doesn't mean he ain't here. The parade is optional, not mandatory. Hell, some cowboys don't even show up 'til time to compete. Don't worry, Stell Bell." Jack gave her a crooked grin. She swallowed hard, hopeful that he was right.

She'd done so much to prepare for this reunion, after all. Her stomach knotted at the thought of seeing Elias again, speaking to him, explaining to him that he was a father. That he had been wrong about her, about his faith in her. But their breakup had been so ugly...

"Hey, it's gonna be alright. You'll get your chance."

Stella gave Jack a bright smile and searched her eyes, taking her hands in his.

What would she have done without him these last three months? He'd been her coach, her shoulder to cry on, her voice of reason when she felt like giving up. He'd been like a second father to her, and she loved him for it.

Jack's motives weren't altogether selfless. He wanted to find Elias as much as she did, which made this plan even more precarious. They all wanted Elias back in the fold. He'd not just left *her*; he'd left his entire family, too. His mom and dad, his sister. Cousins. His uncle and aunt. His friends. Everyone. He'd dropped off the planet...until Jax had heard from a friend who'd spotted him back in rodeo.

"You're right. We have to run into him. It's just a matter of time, right?"

She turned to watch Cash the rodeo clown's practiced performance, stilling her nerves and waiting for this big strategy of hers to come to fruition.

29

"EASY THERE, RICOCHET." Elias patted his horse's neck as the steed caught his breath, his nostrils flaring. He snorted, and Eli laughed. "Good boy."

"Ready?" came the voice of his best friend and teammate, Gabriel Halloran.

"Don't I look it?" Eli asked, but didn't miss the flash of doubt in Gabe's face. "What?"

"Nothin'." The goofy prick snorted.

"Don't nothin' me, asshole. What?" Elias demanded, pulling himself upright in his saddle. "You got somethin' to say? Say it!"

Gabe shrugged his shoulders but kept the smug grin on his freckled face, making Eli want to punch him just for the hell of it.

Elias waited, but nothing was forthcoming. He swore and led Ricochet into the arena from the practice field. He caught the glint of the diamonds atop the rodeo queen's hat and saw blonde hair beneath it as she bowed before the crowd.

"Ha! *Another* blonde queen, you owe me $50." Eli grinned over at his teammate.

"Shit! I was aching for a redhead this time." Gabe scowled, getting a laugh out of Eli.

"Two redheads...nah. That's just itching for a fire."

"You're in a good mood tonight, son. Have anything to do with the night you spent with that stunner *Cassia McCormick*?" Gabe joshed and shoved at him, stopping his horse, Opie, next to Eli's.

"Shut up." Eli grumbled.

"She told Nina she blew you, and I quote, 'like a rockstar.' Maybe I should be the next one in her trailer, if that be the case. Of course, only if that's cool with you." Gabe's knowing smirk rivaled all the world's playboys. Hell, they'd both acted as such since joining back up in the rodeo, meeting women and taking them to bed almost nightly like it was a paid sport.

"Jesus." Eli mumbled, rolling his eyes again. They were pushing thirty years old, but one would think they were still in high school again by the way Gabe spoke about women. It was nonsensical. Then again, Gabe had never been in love. Had no idea what it was like to adore a woman with more than just his dick, so he gave his best friend a reprieve.

Eli simply shrugged a response, for all the world nonplussed, giving his friend a silent, *"I don't give a shit what you do with Cassia McCormick."*

They stopped outside the gate, waiting their turn in the line for breakaway roping–one of the three events that had garnered Elias Kinsen his fame and winnings. As one of the fastest in the IRCA, he was itching to make it to number one. Nothing was gonna keep him from the championship. Not Cassia's blowjob, not Gabe's immaturity...and certainly not the allure of the rodeo queen in those tight-ass sparkly Buckle jeans as she mounted her horse. Damn! What an ass. He'd seen an ass as sweet as that only once before.

The announcer's voice called, "She's gotta go change out of her queen clothes before competition now, folks, so you'll have to excuse little star, Stella Jenkins. Doesn't she make one *fine* queen?"

Sonova– The blowjob he'd gotten earlier had rattled more than his resolve, it would seem, and he frowned. Now he was *hearing* things. *Fuck, fuck, double fuck. Get your head back in the game, Eli!* He peeled his eyes from the back of the curvy queen to the audience. The stands were packed tonight, and he was eager to get them rooting for him. He took a deep breath in, readying himself as his name was called over the loudspeaker, following Gabe's, and led his horse into the paddock.

He gripped his rope and reins, adjusted his Stetson, lowered his brow, and got into position in the box, pulling his horse to the back corner and awaiting the signal. Once he got it, he launched out and in seconds, had his lasso shooting out for the calf's neck.

It was a clear miss and Elias swore aloud. "Dammit!"

"So close," the announcer groaned. "Championship calf-roper, Elias Kinsen, was a day late and a dollar short this time."

Ha ha, so funny, asshole. He'd shoot Cooper Gibbons a bird if he could get away with it, but just rode out of the arena, head down.

His focus wasn't on anything or anyone in particular as he headed back toward the practice field to water his steed. Gabe laughed as he saw him.

"O for one, bucko."

Elias cringed at the name because it reminded him of Buck Jenkins, who reminded him of Stella. What was it today? Stella. Stella. Stella. She was all he could think about. It probably had everything to do with letting that chick suck him off when no other woman had since her. It had fucked up his whole day.

"Fuck this!" Eli shouted and dismounted, pulling his horse's mouth down to a fresh bucket of water before he moved to the fence to cool off. He pulled his hat off and took in a deep breath before replacing it.

Gabe moved beside him then. "You do realize I'm just givin' you a hard time, dude?"

Eli looked over at his friend of ten-plus years. He'd been a good friend and teammate. They'd rodeoed together for a while now. Gabe had been there to listen to him vent and pick his sorry drunk ass up off the ground a few times. Gabriel might not be the most moral character, but he had Eli's back. Suddenly, he was grateful for the ginger asshole he'd known since grade school.

"Yeah, yeah. Give me my fifty bucks, and we'll call it good." He joked.

"You're gonna need it if your next run is as bad as that last one." Gabe raised a brow.

"Fuck you. I'm gonna win the next event with flying colors and fuck the rodeo queen before the night is over," Eli stated with a confidence he didn't feel.

"Did I hear you say you're gonna fuck that fine-ass rodeo queen,

Kinsen?" came the deep voice of Cayden "Mac" McCormick, twin brother of Cassia and winner of All-Around Rodeo last year for a total winning of 60K. "That's rich!"

"I didn't stutter, Mac," Eli replied, preening like a peacock. He still considered himself a decent contender. He was as good-looking as either of the other two.

"Not if I get 'er first, my friend." Mac elbowed Eli playfully.

The rodeo was as bad as a circus or any other close-knit family commune. When a new girl came along, they all turned into a bunch of horny hound dogs sniffing her ass to be the first to try and mount her.

The laughter seemed to break the tension Eli felt. Enough that when the calf roping event came, he placed first for a time of 3.6 seconds and beat Gabe's time by a full second–much to his buddy's annoyance.

Gabe was remiss to congratulate him but pulled his weight as the heeler when they were up for their team-roping event. They placed second to Mac and Dustin Foster's time of 4 seconds. Overall, Elias was pleased with his performance tonight, despite his early pull in the breakaway roping event.

He headed back to his trailer when the rodeo queen's hair caught his eye once more. He figured if he planned to "fuck" her, he needed to at least introduce himself. When he looked up to do just that, the familiar face nearly knocked him off his horse. All right, he *had* to lay off the liquor.

Stella. His Stella? No, it couldn't be. She wasn't the girl there on that buckskin mare preparing to head into the barrel-racing event. He had no idea *where* she was, but she wasn't here, not in El Paso at a rodeo. Right?

Eli shook his head, trying to wake his brain up, even as the gorgeous blonde with unique hazel eyes he'd recognize anywhere nodded to him in acknowledgment. He turned his horse around and looked about, confused.

"And up next," Cooper announced, "is our very own rodeo queen,

Stella Rose Jenkins, whose current time sits at less than fifteen seconds. Let's hear it for the rookie hailing from Abundance, Texas," the announcer stated through the loudspeakers, getting a roar from the crowd.

No way! He hadn't just said–

But the girl turned back to look at him, and he scrutinized her face again. *Holy shit!* It *was* Stella! *His* Stella...

No, no, this isn't happening.

But it was. The stunningly familiar blonde tipped her hat at him and headed into the arena at a full gallop.

CHAPTER 4

That money barrel is the key. Get it fast and you're golden, Natalie's words echoed in Stella's head as she rounded the first barrel in record speed, her focus solely on showing Elias Kinsen what a fighter she truly was.

She pitched her body into the turn with the horse as they rounded the next barrel and sped to the third and final one. They were lightning fast as she and Salvation headed out of the arena. The roaring crowd grew louder at her retreating back.

"Man, oh man, we need to name her Shootin' Star after that run. Y'all, guess what her time was that time?" the announcer exclaimed.

Stella held her breath as she looked up at the board. Fifteen point twenty-seven seconds. Damn! That was faster than her previous record. She sighed and patted her breathless mare. "Good girl, Sally."

"Nice run, rookie." A menacing feminine voice sounded from the shadows as a stunning brunette came forth atop a painted stallion. "Bet I can beat it, though." She winked defiantly and hauled ass into the arena, leaving Stella to watch in awe.

Stella's concern wasn't for the other riders' performances,

though. She felt like she might puke now that her run was over and she'd finally seen Elias.

He'd not looked much different than the last time she'd seen him, his eyes still hard and his manner still closed off.

But she'd come here with one purpose. Now the Band-Aid had been ripped off, giving her the opening she'd sought for so long.

She shook as she came to a stop at her site, dismounted, and took Jack's outstretched palm.

"You ok?"

She nodded and took the water bottle from his hands, throwing it back and gulping it with shaky hands.

"Damn fine job, honey," Jack said, patting her back.

"Thanks, UJ. I finally saw him."

She'd not missed Elias's events, holding her breath as he gracefully performed with an ease that appeared as natural to him as breathing. Eli was born to be a cowboy. She'd known that the first time she'd seen him calf-rope at the Abundance rodeo with Jackson, but that fact had never been clearer to her than it was tonight. Had she truly held him back these last several years? Had she even been aware that she *was* holding him back?

Stella had much to reassess about her life in the last year, but the last four months had been the toughest. Researching how she could break into the rodeo lifestyle as an inexperienced rookie, how to become a cowgirl, and learning every nuance from the gurus of horsemanship themselves–the Kinsens, the very family she'd sought like hell to become a part of.

She'd walked away from the life of luxury and acting, and focused solely on getting the man of her dreams back. She'd jilted her former assistant and had only recently accepted his apology. Her mom and dad had no idea what she was up to. She'd simply told them she was staying with a friend in El Paso. Meanwhile, Natalie and Savannah took turns babysitting Toby in a nearby hotel room while she chased this pipe dream of hers.

She'd given birth to her precious baby boy, Tobias, in May and had indulged in the rewards of motherhood, falling in love all over again. She'd never known how incredibly wonderful life truly was until she held her baby boy in her arms. She'd sobbed in both joy and misery, equally. Joy that she had another piece of Elias Kinsen to love, and misery that he wasn't there to share her pivotal moment.

Now, she could finally share the knowledge that she'd been unable to gift him for ten long and grueling months. And she prayed with everything in her that Elias would give her a chance to expel her secrets.

"DUDE!" Gabe gaped in shock. "Was that–?"

"Yes."

"But... So, the announcer wasn't tripping earlier? Stella–*your* Stella is th–the–?" Gabe stuttered.

"Yes!" Eli shouted as he attempted to catch his breath.

"Did you know? You know...when you said you were gonna... fuck the rodeo queen?"

"No." Eli closed his eyes to keep the world from spinning.

"Why is she here? In El Paso? At a rodeo? I didn't know she even raced."

These were questions Eli didn't have answers for. No, she hadn't raced, not that he'd ever known anyway, even if she could ride with the best of them.

To torture me. Destroy me. Finally take the last shred of my humanity away as she plunges the knife through my heart and bathes in my blood?

"I don't know, Gabe," he stated honestly.

"Do you wanna–?" When Gabriel held a bottle of Jack up, Eli took it from his grasp.

"Hell yeah, I do. I wanna be wasted when she comes over here."

"Comes over *here*? You're not gonna–?"

37

"Nope. No, I'm not."

And so Elias set about the task of getting shit-faced drunk.

"WHERE YOU COMIN' in from, darlin'?" A dark-haired, tan cowboy grinned at Stella as she brushed her mare down.

"Oh, uh... We're–"

"From Abundance, Texas," UJ interceded and moved beside her. Stella looked up to Jack then back to the young man who'd come calling.

"Oh, pardon me, Pops. Didn't realize she had a *chaperone*," the handsome cowboy smirked.

Pops, indeed! Let Jack pull up his sleeves and this cocky cowboy would be seeing who could tangle with whom.

The man didn't take Jack's subtle warning though and continued, "I'm Mac McCormick. Figured I'd introduce myself to the queen. My name's one you won't be apt to forgettin' anytime soon, seeing as I aim to win All-Around this year...not unlike last year, mind you?" He tipped his hat, grinning broadly.

Stella gave the cowboy a nod and soft smile. *Man*, eighteen-year-old Stella would have been drooling all over herself by the likes of a looker like Cayden "Mac" McCormick: tall, muscular, deep brown eyes...but the Stella who'd come to El Paso had only one man in mind. She'd also learned the hard way that men like Mac promised nothing but heartache.

"It's good to meet you, Mr. McCormick. I wish you luck in your endeavors."

Stella turned back to her horse, only to have Mac ask, "D'you ever meet Jennifer Anniston or Jessica Alba?"

She'd gotten that question many times over the years and

38

answered honestly with, "Yes. They're both lovely. Very talented actresses."

"I bet y'all all say that same B.S. about each other, huh?"

When Stella didn't reply, he attempted another shot. "Well, if you need *anything*, you be sure and let me know, alright?"

"I appreciate that. Thank you."

"Or if you wanna get out from under Daddy's prying eyes for a bit, ya know..." He winked, and Stella almost rolled her eyes at his brazenness.

"*Daddy* don't much like to share...if you get my meaning." Jack separated the distance between them, placing an arm around Stella's waist and tucking her into his side.

Thick brows rose, and Mac almost stumbled in shock.

"Oh! My bad, Pops. Didn't realize you were uh..." Mac coughed, covering his mouth, the insinuation obvious.

"Son, just don't," Jack growled in irritation.

"Right." He straightened. "I'll, uh, I'll see ya around, Stella." McCormick quickly turned on his heel and ambled off.

"Damn disrespectful millennials!" Jack swore, getting a laugh out of Stella. "Sorry, darlin', but I was afraid if I didn't do something, he'd never leave."

Stella giggled again. "No, I'm glad you did. Thanks, UJ."

"Here. Let me take care of her. You go on inside and rest up. You got a big day tomorrow."

She nodded and handed the brush over to Jack.

Before Stella could head inside, another dark head shot into view. It was the cowgirl who'd crushed her time...before two others had also done the same.

"Not bad for your first real rodeo, Queenie," she said.

"Thank you," Stella gritted, wanting to tell her to go to Hell instead but didn't want to be rude.

"I'm Cassia, by the way."

"Stella."

"Oh, I know who you are." The pretty brunette smirked and crossed her arms beneath her chest, pushing her ample breasts up.

Stella looked briefly up at Jack before pulling in a deep breath. She was glad she did because, when she turned, Elias was standing right behind the woman.

Nothing could have prepared her for the look on his damaged face. He held the same grim mask in place, the same one she'd seen that awful day ten months ago when he walked out of her life believing she'd aborted their unborn child.

"*Everyone* knows who you are," Eli stated with repugnance. "What we *don't* know is why the hell you'd slum it with us country folk to come play rodeo queen. Wouldn't you rather your servants bring you caviar?" The moss green eyes that burned into hers were unfamiliar, cold as ice.

She'd made a huge mistake coming here, she suddenly realized, as her heart broke in half.

As much as she'd changed over the last year, Elias apparently hadn't. Not at all. He clearly hated her. It hurt that he would say such a thing. She'd never even eaten caviar in the time they'd been together, despite that she did have a couple servants...well, she didn't now, not anymore.

"Nephew." It was Jack who spoke first. "It's good to see you're still alive...although I can't say you're looking well. How about giving your folks a call? I'm sure they'd love to take the Missing Person posters down."

Stella had never heard Jack so sarcastic, and her brows rose.

Eli had the audacity to laugh at his uncle, the one he—unlike her—actually shared blood with.

"Ah, Uncle Jack. How do my leftovers taste?" He snorted and spit onto the ground.

Stella gaped, floored by his words and mannerisms. When she began to step forward to speak, Jack stopped her with a strong forearm.

"Think you got the balls to tangle with me, Elias, go right ahead, but leave Stella out of this."

"So, are you gonna answer the question, Rodeo *Queen?*" Eli's hard glare was back on Stella, leaving her speechless. It took her back all those months ago when half her heart had disappeared, leaving a void the size of the state she loved so very much.

"Stella here's just broadening her horizons," Jack finally answered, seeing as Stella's voice wasn't working. She simply stared back at Jack, unsure how to speak to Eli in his volatile state.

"And what do her *horizons* have to do with you, *uncle?*" Eli's words were straight venom, leaving little doubt at the implications of his words.

About that time, Cassia looped her arm around Eli's shoulder in such a seamless gesture that it cut Stella to the core.

Before Stella could respond, Jack was wrapping an arm around her waist once again and pulling her into his side.

Her immediate instinct was to pull away. She didn't want Eli thinking she'd shacked up with his uncle in his absence because nothing could be further from the truth. But she held her ground, having faith in Jack's methods, and waited to see what Eli would say or do on the matter. His lip twitched, then he scoffed.

"Figures! You always were desperate for Kinsen cock. Looks like you got yet another one." He sounded equal parts defeated and outraged. "Careful, Uncle Jack. That little viper has a fierce bite."

She felt and heard Jack's deep intake of breath, fighting his instincts to defend her, but he stayed silent.

Cassia was the first to break the awkward tension. "C'mon, cowboy. Let's go." Her nose brushed Elia's scruffy jaw, and Stella's heart fluttered in jealousy.

Cassia kissed his perfectly chiseled jawline with familiarity and nuzzled his ear. All the while, his eyes didn't waver from Stella's. She held the stare, trying to instill her emotions through her eyes.

I'm here, Elias. I love you. I'm still fighting for us. I have so much to tell you. Show you. Please just give me a chance.

41

But Eli's sneer said it all too well. Even if he'd "heard" what she was emitting, he didn't care. He was turning away. Away from her. Away from their baby, their future, their...

Who was she kidding?

"Oh God. What am I doing?" she cried when they were out of earshot. "I was a fool. Why did you let me do this? Why did I ever think–?" her voice was ragged with the sudden tempest of emotions building within her with the force of a hurricane.

"Shh, there now," Jack said and pulled her into his arms. He cradled her head to his chest, and stroked her hair. His deep voice comforted her and the sound of his steady heartbeat lulled her panic. He held her for a time, letting her cry out her frustrations before pulling back and taking her shoulders. "We knew this wouldn't be easy, sweetheart."

Stella simply nodded in agreement.

"We knew he probably wouldn't be receptive in the beginning, right?"

Again, she nodded.

Yes, she'd known this wouldn't be a walk in the park. So far, it had been the hardest damn thing she'd ever done, second only to giving birth.

She'd worked her fingers and toes–and chapped thighs–to the bone for this. For the chance to prove to Eli that he was wrong about her. That she wasn't just some rich, entitled, selfish brat. She was worthy of his love. Worthy of his affections. Worthy to be the mother of his child.

"Now, I was taught that anything worth having is worth fighting for. Don't you agree?"

It *was* worth fighting for. Elias was worth fighting for. The thoughtful, giving, kind and selfless man she'd fallen in love with. Even if this Elias imposter didn't seem to want her back. But fear clenched at her heart. Was her hard work all in vain?

"What if...?" she couldn't say it aloud. "What if his love for me is really and truly... gone?" she whispered the last word and looked up at her Uncle Jack in fear. Eli had said as much that day in the high-rise condo. What if he couldn't be reached? What if...?

"C'mon now, Stells. Didn't you see his reaction when I put my arm around you?" Jack gave her a crooked grin. "I was testin' the waters, and he didn't like that I was so familiar with you—not one bit. If I was a betting man, I'd say that was straight envy I saw in his eyes."

"Oh? All I saw was him eager to play tonsil-hockey with the slut draped over him," Stella smarted.

"C'mon now, darlin'. You had to know what would happen—and him a young man in the circuit." Jack shrugged at the obvious fact.

Where her world had stopped without Eli in her life, his had obviously gone on. Including his sex life. He was single, technically, and there were, after all, many available women to catch his eye. But thinking it and seeing it firsthand were two different things. She'd not been prepared to see him with another woman slung all over him. Somewhere in her mind, she had held onto the hope that, deep down, he still loved her. That some small part of him hadn't completely given up on her, despite all the awful things he'd said.

Even if he doesn't love you, you still owe it to him to confess your secret.

As if sensing her inner turmoil, Jack sighed. "Let's call it a night, huh? It's been a really long day."

It had...been a really long day, and Stella needed rest.

She needed to recover her weary body, and she needed to meet him in her dreams. A place where she could see the old Eli, the gentleman who'd rescued her and stolen her heart all those years ago when a shooting star he'd named after her had granted them the greatest wish of all.

"I'm really sorry about what happened tonight, Stella."

Tears once again burned her eyes as she thought of how heart-breaking it had been. First, she'd hurt Cassidy. Second, she'd been jilted by Jackson. And third, she'd been humiliated.

43

"I should have known it would come to this." She'd known Jax wasn't over Cass, but that hadn't stopped her from pursuing him, hadn't stopped her from falling even harder for him, hadn't stopped her from throwing herself at him like some sex-crazed harlot. God, she was a fool. "He's loved her as long as I've known him. Why did I ever think I had a chance?" Tears streamed her cheeks, no matter how much she tried to stop them.

"Don't beat yourself up. You're great, Stella Rose. You deserve a man who'll worship you. Jax just isn't that man. You'll find the right one, though, if you haven't already." He gave her a wink as they came to a traffic light, and she couldn't help the giggle that came from her throat.

Elias Kinsen, Jax's first cousin, was charming, she'd give him that. And he'd defended her against Jared tonight, twice. And now he was taking her home. She was grateful for him and told him so.

"No need to thank me, m'lady. I was only taking care of a damsel in distress. What kinda man would I be if I didn't rescue you?" Another sexy wink, and she could feel her tears starting to wane.

Elias was handsome. Tall. Muscular. Rugged. Dashing. And a cowboy, to boot. All the qualities she loved. Why in God's name was he single? Perhaps he just hadn't found the right one yet, himself. She wanted to ask him but refrained as he looked over at her for directions.

"Oh, sorry. Turn left here." She pointed and guided him from there.

He was silent, giving her time to gather her thoughts. He finally spoke as he pulled into the long, paved driveway of her home. She gave him the numbers to punch on the keypad and he did so, waiting as the heavy wrought iron gates opened before pulling through them.

He stopped in front of the garage, the motion sensors kicking on as he cut the engine. He turned to her then and sighed heavily. "Look, I know Jax needs to apologize to you, but tonight, I'm gonna do it for him."

"You're a good man, Elias Kinsen, and a good cousin." She smiled into his dimpled face, noticing them for the first time as he returned it.

"Well, love makes men do stupid things, or so I'm told anyway." He laughed, the sound comforting to Stella's ears.

"Thank you, Eli. For not making me feel like an idiot or a floozy."

"You aren't either of those things, and I'm sorry you were made to feel that way."

"You have nothing to apologize for, but, all the same, thank you for your kindness."

He gave her a nod and said, "I'll walk you to the door and see you inside."

"You honestly don't have—" she was interrupted as he opened his door and stepped out. He came around to her side and opened the passenger door, extending his hand to her. She took it, blushing, and let his hand interlock with hers as he shut the door with his other hand. He looped her arm through his and walked them laconically to the house.

"It's a beautiful night. Such a shame it had to end like it did." He looked up.

"Agreed," Stella stated and, too, looked up into the cool, starry night.

"Oh, look," Elias stopped and pointed. "A shooting star. Quick, make a wish."

She giggled even as she watched the sudden flash of a meteor's entry into the atmosphere. She closed her eyes and wished for true love, as silly and cliché as that was. When she opened her eyes, Elias was grinning down at her. "What?" she asked.

"That's good luck, ya know?"

The beauty of his beaming pearly whites made her giggle again. "I need some good luck after tonight."

"Well, I'd say your wish might be coming true then, don't you?"

His gaze left her breathless. She was all too aware of his powerful sex appeal, his clean, fresh scent mixed with leather and beer, and the ease she felt in his presence. She felt the strength of his hand in hers and smiled, glad he'd been so good to her when she was so vulnerable.

"I best get you inside before Bobby 'Buck' Jenkins has my head."

"Oh, Mom and Dad are out tonight. They won't be home till late." She suddenly remembered. "Would you like to come in?"

His eyes roved her face and stopped at her lips. Tension seized her, sexual, hot, and licking as it coursed through her veins. What was happening?

"I probably shouldn't, Stella," he answered with a frown. When she pulled her lips in and looked down, his big palm cupped her cheek and his index finger brought her chin up. "I want to, believe me. But you're not the only unguarded one here right now."

She suddenly wanted to know why he was "unguarded". Had his heart been recently ripped out too? Was he in love with someone who didn't love him back? And why on earth did she desperately care so much? She gulped, feeling ashamed of her wanton brazenness.

"Hey." He stepped closer and masculine command overtook her senses. She felt his chest bump hers and fought the urge to press her palms into the broad expanse of it, feel the muscles that poked through his tight t-shirt. "Don't look at me like that," he scolded with a crooked grin and a chuckle, his sweet breath on her face causing her to gasp. "I made a wish on that star, too. I named it Stella."

She would have laughed had his eyes not been burning so deeply into hers; she was awestruck. Was he crushing on her? Was he serious? And how had she not noticed how beautiful his facial features were until now, how well-built he was beneath his clothes?

"You're beautiful, Elias," was all she could say as her eyes fell over his muscular, trim frame.

He laughed big even as his thumb stroked her cheekbone. "I thought that was supposed to be my line."

She cupped the hand holding her face, and he pulled a deep breath in. "You could be a model. In fact, Jax was supposed to go with me to a shoot Friday. Dammit." She huffed and looked down, suddenly remembering that she was now partner-less.

"I'll go with you," Eli stated much too quickly, and Stella's eyes shot up to his, evaluating him.

"You will?"

"Yes ma'am." He winked again and his eyes fell back to her lips. "Should I seal it with a kiss?" His brow went up and before she could decide how to respond, his lips were lowering to hers and he was kissing her.

His lips were soft yet firm as they pressed ever so lightly to hers. He slanted his mouth and tugged gently on her lips as her body eased into his,

his arms wrapping gingerly around her. He didn't deepen the kiss, he just lightly caressed her lips with his own plump, full ones until she was aching for more. She moaned even as he pulled back and felt the smile tug on his lips as she leaned into him for one more smooch.

"I've been wanting to do that since I saw you at the rodeo," he confessed.

Her head was reeling and her heart was pounding, unsure of her reaction to him. Was this ache between her legs misplaced? Was she simply pining for Jax and Eli was a good stand-in? What was she doing? This was too soon, right? She simply licked her lips, hungry for more as Elias's index finger touched her nose and his hand cupped her bicep, stroking her with all the tenderness of a lover.

"Give me your phone, Stella," Eli commanded, and Stella pulled it from her jeans pocket and handed it over, after entering the code.

He smiled even as he began putting his number into her contacts. He handed it back to her and took her arm again, leading her to the door as she continued to float away on cloud nine.

He waited for her to take the key out and unlock the door. He saw her in and stood in the foyer, arms across his chest. "I would stay for a bit, but I know myself and I don't wanna rush you into something you're not ready for." His tone and eyes were serious and had her gulping once more. "But I want you to know that I'm just a phone call away. I texted myself from your number, so I got yours now too." He pulled his phone out and shook it at her, giving her a crooked grin. "I'll call you and we'll go out, if you'd like."

How could she say no to that? She nodded.

"Well, m'lady. I hope you sleep well then." He winked and leaned in to kiss her cheek, her heart hopping up into her throat as his soft lips lingered there for a moment before he turned to leave. She shut the door behind him and locked it, turning and falling against it in overwhelming shock and elation.

She pulled out her phone suddenly and searched for his name in her contact list, scowling when she couldn't find it. She then checked her last text message and laughed aloud as she read, "Beautiful Elias."

Wow! He was beautiful. And he'd just turned her night from horrific into heavenly. Who was this guy?

47

CHAPTER 5

"Evenin', my love. How are you?" Jack asked his wife of thirty-three years, speaking quietly into his cell phone as he FaceTimed her.

He'd waited until Stella showered and went to bed before checking in, not wanting her to overhear the conversation. The poor girl had enough on her plate and didn't need an old man's musings.

"Me and baby Tobias are great. He just drank his whole bottle down and is snoozing away. Such a sweet boy. He has those Kinsen lips, so perfect...and kissable." Natalie giggled, looking down at the bundle in her arms.

Jack couldn't keep the grin off his face. All the Kinsens—himself included—his brothers and their children, too, had inherited those "kissable" lips from his mother, Lillian Kinsen.

"How's she holding up?" Nat asked.

"Surprisingly well, considering," he answered honestly.

"What happened?"

Jack propped his socked feet up and leaned back on the large pillow of the pull-out bed of the fairly large camper. Stella had spared no expense on having decent accommodations for them to travel in, and Jack was grateful. His back was killing him.

He proceeded to tell his wife all about their run-in with Elias, how crude he'd been, and how well Stella had done racing.

"You'd be so proud of her, Nat. She reminded me so much of Viv today. This girl has her mother's tenacious heart."

"And her Leo father's pride," Natalie said with a laugh.

"God, I miss you, baby," he murmured.

"You saw me yesterday, my love," she teased.

"I know, but I want to hold you, inhale you..." Jack didn't finish, but Natalie knew what he wanted. She always wanted the same. They weren't completely whole when they were apart, and he knew she felt it too.

"I miss you too, husband. And holding this little angel baby in my arms makes me eager for another grandbaby." She smiled down at little Toby, and Jack grinned, himself.

"Oh lord, don't tell Austin." Jack sighed heavily. "He'll gladly start working on that for you."

"If he hasn't already." Nat smirked, a perfect brow rising.

"Jeez, don't tell me... Is Vanna pregnant again?"

"Don't say anything. She wants to tell you herself. She's tickled pink."

Jack smiled at his wife's blush, thinking about his daughters, Savannah and Dallas, and granddaughters: Lily, Gracie, and Rowan. Seven and three quarters, four, and two—and now, another on the way.

"I think Vanna's hoping for a boy this time, but you know Austin. He'd be fine with another girl."

Jack laughed. "Hell, knowing that rebel he'll keep at it until he gets his boy, no matter if they have ten girls."

Jack was happy for his daughters...and his son, Jax. Dallie and Cole, Savannah and Austin, Jax and Cassidy, they were all happy in love. They'd been blessed, as had Jack and Natalie.

49

As if sensing his thoughts, his wife sighed pensively, "Jack? Is this gonna work?"

Jack swallowed hard and rubbed his stubbly jaw in thought. "I sincerely hope so, sweetheart."

"How lost is he?"

"No more lost than this ol' cowboy was, I don't think." Jack was a pretty good mess himself before love found him. Surely there was hope for his nephew. "It's gonna take a mighty fine woman to be strong enough to stand up to him."

"She can do it. She's grown so much."

"I think so too, Nat. I think so too."

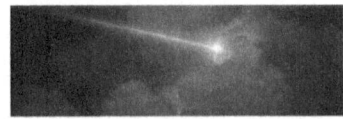

"MMM, YES, RIGHT THERE."

"Here, angel?"

"Oh, Eli. Please?" Stella begged even as he thrust harder and deeper. "God. How do you do that?"

"Me?" He groaned in pleasure and kissed her lips, slowly, passionately. "I thought that was you." His grin was silly, love-drunk, and utterly gorgeous as it overtook his face, making his deep green eyes twinkle.

Would she ever tire of this view? Tire of him loving her with such tenderness that her entire body quaked in answer to his call?

"Eli... Eli, oh my..." she cried out as she succumbed to the stroking of his shaft within her.

He was soon to follow, spilling himself deep as his thrusts became frantic and hard.

When they both came down from their blissful, sexual highs, he stayed inside her and she hugged him tightly to her frame, never wanting to part with him. Her fingernails skimmed his broad back, and Stella giggled when he shivered.

He was sweaty but smelled of sandalwood, leather, and...Elias. Her beautiful cowboy.

STELLA AWOKE to the smell of coffee and wiped the tears from her eyes. That memory was as poignant as the rest, for it was on that vacation to Paris where they'd conceived sweet Toby.

When Stella turned, she smiled over at her uncle, who nodded to her with a cup of coffee. She returned it. Yes, she wanted coffee and lots of it.

He was fresh from a shower, brown hair well-salted with silver strands, his tall, broad frame still as impressive as she ever remembered. He wore a brown gingham button-down and Wranglers, with brown ostrich skin cowboy boots. His usual cowboy hat was missing, at least until they got outside. This man was straight cowboy, his roots as deep as they went.

She'd admired—and maybe even crushed on—Jack Kinsen from the time she was a child, his cowboy lifestyle calling to some ancient pioneer part of her. Her own father had always worn a cowboy hat, despite that he'd failed miserably in his youth as a bull-rider. Bobby "Buck" Jenkins had given that same cowboy hat to the boy who would eventually father his only grandchild; irony in its truest form.

Funny how life came full circle like that.

Stella stood and stretched, feeling the stiffness in every muscle of her body. "Oww," she whined and took the coffee given to her. "Thanks."

Jack gave her a knowing grin. "The only remedy for that is more riding."

"Says the cowboy," she smirked.

Jack gave her a shrug, looking younger than his sixty-three years. Stella giggled.

"Today is gonna be harder than yesterday. You ought to know that. Yesterday, you showed them what you got. Today, you gotta aim higher, ride faster, hit harder."

"Got it, coach," she muttered, feeling unsure of herself. Hadn't she given it her all yesterday?

"Hey, remember: you want it bad enough, you'll do what it takes to get it."

Damn, he was persistent...but right. She'd never really worked "hard" for anything, until now. Not really. Having celebrity parents had given her an in into the world of fame and fortune. She'd not really "earned" her endorsements, product lines, model status, or auditions. Well, not in her opinion. She'd always felt like she had to live up to her mother's name, push herself to be as good or better than Vivian Alexander, just as she—and everyone else—knew that she was no Vivian Alexander, even if she was talented and beautiful. Living in that shadow hadn't been easy, but now she was good at something no one else in her family did. She had a new path, a path forged in self-determination, and she wasn't backing down without a fight.

Even if that fight meant physical and mental exhaustion—and muscles that screamed in pain daily. She simply had to succeed. Her future, her son's future, the love of her life depended on it.

She nodded again.

"Alright, I'll go warm up Salvation. You get dressed."

She grinned and nodded again, sending silent gratitude his way.

Jack Kinsen had stepped up to the plate when Stella had first considered this outlandish idea.

"UH...WHAT?" Cassidy Boyd asked. "You're serious?"

"She can do it." Natalie rubbed her chin in thought.

"Not without a lot of training." Jack scowled. "But it could be done. Depends on how hard you're willing to work, Stella."

"I want to do this," Stella beseeched them. "If Elias is back in the rodeo circuit, then that's the way I can win him back."

Natalie patted her hand then. "Oh, sweetie." The look on her face was sympathetic, but ate into her guts.

"I'm not giving up on him!" She shot to her feet and held her big pregnant belly. "My parents already think I'm nuts. Not you guys, too. Aunt Nat, you know I can ride and well."

"Umm, forgive me for stating the obvious here, but right now, you can't ride—let alone train." Jax shook his head in finality as he motioned to her pregnant belly.

"I'll be ready to train next month."

The skeptical eyes of the Kinsens, and Cassidy, bounced around the kitchen table only to settle back onto her.

"As a labor and delivery nurse, I must highly advise against that," Cass was the first to explain.

"Stella, sweetheart," Nat consoled and reached out her hand. "The recovery is sometimes upwards of six weeks, and that's a pregnancy with no complications. Trust me, I've done it three times now."

"I can do this, Aunt Natalie. I'll be ready."

SHE RECALLED her Uncle Jack's words. *"Ride well or not, this is an extreme sport that's gonna test every limit of your mind and body, a body that'll have just given birth for the first time. I'm not saying it isn't possible, but it's gonna take every last ounce of willpower you have to make it to qualifying, at this rate. I can't guarantee you anything, but if you want it, we'll do our damnedest to get you there."*

Stella had almost jumped for joy, but her heavy belly prevented that, instead she'd begun to cry and thrown herself at her uncle, the best uncle she'd ever had even if he wasn't her biological one.

And get her there he had—through rain, tornado warnings, sunburn, tears, pulled muscles, sprained ankles, and a hell of a lot of determination from the both of them. She wasn't sure why he'd been so patient with her, his will tested alongside her own, as he pushed her, and the perfect horse they'd finally found, to their breaking points.

It had been one night in particular of her falling onto their living

53

room couch in sheer exhaustion that she'd heard her aunt whisper, *"Oh, Jack. This is a fool's errand."*

Stella's groggy mind remembered hearing Jack's boot steps approach his wife and the sounds of a soft kiss.

"I won't give up, Nat, not until she does. And do you want to know why?"

"Why?"

"Because I believe in the power of true love. Elias is all but lost to us. I know what being lost in heartache feels like, and if Stella is his Natalie, then I have to place her back in his path. This is what she feels compelled to do and who am I to tell her she isn't strong enough? She's a fighter, baby. And anything worth having is worth fighting like hell for, my Dad always said."

And Stella had fought like hell: for herself, for Eli; to prove to his family, to his uncle, that she was worthy of their bloodline, worthy of Elias Kinsen and the Kinsen name. Stella Rose Jenkins was born to be a star, even if that star didn't belong on Hollywood's Walk of Fame but in the vast Texas night sky.

She got dressed, pulled her hair back, donned her cowboy hat, and straightened her spine. Today, she was beating her record. Her will was as strong as ever.

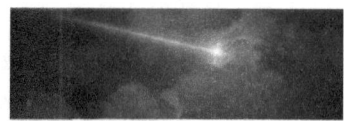

ELIAS WOKE to a raging hangover and puked his guts up first thing. That's how his morning started.

Last night hadn't been much better.

Cassia had been hella pissed when he'd told her to–verbatim–get the *fuck* away from him. She must have gone whining to her twin brother, Cayden, who'd arrived soon after, threatening to kick Eli's ass for *"messing around with his sister."* To which Gabe had boldly–and dumbly–responded to Cayden with, *"Well, if that slut would mind her own damn business, she wouldn't be talked to that way."* Cayden had ended that conversation with a punch to Gabe's right eye.

Eli hadn't bothered to mention to the fuming Cayden that Cassia had "messed around" with a fair number of cowboys in camp, if the rumors about her were true. He sure as shit didn't want, or need, a shiner like the one Gabe now wore.

The whole incident might have been funny if Eli's head wasn't splitting and his heart wasn't sputtering as he watched his uncle Jack and Stella in the practice field together.

She'd never been more beautiful as she was when she rode. They hadn't gone horseback riding much, but when they had, she'd always been elegant, riding with an innate grace. His Aunt Natalie had been the one who'd taught her as a child, unsurprisingly so. Stella appeared to be one with the creature she was atop, as if they were a single entity racing together.

"Dude! Did you hear what I said?"

"What?" Eli snapped back at Gabe from his horse.

"I can't fucking see out of my eye." Gabe whined, pointing to the usually blue orb that was now swollen closed and turning purple.

Jesus Christ! "Well, maybe you shouldn't be stupid and smart off to angry brothers about their twin sister's promiscuity."

"In my meager defense, I was drunk," Gabe explained. "And don't use big words like that. My head hurts."

Elias rolled his eyes, pinched the bridge of his nose, counting to ten.

"So, are you forfeiting tonight or what?" he demanded.

"No, I just...I think I need to go lie down for a while."

"Fine. But if you forfeit, I'm gonna be pissed the hell off."

"I ain't forfeiting, man. I'll be fine come competition. I just need some Advil or somethin'."

Eli wasn't so sure as his friend dismounted, stumbled, and righted himself. *Fuck!* This was the last thing they needed today. Mac and his heeler, Colt Murphy, were up in the standings.

He patted his steed's neck and guided him out of the practice field, leading him onto one of the back trails. He didn't miss the subtle grin Stella gave him as he looked back.

It took him back to when he was happy, when nothing existed but her and the love he had for the stunning star who had stolen his heart so quickly. He hadn't been the same since he'd left her. Even if he had been right in what he'd told her that day, it didn't change his heart. It didn't take away the fact that he was still in love with her. As much as it pained him to admit it to himself, it was the God's honest truth.

In the three years they'd been together, at times, she *had* been selfish, self-absorbed, and solely focused on her fame. He'd still adored every inch of her five-foot-seven-inch frame, adored how she'd loved him, how much fun they'd had together.

But something was bothering him greatly as he tried to calm his anger and trepidation, riding beneath a grove of trees whose leaves shaded the mid-morning sun. Why was she there? And with his uncle Jack of all people? What was going on between the two of them? What had happened in the span of a year? He'd not been in contact with his family at all in that time, and now, suddenly, he felt incredibly guilty. He should call and check in on his mother, father, and sister…and of course, his first cousin, Jax, who'd been like a little brother to him.

He'd spent most of the last year in a foggy blur, trying to focus beyond pining for the woman he once loved with every ounce of his being. He soon discovered himself ambling back into the sport he'd once loved almost as much, and reconnecting with his childhood buddy, Gabe, when they'd met at a rodeo on the border. He'd been attempting to lose himself. Or he'd been trying to find himself, perhaps; figure out who Elias Kinsen was without Stella Jenkins.

He'd forgotten the man he'd even been before she'd burst into his life like starfall. Now, he wasn't so sure he even liked who he'd become. He had no strong purpose, his life lacking a set direction.

The engagement ring he'd had customized specifically for his "little shooting star" sat in a box beneath his camper bed, burning a hole in his heart with each passing night he dreamt of her. Which seemed nightly, as of late.

The more he led his horse down the trail, the more melancholy he became.

Dammit! This was supposed to have been a relaxing stroll.

"Alright, Rich, let's head back. I need to go grab a bite, and I'm sure you could use a treat for your troubles."

He turned his mount around and led him into a jog as they approached their campsite. They came to a dead stop as he saw something that made his blood boil.

Stella had dismounted her horse and stood in front of Eli's uncle, looking up at him. He smiled and cupped her face with such raw tenderness that it took Eli's breath. When Jack leaned down to kiss Stella's forehead, Eli could have roared in envious rage. How long had his ex-girlfriend and his uncle been so friendly with one another? Did his aunt know how close they were? What was going on? And worst of all, how many men had touched her with such familiarity since he'd left?

Elias didn't want these answers and cursed himself for ever being so naïve. What if this had been her game all along? To infiltrate the Kinsen family, to go after Eli only to have her target set on his uncle Jack all along. When she couldn't have Jackson, she'd gone after Elias. Could there be a pattern, and now she'd moved on to Jack? *What the actual fuck?*

He wouldn't put it past her, though. It fit her drive to "shoot for the stars," but something wasn't adding up. Whatever reason she and Jack were together didn't explain why she'd come to El Paso to the International Rodeo Cowboys Association, why she was barrel racing, or why she'd become rodeo queen. Had his uncle and aunt split up for some crazy reason? Was this Jack's late-life crisis kicking in, running off with the young starlet who'd broken his nephew?

Eli knew Jack wouldn't leave Natalie under any circumstance in the world. They were–and always had been–inseparable. They worshiped the ground the other walked upon, not to mention their magnetism. Besides, Jack had a successful multi-million-dollar horse ranch to run.

But that still didn't settle his envy and disgust. When they looked up to see him staring, he tore his eyes from the two of them, scowling at the ground.

Jack stepped back and dropped his hands.

Yeah, you should *feel guilty, you dirty old bastard!* He wanted to shout.

He lowered his head and headed to his camper, aware that he and his uncle would be having a talk soon...very, very soon.

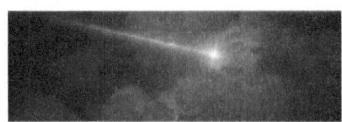

"TAKE A BREATH," Stella heard Jack say as she opened her eyes. "Are you alright?"

"Yes."

She'd just completed her run and came close to falling off her horse when Sally slipped rounding the final barrel. She had held on with all her might and still managed a time of fifteen point seven seconds. However, her right ankle had gotten smashed between Sally and the ground, and was now throbbing fiercely.

She reached down, grunting as she pulled her foot from the stirrup.

Jack grabbed for her boot, and Stella hissed when his touch made the pressure explosive.

"Damn, I'm sorry. Let's go ice this."

He moved to pull her from her mount and eased her to the ground, where she put her weight on the opposite leg and hopped, letting Jack assist her to the camper. Salvation followed obediently behind.

"You can't catch a break can you, rookie?" came the amused voice of Cassia McCormick out of nowhere.

Stella rolled her eyes as she fell into one of the chairs they'd pitched up out front. Jack elevated her ankle, resting it on an adjacent chair. She hissed in pain again as he pulled the boot off.

"Damn!" she and Cassia stated simultaneously, seeing the red and swollen flesh beneath her sock.

Stella glanced sharply up at the intruder, wishing she would take her imposing ass far away.

"Must be nice to have a *Daddy* to tend to you like this one does." Cassia's eyes alluded to the kind of "tending" she was referring to, getting a blank-faced Stella. "Let me know when you tire of this one too, won't cha, Hollywood?" With a little giggle, she turned and sashayed off before either Jack or Stella could respond.

"Dammit!" Stella shouted, her frustrations besting her.

Jack waited for her tantrum to pass before he headed into the camper for ice. Stella kept her tears at bay, holding onto the thin veil of her composure. This was the last thing they needed. Having an ankle injury could put her completely out of competition. Right now, she ranked dead last anyway. But she did, at least, rank...

She pulled in another deep breath and closed her eyes, sending up a silent prayer for strength, patience, and healing. When she opened her eyes again, Eli was standing there, arms crossed over his chest, looking her over.

His frown wasn't as hard as it'd been yesterday. Instead, it was one of concern. She held her breath as he walked closer.

"I saw your run. It was really impressive how you managed to stay on your horse."

She could detect no cynicism in his tone and was held captive by that fact.

When his eyes fell to her battered ankle, he continued, "That looks painful."

Stella wiped the tears leaking from her eyes, and Eli scowled in sorrow as he caught sight of them.

"What are you doing here, Stella? Honestly."

For a moment, she was back in time–close to a year ago, when their life had been so full of love and laughter that it had felt almost too good to be true. Before all hell had broken loose. The few times Stella had been hurt then, he'd been the one to take care of her, hating that she was in pain and crying. Her tears had always appeared to pain him. Perhaps it had been good that he'd missed the birth of their child. He wouldn't have been able to bear it.

Jack came out of the screen door of the RV about that time and stopped dead in his tracks as he saw Elias.

Eli's eyes changed then, the green darkening as he narrowed them at his uncle.

"Eli," Jack stated with a nonchalant nod and went to work setting supplies down in the empty chair next to Stella. Eli stood motionless, unsure what to do or say next. Stella watched as Jack crunched up the ice bag and opened the compression wrap.

Elias stepped forward, then back, wanting to help but hesitant to do so. Stella simply observed his behavior with bated breath.

"You, uh, you need to wrap it first, then ice," he told his uncle like he'd never treated an ankle sprain before in his sixty-plus years.

Jack eyed his nephew in both amusement and annoyance equally before grabbing the wrap up.

"I–I can do it." Stella made a move to grab for the bandage, but Jack shooed her hands away.

"I got it, darlin'." He winked with a gratuitous grin.

Stella heard Eli growl and saw his lips tighten with frustration.

Jack ignored him and began wrapping Stella's ankle with the patience of Job, while she noted Eli's shuffling feet. "Why don't you go grab a couple pillows so we can elevate this leg?" Jack asked, motioning to Eli, who huffed off and did as he'd been asked.

When Jack's eyes met Stella's, he gave a look that she couldn't interpret, but didn't speak.

Eli came out with multiple pillows of varying sizes and stepped forward as Jack moved to take them from him.

"That one needs to go on the bottom," Eli stated to the longer of the three, getting a smirk from Jack when he did as requested, gently lifting Stella's leg.

She watched Salvation move behind Eli to sniff and nuzzle at him. He grabbed her reins and patted her muzzle then looked back at Stella.

She gave him a smile, wishing he could see her heart and how much it bled for him. He gulped and nodded when Jack motioned to her ankle with bouncing eyes, silently asking if his work was up to par.

Jack's expression stayed light-hearted even as Eli took in a deep breath.

"I'll take 'er." Jack pointed to Sally's reins, but Eli shook his head.

"No, I... I'd like to talk to you, Uncle."

Stella's brows hit her forehead then.

Jack's smile tightened and he glanced back to Stella. "You need anything else, darlin'?"

"No, I'll be ok for a little bit."

With that, the two men ambled off, toward the temporary enclosure they'd set up for the mare at the back of the RV.

ELIAS CLENCHED and unclenched his free fist at his side as he led the horse away and through the small fence. The shelter was small but adequate, he noted, and began removing the horse's tack and throwing it over the saddle rack next to the pen. He inhaled deeply and exhaled slowly, attempting to ease his anger.

He'd been fairly pleased with his performance in his events this evening. He'd beaten his time, and—thanks to a hearty steak—Gabe's eye had deflated enough for him to be a decent enough heeler in their team roping event. It seemed Eli's mood had shifted—that was,

61

until he'd seen Stella's horse almost fall. His heart had frozen stiff in his chest.

He recalled seeing it happen, certain Stella would topple right off, but she held fast, finishing the performance despite having her ankle almost crushed. He'd been proud as hell at her perseverance. Stella was anything if not tenacious. It was what originally drew him to her. His little star, always shining so brightly no matter the rain clouds surrounding her.

Jack took over, brushing the mare down as if he had all the time in the world, as if nothing were amiss. Meanwhile, Elias felt like his head might blow clean off at the intense rage building within him.

"What are y'all doing here, Uncle Jack?"

"Competing in a rodeo."

"Dammit, but why? Why is Stella Jenkins competing at all? When I left her ten months ago, she was living the life of a celebrity. What is all this? Some part? And why in hell are *you* here? Don't you have a fuckin' ranch to run? And a wife, not to mention?"

Jack shrugged nonchalantly.

"Dammit, Uncle Jack. Are you and Stella...?" he trailed off, he couldn't form the words. It was utterly ludicrous. He pulled in another deep breath. "Are you two *together*?"

His uncle's eyes shot to his, the tight expression on his face unreadable. Elias waited long moments, knowing deep down he didn't want to know the truth despite that he did; he was *dying* to know the truth.

Right before his anticipation got the best of him, Jack straightened and cleared his throat, shaking his head. "What do you think, Eli?"

Elias scoffed but before he could respond his uncle continued, "Are you really that blind to what's standing right before you?"

Eli's eyes narrowed. What was his uncle saying?

"To be so intelligent, son–and of my bloodline–you're acting like a total idiot right now."

"*Excuse* me?"

"Open your eyes, kid! Why do you *think* we're here?"

"If I knew that, I wouldn't be asking, now would I?"

Jack rolled his eyes. "She's here because of *you*, Elias."

"Me? Why?"

"Damn, boy! Have you killed all your brain cells or were you always this stupid?"

"If you're gonna continue to insult me–" Eli growled, fist clenching, teeth gnashing.

"Eli! She's trying to win you back! She's killed herself to become a worthy barrel-racer and rodeo queen. She's trying to show you how committed she is, impress you, play the game at your level? Why else would she go to such extremes to do all this? Hello! Open your freaking eyes."

Eli felt like the idiot his uncle Jack was accusing him of being. Why would she do that? After what she'd done? After knowing she'd lost him? And why wait so long? It'd been almost a year since they'd broken up. What had she been doing all this time? Training? Seriously? Eli frowned.

But it had all been for naught. As much as he appreciated her efforts, and knew he would never love another woman, he couldn't take her back. She'd wronged him in a way that was unforgivable. She'd destroyed a part of him, a piece he could never get back, without his knowledge or his consent. She'd betrayed his trust, his love.

"Did she tell you *why* we broke up, Uncle Jack?" Eli crossed his arms over his chest. "Why I *left* her?"

He watched his uncle's face, the no-nonsense set of his jaw, then his eyes and the corner of his mouth ticked up. "Eli," he began only to lower his eyes.

"She didn't, did she? Not the whole story, I'm sure. There's always two sides to every story, as you well know." He drove his point home. "I'm not the bad guy here; she is."

Jack's mouth lifted in a sarcastic smile. "Perhaps *you* should've heard the whole story, then, before you up and left."

Eli groaned and rolled his eyes. "I'm sure you would have done something different, wouldn't you? Because your life is perfect. I'm sure you've never made a mistake where Aunt Natalie was concerned."

"Oh, my life is far from perfect, young man. I made a hell of a lot of mistakes, I'll be the first to tell you that. There was a major miscommunication between Natalie and I that almost kept us from being together before our relationship ever really began. Because you know what? Communication is the key."

"Right. So now this is all *my* fault?"

"Go talk to Stella, Elias. Listen to what she has to say. All she wants is a chance to talk to you."

"Well, I have nothing to say. And I don't want to hear her excuses! I was done. Thus, why I left. I'm not wasting my time doing the same song and dance again. It's over."

"Look, I'm not asking you to–"

"Why can't she ask me herself?"

"Because you haven't given her a chance to speak to you. You wanted to talk to *me*, remember? Well this is me, your uncle, your elder, your *blood*, telling you to go talk to the woman who loves you so much that she's given up everything to come find you. And in the meantime, pull your head out of your ass while you're at it!"

Jack tossed the brush at him and walked toward the RV.

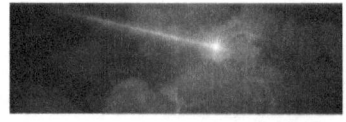

STELLA HELD her breath as Jack rounded the corner and gave her a shrug, as if to say, *"Ball's in his court now."* He headed up the steps of the camper and went inside, closing the door behind him. No doubt she'd overheard their raised voices–not able to distinguish everything that'd been said, but enough to know that he'd handed Eli his ass.

She didn't have to wait too long as Elias approached from her periphery. It was a clear Texas night with brilliant stars lighting an onyx sky. The sounds of crickets lulled her senses, and floodlights from the nearby arena illuminated her beautiful cowboy's face.

"Elias," her whisper brought his head up and his frown deepened, making her heart ache in her chest.

How she'd longed to see a genuine smile light his face again, hear his voice, smell him, feel him pressed against her. It made her teeth chatter and her skin prickle as he came closer.

But his head was down, cowboy hat shielding his face from her view. She longed to pop up and throw herself into his arms, the arms that had sheltered her for three years. She wouldn't be able to stand on her injured ankle, but he would catch her... Wouldn't he?

"Stella, you should go home," he mumbled before she could move.

Home. Where *was* home, exactly? Neither Austin nor Abundance had been home, not since he'd left a giant hole in her heart. Home was where he was.

"Go home before you hurt yourself."

"Please, Eli, I need to—"

She reached out, if only she could touch him.

"I have nothing to say to you. I don't know what you want from me, but I'm not who I used to be. You broke me, Stella. Don't you see that?"

"Eli, I— I didn't—"

"I still love you. A part of me will always love you, but I can't be with you."

"Look at me."

He shook his head and bowed it further. "It's better if you just go. Leave. Now. I won't ask again. You don't belong here, Stella."

"I belong with you, Elias Kinsen." When she moved to rise, he held his hands out to her.

"No, you don't. I don't want you, Stella. I can't trust you. You betrayed me so badly..."

"But that's what you don't—"

"I don't *forgive* you," he interrupted. "I'll never forgive you for what you did to our unborn baby, without my knowledge or consent. Now go home, and don't come back. I meant it when I said I never wanted to see you again. This changes nothing!" He pointed to her foot. "Hell, you probably did it on purpose, didn't you? You're such a good actress. Jesus. You'll do anything for attention."

"You should stop before you say something else you'll end up regretting," Jack's intimidating tone came from the open door of the camper then. "You're *still* not listening, nephew."

"No, the two of *you* aren't listening. I don't want you here. I want to be left alone. I chose this lifestyle, and you have no one but yourself to thank for it."

Stella's jaw dropped as he moved away, back in the direction of his trailer, her body stinging at his hurtful words.

Jack sighed and noted the shiver that crept through her as he moved to her side.

He shook his head. "Stella—"

"I know. It was a mistake. I'm sorry. I'm sorry I dragged you into this. Took you away from your family, your responsibilities, to bring you on this wild goose chase. It doesn't matter. It never mattered, I guess. I should've known, but some silly, romantic side of me was convinced that if he knew his child lived, all would be forgiven and—what? We'd ride off into the sunset together? Jesus. I'm such a fool." She pulled her hands to her face as sobs racked her frame and sorrow filled every cell of her body.

She couldn't control her emotions as they took over her, bringing hysteria to the surface as reality finally sank it. She'd failed. The one thing she'd wanted more than anything else, that she'd worked harder at than she ever had before, hadn't worked. She was a failure, a letdown, a flop. She'd come so close, only to have the finish line fall off the face of the earth. It was useless. She was useless. She'd have to go home and accept that she would forever be a single mother, a single mother with a baby who would never know his father, never know that his father never knew he existed. All because the man hadn't given his mother a chance to tell him about the child.

When her grief was finally spent, and she peeled her hands from her eyes, a thermos lid of amber liquid was thrust at her.

"Here. You could use this. It'll help with the pain."

Stella wasn't sure if Jack was referring to the pain in her ankle or the pain of heartache, regret, and disappointment, but took the cup all the same. She downed it, nodding when he moved to fill it back up.

"You know... Nat was hurt at me early in our relationship."

Stella shook her head. No. She hadn't known that.

"I didn't tell her that I was a millionaire."

Stella's brows rose.

"It's kinda silly now when I look back on it. The reason she was upset, I mean. But it wasn't me being a millionaire that angered her. Hell, she was too. The fact of the matter was that I hadn't told her I had come into money. I gave her subtle hints but never... I wasn't keepin' it from her. I didn't care for her knowing, and why would I?"

Stella watched him as he told the story, letting the man give his audible reverie. He had such a soothing voice as it was.

"Thing is, Nat had an ocean of insecurities to swim through. She'd been betrayed in the worst way possible by her ex-husband. The things he did..." Jack took a deep breath in, closing his eyes. "Needless to say, she didn't trust anyone–especially not me. For one, because I was a man, but also, by not telling her that simple little thing, I made myself appear untrustworthy in her eyes. It was enough to raise doubt. As she saw it, if I could 'lie' about that, what else was I keeping from her?"

Stella nodded. She understood.

"But the truth of the matter was, I thought the money was incon-sequential. It didn't matter, but she didn't see it that way. Two people are never going to see eye to eye on everything. It just isn't going to happen. There are lies we tell ourselves, lies that we live with on a daily basis, but there are lies that we also have to expel and see for what they are—falsehoods. Natalie's lie was that every man was untrustworthy. My lie was that money doesn't matter. Your lie, Stella, is that Eli won't forgive you. What's his lie?"

"That I destroyed him?"

Jack gave her a weak smile when she shivered. "Let's get you inside now, darlin'. You're shivering."

She noticed her hands were numb, but it wasn't cold outside. It had to be the booze. What the hell kind was it, anyway? Her eyes were already crossing.

The ice pack was moved from her ankle, and she was being lifted then cradled in Jack's arms. Her head fell to his collarbone, and she wrapped her arms around his neck.

She moaned at the smell of him: spice, livestock, leather, sandalwood. The smell of a cowboy. Earthy, manly...and, oh so sexy. Her nose hit his jaw, and she nuzzled the stubble there. She was aware of the door opening and the screen slamming behind them as he moved into the RV.

Lights came on as she was carried into her bedroom and laid down with ease, her injured leg elevated. But she was focused on the square jaw in her line of vision, perfect lips—so much like Elias's. Their eyes held for a moment, and she could see green irises, eyes so similar to the man she loved. For a moment, he was there. Her Elias. Her beautiful cowboy.

Stella gripped his face and pressed her lips to his, needing to feel the warmth of them on hers once more.

When he tried to pull back, she held fast and kissed him harder, testing the fullness of those beautifully plump lips.

Strong hands gripped her shoulders and wrenched her from him.

That's when she opened her eyes and realized it wasn't Eli she was kissing.

She'd just kissed Jack.

CHAPTER 6

Stella awoke the next morning to a headache and a stiff ankle, although apparently someone had still been doctoring it. There was fresh ice atop her sock, and her foot was propped on a pillow.

Tears stung her eyes as she thought of her generous and kind Uncle Jack. Ever the gentleman, she'd always loved Jack Kinsen–all the Kinsens, really. Natalie, Dallie, Savannah, Jackson, Gavin, Veronica, Avery, Eli... And although she'd only seen them a couple times Carson, Olivia, Alex, and Ethan–and all their children as well. All the Kinsens were good, honest, hard-working, and lovable folks. The best people she'd ever known. As Elias had said last night, Stella had always wanted to be a part of them–and it would appear she wouldn't stop until she was. What if Elias was right? What if this was all some weird fetish of hers?

Before she could contemplate further, a knock came at the door.

"Come in." She sat up straighter and flattened her tangled hair.

Jack Kinsen's large frame entered with a cup of coffee and a plate of eggs, turkey bacon, fruit, and wheat toast.

"Mornin' darlin'. How'd you sleep?"

Oh, you know... When I wasn't dreaming of Elias, it morphed into you.

"Good. You?" she asked, avoiding his eyes.

"Look, Stella, about last night..."

"I'm so sorry, UJ." Her hands covered her eyes as mortification set in.

A heavy sigh answered her, and the bed creaked and shifted as his weight came to her side. Her hands were moved from her face, only for tears to follow.

"What would Aunt Natalie think of me? I'm so ashamed. I had no right."

"Don't be so hard on yourself, Stells." His palm squeezed her bicep.

God, that was Eli's nickname for her, too.

"Besides, Aunt Natalie doesn't have to know...or anyone else, for that matter."

When Stella looked up at him in surprise, he gave a short laugh.

"I *know*. I don't keep secrets from my wife. And as you've learned the hard way, secrets only hurt those we love. But in this case, what happened last night changes absolutely nothing. I'm not going to be any different with you than I have been...and you're not gonna go and get all weird on me now, are ya?" He elbowed her arm. She giggled.

"Truth is, Stella. I've never once done anything to betray my wife's trust, nor would I. Since I met Natalie, I've not desired or even thought of another woman. She's always been enough for me.

"Perhaps there will come a time when I *will* tell her about it in the future, but it isn't necessary. Like I said, it doesn't matter. You were drinking last night, thanks to me, and you were upset for more reasons than one. My nephew said some pretty awful things. I'm not upset with you, and I do understand. Not to say I'm not flattered, but you're like my daughter, Stella, and I love you like one."

Stella stifled a laugh and wiped at another tear that fell. "I love you too, UJ." She took a deep breath in, needing to unburden her thoughts. "Maybe when I was a girl, it was more than the love I have for you now." She frowned as she looked up into his handsome face. "Please know that I would never do anything to intentionally hurt you or Aunt Nat, or the girls. I guess my only excuse is that all you Kinsens look alike." She shrugged, and Jack gave a hearty laugh.

"So I've been told..." He shifted and brought her chin up to look at him. "Although I'm sure I'm a better kisser than my nephew." He winked.

That got a full laugh out of Stella, and Jack followed, pulling her into his steel arms for a big hug. He kissed the top of her head and patted her shoulder as she sighed in relief.

"I gotta give you credit though, kiddo. You're one *tough* cookie, Stella Rose, and if your parents were here, they'd be mighty proud of you. I know I sure am."

"Thanks, UJ." When he pulled back and handed her coffee, she took it. "But I think it's safe to say that we should take Eli's advice, tuck our tail between our legs, and wave the white flag."

"Is that what you really want?" He arched a brow. "After you've worked so hard for this for so long?"

"I failed."

"No. You haven't. Failure is not trying in the first place. Failure is refusing to get back up and fight. What you've done thus far is not only admirable, it was damn near impossible. Yet here you are, months after having a baby, both a barrel racer *and* rodeo queen–just as you said you'd be. All because you didn't give up on love." His grin got one out of her. "Here, let's check your ankle."

Stella was surprised by his words of encouragement.

Jack moved to the end of the bed, slowly moved her foot from its perch on the pillow, and unwrapped the compress. To her utter shock, it was barely swollen, a dull purple, and she could move it without pain.

"Oh, wow!" she said.

"Impressive... See, fate's on our side. It wasn't too bad an injury, after all."

Stella couldn't help but smile. His enthusiasm was contagious.

"Now, get dressed, eat, and pop a few of these anti-inflammatories. Today, I'm gonna teach you the meaning behind the term 'Cowgirl up,' darlin'."

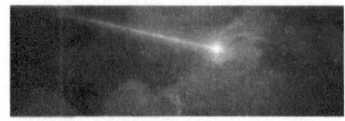

"OPEN THIS DAMN door right this minute, Elias Edward Kinsen, before I break it off its fucking hinges," came a familiar voice Eli didn't want to hear right now.

He padded barefoot to the front door even as the pounding on it–and in his head–sounded again.

"*Fuck!* Give me a sec... damn."

He unlocked the interior door and pulled it open to see a face not so dissimilar to his own through the screen.

"Avery, what are you doing here?"

"I could ask you the same freakin' question. Now, open this freakin' door, and let me in."

Elias pulled a deep breath in and did as his younger sister said.

"What do you want?"

"What do I *want*? Is that a joke, Eli? I don't know what breaking up with Stella did to you–" Stella, there was the name again, the one that would apparently haunt him forever, "but you have a lot of explaining to do, big brother."

A hard slap came to his face as his sister pounced on him.

"Do you *know* what it's like to have a family member *missing* for almost a year? Huh? No, because you don't care about anyone other than your damn self. I could literally throttle you right now." She snarled, lips curled back.

"Do Mom and Dad know–?"

"Why? You afraid they'll come too?" A shove came at him, and he grunted.

He was hungover...again. After encountering Stella and telling

72

her how he felt, he needed to drown her image out of his brain. But the booze hadn't helped. He'd still dreamt of her all night long, per usual.

"I'm *so* damn mad at you, Eli. I've never been more grateful or angry in my life. I can't believe you would do this to us. We sure as hell didn't deserve it." Tears overflowed from Avery's green eyes, followed by another hard shove. "I hate you, even if I do love you, you asshole. You suck, and I want to punch you right in the nose. After I give you a hug."

Eli grinned and pulled her shaking frame to him. He squeezed her tightly, enfolding her in his arms and inhaling her honey-brown hair. It always smelled like strawberries and roses. "I missed you too, Ave."

"Fuck you." Avery sobbed.

Eli laughed. "I deserve all your anger. I'm sorry."

"And a punch in the nose."

"*And* a punch in the nose," Eli agreed.

"You could've at least told us what you were doing. Where you were. Stayed in touch. A phone call every now and again would have sufficed."

"I'm sorry," Eli sighed. "I know I didn't handle things well."

"No, you didn't."

"I'm sorry," he repeated and meant it that time. He kissed his little sister's forehead, even as she continued to cry into his chest. His palms settled on her back, and he continued to hold her to him. He *had* missed her...and his mom and dad, if he were being honest. And Jax and Savannah and Dallie and... *Don't say her name...* Stella.

Avery cried for a time before she wiped her face and looked up. "Elias, you look like shit."

"Thanks. You look great. How's school?"

"I don't know... I took my senior year off."

"Why?" Eli frowned.

"Gee, I dunno. Perhaps to search for my long-lost brother," she smarted.

73

"Ave–"

"Don't. Don't scold me. I'll finish. But I haven't had the right mindset to do so."

Eli sighed. She'd been pursuing a career in marine biology and was looking forward to working in the field, studying dolphins.

"I gave up an internship in the Bahamas thanks to you, jerk face."

"I'm sorry, Avery. Truly, I am." His eyes held hers for a long time before she shoved at him once more.

"It's fine… I'll figure something out. I plan on going to grad school, anyway, this will give me more time to decide exactly what I want to do."

Eli grinned. He was proud of his nerdy little sister. He'd migrated to livestock while she studied the ocean. Living in Corpus Christi had made that a no-brainer for her. She'd always been captivated by the sea.

"How's Mom and Dad?"

"How do you think they are? Worried sick and annoyed at you as much as I am."

"They know?"

"They know you're alive and back in the rodeo. That's all."

"Did Jack tell 'em?" Eli grumbled.

"*Uncle* Jack wasn't who told me where you were."

"Who did? Stella?" Eli snorted.

"You've seen her?" Avery asked and stepped back.

"Yeah, I've seen her." Eli stared down at the hole in his sock.

"Then you know…?"

"Know what?" He frowned as he looked up.

Avery just covered her mouth and shook her head.

"Know *what*, Avery?" He gripped her shoulder, his brows furrowing.

Avery gulped and shook her head again. "She's here?"

"Yeah, three lots down, on the right. Can't miss that big ol' decked-out RV she and *Jack* are shacked up in together."

"Oh, big brother..." Avery tsked. "You are so stubborn, I swear to God."

"You haven't been here! Have you seen the two of them together? It's sick. To think... What?"

"You're an idiot." Avery rolled her eyes. "Unlike you, I haven't stopped talking to Stella over the last year."

"*What*? Why would you stay in contact with my ex-girlfriend? You're my sister, your loyalty is supposed to be to me."

Avery crossed her arms over her chest. "You don't get to tell me who I can and can't talk to. Besides, I only recently contacted her for the record."

He was in *The Twilight Zone*? This was a bad dream. A bad trip, maybe. Someone had laced his drink last night... Yeah, that had to be it.

"Well, you'll get to see her perform tonight if you're staying for the rodeo. Maybe you should get a banner that says 'Team Stella' on it, since you're clearly rooting for her."

"Gah, grow up, Elias. Shit! You're twenty-seven years old."

"I'm well aware of my age, thank you." He rolled his eyes and threw his hands on his hips. "You just... You don't know what she did, Ave." Eli moved away and sat down in the chair closest to the table. "It was unforgivable. I can't..." Elias trailed off, feeling his heart ache at the thought of the duplicity.

"Eli, you don't know the whole story. You never let her talk."

There it was again. Twice now, he was blamed for their breakup. All because he didn't stick around for another excuse?

"It doesn't matter. Whatever she has to say. Whatever excuse she has to make. It doesn't take away the fact that she didn't even talk to me before going behind my back and..." Welling tears in his eyes rendered him speechless. The pain of the blow felt just as sharp as the day he found out that the woman he loved had terminated his child.

"I never thought my life would bring me here. Never thought I'd be living alone in a trailer, running away from my past. This wasn't what I wanted, but she...she broke me, Ave." His voice cracked and tears blinded him.

His sister's arms wrapped around him then, and he took comfort in her embrace, allowing himself the luxury of finally sharing his grief with someone. It had been a long time since he'd felt security and contentment, and he absorbed it, letting his baby sister's presence calm his inner turmoil.

"How long's it been since you had a decent meal?" she asked softly when she finally pulled back. "A while I see..." She looked his lean frame over. "So, let's do this. Let's go into town and grab some lunch. It's close to noon now. Then when we come back, I want you to have a sit down with Stella, just you and her. No me. No Uncle Jack. No one else, alright?"

"Avery..."

"Please? I haven't seen you in a year. You owe me this much, and you damn well know it."

"Fine, whatever. If that will get you all off my back, then fine. I'll do it, but it ain't gonna change anything."

"Right. Okay...." she smarted. "Don't be so sure of that. And you have to *guarantee* me that you'll allow her to speak, tell you what she has to say. Deal?"

Eli scowled and drew in a sharp breath before finally acquiescing. "Fine. Deal."

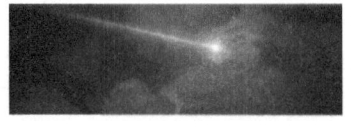

"THERE'S MY BABY BOY." Stella pulled Toby to her breast and kissed his forehead. "I hope he's been good for y'all."

"*Y'all*, huh? You been around Daddy too much already." Savannah Kinsen laughed and swatted at her dad's arm.

"Are you kidding? He's a precious angel baby." Natalie stroked Toby's little arm lovingly.

"Bay-bee," Rowan said and stroked the baby's hair, leaning in to kiss him and getting an "*Awww*," out of everyone present.

"You want one of these, don't ya, Row?" Austin Montgomery, Savannah's handsome blond husband, asked and wrapped his arm around his equally blonde toddler.

"Shh, Daddy. Bay-bee sweepin'," Rowan answered and looked back at Toby with her little finger held to her little rosebud lips.

"Right. Daddy talks too much doesn't he, pumpkin?" Jack asked his granddaughter and smirked at Austin.

Rowan nodded her little head, getting a laugh out of them.

Austin feigned hurt and pouted, getting a kiss from his wife, even as he stroked at her lower abdomen. Rowan settled in her grandfather's arms and continued to monitor the baby, her little hand patting Jack's deeply tanned forearm.

Stella loved being a part of this loving family, even if she didn't share their last name. Her son was of their bloodline and would always be welcomed, as would she.

"We're gettin' a baby too, Rowan," Austin said, oblivious to the fact that he "talked too much." "She should get here by Christmas." He checked his Rolex. "Maybe Santa will bring her, ya never know." He shrugged, grinning at his daughter.

Rowan's hazel green eyes glistened in wonder, and Stella smiled at her.

"Bay-bee?" she pointed to Toby.

"Yup, a baby. Mommy's got one growing in her belly right now." Austin's hand moved over Savannah's very flat lower abdomen again, with so much love that it squeezed Stella's heart.

But Rowan's baby cackle made them all laugh again.

"No, Daddy. No bay-bee." She patted her own tummy and crinkled her little nose.

Another beautiful baby, with Kinsen blood, with those sweet lips, just like her little cousin Toby had and all the other Kinsens. Stella kissed her infant's cheek and watched him snooze. He was such a good baby.

Natalie had been a Godsend. She, Dallie, and Savannah had all helped with the babysitting. Natalie, the woman Stella had modeled after, the woman she'd always admired, loved like a second mom...the woman whose husband she'd kissed last night. Guilt pierced her heart and she sighed and handed Toby off to Savannah.

"Aunt Natalie, can I... Can I talk to you for a minute?"

Jack caught her eye as she stood and tugged at her aunt's arm. He gave her a tight smile, knowing why she would need to talk to her aunt in private. But he didn't look ill at ease, just stoic and perhaps a bit relieved.

"Of course, sweetheart." Natalie smiled brightly and stood along with her.

She led Natalie away from the sitting area of the hotel suite and out the front door. She shut it behind her and stepped into the hallway, pulling in a deep breath as Natalie's blue eyes held hers in inquiry.

"Stella, honey, are you ok?"

Tears stung Stella's eyes and her lip quivered as she shook her head. "I... I did something last night that I'm not proud of, and I need to confess it to you." She swallowed the lump that had formed in her throat. "Oh God, Aunt Nat. I'm so sorry. It just happened. I don't... I drank some whiskey UJ gave me after Eli... well...and..." She pulled a deep breath in, feeling like she might pass out before she could profess her transgressions to the woman who meant so much to her. Her stupid indulgence could change everything. Natalie could kick her out, slap her, tell her to never speak to her again. But Stella had done this to herself, and she must face the consequences of her actions. "Oh, Aunt Nat. I... I didn't mean it. I swear, I would never..."

"Oh, sweet girl," Natalie took Stella's hands in her own, "is this about the kiss?"

Wait! She knew?

Natalie gave her a soft smile and nodded. "Jack called me right after you fell asleep last night. I've never heard my husband so apprehensive to tell me anything in his entire life." She giggled with amusement. "He needed to get it off his chest, bless his heart. Jack is such a good man, after all, such a noble man."

Stella had no words as utter mortification flamed within her cheeks. Her hand came up to cup one of them, feeling the heat, and she tilted her head at her aunt in shock. She wasn't mad?

"I'm not upset, honey. In fact, I found it rather comical. Makes for a great book idea, in fact." Nat rubbed her chin in thought.

Stella gaped. Was she serious?

"Stella," Natalie took her hands in her own again, "I love you both and know neither of you would ever do anything to hurt me. You were missing Eli. You also had some very strong booze when you haven't drank in almost a year. And, let's face it, my husband *is* quite handsome." She winked playfully.

Stella looked down, feeling bad. "There's still no excuse. Booze or otherwise."

"Nonsense. Jack was flattered, as am I, but you definitely took him by surprise. He knew you'd feel horrible about it once you sobered up and didn't know exactly how to handle it, so I worked him through it."

"But he told me just this morning that he wasn't going to tell you."

"That was my idea." Her aunt grinned. "You had enough to feel bad about, after all. You didn't need to worry about upsetting either one of us on top of everything else."

"You know how sorry I am, though, right?"

Natalie shook her head. "Don't be. Just don't go making a habit out of it, ok?"

She laughed and pulled Stella in for a hug.

"I love you both too, so so much." Stella teared up as she squeezed her aunt tightly to her.

"I know, sweetie. And you've been without the love of your life for almost a year now. That has to wreak havoc on your mind and body."

It had. It truly had.

When they came back in, Jack was smiling knowingly.

"Everything alright?" Austin asked, seeing Stella wiping her eyes.

"Just needed to tell Aunt Nat how grateful I am for all y'all have done for me." Stella clasped Natalie's hand as they sat down. She then moved her hand to Vanna's arm and squeezed, getting a grin out of her beautiful cousin.

"We're happy to help. This sweet baby has been precious. So easy." Vanna kissed Toby's head before handing him back to his mother.

Stella looked around at the family who'd accepted her and little Toby with open arms and smiled.

"I have a good feeling about today," Savannah said and took Stella's hand. "Somehow, I just know that Elias isn't completely lost. No matter what he says."

Stella looked down. After the words he'd said to her last night, she wasn't so sure about that.

"I have an idea," Natalie piped in suddenly.

Jack's brows knitted inquisitively, and Natalie's smile made the butterflies flutter in Stella's chest.

"Nat..." Jack warned.

"No, just hear me out. You know I have a flair for the dramatic, but this calls for dramatic, am I wrong?" Natalie's eyes held Jack's, and the love in them tore through Stella's already breaking heart. She looked down to her infant son and took a deep breath in.

Hell, Eli already thought Stella was dramatic. What was one more rehearsed performance at this point? Stella nodded for Natalie to continue.

"Ok, so, here's my idea."

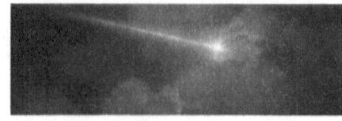

GABE ALMOST FELL off his horse when he saw Eli's little sister, Avery, on the stairs of Eli's camper.

"A–Avery?"

"'Sup, Gabe?" Avery's grin was slightly playful.

Eli's brows drew. Why the hell was Gabriel all frazzled over his baby sis? Eli's eyes narrowed as he looked his friend over, ready to throttle him if he didn't get his tongue back in his mouth.

Gabe continued as if Elias wasn't even there. "Wow, you, uh... You look... Wow, you look great."

"Hey, thanks." Avery looked down at her skinny jeans, UGG boots, and caramel-colored turtleneck shirt beneath a fleece white vest then back up at Gabe. She'd always been sensitive to the cold, despite living in a state where the temperature was in the mid-seventies on average and rarely dropped below fifty. Not to mention the humidity. But it was fall time, and they were in Amarillo. It was a bit colder here with the day's unseasonable chill.

"If you're done appraising Ave's latest fashion attempt, can we go practice now?" Elias smarted, annoyed.

Gabe's goofy grin didn't leave Avery's face. Elias had to clear his throat several times and finally slap at his best friend to get his attention.

"What?" the ginger asked, looking dazed and confused.

Eli shook his head. *Jeez, dude, get a grip!* "Practice! You know since we're neck-and-neck with your buddy, Mac?"

"Oh, uh… Yeah, sure. Wanna come watch us, Avery?"

"You know I prefer underwater creatures to livestock, but sure, I'll come hang out with y'all." She shrugged and pranced down the stairs.

Great! Another set of eyes to judge him.

Catching up with his sister today had felt good, though. He could feel the past year's bitterness start to dissipate as she spoke of their childhood, her classes, and their home.

She had cried again while they ate in a little diner in town and Elias took her hand, apologizing once more. *"You know I would never have hurt you guys if I hadn't...*" Elias trailed off. It was still so hard to speak about what Stella had done. He'd worshipped the ground that she'd walked on, and she single handedly ripped his heart from his chest and stomped on it.

"*Oh, Eli, it's imperative that you talk to Stella. There are things that you just don't know.*"

It didn't matter. The past was the past. There was nothing that could be done to change it, but Elias nodded to appease her, wanting to end talk of Stella. He'd asked Avery about their parents, and she'd smiled and proceeded to tell him what all had happened over the last year. At least they'd moved the subject off him, for a change.

They'd finished lunch and came back to the fairgrounds so Eli could practice.

"Did you get a hotel in town?" Eli had asked her on their way back.

"Nope. I figured I could stay with you tonight."

He'd have to change the sheets, but he would gladly give her his bed and take the couch. Which was fine; he *had* missed her.

It didn't look like Avery planned to let him out of her sight though, and he couldn't really say as he much blamed her. He and Gabe tacked up their horses and began riding in the practice field, getting ready for the last performance of the weekend.

Eli hoped to crush his time, until he heard Avery squealing. He looked up to see her hugging Stella. What the fuck?

"Damn, she looks great... doesn't she?"

Gabe's assessment of his sister pissed him off, on top of witnessing Avery's joy at seeing his ex-girlfriend.

"Her hair's longer... She's really grown into quite a beautiful wom–" Gabe's appraisal ceased as Eli's eyes burned into his. "I mean, you know she was just a knobby-kneed kid for the longest." Gabe's cheeks reddened.

Eli crossed his arms over his chest.

Gabe gulped. "I mean, for a kid sister, she's...she's not bad."

Eli remembered another "knobby-kneed kid" who'd grown into

her own and the dazzling blonde starlet's presence never failed to leave him in awe.

She looked so beautiful. Stella. In a pair of tight Wrangler jeans, a checkered pink button down, and her tan Stetson. He longed to raise her, spin her around, and pull her curvy frame to his.

Dammit! What was happening here?

"Practice! Why are we stopping?" Eli shouted.

Gabe gave him a weak smile as Eli turned his horse away from his view of the girls and got his head back in the game.

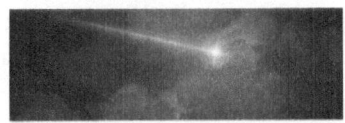

"Wow, Stella, you look amazing," Avery gushed, her heart heavy as her brother rode away.

"You do, too. You grew your hair out. I love it." Stella ran a hand through Avery's long, curly honey-brown locks.

"Thanks." Her voice lowered. "I see you haven't told him yet."

"No," Stella shook her head and looked down. "He hasn't exactly given me the chance to do so. He hates me so much."

"He was always so *damn* stubborn," Avery answered with a sigh.

"A Taurus, through and through."

"Oh, you don't know anything. Try living with him *and* my dad, who's a Scorpio." Avery rolled her eyes, getting a laugh out of Stella. "Where's my nephew?" Avery looked around.

"In a hotel with Natalie, Savannah, and Rowan at the moment." When Avery's brows drew, Stella continued, "I didn't wanna come waltzing on the grounds with a baby and overwhelm him. I thought it best to tell him first, then let him meet his son."

Good point. It was gonna be hard enough for Eli to accept the fact that Stella hadn't in fact gone behind his back and had an abortion as he'd thought, let alone understand that he was now a father.

The last ten months had been hell for her and her parents as they'd desperately searched the country over for Elias. She'd been in constant contact with her entire extended family, calling Jack and Jackson with optimism, and bugging Ethan and Alex, hoping Eli might have gone up to Wyoming. Every week, no news. Until finally her uncle Jack had called her a couple months ago.

"Avery, we found him!"

Avery had literally fallen to the floor in thankful tears when Uncle Jack had told her Eli was back in the rodeo circuit again, competing, moving northward, and following the IPRA.

Jack had a plan, and he'd made her promise not to interfere, which had been difficult. She'd told her parents, and they'd been completely relieved that he was alive and well. But she'd also gotten angry when they didn't seem as eager as she was to reunite with him.

"So?"

Her mom had looked at her as if to say, *"What?"*

"We aren't going after him?" Avery contested in annoyance.

"Why? It's obvious he doesn't want or need our help, Avery?" her father replied.

"Dad! He's your son. He needs you right now. He needs all of us!"

Gavin Kinsen had shaken his head in defeat. *"No. Apparently, he needs no one."*

The pain in her father's green eyes had cut her to the core. Same with her mother. Disappointment. Heartbreak. They were glad he was ok, but they weren't going to suffocate him or beg him to come home. They'd never been the type of people who interceded where they weren't wanted. That knowledge had ripped through her. She silently vowed to bring her brother back into the fold, even if she had to go at it alone.

She'd contacted Stella and was shocked to find out she had a nephew. She'd flown to Abundance to meet him the very next day. Toby was a precious angel that looked so much like her brother that she'd bawled like a baby all over again. Stella had told her every-thing: why Eli left her, how she'd begun training to be a rodeo contestant, and about her plans to win Elias back.

Now, here she was, not interfering so much as helping propel the plan along. If she could aid in this situation in any way possible, she was going to do so.

"Stella, you *have* to show him the baby."

Stella pulled a shaky breath in. "I dunno, Avery. Natalie said the same thing last night, but..."

"Tonight! You go talk to him in his camper, and I'll tell Aunt Nat to bring Toby here. When you're ready, we'll step in and let him see the proof that you didn't do what he thought you did."

"Oh, Avery, I'm so scared." Stella's bottom lip quivered, and Avery pulled her back in for a hug. She shuddered for a moment before pulling back, tears silently flowing down her cheeks.

"What if he doesn't believe me? What if he doesn't think Toby is his? What if–?"

"It's time, Stella. He *has* to know. He has to see him. Then he'll know the undeniable truth."

Stella nodded while Avery stroked her hair and reassured her. Finally, Stella gave her a confident smile, the one that had won her multiple TV and movie awards. "It's time."

Jack walked over and grinned at Avery before pulling her in for a warm hug. "How are ya, sweetheart?"

"Good, Uncle Jack. Better now that I've been able to talk to him." Avery looked back out at Elias, riding hard after a calf, lasso high in the air.

"It's all gonna work out, darlin', I feel it... right here." He pointed to his heart and patted her back as he pulled back. "Stells, let's saddle up. It's time for your final performance." He gave Avery a wink, and he and Stella walked away.

Avery watched Eli and Gabe in the practice field for a time, sitting on a large boulder. Her brother was good at being comfortable on horseback. He also had a knack for calf-roping. She'd never really admired his efforts until now. It was amazing how much one took their sibling for granted. She'd truly thought she'd lost him. It was incredible that he was here before her now. Save for needing a decent meal and to lay off the booze a bit, he looked good.

"Howdy," a voice called from behind her, and she turned to see a dark and handsome cowboy stopped behind her chewing on a piece of hay, hands tucked into a pair of jeans that looked poured on.

"Howdy," she answered back awkwardly. She had never been a cowgirl, herself, so the greeting felt foreign on her lips. The stranger must have picked up on that because he laughed.

"The name's Mac. Who might you be?"

"I'm Avery. Avery Kinsen, Elias's sister."

"Well shit, must be a family reunion in town, huh?" His smirk was one of amusement.

Avery's brows drew. What was he talking about?

The cowboy tried again. "What brings you to Amarillo?"

"A family reunion," she smarted, and the stranger laughed heartily again.

"Figures. You ride too, darlin'?" *Ugh, one of those...* she thought.

"I ride...but not horses." She replied, looking back out to her brother, who was now frowning at her company.

"Oh really?" Mac smirked. "And what is it you do ride?"

Drawn back in, Avery glanced back to the cowboy, his deep eyes trailing over her frame. *Oh shit!* She hadn't meant it like that. She snorted, annoyed with his chauvinistic tone. "Dolphins. I ride dolphins and whales."

The cowboy threw his head back and wailed in laughter, getting a scowl from Avery. She crossed her arms over her chest, waiting for his chuckle-fest to end.

"What is so funny?" she asked even as tears fell from his eyes. He laughed even louder.

Avery huffed and stomped her foot in annoyance.

Finally, Mac wiped his eyes and gawked at her. "Wait! You're serious?"

Avery had no words. This man was insulting her. "Yes, I'm serious."

That got him to laughing again, and Avery put her hand up, shooing him away.

"I'm sorry, darlin', I thought you were jokin'."

"I study marine biology, asshole," she muttered under her breath.

"Sorry," he chuckled again then squatted down next to her as she sat back down on the boulder. "That's cool, but... I mean, you do understand how weird it is to hear someone tell you they ride dolphins and whales, right?" The cowboy covered his mouth with another snicker.

Avery's eyes cut to his, and he canned it.

Yes, now that she considered it, it was probably highly strange that she told him she rode aquatic mammals, but that was Avery–a horse of a different color. She shrugged and propped her feet out to continue watching the practice session that seemed to last a lifetime.

Mac didn't seem to take the hint. "Ya know, I won best all-around last year...and the year prior."

"Oh, that's impressive," Avery's tone sounded the counter opposite as she looked down at her nails.

"Yup. I aim to win again this year if Tweedle-Dee and Tweedle-Dumb here stay out of my way."

About that time, Gabe rode up and stopped a good six feet away. "Avery, is this douchebag botherin' you?" His dark auburn brows were drawn and he sat rigid on his steed, appearing almost regal.

Her older brother's friends had always been protective of her, especially Gabriel. He'd gotten suspended for her one day after punching a bully in the face that had been trying to steal her lunch money. Come to think of it, he'd always been at just the right place at just the right time. *Interesting*, Avery thought.

"Gabriel Halloran, ever the cock-block."

Whoa! How can he be a cock-block when...?

"Hard to be a cock-block when you're talking to *my* woman, asshole," Gabe growled.

"Whoa, wait just a min–" Avery began.

"Really?" Mac bellowed loudly. "*Your* woman, huh? Think you get

87

dibs on *all* the chicks walking around her, Gabe. I don't think so, dickwad."

Jesus, talk about a penis envy. Avery rolled her eyes.

"I'm sure your *girlfriend* here would be surprised to hear about all the women you've bedded this weekend alone." Mac's sly smirk was triumphant.

Gabe's freckled cheeks pinkened before he snorted, taken aback.

Avery wasn't sure whether to laugh, gasp, or retreat when her brother saved her from the decision.

"You boys done comparing dick sizes?" Eli tipped his hat at Mac, who lifted his chin in defiance. "Or are we gonna let our standings do the talking?"

"Numbers. That's where Gabe here excels, isn't it, *Van Wilder?*" Mac responded, his voice dripping sarcasm.

Gabriel's face fell, appearing embarrassed before his blue eyes looked back to Avery's in apology. What would he have to apologize for?

"We'll see who has the last laugh, McCormick."

"Yes, Kinsen. Yes we will. Good luck tonight, boys. I'll buy y'all all a round of beer once I've won. See ya later, darlin'." With that, the handsome, bearded cowboy tipped his hat and turned.

When he was out of earshot, Eli looked to Gabe, whose gaze stayed riveted on Avery.

"Can we get back to doing what we were before he ruined it?" Elias asked and rode off, annoyed.

Avery stared back into Gabe's face.

She'd never noted him to be handsome. He hadn't been a pretty boy in his youth. No Ryan Reynolds or Chris Hemsworth, by any means. He hadn't been in competition for sexiest man of the year... But he looked different now at twenty-seven compared to the soft, boyish features of a seventeen-year-old. Though she'd seen him as recently as a few years ago, it was as if she were seeing him for the first time. The curve of his stubbled square jaw, his long, aquiline nose, his soft lips, a stark contrast to those piercing glacier-blue eyes.

His dark auburn hair peeking from beneath a silver Stetson, the matching stubble covering his cheeks and chin, and those perfectly sculpted brows, drawn in dominance.

Suddenly, he was sexy. Sexy as all get out.

Avery gulped as her eyes fell down his chest, a broad solid chest where a tuft of copper hair stuck out beneath his blue-checkered button-down shirt. He'd rolled the sleeves up his arms, showcasing his freckled, muscled forearms. He was bigger than he'd been in school, and not in a fat way. He was all muscle as her eyes continued to descend his torso and fall to his thick thighs.

Shit! Am I seriously checking out my brother's best friend right now?

Avery's eyes shot up to his, and she took a step back.

"Are you ok, Ave?" When had Gabe's voice gotten so deep and baritone? He'd always just been another annoying friend of her brother's. One who laughed too much and snored too loud when he'd housed a case of beer, but one who she'd always been comfortable around...until now.

"Yes," Avery croaked out, all too aware of her racing heart. "I'm fine."

"Gabe, get the fuck over here before I beat your ass!" Eli yelled, and Avery snickered.

"Guess that's my cue," Gabe joshed and his brows rose. The sexy smile that took his face made his eyes crinkle and the dazzling pearly whites that greeted her made her core tingle.

Gabe tipped his hat and rode off toward her brother.

CHAPTER 7

"Please tell me your dad doesn't know about this guy? I don't want you working with him ever again. He's a sick fuck, and I didn't like that at all." Eli told her, regarding the highly inappropriate behavior of the man taking photos of them during their very sexual photoshoot.

"Eli, I–" Stella's brows drew in protest.

"Stella, I felt like he was watching us hump each other. It was revolting."

"Then why were you so turned on by it?" she smarted back, recalling how aroused he'd been having her almost bare-chested against him. Not to mention how aroused she'd been, herself.

"I was turned on by you. I was touching you, kissing you. You were half naked pressed against me. It was only a natural response."

She crossed her arms over her chest and harrumphed back at him.

"Let me finish," Eli scoffed and looked out the front window, his hands shaking on the steering wheel of his truck. "Your father would have killed that man. There's no way he would have let him talk to you like that. You won't work with him again!"

The finality of his statement couldn't be argued with; he was right. Buck Jenkins would have Nero's head on a spike and come to think of it, the *last two shoots had been even weirder than that one had been. Stella didn't need the gig. She was a model and star all her own, despite her parents' fame. The shoot had only been set up because she was in the area.*

When Eli stopped at a traffic light, she reached out and took his hand. "Thank you, Eli," she stated truthfully. "For taking up for me and being a good sport. I'm sorry."

"You have nothing to be sorry for, my shooting star. I'm sorry if I seem to be overreacting. It's just– I couldn't stand the way he spoke to you, the way he looked at your body like he did. Like he wished he was touching you like I was. It made my skin crawl." Eli huffed out. "I hope I haven't messed anything up with your career. I just couldn't take it anymore."

She just smiled over at him. "I believe I owe you dinner, Elias."

"You don't owe me a single thing. Being in your presence is more than enough." When she frowned, he pulled her hand to his lips and kissed it. "But I have worked up an appetite. I'm all sweaty and sticky though. I'd like a shower first, to wash off more than the oil."

"Yes." Stella laughed. "I need one too." She showed him her sticky hands.

They rode in easy silence before they pulled into the luxury hotel Stella had booked for them. It was a beautiful high-rise right in downtown San Antonio.

"Man, this is nice. I don't know if I've ever stayed anywhere this fancy before, Ms. Jenkins." He tipped his cowboy hat at her, and she practically swooned.

He pulled their luggage from the back and scoffed as she tried to take hers from him. "I'm stronger than I look, Stella. If I can wrangle calves, I can manage two bags." He winked.

She smiled and led them through the lobby as a piano tinkled in the background. The foyer was large with dark marble tiles underfoot and cascading chandeliers hanging from high mirrored ceilings.

After they checked in, Stella taking both their separate room keycards, she waited at the elevator door as Eli pulled their bags in and the valet pushed the button for the eighteenth floor.

Eli smiled over at her and she couldn't help but blush. "I'm still glad I came with you, you know?"

She gave him a grin. "What time do you have to be to the stockyards tomorrow?" She was referring to the rodeo Elias had to perform in starting tomorrow night. They'd worked it out so that the photo-shoot didn't interfere with his calf-roping events which lasted two nights.

"I'll probably go in by four so I can do some practicing."

When the elevator stopped on their floor, they got off. Elias thanked the valet and declined his offer to take their bags. Eli was such a stud, and as she stopped at her room and he saw her in, carrying her luggage and setting it down, she couldn't help but gape at his rippling muscles. He turned to her and tipped his hat again. "Well, I reckon I'll meet you outside your door, say in an hour?" he asked, and Stella grinned and nodded. "I guess I should dress up for this dinner?" His smirk had her reeling. She couldn't wait to see how dashing he'd look in a suit. Again, she nodded. He winked and turned to leave.

She called to him and he stopped and turned back around.

"M'lady?" If he tipped that damn cowboy hat one more time, she was jumping his bones, she didn't care how desperate it made her look. She couldn't stop her audible gulp and bit on her lip. His eyes fell to her lips then and they darkened with what looked like desire. He stepped forward, closing the distance between them. He took her chin between his thumb and index finger. "You're much too good of a person to allow anyone to treat you any such 'a way as that man did, Stella Rose. He doesn't deserve to breathe the same air you do."

With that, Elias Kinsen leaned down and kissed her. He kissed her breathlessly, allowing his tongue to slide in and do incredible things to her insides, unraveling the very fabric of her being, until she was panting and yearning for more. Then he pulled back and grinned devilishly before he left her room.

And just like that, Stella was over his cousin, Jax.

You CAN DO THIS, *Stella, you're strong.* Stella mustered up the last bit of courage she had left, recalling the kind and caring man she knew resided within the now wounded and damaged Elias Kinsen. The man she loved with all her heart and soul.

She'd finished her competition that night, coming in dead last, but was proud of herself for even competing in the first place. UJ had sung her praises as she'd come racing back to the starting gate. His joy had been hers too. She might not be a "winner," but she'd accomplished a great feat, after all.

She'd also watched Eli compete. He had won second place, overall, losing to first Cayden McCormick, then his own partner, Gabe.

Now, before Eli packed up and headed out of the campgrounds, she had to make her move. She knocked on the door, hoping he wasn't sleeping.

It opened slowly, and Stella prayed that stupid brunette—*what was her name?*—didn't appear behind the screen.

Elias stood, green eyes scorching her soul behind the mesh. He wore a white wife beater and tight jeans that hugged his lower half in all the right places. She gulped as he crossed his muscular arms over his chest and took a step back, clearly not pleased to see her but welcoming her in, either way.

His dark brown hair was damp from his shower and his jaw scruffy, but it was his eyes that gave him away. As annoyed as he was by her presence, he looked ready to have this conversation.

"Come on in," he muttered then turned. "Want some coffee?"

Stella came through the unlocked door and closed it tightly behind her, feeling intimidated in the suddenly tight space with a formidable man who seemed much larger now that she was in his territory. His tall frame moved from the sink to the coffee pot as he worked to make some java—whether to keep his distance or actually stay awake, she wasn't sure. She watched his back muscles ripple and a vision of gripping them in passion flashed in her head.

The last time they'd made love, he'd taken her on her back on their bed in Austin. She could remember every kiss, every touch. The feel of his weight on top of her and his hard, thick shaft plunging deep inside her. She remembered the sweat that dripped from his brow, the smell of his masculine scent, the warmth of his big body. Those muscles as her hands roved his back and biceps, spurring him on. His deep moans, his hot mouth, moving from her neck to her collarbone, her breast, and finally covering her nipple just as she split in two.

But it was his eyes, those eyes that held her captive even now, that she'd been taken by, the eyes that told her how much he worshipped her even as his body performed the action.

She'd not been touched or held or kissed in ten long months. Her flesh and womanhood ached for him, along with her heart and soul.

"Oh, Elias," she stated as she collapsed into the booth of the dining area. She tried to hold back her tears but wasn't successful. She'd had them bottled up for so long. "These last ten months have been so hard without you." She tried to speak from her heart. "You have no idea how broken I've been."

"Try me," he answered and turned to look at her. He propped his hips on the counter and crossed his ankles. "As you can see, it's not exactly been a walk in the park for me either, Stella. But you made your decision, and now you have to be the one to live with it."

"That's just it, Eli! I *didn't*. That's what I've been trying to tell you all this time."

There, she finally had his attention. His sexy brows drew, and he tilted his head.

Continue, Stella, tell him your truth!

"I know what conversation you bore witness to between Tony and myself, but I can assure you, I only agreed in order to shut him up. I would never, *never* abort our baby."

Eli gulped, clearly rattled by what she'd just said. She continued, before he had a chance to interrupt her thoughts.

"I fired him, in fact. The very next day. We got into a huge fight when I told him I was keeping the baby. He was more worried about my upcoming movie. I told him that my baby, and you, came first—no matter what happened with my career. If I had to lose the movie, then so be it. We've since made up," she waved her hand in dismissal, "but I didn't speak to him for six months. I was so pissed that he would even suggest that I terminate the pregnancy. Especially after I figured out what had happened, that you'd overheard and thought I'd actually go through with something like that without talking to you first. It hurt me, though, that you just assumed me to be so..." she trailed off, pain contorting her features. "But, God knows, you were right, Elias. So right. Most everything you said was spot on... And coming here," she rose, inching forward toward him, little by little. "Seeing you in your element, my love... God, I never realized I was holding you back, and I'm so sorry if I was. I never–"

"Wait! Stop!" Elias's hands came up, taking her shoulders. The jolt of his touch made her eyelids flutter. "If you didn't have an abortion, then what happened? Did— Did you lose the baby?" The pain in his eyes tore through her guts, but the joy of hope greeted her heart.

She shook her head and smiled. "No."

"Wh– I don't understand. Stella, what do you mean? What are you saying?" He blinked, clearly confused.

"Elias, our *son* is alive and well. And he looks so much like you. He's my beautiful little cowboy, just like his Daddy."

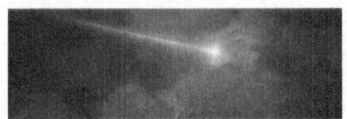

SON. *I have a son.*

Tears came to Elias's eyes as he stared back in awe at the mother of his child. His *child*.

Holy shit. He was speechless.

Stella continued, "Baby, he– God, he's... Oh, wait until you see him. I can't believe he's ours. We made such a gorgeous child."

Ours? This isn't real. It isn't happening. It's a dream. A really, really good dream.

But as Elias pulled Stella into his arms and her head hit his chest, he knew it was real.

"Oh Stella." Warmth spread through him and thawed his hardened heart like butter in a skillet. He felt his anger, pain, and regret all melt away in an instant. She was back in his arms, the woman he'd loved more than anything else in the world. It was a feeling of duality: on one hand, it was as if they'd never been parted; on the other, he felt their separation even sharper, as if it'd been centuries since he last touched her.

Stella. His Stella. His little star. She wasn't the person he'd mistakenly assumed her to be. He'd been wrong. She did love him as much as he loved her. And she'd proved it in every way she could.

His lips fell to hers instinctively, and he savored their warmth–a dying man starving for oxygen, for her, his life, the only reason he lived. She was pulling him from the darkness and into the light, and he embraced her shining warmth.

His hands moved over her back. One tangled into her hair, the other fell to her waist, forcing her harder to his chest. He growled, in turn, as he deepened their kiss. His need for her bordered on desperate, the need to seal this rift between them, to reunite and rekindle, to heal and reconcile.

She was an open well of desire, feeding his flames as she kissed him back with equal passion, her arms wrapping around his neck and her breasts melding to his chest.

"Fuck, I need you, my sweet star. God, I need you so much." His hands moved rapidly over her chest, kneading her breasts before pulling at the buttons on her shirt, his tongue delving deep into her mouth, claiming her as his. Her moan brought his cock full throttle. The bulge ached painfully between the apex of her thighs, yearning for her feminine warmth like a heat-seeking missile.

"Yes, Elias, please?" she begged, and he answered it with a rewarding tongue.

Stella's hands moved to the button of his jeans, freeing his erection. He ripped her shirt and moved to the back of her bra, needing to see and feel her.

"No," she cried and stopped him, as if suddenly remembering something.

She held the bra against her breasts, a blush painting her cheeks, a blush Eli wasn't sure came from her embarrassment or arousal. She fastened the bra back even as she moved forward and took his lips again, her hands falling to grip his hard shaft. He moaned, his body overwhelmed with yearning.

He backed her into the bedroom, and they fell to his bed, Elias atop her as he grappled with her jeans.

Her stroking fist on his member had him quaking, and he sighed with relief when he peeled her jeans and panties from her legs. He smiled as he looked down upon her curvy frame in the dimly-lit room. God, she was just as sexy as he remembered, even more so now that he knew she'd grown and birthed his son. Her body was a verdant garden, his garden. He cupped her upper thigh and moved his fingers through her wet folds, his ears greeted with her moans.

Stella whimpered and arched up into his palm, the heel of his hand grinding into her clit. "Mmm, yes."

His head lowered and he began to kiss and suck at her swollen flesh, thrusting two fingers into her wet heat. "Oh, shit, baby," he murmured, his eyes flickering up to hers, "always so slick and hot for your cowboy."

"Oh God, Eli…"

Stella's whimpering had his dick jerking in longing. At this rate, he'd be lucky if he even made it inside her before he climaxed. The taste of her desire fueled him on as he flicked at her little bud with his tongue, letting her reaction feed his passion. It had been so long since he'd done this act and he realized how much he'd missed it, missed her taste, her smell…

Soon, she was tumbling over the edge, her fists gripping his hair as he brought her to orgasm, licking her slit like she was drenched in chocolate.

After her body stilled, he used the lubrication from her release to coat the tip of his cock before he positioned himself between her legs.

"Wait, we need a condom," she pleaded, but it was too late, Eli was already thrusting inside her.

"Oh fuck," he whined, encompassed by the heat of her, his mind, soul, and body knowing they were finally home. "Just as perfect as I remember, my sweet little star."

"Oh, Elias...baby, yes. Take me." She reached for him as he settled himself atop her, aligning their frames as he took her lips once more.

She arched her hips and climbed with him, wrapping her legs around him and looking into his eyes as he loved her body with his. A love he hadn't been able to match over the last ten months, a love he knew he'd never find in another ever again. She was it for him. His sweet Stella. His shooting star. She was his, and he was hers. They were together again. Finally, his soul had been reunited with its counterpart, and it relished in ecstasy–soul and body.

His thrusts grew frenzied even as he attempted to hold his release back, waiting for her to cave first, but it'd been so long, too long. His love-starved form was finding solace inside her, and he wasn't sure he'd last another minute. He'd somehow become the "five-minute stud" after all, and the wave of disappointment at what he'd done to the woman he loved blasted into him so fiercely, it took his breath.

You cheated on her, you bastard! You fucked other women while she was growing your child. While she was giving birth to your son, you were running away. You're a fucking coward! A piece of shit! You don't deserve her or her love.

Her voice brought him back. "Stay with me, my beautiful Elias."

He grinned, but the pain continued to rip through his heart, even as her sex clenched his and made him grunt in pleasure.

"Love me, as only you can." Her eyes coaxed him on.

And Elias did. Each thrust edged her closer to the edge before his hand moved between her thighs to coax her to submit to him. It was the least he could do, for he'd been so very selfish this past year. So. Very. Selfish.

He pitched his hips, stroking her with his sex and rubbing the delta of her thighs as her cries echoed around the room. Finally, when she split in two, he let go as well, spending his anguish and adoration into her. He continued to thrust hard, gripping her hips in a death grip, spilling himself deep inside her.

"Shit, Stella. Oh God, baby," he groaned as his release continued to wrack his body in delicious spasms. He'd not come so hard since...their last time together. *Damn.*

Eli's heart soared as he came back to earth, holding Stella tightly to him as he looked her over. "I love you, Stella Rose. So damn much. God, I'm so sorry."

He cupped her cheek, and her gorgeous eyes pierced his soul. She gave him a sweet smile of surrender, even as tears streamed from the corners of her eyes. Tears of affliction, tears of regret, sorrow, love, pain, and relief took hold of him all at once. His jaw clenched and his entire body stiffened, knowing it had never been her who was unworthy of him. It was actually just the opposite.

He pulled out suddenly and moved off her, coming to the edge of the bed and letting his head fall into his hands. Grief and shame overwhelmed his entire form. Disgust and regret took hold next.

"Eli?" her soft voice cracked his resolve, and he began to sob. Sob for remorse at abandoning her, his cowardice, the time lost with his baby, with the woman he revered.

Her hands stroked his back and hair, comforting him in the way he remembered, soothing him as only she could. As no one else had been able to since her.

He stopped crying and moved her hands, cupping them in his own.

"I'm such a damn fool, Stella."

"No."

"I am! For not letting you explain yourself. Not sticking around to hear your side of the story. Not stepping in after overhearing your conversation to intervene or fight or tell Tony to go jump in a lake. Believing so harshly of your intentions. Hell, dropping off the face of the planet while you grew and nurtured my child and then gave birth to him." He sighed heavily and closed his eyes. "The things I've said to you, about you. The things I've *done*... Fuck! What kind of man does that make me?"

Violent sobs wracked his body. He succumbed to the emptiness he'd felt for far too long, even as the only woman he'd ever given his heart to pulled him into her sweet arms and cradled him.

"Shh... C'mere, my love."

My love? Like he even deserved her love. He didn't. She was always good to him, despite the fact that he had given up everything to be with her and live as a celebrity's boyfriend. He'd do it all over again because he'd been nothing this last year without her–even if he'd only just realized it.

"I'm so sorry, Stella. I'm a horrible person. What kinda man turns his back on the woman he loves? His child? His family?" Eli pulled his sniveling face up to look at his gorgeous Stella, who simply smiled in understanding at him.

"Eli. I'm here, aren't I? I love you and I forgive you. All I've wanted this last year is a chance to tell you that I never stopped, that I never gave up on you–on us–and, of course, that you're a father to a beautiful son."

Her eyes were so sincere, and it made him feel even worse. "I-I've–" He gulped, unable to form the words. "I've been with other women, Stella." He looked down, unable to meet her eyes. "A lot of women."

"I know. It's ok." The pained expression on her face said otherwise.

"No! It isn't." He huffed, his stomach pitching in disgust.

"Eli, you thought I betrayed you. We weren't together."

"The keyword here is *thought*, Stells. And now I've cheated on you, multiple times with multiple women. I've lived the life of a broken man. I'm not the same person I was before...and you– You deserve better. You've been loyal and faithful and... Jesus." He covered his face again, humiliation consuming him.

"You know the truth now. Things can be–"

"Like they were?" Eli asked sarcastically. "Can they, though? Can they really ever be like they were?" His tone was harsher than he'd intended. "And why were you covering your breasts from me?" He motioned to her bra, the one still firmly attached while the rest of her was bare as the day she was born. She'd never been ashamed to be naked in front of him before, so why was she now?

"I-I breastfeed, so I d-didn't want to leak all over you." Her cheeks reddened then as she looked down.

They appeared to be a bit plumper than before, but Eli thought maybe she was wearing a push-up bra.

He simply nodded, admiring their fullness and imagined his son feeding at Stella's breast. The thought made him smile. *His* son. They had a son.

Stella's hand sought his and his eyes drifted back to hers.

"Look, Elias, I didn't bust my tail to become a rodeo queen and a barrel racer after giving birth to our child, only to throw in the towel because you've lived the life of a bachelor these past ten months. I knew this wouldn't be easy–and it hasn't been–but I love you, Elias Kinsen, and I've fought like hell to win you back. Please, tell me that you sleeping with other women isn't going to be what breaks us now?"

He didn't want it to be. He had lived the life of an unrestricted bachelor, of a rambling man, a cowboy with no code of honor or conduct. But he had a woman who loved him and wanted to be with him, a child, a future. She'd chosen him, despite all his past trans-gressions, and he owed it to her to give her a beautiful life, a life of love and happiness.

"Unless there's another woman you now have a relationship with..." Stella's statement sounded more like a question as she tilted her head. "That brunette–"

"*Cassia?* No. She means nothing to me. Honestly, Stella," Elias took a deep breath in, "It only happened once."

"Well, she *is* really pretty."

"No, Stella...baby," Elias chuckled, relieved, "there's only one woman I want to be with. Only one woman I've been able to make love to in a year, and that's you, my sweet star. That part of me seemed to die when I left you. My dick was its usual self, unfortunately, so I gave it what it needed, but I only did what had to be done. And I always used protection, of course, but I didn't do anything... extra, if you get my meaning." He'd not gone down on any woman since her either, and recalled how delicious she was, how much he'd missed her taste.

Stella looked away and closed her eyes for a moment before holding his gaze again.

"Stella," Eli cupped her cheek in his palm, relishing the feel of her soft skin on his once more, "I never stopped loving you. You need to know that, even if I despised you for what you– What I *thought* you'd done."

"Well, you can stop despising me now, Elias," she stated, tearfully. "Hopefully."

Elias laughed to keep from crying again, himself. "I can. It's quite a relief, you know?"

Stella nodded and wiped the tears from her cheek.

"Look, I know we have a lot of reparations to make. Me, primarily. But I've missed this. You. Our talks, our kisses, just...your presence and how it soothes me." He looked her over, realizing–painfully so–that it was the God's honest truth. "I'm eager to make up for our lost time, if you're willing to let me try. Will you take me back, Stella?"

"Oh, Eli," Stella cried as she threw herself into his arms, tackling him backwards. He held her tightly stroking her long, thick curls and inhaling her sweet scent before kissing her lips lovingly.

She sighed as his hands moved slowly, easily, over her body as if she were a fragile piece of glass, a treasure to be worshipped and revered.

"God, you're so beautiful, so exquisite. You always have been."

"No, you."

Eli shook his head. "I didn't realize how lost I was..." But now he was found once again. Found by his sweet shooting star, the mother of his child. "Stella," he pulled back enough to look into her face, while one hand moved to her plump breast, his fingertips following the curve, "Please tell me about my son. What's his name? How old is he?" His other hand stilled on her waist then moved lower, tracing the lines of subtle stretch marks.

Stella smiled up at him in the moonlight streaming in from the blind-covered window.

"I named him Tobias–Toby, for short–and he's a little over three months old. Born on May 1st."

Elias's face lit up in a smile. "And he looks like me you said?"

"So much." Her hand moved up his arm, over his chest, then down, getting a moan out of him. "He has blue eyes, like most babies do, but your hair color. And he's so sweet and cuddly and eats like a pig."

"Definitely my son." Pride filled Elias's heart then.

"Do you... You want to meet him?"

Eli nodded even as he sat them up, pulled her tightly against him, needing her again, his one true love. "I do... after I make love to his mother one more time."

"Oh Elias." Stella grunted as she aligned her body to his and kissed him fiercely.

He settled her atop his lap, and she began stroking him.

He cried out when she impaled herself upon him and gripped her ass, feeling like he would explode with both love and ecstasy.

As he watched her love him, body and soul, he realized how much he'd lost and gained at the same time. Life was going to be different, fulfilling, *better* now that he and Stella were back together.

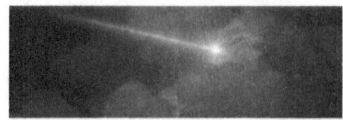

AVERY COULDN'T HIDE her distress as she waited with bated breath while Stella entered Elias's trailer.

"What are you doin'?" came a male voice from behind her, and she whirled around, covering her squeal of surprise with a hand to her mouth.

"Jesus, don't sneak up on me like that, Gabe. Shit... you almost gave me a heart attack." She swatted at Gabe's forearm even as he grinned in amusement.

"Sorry, but you look like you've planted a bomb in there and are waiting for it to go off." Gabriel pointed to Eli's trailer. "You didn't, did you?"

Avery crossed her arms over her chest and gave him a withering look. "Stella just went in there." She looked back in apprehension, worried for both Stella and her brother.

"Well, this is gonna go one of two ways: either a screaming match will ensue, and we'll have to go rescue one or the other; or Stella won't take his shit, and she'll be stalking out the door in about ten minutes because Eli's being his usual dick self." Gabe grumbled.

Avery shook her head. If her brother didn't give Stella a chance to speak this time, then Avery was damned and determined to intervene. This charade had gone on long enough.

"Say... what *are* you doing here, anyway?" Gabe looked her over thoughtfully.

Avery rolled her eyes. "Isn't it obvious? I'm trying to get them back together."

"Why?"

Avery turned her attention fully to Gabriel, surveying his tall frame. "Because she's the mother of his son."

Gabe's auburn brows shot to his forehead and his jaw fell. "Wait... But he...he said..."

"I know." Avery waved her hand in dismissal and shifted her body back to focus on the trailer.

In a matter of minutes, there was movement inside, followed by moaning.

Gabe stepped up behind her, his palm coming to her lower back, as he chuckled. "Well, sounds like they made up fairly quickly."

When a frowning Avery whipped her head to look at him, he pointed to what she assumed to be the curtained bedroom where two silhouettes were indeed melding together in passion on the bed. Her ears got a whimpered, "Oh Eli," before Avery turned her back to the camper.

"Well, that went much better than I thought it would. I was prepared to..."

Another breathy moan had her walking in the opposite direction. She didn't know where to, just out of earshot of the copulating couple. She swallowed, a mixture of relief and envy.

Gabe chuckled again, catching up to her as she strolled the gravel lot toward the arena-side parking lot.

"Glad he finally listened to what she had to say. I'll bet he is too, if I had money to bet," Gabe joshed with a snort.

"Wait," Avery halted. "You *knew*?"

"Knew what?" Gabe asked, and Avery rolled her eyes as if he were the dumbest man alive. "No, I didn't know he was a father. I only knew something was going on because I overheard Jack telling Eli that he 'wasn't listening' to Stella. I figured there might be some unfinished business Stella had with him but didn't realize... Wow, so all this time, huh?"

He'd caught on. Good, it saved her breath. Avery nodded. "Yes, she was still pregnant when he left and tried to find him the whole time. We were all searching everywhere." Her icy glare centered on him for a moment.

"I was sworn to secrecy, Ave. He had some shit to work through."

"Fuck that," she grumbled and shoved at him. "You *knew* we had to be worried sick, asshole. You could have at least told us he was alive without giving away his location."

Gabe's eyes fell to the ground. "He was hurting so much, Ave, and he really didn't want to talk to anyone about any of it. Hell, the only reason he told me was because he got drunk one night and spilled the beans. It was hard enough to convince him to focus his energy on something, *anything*, and when I suggested the rodeo–"

"*You* suggested the rodeo?" Avery frowned.

"He was staying snockered all day, every day. I had to do something! He was wasting away before my eyes. At least, in the circuit, he had something to look forward to, something to drive him. He started eating again, talking to people, and smiling on occasion."

Avery gave him a grin. "You always were his best friend," she elbowed him, "but you still could have told us."

"A shitty excuse for a friend, I reckon." Gabe kicked at a rock with his booted toe.

His cowboy hat shielded his face for a moment before Avery said, "You can make it up to me by buying me a drink. Let's go honky-tonkin'. I mean, I *am* in cowboy country, right?"

Gabe grinned as he looked up at her and stars seemed to sparkle in his eyes.

"Think they'll be alright?" His eyes moved back to the trailer that was now rocking at a dangerous pitch, assumedly from the sex that was being had at the moment.

Avery grimaced. "Looks like they may be there for a while, and I honestly don't wanna hear all...that."

Gabe laughed. "What's the matter, Ave, you jealous?"

"Ha, no..." She looked away, cheeks flaming. "Can't be jealous of something I've never done, now can I, Halloran?"

Gabe's face blanched, and Avery laughed.

"You tell my brother, and I'll kill you. No, seriously. Let's go." She grabbed his arm and looped her own through his.

"Horse or truck?" he asked, playfully.

"Truck. Definitely truck."

CHAPTER 8

Gabe took a long, hard look at Avery Lenore Kinsen. She'd gone from a lanky little girl to a smokin' hot woman in just four years' time. He'd last seen her when she graduated high school as salutatorian.

Tonight, she was anything but scholarly in jeans and a tight, low-cut black tank top that barely covered her full breasts. Her skin was tan from all her time in the Corpus Christi sun, honey-brown hair curled in ribbons–soft and sexy. Her lips were painted coral, and her blue-green eyes danced as her hips swayed to the song on the juke-box–an old country-rock ballad he'd always enjoyed. She held a bottle of beer and laughed while he steadied her.

They'd come to the bar he and Eli had frequented this weekend, Duke's, where they'd reminisced about the past. Avery had proceeded to pound beers like they were going out of style. The talk had started out friendly enough, Ave discussing her field of study, her parents, how relieved she'd been to find out Eli was okay. Then Gabe had informed her about what he'd been up to since high school, his parent's divorce. They'd gotten to laughing about their memories. Memories of the sleepovers he and Eli had had over their many years of friendship–bedeviling her, for most of them–and playing together despite their nearly five year age difference. Gabe had helped Avery learn how to ride a bike at seven, fought off a bully when she was just a freshman, and driven her home. They'd played hooky one day after she started her period during her first class and ran into the hallway, only to crash into him and break down into hysterics. He'd been unable *not* to assist when her devastated eyes slashed his heart like that...

Thanks to the alcohol, their banter had begun to turn flirty. Now Avery was on her fifth beer, while Gabe trailed her by one.

Other cowboys had started taking notice when the glasses and sweater had come off. Avery claimed to be hot–and damn, she wasn't kidding. She *was* hot, in every sense of the word.

Gabe wasn't sure when he'd developed the secret crush on his best friend's little sis, but it had started when she hit high school and gone from an annoying, buck-toothed kid to a sweet and sassy girl of interest. The once subtle softness of her womanly body had developed into dangerous curves. Curves he wanted to explore with his hands and lips and...

"Gabe, dance with me." She grabbed his hips and pulled his pelvis to hers.

He stifled a groan and wrapped both arms around her waist, crossing them in the back as her arms came around his neck, the butt of her beer bottle settling against his shoulder blade. He grinned back into her beaming smile, recognizing the slow song.

"So, when did you start drinkin' beer?" he asked, curious as to the secrets this college girl held.

He'd been shocked to learn that she was a virgin–even more shocked that she'd admitted it aloud, and while she was sober. He hadn't known whether it'd been a warning or an invitation, but he hadn't heeded either. He'd just been stunned, left in awe of her dazzling wake.

She'd proceeded to drag him to this bar and get buzzed. What was her game? Was she blowing off steam, or trying to have some fun of her own now that her brother and Stella had finally reunited?

Stella had been Eli's white unicorn–*or was it whale?*–the one who'd gotten away, the one who'd owned him. Despite that Eli had bedmates over the past year, he'd not cared for anyone since her. It had been glaringly obvious to anyone with eyes. Eli was deeply in love with her.

Gabe was the opposite; he'd never known love. He'd known sex and passion and lust... and lots of it over the years, but never love. Women warmed his bed and he'd gotten all wrapped up in their allure, but none had ever warmed his heart. Relationships were foreign to him. After his parent's divorce, he'd sworn them off completely. He realized long ago that it was trust issues, but then again, looking at Avery Kinsen now... Maybe he'd just not been with the one he really wanted.

"You're one to be talkin'," her accent thickened with the alcohol, and he couldn't help but grin. "You've had a beer in your hand almost every time I've ever seen you." She puckered her lips.

Gabe set his beer down on the top of the jukebox and showcased his hands. "Empty now." He settled his hands back on her slender waist, tempted to slide them lower to cup her plump ass cheeks, the ones enticing him beyond all measure. As if her hips on his weren't eliciting a hard-on already. He cleared his throat, trying very hard not to look down her shirt. Her breasts felt so good against his chest, firm and soft. He wondered how they would feel in his palms, her nipples peaking to the teasing of his fingertips.

"Was that Mac guy right about you?" she asked.

Gabriel frowned, unsure what she was talking about as the blood drained to his favorite body part, pulling it taut between the two of them.

"You bein' the rodeo circuits' stud." Her brows went up in surprise.

The last thing Gabe wanted to talk about was what a man-whore he'd been. Just nights ago, he'd been proud of the fact–a braggadocio to anyone who'd listen. The ladies all loved him, wanted him, his cock... But admitting his promiscuous ways to Avery... He wanted the world to swallow him whole at that moment.

Avery laughed audaciously. "You like women, man. Nothin' to be ashamed of. I thought that was a good thing, to spread your seed and all that. The more women, the more *experience*, right?" The way she said the word experience had his scowl deepening. He suddenly didn't want to think about "spreading his seed," unless he was spilling it inside *her*.

What the hell was happening here?

"What would a virgin know about all that?" He baited when she pinched his reddening cheek.

"It's all biology, right? Men are genetically designed to be polyamorous. It's like a survival of the..." Avery frowned suddenly. "You're right, though. *I* wouldn't, now would I?" she snorted. "Nothing about men or their cocks. Never even touched one." She sighed.

Why was she telling him all this? And why was he so relieved about her not seeing one up close and personal?

"Why?" he asked because he couldn't help himself. Not to mention, he was surprised she hadn't.

She shrugged. "Got better things to do. Like ocean conservation, studying the mammals of the deep, the mating habits of penguins... No guy wants to connect with a weirdo who talks about things like that..." Avery hiccupped then blushed, searching his eyes. "Men want an easy piece of tail with fake tits and a butt the size of our great state. Women who wanna do naughty things and twerk and go buck-wild in bars. They want a woman who'd rather ride in a dirty truck than discuss the effects of not recycling on our planet's ecosystem."

Well, she had a point, but...

"I'm twenty-four, and I haven't even been kissed. How pathetic is that?"

Not been kissed? *Really?* But her lips were so alluring, plump bottom and cupid's bow-top as she pouted up at him. He was having a hard time not imagining their softness against his, that pink tongue licking the tip of his...

"I bet you're a good kisser aren't you, Gabriel?"

That statement, and her sparkling eyes, had him licking his own lips and gulping. "I-I've been told I am." Why was he feeling so self-conscious about himself right now? This was new.

"God, I bet you are. Look at your lips. So big and full and..." Her eyes on his lips caused him to stifle a moan. She bit into her bottom lip herself as if restraining herself, and Gabe's erection went from chub to full-on in seconds before her fingertips came up to his jaw. "When the hell did you get to be so damn hot, Gabe?" she asked.

Gabe all out gaped at her. Did she just call him hot?

"Uh..." he was at a standstill, debating whether he should close out the tab and take her home to sober up or slam her against the jukebox and show her how hot he was...how hot he was for her.

As if reading his mind, she said, "You know, Gabriel..." Her brow arched. "I wouldn't mind losing my virginity to you. I bet you'd know how to show me a good time, wouldn't you?"

He'd been with so many women over the years he'd lost count, but he'd never had a woman invade his senses in the mere half hour this one had, crawl under his skin like she was doing, and make him crazy. Crazy horny, crazy to claim her... But she was, indeed, a virgin—*and his best friend's sister!* And that was territory even Gabe had never entered.

Gabe's heart hammered in his chest. He was certain he needed an ambulance right that moment as her hand trailed his collarbone, settling at the notch of his throat.

"I've noticed the way your hips move in the saddle when you ride your horse. Is it like that? How you move?" Her eyes shot up to his, and he could swear he'd just ejaculated in his jeans. He could feel it weeping from the tip of his cock, as if drawn to her, his essence seeking hers.

He was dumbfounded. Who was this woman he no longer knew? Definitely more than met the eye. Was she just drunk and venting?

Alcohol loosened the tongue, definitely loosened one's inhibitions. But Gabe knew deep down that a sliver of truth always came out when a person was drinking, thus why many people called it truth serum, liquid courage. He decided to call her bluff.

"So you wanna fuck, huh, Ave?" He looked her over in piqued interest. "What do you think Eli will have to say about this? His best friend taking his sister's virginity?"

"I don't really give a shit what my brother has to say about it. He hasn't been around to care what I do, now has he? And dammit, personally, I'm tired of being the only damn virgin in the whole FUCKING bar!" She yelled, causing Gabe to jerk in response.

He looked around and, much to his dismay, the majority of the tiny bar had heard her statement. *Shit!* The mix of young bucks and dirty old men was morphing into wolves circling a cornered deer. Gabe braced himself for a fight. Alcohol always seemed to fuel tempers, territorial disputes, and drama. He was tempted to pee on her, mark her as his territory.

"What age did you lose yours, like fourteen? I'm like a decade behind everyone else." She pouted once again.

She was too loud. He needed to get her out of here before something bad happened to one or both of them. He didn't mind getting another black eye, even if his right one was still green and recovering from the last punch. He'd take another, if it meant keeping Avery safe from the hard-up goons now checking her out as if she were the Porterhouse on a steak menu.

Avery couldn't be more oblivious to her allure as she fingered the chest hair peeking out from his half-unbuttoned shirt. "At least it'd be with someone I know and not some random stranger, ya know?" Her eyes beseeched him.

God, how tempting it was. She might as well be dangling a fresh leg of lamb in front of a lion because Gabe was drooling at the prospect.

He tried to think of every valid reason on God's green earth why he should shut this shit down, and came up with at least a dozen.

There was no good that could come from sleeping with his best friend's baby sister. He'd practically have a target on his back for the entire Kinsen clan to be out for his blood—and there were lots of Kinsen men, not limited to in-laws and such. But her pleading sea green eyes held him captive.

"Did I hear her right, Halloran? Your *girl* is a virgin?" a deep voice came from behind them, and Gabe turned to see Cayden McCormick looking a bit too smug. "I find that quite hard to believe, given your reputation." He then stroked his eyes over Avery. "I can handle that problem real quick for you, darlin'."

"Mind your own business, McCormick." Gabe growled. "You're still seething from losing to me."

"Let's just say, I disagree with the judges is all," Cayden simpered and propped himself at the wall just four feet away.

"Disagree or not, I won and you lost. Just like I told you that you would."

"I'm sure you're feeling on top of the world right now, aren't ya, Gabe?"

Cayden's eyes flickered back to Avery who'd pressed her nose into his sternum to inhale him, causing his erection to jump in reaction. She was either clueless to Cayden's presence or simply didn't care. Her head moved to rest on his collarbone, and she squeezed him tighter.

"I'm a lucky bastard, what can I say?" Gabe hated to gloat, but he felt pretty damn lucky at the moment, considering. Plus, he couldn't stand Cayden McCormick and wanted to rub anything he could into the arrogant prick's face.

"Well, luck can always run out. Besides, there's always next weekend."

"Speakin' of, how come you ain't on the road yet?" Gabe asked, needing him to shoo.

"I could ask you the same question, Halloran, but it appears I'm looking at the answer."

Was Mac jealous? Because he sure appeared to be. There was

almost pain on his face as he took in Avery, soft and sweet, cradled in Gabe's arms and looking like an angel.

Her eyelids were closed and a smile tugged at her perfect lips as if she were the epitome of happy, perched against him–and damn, did she feel like Heaven. Gabe grinned and brushed his lips across her forehead, his palms moving over her back.

"I'll settle your tab, *champ*. You take that girl home and give her everything her heart desires. Or someone else just might," Cayden smarted and turned on his booted heel to the bar, not looking back.

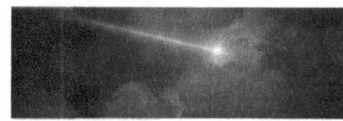

"OH GOD, THE WORLD IS SPINNING..." Avery whined and fell back to all fours again, puking onto the grass just inside the parameters of the campground parking lot.

Gabe's warm palm settled on her back, the other hand pulled her hair back from her face as she wretched the contents in her stomach up again...and again...and again.

He stayed silent for so long, Avery thought she'd imagined him there. When she moved to turn and reaffirm his presence, she got a scowl from his handsome face.

"Sorry," she whimpered. "I'm sure you're completely grossed out right now." She sat down and avoided his eyes.

"Not in the least, darlin'. It takes more than regurgitated booze to scare me off. Try birthin' a calf in the middle of a hurricane, covered in mud, blood, and feces, even dealing with a colicky horse–not to mention the putrid smell of hoof rot."

"I'm gonna stop you right there." Avery pulled her hand to her mouth, trying to get the smell out of her nose at the mere hint of rot. She stifled a gag.

"We should get you some Gatorade and water."

"I never even wanna smell another beer again." She whined.

"The beer didn't do this. The three shots of Jose you housed after is probably what did you in. I'm sure Eli will have my ass for–"

"Fuck that! You aren't my keeper and neither is Elias. Besides, I've drank more than this before."

"Oh, you have, huh, tough girl? When?"

"A year ago, at a frat party..." she explained. "Just because I'm a virgin doesn't mean I haven't had my fair share of good times."

Gabe showed his palms in surrender and laughed, sitting down beside her. "Ok, I yield." He swiped a piece of hair away from her face and tucked it behind her ear. "But I *am* curious, how does one attend one of those wild frat parties and still remain a virgin?" His smile was playful.

"I was drinking with my equally as eco-savvy friends, while the 'wild' frat brothers danced with the 'wild' sorority girls." She used air quotes, getting a crooked grin from Gabe.

"I have a hard time believing not a single guy there found you interesting enough to try to dance with you, let alone take you up to a room to play."

"Maybe I have RBF, or maybe I'm intimidating or something, who knows?" She shrugged.

Gabe shook his head. "I think you being smart as fuck is the biggest turn-on I've ever seen."

"Even bigger of a turn-on than a set of fake tits and a huge ass?" she smarted.

"There's nothing wrong with your tits, Ave. They're perfect, fit-in-your-palm sized." He even raised his cupped palm as if to show her, sending an electric jolt slicing through her to settle in her center at the thought of how it would feel. "Same for your ass. It's definitely squeezable."

Something in the way he looked at her had her shivering, and she recalled their earlier conversation at the bar. "So... you *would* be interested in taking my virginity?"

"Avery," God the way he said her name, his deep, smooth voice, "I think you've had too much booze tonight for us to discuss serious matters like this, ok?" His blue eyes pierced hers, and she had to act fast before she lost her nerve.

Her palm settled on his pec and she scooted closer, letting her thigh cover his. "Gabe... tonight is as good a night as any. I need the booze to take the edge off, honestly. Otherwise, I'd never be able to let you see me naked."

"Please," Gabriel scoffed. "I've seen you in a bikini and trust me when I tell you: Based on what I saw, you have no reason in Hell to be shy about being naked."

That's right. He'd seen so much of her skin over the many years of his and Eli's friendship. That's why he was perfect for her first time. She smiled, feeling her confidence restored, despite that he'd seen her hurl her guts up minutes prior. He'd seen many women naked, and she reminded herself that bodies came in all shapes and sizes. As a promiscuous man, he could surely appreciate them all.

He frowned again. "Why are you so hellbent on losing it in the first place? Don't you wanna save it for like...your husband or whatever?"

Avery tilted her head and puckered her lips at him in disdain. "Ok first off, this isn't 1952. Second, how many people actually *do* that nowadays? Most people have lost their virginity long before twenty-two. And three...what's so sacred about it? It's no more a rite of passage than riding a bike for the first time or eating your first birthday cake or..." She suddenly huffed and crossed her arms over her chest. "*What* is so damn funny?"

Gabe was laughing so hard his entire body was shaking. "You talk about sex like it's akin to ripping a Band-Aid off. You do understand that once you do it the first time, you're opening a giant can of worms, right?"

She scowled at him. What was he talking about?

"I mean, c'mon, Avery. You've never even been kissed, what makes you think you can just jump right into having sex? For most women, it's about connection. For dudes, it's just...well it's...conquest." He gave her an apologetic smile.

116

She appreciated his honesty and understood what he meant, but she'd never had a real connection with a man anyway, so what did it matter? "Because I just wanna get it done and over with, dammit. See what the big freaking deal is. Besides, why do my reasons matter? I'm a woman who wants to have sex with you, so dammit, just...just *do* me already."

Gabe shook his head but grinned. "Avery Kinsen, you are just full of surprises, you know that?"

"Sure, I guess so." She scowled and looked up at Eli's eerily quiet trailer as if waiting for the rocking to start again. "Guess I can't go back in there for a while. Can I bunk with you tonight, Halloran?"

"What, so you can badger me into having sex with you some more?" he teased even as he pulled her to her feet.

"Don't act like it's such a hardship, sheesh." She shoved at him.

"It's no hardship at all. Quite the opposite, actually...but you do understand the predicament you're putting me in, right? If I take your virginity while you're drunk, that violates all kinds of sacred laws of civility."

"What are you, the secret order of the virgin police?" she grumbled as he led her up the steps of his trailer, realizing he was laughing again. "Dammit, that's the last time I ask a man to sleep with me."

"Good, you shouldn't make a habit of it, you know? Men might get the wrong idea about you." He snickered again as he unlocked his camper door and helped her inside.

"Oh can it, Gabriel. You've made me feel bad enough about myself. Fuck it, where's Mac's trailer?" She made a move to go back out the screen door she'd just come in, only to have Gabriel's grip her arm and sit her down in the built-in chair.

"The last person you need to shack up with is Cayden fuckin' McCormick. It'd be like sending a lamb to a slaughterhouse. Nope, sorry, angel. You're stuck with me for the night."

"Joy! I can't wait to see what kind of prudish games we play." She huffed and crossed her arms over her chest. "You're a party pooper, you know that, Halloran?"

Gabe rolled his eyes and moved to the coffee pot to make coffee. "Be mad at me all you damn well please, Avery. Come tomorrow, you'll thank me for it."

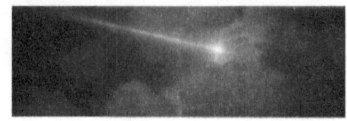

GABE SET Avery's mug of coffee on the table in front of her even as her pout began to unravel his resolve. "Here, drink this."

He took a sip from his own mug and sat down beside her, watching as she took a sip from hers. "Now, tell me truthfully. Where's all this coming from? Why the sudden urgency to lose the virginity you've had your entire life? What's really going on?"

"Well, Dr. Phil, it all started when my brother went missing..." she sassed, and Gabe came close to spewing his coffee all over the floor. "Don't try and psychoanalyze me, jerk. I'm just ready to end my dry spell, ok? I don't need any more reason than that." She shot him a bird and jerked up to stand.

Gabe followed. "Ave, c'mon, I'm sorry. I didn't mean it like that."

One hand cupped her bare bicep, the other moved to her waist.

"Where's your bathroom? I need to pee...and brush my teeth."

Gabe released her and pointed to the bathroom, grateful he was tidier than Eli was.

"There's toothbrushes under the sink. I keep extras."

"For all your one-night stands? Isn't that sweet," she snorted.

Suddenly that fact embarrassed him, and he lowered his eyes.

Avery said nothing as she moved off to the bathroom, and Gabe returned to the table and his coffee.

He realized that if this was any other girl he'd be obliging her right this moment, drunk or not, and that thought gave him pause. Was he really a wolf in sheep's clothing? He felt bad. He'd not had sex too many times when he–or his partner–was shit-faced drunk. Buzzed? Yeah, plenty of times, but not trashed.

But this was Avery. His best friend's little sister. Eli would throw a conniption if he knew the topic of conversation they'd been having. Gabe could tell Eli wasn't happy about the way he'd looked at her since her arrival this morning.

Women hadn't always come easy for him. He'd been the ugly ginger duckling who'd risen to a great swan after he'd gone into the military as a punk kid and came out a respected–and chiseled– Marine. He'd been running from the shock and grief of his parents' divorce, unsure what direction he was headed. After he'd served his eight years, he decided he liked playing in the dirt with his horse more than sitting behind a desk all day. Besides, the rodeo lifestyle was tranquil compared to the horrors of war.

Women seemed drawn to his easy nature and his no-strings-attached attitude–and hell, apparently, he was good in bed. He could fuck for much longer than other men and go again and again, which made him a stud in their eyes. So, he capitalized on the advantage.

When Avery came out of the bathroom, her arms were crossed once more and she looked miffed as if she just realized something.

"What's wrong, little mermaid? Still mad at me?" He pushed his bottom lip out in a pout and got a snicker from her.

"I don't have my overnight bag. No PJs." She shrugged.

"I got a t-shirt you can wear." Gabe motioned to the inset drawers between the bathroom and bedroom, and Avery pulled on the second one. "Take your pick."

"Wow, Gabe. Do you *iron* these?" She unfolded one and held it up, surprised at how tidy and neat it was. Gabe shrugged as if to say, "Guilty."

Then she did something completely unexpected. She began to undress. First, her shirt came up over her head, revealing a flat stomach and a lacy blue bra that begged to be unlatched. Then, she unbuttoned her jeans and slid her hands into them, revealing a pair of lean legs and silky white panties covering the apex between them. Gabe gulped aloud and felt his cock stiffen in salute.

"Holy shit, Ave," he breathed out.

"Sorry, yeah. I guess for a girl who wanted to go and throw her virginity at you, I should have matched my bra and panties, huh?" She looked down at herself, perfectly gorgeous and so close to naked it was downright torment. Gabe bit into his bottom lip, close to drawing blood, as he imagined how good her curves would feel beneath his palms, how good she would smell, how slick her wetness would be.

She didn't flinch as she took his clean shirt and threw it over her head. It swallowed her whole and the hem hit her mid-thigh, making her look like dessert in his book. He stifled a moan and adjusted his rock-hard erection in his jeans.

"This will work," she stated as if she had no idea what torment she'd just put him through. He was definitely gonna have to get his rocks off in the shower before bed, if he had any hope of survival tonight. Even still...

She came to sit at the table and picked her mug up, sipping her coffee. She crossed her legs beneath her, and Gabriel's imagination ran wild, seeing those sexy undergarments of hers. He'd never been this turned on in his life before. Fuck the fact that there were so many reasons why he shouldn't want her.

"I guess I'm just feeling... I don't know the right word... Left out?" she suggested and looked down. "I mean, seeing the way Elias looks at Stella, the way she looks at him. I want someone to look at me like that, too. I've met many guys in college. I even have male friends, but none that–well, you know–that I want to have sex with. I just wanna know what it feels like. Sex. What all the fuss is about."

She looked so comfy sitting there at his table, sipping from his coffee mug, in his shirt. It was so natural that it took his breath. He had no words. He couldn't breathe. He wanted nothing more than to rip that shirt in two, take her to the floor, and show her exactly what all the fuss was about...as she screamed his name in orgasm.

"Gabe?" She reached out and touched his arm, and he grimaced as if scalded. Avery even pulled her hand away as if she had and was horrified by it.

She popped up again, looking all frazzled and out of sorts.

"I'm sorry. I-I should..." She looked at her discarded clothes on the floor. When she made to move, Gabe made his.

His hand enclosed her forearm and whipped her around, hauling her into his chest. She gasped as one hand fell to her hip, the other bringing her chin up as he lowered his head.

The brush of her lips on his was as sweet as he imagined it could be. Her breath was minty from the toothpaste, and her moan was deep as he pressed his own lips gently but firmly onto hers. He angled his head and deepened the kiss before his tongue flitted across her own pliable one, getting her body arching against his.

He pulled back at the movement to assess her...and warn her. "Tell me to stop. Right this minute, Avery. Tell me."

She glanced at his mouth before her eyes darted back to his, and she shook her head. "No. Don't stop, Gabriel."

His name on a set of beautiful lips had never sounded more erotic than it did at that moment, and he indulged in her, in this feeling, and ran with it. He pulled her tighter to him, his mouth fusing with hers in a dance of tongue and lips and teeth that had them both panting and fumbling. His hands moved over her back and down to her bottom, testing the firmness he knew resided there, pulling and opening as he picked her up and she straddled his waist.

He moved them from the kitchenette into the bedroom, ducking to ensure he didn't hit their heads before falling with her to the bed.

"Mmm," Avery cooed as his hand cupped her breast and squeezed gently.

"My shirt has never looked hotter on anyone," Gabe assured her. "But it really spoils the view of what's underneath."

He began pulling the hem of his shirt up her torso, stroking those sexy thighs before he peeled it off her head. "I nearly busted a nut when you began stripping."

"Really?" she smirked, her face reddened.

"Sorry. I mean, you're beautiful," he corrected.

"No, screw that. I mean, you *really* almost busted a nut? Just by looking at me?"

Gabe chuckled. "Hell yeah! Wanna see the proof?"

He pulled her hand to the erection painfully restrained behind his zipper.

Her mouth fell into an O, and he didn't know if her shock was from fear or...

"Damn! You're...you're big, Gabe. Like really big."

Gabe's head fell back in laughter. "How the hell would you know, *virgin?*" he teased and began fingering the lace of her bra, watching goosebumps form on her flesh.

"I-I've watched porn. I've seen dicks before," she offered helplessly.

"Never felt one though."

"No. It's...curious."

He grinned again as she began to tease at his jean-clad shaft with her fingertips.

"Mmm, can I... Can I see it?"

Gabe's brows bobbed as he raised to his knees and Avery sat up, looking like a kid about to open a coveted birthday gift. If he wasn't ready to explode, he would have laughed. Now he knew what the dancers at Chip N' Dales felt like. He'd never seen a woman so eager to see his sex. It made him feel like a king.

He unbuttoned and unzipped his pants slowly, then felt his member bob as he slid his jeans and boxers down his hips, watching her face as she took it all in. She gulped and licked her lips and his cock jerked in response.

"Wow," she said and reached out to touch him tentatively. Her fingertip grazed the tip before her fist gripped the base of his shaft, and he whimpered. "It's amazing."

"Glad you like my cock, princess," he grated out, gritting his teeth as she began to pump him with curiosity. He watched a bead of precum come to the tip as she milked him and became as fascinated as he was by her fascination, especially when her other hand discovered his scrotum and began tickling him into a new erotic torture.

After several minutes of restraint, he said, "Avery, I don't know if you understand how a man's body works, but I'm about to soak your face in cum if you continue this much longer."

"Oh, I'm sorry." She immediately moved her hand from his cock, much to his relief and dissatisfaction.

"Don't be sorry. I'd just rather finish inside you than in your hand, if you get my meaning." He winked and she blushed. "That is, if you still wanna–"

"Yes!" she blurted out, and he stifled a laugh at her enthusiasm. "What uh, what next?"

"Well, usually I start here," his fingers drifted back to the soft mound of her breast and he began laying her back onto the bed, "and work my way down, but we can start wherever you want."

"No, uh, that works." She moaned when his mouth came back to hers in a searing kiss. His hand cupped her breast before he moved both hands behind her, to unfasten her bra. She didn't protest as he let the garment slip from her skin and he licked his lips as his eyes beheld her round breasts with small, pert pink nipples.

"Beautiful," he muttered before he kissed her again.

When they pulled back for breath, Avery said, "I really like kissing you, Gabe."

"I like kissing you, too, Avery. Let's see if your tits like kisses as much as your lips do."

She cried out as his lips settled over her erect nipple and pulled it into his mouth. He gave it a little nip and flicked his tongue over it, rewardingly.

"Oh my God, Gabe. Holy shit... Mmmm."

"Like that?" His eyes held hers as he repeated the motion again, letting one hand drift to her opposite breast to attend to her other hungry nipple. The other hand began moving down her hip, to the edge of her panties. Her hips arched up against his, and he answered her moan of pleasure.

He feasted on her breast for a few moments before moving to the other, her hands gripping his shoulders and falling into his hair.

She was panting before his hand moved to her panties and stroked her through the fabric. She gasped and arched against him again as he pressed his heel into her, savoring the sound of her pleasure.

"Let's see how ready you are, sweetheart." He peeled her panties down her hips and off her legs before sliding a finger through her folds. He swore when he felt how drenched she was. "Fuck, Ave... You're soaking wet."

He thrust a finger inside her and used the heel of his palm on her again, grinding as his mouth fell back to her breast. Her head shot back and she moaned again. "Oh, shit."

"Mmm, yeah... Come for me, baby. I can't wait to fuck this tight little pussy."

"Oh, God, Gabe." She arched again as he moved his finger faster and suckled her nipple harder. He felt the moment when she split and her hands held onto his shoulders as she spasmed, her womanhood clenching his finger so deliciously.

She was still panting when he pulled the nightstand drawer open and grabbed a condom. He ripped the packet and had himself sheathed in record time. He settled between her legs and peeled his shirt over his head, then gathered her in his arms. He kissed her lips and moved his hands over her, feeling her quake before he pulled back and looked into her face.

"It's not too late to stop this, little mermaid. It'll suck, and I won't be happy about it, but if you don't want–"

"No, I want to. I do. Please, Gabriel?"

Her answer made him smile, and he cupped her cheek. "You're stunning, do you know that? This is for you. All for you, Avery." He grabbed his shaft in his hand. "Now, you know this is gonna hurt at first, right?" She nodded in answer. "I'll go slow. But still..."

"I know. It's ok. Let's do it."

He nodded before stroking her folds with the tip of his shaft, skirting the entrance of her body. When he shifted his hips, the head of him entered her and he thrust in gently, slowly. Suddenly the feel of her began to overwhelm him, and he felt like an inexperienced teen about to shoot his load. Fuck, she was tight. So damn tight. He gritted his teeth and braced the hand that was guiding his cock inside her against the headboard, needing a break.

"Fuck, fuck, fuck..." he breathed.

"Gabe, what's wrong?" she asked and held his eyes, concern echoed there.

"Nothing, princess. It's just... shit, baby, you're so... I've never been with a virgin. You feel fucking amazing."

"I'm your first, huh?" her brow arched and he almost laughed, causing him to whimper in agonizing sexual bliss.

"Jesus Christ, I'm gonna cum, seriously." He breathed out. "Give me a sec."

Inch by inch was straight torture by silken heat until he was fully seated within her. His finger stroked her cheek as he asked, "You ok?"

"Yeah, it's just pressure, but it doesn't hurt."

"Thank God," he answered, honestly. "I'm gonna move now, alright?"

Her nod was all he needed as he withdrew and plunged back inside her. She gasped, and he stilled cautiously, but her wrapping her legs around him was his answer to keep going, so he did.

He withdrew and thrust again, deeper this time... and then something happened. He wasn't sure if it was her body, her moans, or her fingernails digging into his back, but suddenly he was all encompassed by this gorgeous virgin, enthralled, entranced.

She had him under a spell as each dip of his hips brought them closer and closer to oblivion. His grip on her tightened as he held her gaze, watching her reactions as her womanhood took every inch of him within her, accommodating him as no other woman had before. This wasn't just sex, it was something more, something deeper. He immediately felt a connection.

Maybe it was because he'd known her for years, they'd had an association that went beyond their physical one, but Gabe felt as if he was touching some pinnacle he never had, in the bedroom or otherwise.

As her body yielded to his ministrations, his heart felt fuller, as if it might explode, and when her sex contracted around his, he roared a mighty pleasure cry as they came together.

His groan was one of surrender as he spilled himself, continuing to rock into her until he was spent. He held her while their bodies continued to savor the last of their sexual union and he looked into her blue-green eyes, eyes that swirled like waves in a churning sea.

"Wow," he said in shock and awe.

"Wow," she agreed.

"Oh, we're *so* doing that again," he said and kissed her.

"Mmm," she agreed and returned it, her tongue stroking across his. "So, porn wasn't lying about that?"

"Not where I'm concerned. I can go again and again. You just say when, darlin.'"

Avery ran a finger across his jawline and smiled. "Thank you, Gabe."

"No, thank you." He looked down at her ample bosom, red from the chafing of his stubble. "So you see what I was talking about now, huh?"

"Oh yes...can of worms for sure."

Worms, hell... Gabe knew he had just opened Pandora's box. But he was more concerned about what Eli would say if he knew. Only, Eli didn't have to know. Not right now, anyway. Not when he had a beautiful woman tracing the lines of his pecs and bringing his erection back like Avery was right this moment.

Gabe would worry about his best friend tomorrow. Tonight, Avery Kinsen was his.

CHAPTER 9

*E*lias couldn't contain his nervousness. He was meeting his son. His *son*. The child he'd dreamt about, the one he'd wanted since he heard Tony tell Stella to abort the pregnancy, the one he'd mourned...

Stella gave him a weak smile as she rapped her knuckles on the hotel room door. Eli took a deep breath and held it as his uncle Jack came into view.

Jack beamed at a still smiling Stella, then Elias. "It's about damn time." A huge weight seemed to lift from his shoulders as he pulled Eli in for a half-hug. "I knew it wasn't too late."

"I guess I owe you an apology, Uncle Jack."

Jack shook his head. "Nah, we're square, kiddo. No need for all that. It's been a rough year. I'll cut you some slack." He slammed his palm down on Eli's shoulder blade as Eli stopped in front of his Aunt Natalie, who held a small blue bundle in her arms.

"It's good to see you, Eli. Would you like to meet your son?"

Eli turned to Stella, whose lips quivered in both joy and sorrow equally. She nodded as Natalie stepped forward and held out the baby for him to take.

He gingerly took the infant in his arms and felt his heart swell to bursting. The babe was so small but plump with health, a set of perfect lips, full, thick eyelashes that sat on his tiny cheeks, a pert little nose, and a head full of brown hair.

"Oh Stella." Eli felt tears brimming in his eyes and couldn't hold them back. He settled his child in the crook of his arm and stared in awe. "He's beautiful."

"I told you," she whispered. "Just like his daddy."

Eli swallowed the sob in his throat and looked at her. "You're amazing. You did so good. *We* did so good. Wow, I-I'm stunned." He began peeling the blanket off, needing to see how perfect his son was. He was pleased to find ten fingers, and although his toes and feet were covered in the footed onesie, he felt the little feet to verify it. "Are we sure he's a Kinsen, though?" Eli laughed as he looked up Stella. "He's awfully little."

Natalie glared at him in shock, and Stella balked, elbowing him playfully.

"He's the second smallest male Kinsen on record, weighing in at a full pound more than your dad, Elias," Jack stated.

"Dad was the smallest?" Eli asked in surprise, although Gavin Kinsen was still the shortest of them all at five foot ten. "Who was the biggest?"

Natalie smirked. "Jax was, believe it or not, but don't worry. Toby may be small now, but one day he'd be as big as you are Eli."

That didn't seem possible. Not as Elias threaded his finger into his son's itty bitty palm and grinned, falling in love.

"For the record, my little cowboy here is about thirteen and a half pounds, so he's not super small."

Eli grinned at Stella before beholding his son once more. "I've never loved anything so much in my life." Tears continued to stream down his face, and he brushed a knuckle across Toby's cheek. "And yet I missed it. All of it. Because I was so…"

"Please don't beat yourself up. You're here now, and that's all that matters," Stella pleaded, looping her arm through his. He gazed at her gorgeous face, awed by her strength, her determination, her love–for both him and his baby.

"You didn't give up on me."

"I couldn't. Not until you knew that your child lived. Until you got to meet him. If you'd turned your back on me, fine, but I knew you deserved to know you are a father."

Toby began to pout. Eli was surprised at the set of lungs on the kid as he cried out. "Uh oh..." Eli grimaced.

"He's probably just hungry. He was sleeping so good that I didn't want to wake him, and I figured you'd want to feed him yourself." Natalie patted Stella's arm.

"Oh yes, thank you. I'm full...again." Stella scowled down at her swollen breasts.

"It never ends, especially in the infant stage. I felt like a dairy cow with mine." Natalie winked.

Eli reluctantly handed Toby over to his mother. Stella sat on the bed, cooing to him. It was the most adorable, heart-rending thing he'd ever seen. He wanted to fall to his knees and beg for her forgiveness, confess his undying love, and swear never to betray her again. But he stood there, dumbfounded, as she propped the babe between her crossed legs and began to unbutton her shirt.

"We'll head out and give y'all some privacy," Eli's aunt told them, grabbing for her purse.

"You don't have to, Aunt Nat. You know I don't mind." She really didn't seem to as she pulled a nearby baby blanket over her shoulder to cover herself, cradled the babe to her breast, and unlatched her bra. Eli felt a sense of masculine pride as he heard his son latch on and begin suckling.

"How about y'all take the room tonight, and we'll head back to the RV? I'll text you in the morning, then we'll pack up and head out."

"I hate to inconvenience you," Stella protested.

"Nonsense. The crib is already set up here, no sense in you having to move everything. Get some rest." Nat leaned in and kissed Eli's cheek, patted Stella's, then turned on her heel to exit the room. Jack followed, tipping his cowboy hat with a grin.

They were alone with their son for the first time ever.

Eli stared after his aunt and uncle, the one's who'd done all this...for him. Well, for Stella, but ultimately for him.

The room grew quiet as Stella pulled the blanket back to peer down at their child while he fed. She grinned down at him, and Eli was entranced by the scene before him. The babe gazing up at his mother, the greedy suckling, the murmur of Stella's voice as she cooed to their son.

Eli fell to his knees before her, needing to feel that connection, the one he'd thrown away on a whim. He cupped Stella's knee with one hand and the back of Toby's head with his other.

"I realize that I didn't ask you how it was? The birth. I just...moved right in and had my way with you. I didn't hurt you, did I, my sweet star?" His palm settled on her lower abdomen.

"No, not at all. I've been healed for a while in that area." Stella winked. "But the birth was intense. Not to say I wouldn't do it again, but..."

"Does that hurt?" he asked, looking at his son's mouth on Stella's nipple.

"It did in the beginning. I'm used to it now, though. It's our own time together–right, little one?" She brought her fingertip to Toby's nose and tapped very lightly.

"I can, uh...go grab us something to eat if you want some privacy." Eli made to stand, but Stella gripped his arm and shook her head.

"No, I didn't mean it like that. It's... I never realized how valuable breastfeeding would make me feel." When Eli cocked his head in question, Stella elaborated. "Like, I'm his sustenance, my breasts, my milk, my body, what I decide to fuel mine with. It all affects him and his health. Certain foods I eat can upset his stomach, so I have to be careful."

"Really? I didn't know that."

"Yeah, me either, until I gave birth and started lactating. It's been eye-opening but also so rewarding, despite the sacrifices."

"Sacrifices?" Eli frowned.

"Well, little things, really, like less caffeine and no alcohol, nothing major. Since I've had him, it's been so different. Obviously I didn't drink or anything when I was pregnant, but foods like cabbage and broccoli upset his tummy so I avoid those altogether."

"It's cool, bud. Daddy doesn't like broccoli either." Eli stroked his son's head, listening to his mewing sounds as he continued to eat his dinner, his little eyelids drifting closed. When Eli looked up smiling, he saw tears running down Stella's face. "Stella, my love, what is it?"

"You called yourself Daddy."

"Yeah, well, if the shoe fits and all," Eli gave her a crooked grin, but he understood, he was feeling all the same emotions at that moment.

"Oh, Elias... You have no idea how happy I am right now. How much I've waited for this moment. For you to meet and hold your son, know how much I love you both, how much I wanted you here with me from the start." Tears spilled down her cheeks, stopping Eli's breath.

He lowered his head, reverently. "I'm so sorry, Stella. I never should've–"

"No, I should have stood up for myself, for you, but I didn't. I let Tony dictate both of our lives. I let my career sway me, left and right, until I wasn't even sure who I was any longer. But now I'm a mother and all I want is to love and protect him...and be with you, Eli."

How had he gotten so blessed? He had a woman who adored him, who'd given him a child, become a barrel racer and rodeo queen in order to get his attention, a woman who'd not given up on him even when he'd given up on himself.

131

"I'll never let you down again," Stella whimpered and gripped his collar.

"No, baby, it's you *I* won't ever let down again. I fucked up. Like really *really* badly, and I feel horrible. I missed–" Sobs tore at his throat, but she needed to hear him out. "Your entire pregnancy, feeling my baby kick inside his mother, the birth of my child. You don't know how broken I was without you. I swear never to doubt your love ever again. I have much to make up for, but I'm starting today–right this instant. I'm never leaving you again. I'm here. Now and forever more."

He leaned up to kiss her, and she held him to her by the crown of his head. He chuckled as he pulled back then looked down at her with a smirk. "Your breasts are super sexy, all big and full of milk, especially from this view...just sayin'."

"Perv," she teased. "Here, burp your son. He needs to switch sides."

She pulled the milk-drunk babe from her breast and threw the burp cloth over Eli's shoulder. When she handed Toby off, she laid him facing Eli and instructed him on how to go about burping a baby. Sounded fairly simple. Eli patted his son's back and grinned at how his eyes had come open, alert and awake, probably with a new smell and face. Eli finally got the anticipated belch, and with it came a splash of breast milk.

"Uh oh," he said, "looks like he's spit up."

"Oh that's nothing. He does that every feeding."

Eli shrugged and kissed his son's fleshy little cheek before handing him back to Stella, who got him latched onto the other breast where he settled, eyes half-lidded again–as if her milk was laced with melatonin or something.

"I guess I'll call Gabe and tell him I'm pulling out of the competition." Eli ran a hand through his hair.

"What? Why?"

"*Why*? Because nothing matters more to me than you and Toby,

Stells. To hell with the rodeo. I'll go work for Uncle Jack or Austin, even. Get us settled back into Abundance. I know how much we both loved it there."

"But you love calf-roping, the rodeo."

"I love *you* and my son. The rodeo circuit isn't the place for a baby. Besides, who'll keep him while you and I practice and–"

"Aunt Natalie and Savannah have done a super job, and I'm sure my mom will be on board too when I–"

"You haven't told your mom!"

Stella looked down, her eyes cautious.

"You haven't told your dad either, huh?" Anxiety filled his veins at the thought of her parents. Buck Jenkins was liable to have his head in a vice when he found out what she'd been doing behind his back– trying to win back the man who'd left her high and dry. "Shit."

"Don't worry, Eli."

"We gotta go back, Stella, sort things out with your folks...and mine too."

"We should finish the circuit," she insisted.

"What, two more months?"

Stella nodded.

"Then what?"

"Then Natalie and I have a great idea," she grinned, looking so hopeful that Eli couldn't hide his own smile.

"You really wanna do this? Finish out the circuit? What if you get hurt again?" He remembered her close call, and his heart ached at the thought of it happening again.

"Eli, I didn't become a barrel-racer and rodeo queen just for you, you know?"

Elias smirked. "Oh? You got another cowboy whose heart you aim to steal, my little star?"

She blushed, and he sat down beside her, wrapping his arm around her and tucking her into his side. He stroked Toby's little arm and felt like he'd just been given the whole world. "You are ever tenacious. No one can ever say different about you, Stella Rose Jenkins."

"I just...I want to see this through. I want to see if I can qualify for the finals. I'm invested."

Eli chuckled. "Well, darlin', I'm not one to shoot down a rodeo queen's dream or nothin' so... looks like we're a rodeo family for a little while, then."

Stella took his hand. "Thank you."

"No, Stella baby, thank you. I feel so undeserving of you both. I was a fool to ever doubt you."

"And I was a fool to take you for granted."

He leaned in to kiss her and savored the taste and feel of her, the smell of her–still wholly Stella, but now with Toby mixed in too. He pulled back and grinned, rubbing his nose across hers. Then a thought came to him.

"Wait... Is your trailer big enough for all three of us? And where's Uncle Jack and Aunt Nat gonna stay, in mine?" He knew his Streamline was too small for two and *really* too small for three.

"Funny you should ask that," Stella smirked. "They literally just went and looked at one this morning."

"But he didn't know we would–"

"He said he had a gut feeling about it, and his gut had only been wrong once in thirty something years."

Eli rubbed his chin, then another thought came to mind. He'd been so wrapped up in Stella and the baby that it had completely slipped his mind where his sister went off to.

"Wait! Where the hell is my sister?"

Stella looked around, too, as if she weren't sure why Avery wasn't there. "Uh, when did you last see her?"

"Before competition." He might have seen her in the stands during the rodeo, but he hadn't been paying attention to the crowds. "But she was supposed to stay with me tonight and well, hell... I guess I dropped the ball." He grimaced, feeling like an ass all over again.

Stella looked thoughtfully at him, then smiled reassuringly. "Oh, I bet she's with Gabe. He wouldn't have let any harm come to her. I saw how protective he was of her around Cayden. It was kinda funny actually."

Eli scowled. He hadn't thought it'd been a damn bit funny, but Stella was probably right. Gabe would have stepped in and made sure she had a place to sleep for the night, surely. "Still, I should try and call her, make sure she's ok."

"It's past midnight. She might be asleep." Stella offered, looking at her watch.

"I'm still gonna call. I can leave her a voicemail at least." Eli shrugged.

When Avery's phone rang five times and went to voicemail, he left a message. Then hung up, worried, like any good big brother would be.

"Don't fret. I'm sure she's ok." Stella patted his thigh. "She's got a good head on her shoulders. She might have even gotten a hotel room. She had a long drive in from Corpus Christi... Besides, Gabe would have called if he hadn't seen her, right?"

"But what if Gabe *hasn't* seen her?"

"Wanna try callin' him?" Stella stroked his arm placatingly.

Eli nodded even as he dialed.

Anxiety got the best of him, and he waited with bated breath for his best friend to answer the phone and give him some relieving news.

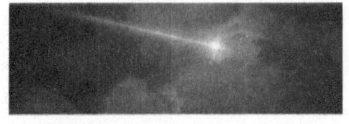

GABE PICKED up on the third ring. "What?" he grumbled, trying to sound like he'd been asleep. Though Avery had fallen to sleep not long after they'd made love the last time, Gabe had spent the better part of an hour watching the floodlight bathe her beautiful skin as she lay next to him in his bed.

"Thank fuck! You seen Avery?" came Elias's concerned voice.

"Looking at her right now." He realized what he said too late and could kick his own ass for giving them away. Luckily though, Eli missed the truthfulness of what he'd said. "What's wrong?" He tried to play it off.

"Nothin', I just wanted to make sure she was ok. I left her high and dry tonight. She was supposed to stay at my place, but I'm with Stella in a hotel room."

Gabe laughed in exuberance. "About fuckin' time. What'd you think of your son?"

"How the hell did you know I have a son?" Eli smarted even as Gabe could hear a smile in his tone.

"Ave told me. Hey, congrats man. That's awesome. I can't wait to meet him," Gabe stated honestly.

"Thanks. It's insane. I can't believe it, honestly. It's a little surreal."

"I'll bet." Gabe laughed again. "So, I take it you and Stella made up? Not that the entire campground didn't realize it with all the noise y'all were makin'."

Eli snorted. "Yeah, I'm not gonna apologize for that. Sorry, not sorry."

Gabe laughed again. "No need, brother. No need. Hey, enjoy your girl and your kid. I'm happy for you guys." Eli deserved to be happy for a change.

"Thanks, man. Hey, tell Avery, we'll be back midmorning to pack up if she wants to ride with us. I'm sure she's beat. I left her a message telling her what was going on."

"Oh, uh... Yeah, sure." Guilt tore at his guts. While Eli was repairing his family, Gabe had moved in on his sister like a damn thief in the night, stealing her virginity. Not like he'd actually *stolen* anything. It'd been given freely...but still. "She sure is. Passed out cold. I think that ride in did her in."

Lord, forgive me for lying to my best friend. Truthfully though,

136

Corpus Christi was almost ten hours from Amarillo, and she'd driven that–plus, she'd drank a fair amount for the tiny little thing she was before he'd worn her the rest of the way out.

"Well, thanks for taking care of her, buddy. I owe you one. Hope she didn't drive you too crazy."

Crazy in every sense of the word, getting under his skin and working him into such a frenzy he'd been bewitched by her...and the sex they'd had. Gabe closed his eyes. There was no way he could tell Elias what had happened. He'd no longer be his friend if he did so.

"Nah, it was no problem, bro. I got you. Your family is mine, you know that." Hopefully Eli would remember that when he came to murder Gabe tomorrow for pouncing on his sister.

"I appreciate it. See you tomorrow."

"Later."

Gabe ended the call and looked back at the angel laying in his bed, round bottom covered by the sheets, tanned back bare, her hair draped over her like rivulets of honey. His erection went full throttle. He couldn't stop himself from moving up and kissing that velvety soft skin of hers. She moaned as his mouth moved from her shoulder blade all the way down her back, his tongue lapping at the dimples of her lower back. He squeezed her ass cheeks and spread her legs wide as he moved the head of his cock along the slit of her silken heat, needing her more than he needed his next breath.

He groaned, a man in bittersweet agony as her arousal answered his stroking.

"Mmm, Gabriel."

He could climax at the sweetness of his name on her sexy lips. Had it always sounded like a call to his heartstrings, the answer to an unspoken prayer?

"I want you again, baby. Do you want me?"

A shy smile tugged at the corner of her lips and she glanced back at him, her eyes telling him all he needed to know. He thrust into her, whimpering as her tightness devoured him, inch by enticing inch.

He sank in, easing himself achingly slowly, as if slipping into a too-hot bath. Knowing it was temperate enough to scald him but unable to resist the pull of its alluring warmth.

Gabe sighed as he was fully seated within her and snaked his hands beneath her, pulling her body tighter to his own. His mouth settled at her neck. She gasped, arching her bottom, her sex fisting his in the most exquisite embrace he'd ever felt. He could stay inside her all fucking night and not be sated, he realized.

Yup, I'm in deep, deep shit, he told himself and let her cry of ecstasy be his death toll.

AVERY AWOKE to the feel of a solid chest pressed to her cheek and grinned in delight, cuddling even deeper into Gabe's muscular arms.

Last night had been... well, for starters, much more pleasant than she'd imagined possible, and second, it had been eye-opening. Sex was the polar opposite of what she'd been expecting. Gabe had been a generous and giving lover, flooring her by the number of times he'd been able to rally to the occasion. A comfortable soreness already stung the flesh between her legs, and she smiled sheepishly.

She was very glad that she'd chosen well, giving her virginity to a respectful and thoughtful man like Gabriel Halloran and not some random hothead egotistical jerk at a bar or frat party who would have left her feeling shameful for entertaining the natural curiosities of intimate inclinations. At least he was someone she knew well and truly trusted with her body...her secrets. Even if it meant her big brother would shit a squealing worm if he ever found out. He would feel betrayed and personally violated, seeing that, in his eyes, Avery was–and always would be–his baby sister, and nobody but him dare mess with her, or else, they'd feel his wrath.

Well, this would just have to remain her and Gabe's dirty little secret, then.

But at least the deed was now done, and Avery could move on with her life having garnered the confidence that she wasn't entirely clueless to the world and its ways. She felt grateful to Gabe. She'd have to get him something more expensive and valuable for Christmas this year than a pair of Snoopy socks or a Lone Ranger t-shirt. She'd always gotten him outrageously ridiculous gag gifts just for the heck of it. She wasn't sure when it had originally started, who had bought who the first gag gift, but it had quickly stuck.

"To remember me," she'd tell him, getting a laugh and shake of his head. But he always wore whatever she got him, even if only around her, so he must have liked her tastes. Either that or he was just trying not to hurt her feelings. The latter gave her pause.

A big palm moved to cup her breast, and she felt his erect shaft poking into her butt cheek. She couldn't stop the moan from escaping her throat if she'd tried. This feeling of consuming passion was unlike anything she'd ever felt before in her life. When she headed back to school in a few months, she'd have to find someone to fill the void she would feel after she left this trailer. When Gabe warned her she'd be opening a can of worms after discovering sex, he hadn't been kidding. No wonder he'd gotten the title of stud and couldn't get enough of it. It felt incredible.

"Mmm, have I told you that your tits are the most beautiful set of tits I've ever seen before?"

Avery laughed. "Good try, stud. I'm sure you say that exact same thing to every girl who's graced this bed."

"Negative, Ave. Never said it before, I swear. And your skin is like sheer velvet."

"Your cock is like velvet, too." She gripped it in her fist and stroked, getting a strangled groan out of him. "It's such a curious thing...so hard, yet simultaneously so soft."

"I'm not a science project, FYI."

"Could've fooled me." She laughed again and tilted her head back

139

as his lips moved to her neck, putting a lid on her tom-foolery. She gasped, feeling his other hand slide between her legs. "I'm so sore, but dammit, I don't want you to ever stop."

"Did I hurt you?" He ceased his ministrations, his face falling into a frown.

"It's ok. It's a good burn."

He smiled and took her lips, making her forget every thought in her head. She quickly twisted in his arms, deepening the kiss, and wrapping herself around him,

He guided himself into her, and she grunted at the sting of the intrusion before moaning as it yielded to blissful pleasure and gripped him tighter. Like ivy hugging a massive oak tree, her fingernails dug into his sinewy, freckled shoulders. He withdrew and thrust in again, getting a cry from her throat.

"Oh shit, Avery," he moaned and leaned his forehead against hers, "how does it just get better and better each time?"

She'd been about to ask him the same thing. Despite the irritation, her womanhood was absolutely relishing him filling her once again, as if they hadn't done this same thing mere hours earlier. It was simple biology, right? Chemicals and chemistry, pheromones and natural selection, the need to reproduce, to breed and insure the next generation...

"You're thinking about fuckin' science again, aren't you?"

Before she could shrug and laugh, he was increasing his speed and gripping her hips, angling her bottom up for even closer contact. He moaned loudly this time and his mouth moved back to her throat where he licked and sucked her into a blissful stupor.

Her body rattled as he pounded into her without pause, coaxing her into sheer ecstasy where she cried his name and clutched him to her, aware that they might just form one being by osmosis alone. His release soon followed suit as he quickly pulled out and ejaculated onto her stomach, his pleasure equally as magnificent–if his roar was any indication.

Their breathing intermingled before Gabe spoke first. "Shit, I'm sorry…" He looked down at his mess, but Avery thought it was kinda sexy, his lack of inhibition, being covered in his essence. "I really hope you're on the pill."

Avery gave him a smile. "Of course I am." She winked. "I'm smarter than the average bear, aren't I? I mean, a girl can't be too careful nowadays."

Gabe's scowl returned even as he moved off her to go and grab a towel.

When he came back, she took it from him as he crossed his arms over his chest, looking thoughtful. "So…you planned this?"

"What?" She wiped between her legs before removing his cum from her belly, then looked up.

"Losing your virginity this weekend."

"I mean, yes and no. It's been on my mind a lot lately. The opportunity just happened to present itself last night, so…"

"Avery," Gabe sat and took her hand, "not all guys will be thinking about your safety, your well-being. You're gonna…"

A pounding came to the door, and they both jolted like a gun had gone off.

"Fuck!" Gabe lunged for his jeans and stepped into them just as Eli's voice said, "Up and at 'em, Lady Killer."

"Oh my God!" Avery whimpered and moved off the bed. She had no idea where her clothes were, but Gabe threw a t-shirt at her and told her to put it on. She did, then searched the floor for her panties.

"Don't make me use my key…" Eli warned and jiggled the door.

"Shit, you gave him a *key*?" she screeched.

"Hell no. He's bluffin'." Gabe was helping her search the floor for her undergarments until the lock began to turn. "Fuck it, I'll find 'em later." He jostled his hair and threw his comforter at the couch, where it landed in disarray just as Eli threw the door open.

Avery pulled at the hem of Gabe's shirt, grateful it was long enough to cover her vagina and blushed at her brother, who scowled.

Elias's gaze moved from Avery to Gabe, who stretched with a

141

yawn and reached to fold the comforter, making it appear as if he'd slept on the pullout. "Dude, you don't have to tear the door off the hinges."

"It's 11 o'clock. Y'all planning on sleepin' all day?"

Eli's gaze hovered to Avery's bare legs then back to Gabe. "How much did you drink last night?"

Gabe tilted his head in question. "Not that much. Not my usual. How come?"

"I was talking to *you*," Eli said, his eyes assessing Avery.

"Uh...I don't know. W-why?" she stammered.

"Cayden said you were pretty shit-faced."

Damn that Cayden fellow. He was a shit-starter. He better not have blown it for her. "What does he know? Besides, you aren't my keeper, brother. I can drink all I want. I'm over the drinking age." She crossed her arms over her chest.

Eli held his hands up in surrender. "Point taken." He looked around the trailer at the coffee mugs, then the bed behind Avery. She prayed he couldn't see through their guise. As much as she didn't care what her brother thought, she didn't want to hear it. "Did y'all..."

Gabe gulped, eyeing Avery with caution before he crossed his arms over his beautifully naked chest, and gave Eli a frown. "Did we *what?*"

Eli took a step forward, jaw clenching. "You didn't take advantage of my sister last night, did you, Halloran?"

Gabe separated the distance between them, and Avery realized he actually was an inch taller and a tad broader than her brother. "What do *you* think, Eli?"

How brave... Avery was sure Eli would be able to smell the sex oozing from his pores, on his breath. Mortification took hold of her, and she acted before this turned ugly.

"Elias Edward Kinsen! How dare you! As *if!*" she snorted and gave Gabe a look of disgust.

Eli continued to stare Gabe down before looking back at his

sister, relief seeming to relax his shoulders. He attempted a grin. "Yeah, I didn't think so but... Hell, I guess it's always smelled like sex in here. Probably should've thrown a tarp over that mattress before you slept on it, Av. You might need to go to a clinic and be deloused." He laughed and turned. "We need to head out by one. How long before you can be ready?"

Gabe shrugged. "Not long."

"Well, Uncle Jack and Aunt Nat have already started out. Stella's feedin' Toby, so we'll be ready soon. Was gonna grab a bite at the Denny's before we ride. Y'all down?"

"Yeah," Avery nodded, "let me just hop in the shower, and I'll be ready in like fifteen minutes."

"Gabe?" Eli asked.

"Yeah...same. Just need a quick shower."

"Ok, cool. Sounds good." Eli tipped his hat and headed out the door.

When it was closed behind him, Avery sighed heavily. "Sheesh, that was so close."

"No shit." Gabe held Avery's gaze for the longest time, as if he wanted to say more but didn't.

"Well, you should probably shower first, huh? Since you need to hitch up the camper and stuff, right?"

"Yeah, I'll be quick and save you some hot water. Unless..." he grinned and Avery's insides hummed at the hint in his eyes, "you wanna join me?"

God, it was so tempting, even if the shower was tiny, but what if Eli came back?

"Uh, probably not the best idea–or even plausible with your height, I'm sure."

He nodded quickly and turned.

"I'll clear up our mugs from last night and make some coffee for the road."

"Perfect. I'll be out in five." He winked. Avery bit her lip, reminded of the tenderness of his kiss and love-making.

143

When he closed the bathroom door, she began clearing the cups and brewing coffee. She knew things would be different between her and Gabe now that they'd slept together, but she really didn't want the awkwardness that would surely follow.

She'd been a virgin; he'd remedied that. No need to label it as anything more than what it was. Besides, she was simply the latest of many girls he'd had over the years, so the last thing he'd want was her expecting anything more than one nocturnal session beneath the sheets. Last night was a means to an end, nothing more.

So why did the thoughts of him being with someone else suddenly make her nauseous?

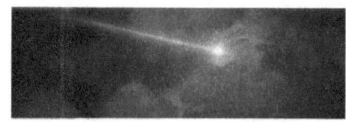

GABE LET the hot water run over his head. The blow his heart had taken from Avery's words was like that of a violent stab from a great sword.

As if!

The statement echoed inside his head again and again.

As if!

As if she would lower herself to share a bed with a man-whore like him.

As if she would let herself be defiled by a roughneck nobody like he was.

As if he hadn't made her scream his name over and over again.

What the hell had he done? And with his best friend's little sister? The one who used to play Barbies while they played video games in the next room over, the one who's boo-boos he'd help tend when she'd fallen off her bike, the one whose honor he'd fought for like she was his own flesh and blood.

That was the problem. He'd always had a soft spot for the innocently beautiful and unaware Avery Lenore Kinsen. So when she'd been so eager to throw her inhibitions to the wind last night and play her "who wants my virginity?" card, Gabe had been the first to brave the gauntlet.

Now he was all out of sorts. He could think of nothing else as he let the water wake him and washed himself robotically. Problem was, he still had a raging boner that he couldn't seem to dispel and the only thing he could think of was how amazing it felt being inside her.

He'd never been with a virgin before. Ok, maybe he had...but he'd not been told of it.

She'd been as naive and soft and sweet as he expected. Her inexperience had been both endearing and highly erotic. It had turned him on unlike anything ever had before. Perhaps he was a sick pervert... or perhaps it'd just been that way because it was Avery. She'd always been able to crawl right under his skin.

She'd burrowed there long ago. Now he was infested with her.

He cut the water off and got out of the way-too-small shower stall. Despite that it would have been practically impossible to claim her in there, the very thought had his heart racing and his cock throbbing. He grabbed a clean towel from the rack and began drying off.

He knew she wasn't out of his system, had known moments after he'd entered her last night that once–one *night*, even–wouldn't be enough. He wasn't quite sure how he was going to be able to slake this lust, this chemistry, between them–or, furthermore, that he *wanted* it slaked. What he did know was that he needed more time. Time that he didn't have. So he had to stall. Think of ways to continue this fling somehow. To figure out what he wanted from her, what these thoughts really meant. Because he knew she was already making plans to move onto the next guy, planning her next sexcapade beyond him. And Gabe couldn't have that. Not yet.

But I was just the endgame anyway, right?

She'd used him. The player had been the played, and boy, was Gabe reeling. Was he getting a dose of his own medicine? Was that what he'd done to the girls he'd been with? Had he played with their emotions? Had he used them? *Mis*used them? No. It had always been mutual. They'd wanted him as much as he'd wanted them. He'd never had non-consensual sex, even drunk. He'd never been *that* guy and never would be. He hated fuckers who took advantage. No meant no.

In regards to using, or even misusing, them... as far as he knew he'd never out-right broken any hearts. He'd not promised anything he wasn't apt to give, never made his one-night stands out to be more than just that, never given a girl any reason to assume he was the settling-down type.

Sure, he'd had the same girl more than once, but rarely ever than for more than a week or so. Once they even hinted at getting all clingy, he made like horseshit and hit the dusty trail.

But that smooth-talking ladies' man was the shadow of his past now. There was only one lady on his mind, and somehow, he had to convince her not to end their amazing sexual connection just yet.

He decided to test the waters and see if he could pick up on her vibes. Was she feeling as high as he was? Did she want it to continue as well?

He stepped out into the main room, towel over his head.

"Shower's free now, darlin'."

"Oh, thanks." Avery turned and swept her honey-brown hair behind her ear. She gasped as she saw he was buck naked. "Jeez, Gabe!"

"Nothin' you ain't seen, little girl'. Like barely more than ten minutes ago, in fact."

He didn't miss her eyes on his dick and didn't hide the fact that it was once more rising to the occasion.

"Here." She looked flustered as she handed him a thermos.

"Nectar of the gods." Gabe grinned. They both took a sip and looked expectantly at one another. Gabe spoke first. "Listen, uh, you don't have to worry about me tellin' anybody about last night, especially your brother. I would never hurt or betray you on that, you

146

can rest assured. This is always just gonna be our little secret, Avery. Something only we know."

"Yeah, I know." She smiled and the sight made his heart melt. "And thanks for... well, you know. I'm glad my first time was with you. You were really *really* good at...well, all of it." Her cheeks flamed red, and she looked down at her toes. "I mean, I just... I don't want things to get weird or anything between us."

"No, of course not. We won't let it." He *couldn't* let it, no way, no how. "But...uh, look, I mean, you're gonna be stickin' around a little while, right? You're not going back to college for a few months."

"Yeah?" she frowned, as if unsure where he was going with his comments.

"Well, I could... I mean, if you're up to it, I can show you some other stuff, too. It doesn't have to end here...if you don't want it to, that is." He pulled the towel from his head and slowly covered his lower half, watching her eye him. God, he could take her right then and there without any hesitation.

Avery's mouth opened to reply, but she closed it again. She bit her lip, contemplatively. "I don't want to interfere with what you got going on here with the other ladies. I'm not trying to rain on your bachelor sex-pad parade or anything. But I am still curious about a few things..."

"Yeah! Absolutely," he said with a little too much enthusiasm, and sighed in relief. "We should probably go to a hotel next time, though. Probably the best way to avoid your brother finding out. There, we are less at risk of anyone suspecting."

He pointed behind her, to the door, recalling how her brother just showed up unannounced and almost found out their naughty little secret in the worst way possible.

"Yeah. Ok." She shrugged.

"Cool."

Gabe tried hard to play it cool, all the while desiring to grab her up, tear her clothes off, and fuck her against the wall until she cried his name in bliss. Instead, he took another sip of his coffee. Avery followed suit, avoiding his eyes.

Just when he thought she would back out of the impromptu arrangement, she set the Thermos down. "Let me rinse off, and I'll be ready in ten."

Out of the frying pan...and into the fire. But damn, was that fire of theirs ever toasty.

CHAPTER 10

Stella smiled over at her baby in his father's arms while Elias held him and perused the menu of the diner they'd decided on.

She'd never felt more complete than she had last night as Elias cried at the sight of his child. It had been such a beautiful and heartrending moment.

Once she'd gotten Toby to sleep, they'd made love again and again. Until Toby had woken up and cried, needing to be fed. She'd pulled her infant to her breast and laid him in between herself and Eli. Eli had stroked the crown of his head and kissed his little cheeks, making Stella giggle as he cooed to their baby boy and told him how sorry he was, how much he adored him, and how he couldn't wait to make up for lost time. Eli cuddled Toby's back and nuzzled the baby's head, both of them soon falling sound asleep. It was then that Stella had allowed the tears to come, crying tears of joy and singing praises to God for reuniting her family. It was surreal. The plan had actually worked, her ultimate dream had come true—winning back the man she worshipped with her entire being.

Stella couldn't remember a time she'd been happier, not the night

149

Eli had stolen her heart, not the first time they'd made love, not even the first time he'd told her he was madly in love with her. No, last night was as close to true happiness as she'd ever felt–and in the presence of the males she adored with every beat of her heart.

Her heart was now completely full, and her family was finally together. By the way Elias looked at the two of them right now, she knew she'd had him back. She hadn't given up, though many times it had been tempting, and she was being rewarded for that perseverance and selfless love. Her blood, sweat, pain, and tears had all paid off. She had her man...well, her man *and* her little man.

"Yes ma'am," Eli told the expectant waitress, "I'll take the big daddy breakfast with scrambled eggs, bacon, hash browns, grits, and pumpkin pancakes." He snuggled Toby tighter as he set his menu down on the dinner table.

"Ok, *big daddy*," Avery laughed as if he were taking on more than he could handle in such a big order. The waitress looked at her next. "I want the yogurt and fruit with granola."

Gabe sat beside Avery and grinned up at their server. "And I'll have the same as big daddy over here, only I want cheese in my grits and regular pancakes."

They all laughed, even the waitress named Peggy. "You got it. Refill on those coffees?"

"Yes, ma'am. Thank you." Gabe tipped his cowboy hat at her, and Stella couldn't fight the smile that dawned her face.

Something was going on with Gabe and Avery, and if Stella had her opinion on the matter, she'd say they'd gotten intimate last night. Gabe seemed more on edge than usual, and Avery blushed every time his elbow bumped hers.

Elias hadn't seemed to notice. He was too enthralled with Toby.

"God, he smells so good. How do babies smell better than anything else?"

Avery smiled up at him. "Brother, you look so good with a baby. I haven't seen you smile this much since..." She didn't finish, not wanting to head down that road again.

Eli looked to Stella, and her heart skipped a beat. "I mean, you smell like Heaven, my little star, but he just... Gah! He's one good-lookin' kid, ain't he?" he looked over at Gabe, who shook his head.

"Thank goodness he took after his momma," Gabe joshed, and Eli scowled.

"Whatever. You're just jealous, Uncle Gabe. Ain't he, Toby?" Eli took Toby's little palm in his and leaned down to kiss his tiny knuckles. "I can't get over how small he is either. Baby, you are amazing, have I told you that?" Eli cooed and kissed her cheek.

He had, about a million times now.

"How did you do it? Tell me, please. Although a part of me hates to hear it, I need it, too. Naturally?"

Stella smiled. "Yes. It was hard as hell, but my mom and Aunt Natalie were there coaching me through it."

"I'll never forgive myself for not being there when you were giving birth to my son, that I up and abandoned you, assuming the worst. You know that, right?" His hooded gaze said all he felt.

She nodded. "Eli, please don't. No more sorries, remember? We agreed."

They had, but she knew by the look on his face that more would always come. He'd never stop beating himself up for what he'd done.

"If it's any consolation, we'll start working on the next baby as soon as you want."

That brought his head up. "You want more?"

"Don't you?"

"Yes. A dozen more, just like him." Eli grinned over at their baby and took Stella back in his arms again.

He began kissing her everywhere and soon was pumping inside her, unable to quench the unending hunger they both seemed to be overcome with.

When he was done, he stroked her face and held himself over her as their bodies stayed joined and their slowed breathing synced. "So, he's three months old. When did you start training for barrel-racing?"

He stroked her hair as her eyes fell to his chest, tracing the sparse chest hair there and the sinewy muscles beneath. "Barely four weeks after giving birth..."

"Holy shit, Stella. You were able to be good enough to qualify in just...three months?"

She smiled triumphantly and looked up into his gorgeous face. "And win the beauty pageant, too." She laughed at his widening eyes. "You sound as surprised as Jax was. He didn't think I had it in me. But I had to prove everyone wrong, even myself. I can't tell you how many times I failed, how many times I wanted to give up, but Aunt Nat wouldn't let me. Every day she came in with a new motivational tag, and every night she filled the tub with ice."

"Jesus. All for me."

"And me...and him." She nodded her head to the baby who slept so soundly in his bassinet. "He's so perfect, isn't he?"

"Just like his mother." He ran a finger over the swell of her leaking breast. She knew she was soaked in breast milk, but neither of them seemed to care. "I don't deserve your love, Stella. I've been so–"

"Let's just pick up where we left off, this last year is behind us, nothing stands in our way of a bright future now, not even the regrets."

With that, he kissed her and began loving her all over again.

HE SEEMED to be remembering the same conversation as the love echoed in his eyes.

"So, what's the plan?" Gabe asked, pulling them from their silent conversation. "I mean, I'm a bit surprised you didn't pull out of the rodeo."

"I was going to. I mean, I got a kid now to support–a family." Eli pulled Stella's hand to his mouth and kissed her knuckles, one by one. "But Stella wants to finish the circuit, and I can't leave you hanging either."

"I appreciate that," Gabe snorted. Stella could see he wasn't fully satisfied with the answer, but Gabe had been there for him this past year. It was the least Eli could do.

She nudged Eli's hip. "Stella and I are actually coming up with a business plan. We could do with an experienced heeler such as yourself."

Gabe scowled at him. "You mean hang my hat up? Settle down?"

"Call it what you want, dude, but we ain't gettin' any younger. And you know there's no such thing as an old rodeo champ. It's kinda like football. It's a young man's game." Eli shrugged.

Gabe looked down then to Avery, who grinned at him.

Headers and heelers lasted much longer than the other cowboys and cowgirls of more extreme events like bronc-riders and bull-riders, but Stella let Eli's words linger a little longer before saying, "We plan to head back to Abundance. We've always considered it home, and well, with the ranches and the famous Dr. Dallie, we figure a rodeo school could come next."

Avery laughed. "Wow, that's awesome, you two. What a fun idea! Have you pitched it to Uncle Jack and Aunt Nat yet?"

Stella shook her head. "No, but I have a feeling they'll love it."

She knew Jack and Nathan both rode bulls back in the day, and Natalie had experience in barrel-racing. As if she didn't have enough to do with her own grandchildren and her writing, but Stella was willing to step into lead. She just had to win some ribbons first.

As if reading Stella's thoughts, Eli said. "I mean, we ain't talking like tomorrow, Gabe. It may be a year or so down the road, we ain't in no hurry to quit. It's just a future plan, you know? Once we get tired of all the traveling. We'll hire a nanny soon, so Aunt Natalie can go back home–and Uncle Jack too, if he wants. But where we plan to end up is Abundance. It's where we first hit it off, where we belong."

Eli looked at his sister, almost regretfully, but she smiled lovingly at him, tears brimming her eyes. "I'm so happy for you guys. To see you finally get back together. That you now know you have a son and..." She wiped at the corner of her eye. "I'm sorry, I don't mean to be emotional."

Elias grinned and took her hand across the booth. "I love you. I know I haven't said it in far too long, Avery, but I do. You know that, right?"

Avery nodded. "I love you too, big brother." She puckered her lips and smiled again.

"Corpus Christi will always be special to me, but it's not where my heart is."

"I know, Eli, your heart has always been in Abundance."

"Yes," he looked back to Stella, and she swore she saw stars in his eyes. "Yes, it has."

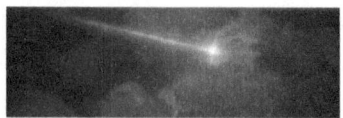

AVERY WASN'T ENTIRELY sure what the hell she was doing.

The plan for the next few weeks was for her to bunk with Gabe, and much to her surprise, it had been Gabe's idea.

"So you won't actually be needing your camper, then," Gabe had said to Eli before they'd finished their breakfast.

"Well I mean, Avery can stay in it." Eli had shrugged.

"So, you're gonna haul yet another trailer? Just for her?" Avery had frowned over at him, hurt at the tone in his voice, before he continued. "She can stay with me. There's no sense in you two having to ride separately. I'm sure Avery hasn't even driven a truck with a trailer. It's no easy task."

As it was, Avery had volunteered to drive Eli's truck to their next stop, Lubbock, so that Eli and Stella could ride in her truck with the baby together. Nat and Jack had insisted on staying this morning, so that Jack could drive, but Stella had sent them on, saying if she was strong enough to enter the rodeo circuit she could haul her own trailer to the next town in the circuit.

"I'll manage, thanks very much." She might be young, but she was

154

one hell of a driver, and a F-250 with a camper didn't intimidate her in the least.

"Point is: it's silly for us to all have so many campers when it ain't necessary. Besides, Avery isn't a contestant. She can stay in mine. It's not a big deal."

Stella grinned as if housing a secret. "But...won't that put a damper on your nocturnal exploits, Gabe?"

Gabe looked down, blushing. His reaction surprised Avery until he smirked and said, "Don't worry. There's other places I can work my magic."

How many places could people do it? For Avery, it was automatic. It took place in a bed...but she'd known others who'd done so in a bathroom, on a table, couch, countertop. And him being a cowboy, he'd probably done the deed in a barn, too. She didn't want to think about Gabe doing it anywhere else. Not if it didn't involve her.

Why was she being so strange? He'd taken her virginity. She had no stake on him. And men didn't like clingy women, especially not free spirits like Gabe. She needed to get a grip.

"I don't mind, honestly," she'd insisted again.

"No. Gabe's right, Ave. It's just another vehicle to have to transport, and I don't like the thoughts of you staying in there alone." Eli frowned. "Rodeos can sometimes attract rough crowds."

Avery rolled her eyes but figured this worked to their advantage, her and Gabe's, if they were planning to continue their taboo fling. She shrugged, not apt to argue.

"I think Jax said he was heading to Abilene soon for a pick up. Maybe I can see if he can bring someone with him to transport my truck and trailer back to Abundance," Eli had told no one in particular.

And that had been the end of it.

Now Avery was behind the wheel of the duelie and headed south down I-27, hauling Eli's camper, rocking to some oldies, and feeling like a new person. She was about halfway into the trip, following Eli in Stella's Silverado, with Gabe behind them in his GMC Sierra.

Stella had left her horse trailer back in Amarillo on the fairgrounds with the city's permission. Gabe and Eli had long ago hired someone to transport their horses to and from the rodeo events. His name was Pedro, and he'd been cool with adding Stella's horse, Sally, to the mix.

"*No problem, ese,*" he'd said with a tip of his hat, even as Eli had handed him an envelope, assumedly with the extra cash for the additional horse.

"*Good thing I bought a three-horse trailer last year,*" Eli had smirked and tapped his temple, getting a laugh out of Stella.

Jack was sending someone from his ranch to transport Stella's horse trailer back to Abundance in a few days' time.

Avery decided to call her best friend, Scarlett, needing to announce to someone about losing her virginity. She knew Scarlett would be eager to hear that the deed was done. Avery had only been talking about popping her cherry for months now.

Scarlett answered on the third ring. "Hey, girl! I was literally just about to call you. Or send out a damn search party. It's been two days!"

"Talk about good timing, then."

"What's up? Did you find your brother?"

When she left Corpus Christi, she hadn't explained much about where she was going or how long she'd be gone, only that she'd gotten word from her family that her brother–who'd been practically missing for a year–was in Amarillo.

Scarlett would have come with her, but she was in her last semester of college and had finals she couldn't miss.

"I did. And his ex-girlfriend."

"Aww... Did he get to meet his baby, finally?"

"Yes, and he's so freaking cute with him, I swear." Avery smiled brightly.

"Good. I'm so glad. So, you think they'll get back together?"

"Oh, yeah. If the look on his face is any indication, they're already together and don't plan to break up ever again."

"Aww, what a sweet story. I love a good second chance ending." Scar sighed heavily.

Avery rolled her eyes. Her BFF was definitely the romantic one of the two of them. The girl had seen *While You Were Sleeping* like a billion times and still cried every single time.

"Tell me everything," Scarlett pleaded.

Avery told her as much as she knew up to that point—well, what Eli had filled her in on, anyway. From Stella entering the rodeo as a barrel-racing contestant and rodeo queen to all the drama that had happened before Avery had shown up. Scarlett was well aware of the breakup as Avery had already told her the sordid tale of misunderstanding. It had been like a soap opera for the dramatic Scarlett, and she'd eaten up every detail, even helping search for Elias too when she wasn't in class. Together they'd contacted numerous law agencies, hospitals, even news outlets to get the word out. Scarlett was fully invested, and her tears on the other end warmed Avery's heart.

"I'm so happy for them," she sobbed.

"Thanks, lady, but suck it up, would ya? Sheesh." Avery couldn't contain her laugh at her theatrical friend.

"Sorry, I'm premenstrual and cramping like a sonovabitch. I've just watched *Steel Magnolias* and eaten a full pint of Haagen Daz. I needed a break from studying. I swear my head was about to explode."

"Are you ready for your final on Thursday, you think?"

"I'm gonna be. Even if I have to stay up all night on Wednesday."

"You can do this. I believe in you, Scar."

"Thanks, girl. I dunno what I'd do without you. My mom called, being a bitch, and dad is on my ass about working again. I swear I can't deal with their shit right now."

As an only child of divorced parents, Scarlett had her fair share of drama. Her mother was a successful lawyer and her father, a real estate broker. To say Scarlett was a spoiled rich girl was an understatement, but she was also trying to break out of her parent's financial—and helicopter—hold on her. She worked as a barista at Starbucks, despite her generous weekly allowance. She was trying to earn her own keep in the world, explore new paths, and had really blossomed in college. Avery was so proud of the person her bestie had become, a far cry from the shallow girl she'd met during their first class in college together: Psychology.

Scarlett no longer looked at brand names when they shopped together nor judged people based on their appearances alone. She'd learned the hard way that a book couldn't always be rated simply on its cover.

"I'm sorry. Hey, how about you come to Abilene next weekend for Spring Break? I'm hanging with this crew for a little while. In fact, I'm transporting my brother's camper right now as we speak."

Scar gave a big laugh. "OMG, I just got a visual in my head. You are too funny. Has my little mermaid become a landlubber, after all?"

Avery had been waiting for a way to tell Scar about what she'd done. This was it. "Well... let me tell you, the view in the rodeo has definitely improved since the last time I came to one." Boy had it. The cowboys were hotter, jeans were tighter, and muscles were steel death traps for panties in general.

"Uh oh. Why do I feel like you're about to tell me something that might send my ass to come get you?" Scar's tone thickened, concern peeking through.

"You'd be proud to know: this girl is a virgin no longer."

The squeal over the line hurt Avery's ears. "Avery Lenore Kinsen, you didn't!"

"Oh I *did*." Avery smirked, remembering the feel of Gabe's chiseled body on top of hers. His lips. His hands. His cock.

"Holy crap, I'm stunned! I was convinced you'd die a cat lady—or, better yet, a dolphin lady. How'd it happen?" Scar's question made Avery's belly take, as if riding a rollercoaster, eager to give her all the juicy details.

After swearing her to secrecy for life, Avery told Scar about seeing Gabe again, how fine he was now, how swoony he was, and finishing with her plan to continue having sex with him for a little while longer behind her brother's back.

"Holy fuckin' shit! Gabriel Halloran, your brother's best friend! The ginger? No way! I'm flippin' shocked. I just fell off my couch. Seriously."

Avery laughed again. "I know. It wasn't exactly planned, but isn't that how it works?"

"Gah, I'm so happy for you. This day has just turned the corner, girl. The sun is coming out, and I think I may go outside and sit at our coffee spot and study again. There is hope for this world, after all."

"Oh, shut up, jerk," Avery scolded with a blush.

"Seriously, though, I would never have guessed he was your type, Ave. You always like those quiet, broody, yuppy guys."

No, Gabe wasn't her type—at all. He was too flirty, too outgoing, too self-assured. He was sweaty and smelled of livestock...and leather, and sweat...and sex. Shit, she was drooling again.

"I mean, wait 'til you see what I mean. There's just something so sexy about a dirty cowboy, I dunno, Scar. It's..."

"Sounds like you got it bad, lady. I may have to take you up on your offer though and not just for the stinking hot cowboys, pun intended." She laughed. "My dad said he would pay for me to fly anywhere in the world I wanted to go for Spring Break if I would quit working until after I graduated. Isn't that the dumbest thing you've ever heard? God, I swear I'm moving to Antarctica when I graduate."

Her father was afraid her job was affecting her grades, but it wasn't her job. It was just Scar. She had bad test anxiety and had to see a therapist for it—which was something her folks didn't know. Scarlett was too ashamed to admit what she thought was a weakness to two of the brightest people she'd ever known.

"Oh, Scarlett, my sweet Scarlett. Just think, two more months, and you're done."

Then she would be free to make her own decisions...until her parents attempted to bribe her with more money.

"Yes, and I'm already looking at jobs abroad. I can't with those two. I can't believe they are still trying to suffocate me with their type-A personality bullshit."

Avery wouldn't point out that they were the ones footing her tuition, fees, and housing. She just let that slide.

"Well, you keep fighting the good fight, girl. We're almost to Lubbock. Text me later on, and keep me posted if you decide to join me next weekend. I miss you. Good luck studying."

"And good luck on getting your much needed–and deserved–Vitamin D." Scar giggled. "I'm proud of you. Just don't become a slut now! Your mom and dad would shit if they knew."

She knew that, which was why they never would.

"I don't plan to, but man... It's kinda different than I thought it would be."

"I'm glad your experiences with sex have been better than mine." Scar sighed.

Avery frowned. Scar had lost her virginity at fifteen to her long-time high school boyfriend, Grant, but they'd broken up her freshman year of college after he'd cheated on her with her room-mate. She'd been single for a little while before dating a guy who'd turned out to be a total stalker. She'd had to get a restraining order put on him not long before he'd OD'd on coke at a party and died. Next up was a jock with anger issues, thanks to his addiction to steroids, who'd beat her pretty good. And finally, the cherry on top of that dumpster fire sundae, was her rape at a frat party last year, causing her to write off relationships, men, and sex for good. She'd even considered going into a convent following a three week stay in a luxury mental health facility. It had taken lots of hugs, lots of therapy sessions, and lots of time for Scarlett to ease back into even talking about–or to–men. She'd been focusing solely on herself this past year, proving herself a true fighter. She'd thrown herself into her studies, saving the romance movies and books for entertainment purposes only.

Now, perhaps, she was finally ready to move on from her tragic past. Avery would do whatever she needed to help pave the way. Her BFF deserved a good man, and she knew eventually Scarlett would get him in the end. Fate favored the bold, or so the saying went.

Avery told Scar she loved her and to call her later.

She sat pondering her life during the last leg of the short trip from Amarillo to Lubbock. How her own life had been fairly anticlimactic, until her brother went MIA, especially when compared to her bestie's. She'd been the shy one of their duo, the one in the background. The one boys didn't seem to pay any mind to because she'd not been flashy, never seeking attention–just there, attempting to blend in.

Unlike Scarlett, college hadn't been an escape for Avery so much as just an avenue to her dream job of working with marine life in her hometown of Corpus Christi. She was so close to it. Despite that she'd taken a minor detour from her future, taking the last year off to search for her missing brother, she was eager to get back and do what she loved, get her degree, and head on to new tropical adventures.

The sea called to some ancient part of her; it was in her soul. She missed the salty air, the sight of the seawater at sunset, the feel of the breeze in her hair, the sun on her tanned skin.

For now, though, she was enjoying not having a set plan–nothing she had to do, no test to study for, no assignment due. She was happy to have her brother back, glad to see that he was getting the happiness he'd missed out on in the last year, glad he was able to piece things back together with the love of his life. Fatherhood looked good on him.

She hoped, in the long run, she wasn't interfering in his time with Stella and his son, but neither he nor Stella were selfish. They'd be upset if she even stated her doubts. She was there to support them, and truthfully, she was enjoying herself, even if she hadn't been much for rodeos or cowboys...until Gabriel Halloran.

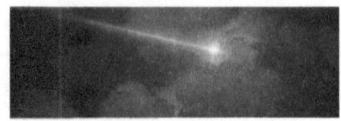

"LUBBOCK, HUH?" Cassidy Boyd asked her longtime boyfriend, Jackson Kinsen, that night as she washed her face and brushed her teeth, getting ready for bed in her flat in Monterrey, California.

"Yup. I'm gonna meet up with Stella and Eli there and bring his camper back home. We got a pickup to make in Sweetwater anyway, and I figured you might enjoy the change in scenery."

Change in scenery had been her story for some time now. She'd graduated top of her nursing class a year ago from Emory University and had taken an immediate job in Atlanta. She had worked night shifts as an ICU nurse there, finding her niche in critical care. She'd gone home as often as she could and Jax had come to visit her too. After an interesting job opportunity came up just a few months later, taking her all the way to London, England, she'd been swept up in travel nursing. Thus far, her career had taken her as far away as Florence, Italy and as close as New Orleans, Louisiana. Jax had come to tour the new places with her, compromising as he promised he would—something that had been quite a hardship on their relationship.

She'd gotten the life she'd wanted, traveling and nursing, and he'd done what he loved, ranching. Their time apart far exceeded their time together and made getting to know one another again a new experience each time. Each time, Cassidy realized how much the distance affected them. Despite their love for one another, they were still worlds apart—in more ways than one.

It was interesting and fun too getting to relearn her lover's body, his pleasure, what he liked. Kinda like she got a new man every few months. But she also had to get to know him all over again, missing out on little things. At times, she could see the strain of frustration overtake his facial features. He'd been patient, he'd been fair, he'd been amazing.

But this distance was as taxing on them both as it was rewarding. Cassidy felt it in her bones. Jax was growing tired of this charade, and he loathed flying and travel. He was getting too old for these games. He was twenty-four, soon to be twenty-five, and he wanted a family, a home, a wife.

Could she be that person? Was she ready to stow away her carry-on for good?

Those thoughts plagued her dreams. She'd just gotten into a career she loved. If she came home to stay for good, she'd be giving it all up. Would it be worth it? Would marriage change them more than time already had? Cassidy loved Jax Kinsen more than she'd ever loved anything, anyone. She'd never known but one man in her life and never wanted to know another. But she feared having regrets about giving up her career. Why did she have to choose?

But she feared losing the man she loved, too, as much as losing herself.

She'd almost lost him once before, just four years ago. She couldn't bear to do so again.

"Yeah, I can go," she sighed with equal parts relief and apprehension. It'd been a month since she'd seen him, and she was desperate to feel his arms around her, kiss his lips, make love with him, even if it had to be in a camper. "You know I'm not the camping type though, Mr. Kinsen," she teased and got a laugh out of him.

"I know. That's why I rented a hotel room. It even comes with a continental breakfast and everything."

"A man after my own heart." That got another laugh out of him. "You've won me over. I'll hop a plane home Wednesday."

She had five days off in a row, which hadn't happened since her assignment had started a month ago. She'd worked her tail off and specifically requested the schedule haggling. The supervisor had agreed, and Cass was grateful. She was enjoying California but needed to come home and see her family, her man. She realized was homesick for the first time in four years.

"Perfect. I'll be there to pick you up at the airport."

"You'll have to backtrack. Want me to just rent a car and meet you in Abilene?"

"Hell no! Then I'll have to worry about you more than I already do. I'll pick you up at the airport," he repeated, gentleman that he was.

She knew he could see her eyes rolling from the other end of the phone. That was another problem. His extremely overprotective side. The one that worried about her traveling alone, living alone, walking to her car at night because someone might kidnap her, rape her, and/or murder/human traffic her. She had a can of mace on her person at all times, always had security walk her out after hours, *and* had been coerced into taking self-defense classes–with the blessing of her father, Luther Boyd, no doubt–before Jax ever agreed to be okay with her traveling all the time.

"Fine," she acquiesced because she didn't have the energy to fight with him. "I love you, baby." She smiled. Despite his demanding, caveman ways, it was the absolute truth.

"I love you too, angel." He sighed heavily. "I miss your kiss, your body, every single part of you. I can't *wait* to see you."

She tingled all over, crawling into bed and settling her head on her pillow. "Tell me exactly what you miss, lover," she cooed seductively.

"Oh. We playin' this game tonight, huh?"

"Mmm, yes, it's my favorite one. Wanna FaceTime?"

"Fuck yes," he agreed. She hit the button on her phone, grinning brightly as his face filled her screen. "There you are, my gorgeous girl. I swear, you get prettier every day."

She wouldn't call him a liar because she knew there were bags under her eyes, but that his eyes held such conviction touched her heart.

"Where are you?" she asked and tried to see beyond him but couldn't tell.

"Dad's office. Waitin' on the boys to bring in the last mustang. They're about an hour away...so I got time."

Cass giggled, feeling giddy with need and desire for him. "Time to play?"

"You wanna play, naughty girl?"

"I always wanna play with my cowboy."

"Mmm, and damn does your cowboy want to play with you, darlin'."

He sat the phone on the desk and reached for his fly. He unbuckled his jeans and unzipped himself then stalled, grinning like a possum.

"Hey, who told you that you could stop?" she teased and bit into her lip.

"I don't show 'til you do, baby. You know the rules."

Cassidy giggled again and began unbuttoning her top. When her breasts spilled out, Jax groaned. "Fuck, Cass, you're so sexy. I wish I was touching you right now." His hand moved to the thigh of his jeans, and he stroked himself through the denim. She moaned, remembering how beautiful his cock was.

"Here?" she asked and cupped her breast.

"Yes. Flick your nipples, baby, make them hard. Hard like you're making me."

"Am I making you hard? Just from seeing my tits?" she teased, knowing he was always up for phone sex, especially if he could actually see her.

"Oh yeah, your tits are perfect. Now show me the rest of you."

"Your chest, first."

He grinned and unbuttoned his shirt, achingly slow, to reveal his tanned skin, broad chest, and washboard abs, well-honed by a combination of workouts and hard labor. "Fair?"

"Mmm, yummy. I want to lick those perfect abs before I pull your dick into my mouth and suck on it like a lollipop."

"No fair." Jax whined before imploring, "Show me yours, bad girl, and I'll show you mine."

She moved the phone back and slid her shorts down, along with her thin, lacy panties.

"So beautiful. Now spread your legs and touch yourself, darlin'. Show me how wet I'm making you, Cassidy."

"Mmm, Jax." She did as he requested, sliding a finger through her wet folds and watched him lick his lips as she did so.

"Oh God, Cass, I swear I could come right now. This is the best view ever." He growled.

She giggled again. He'd always known how to make her feel like the most beautiful woman in the world.

"Finger yourself. Let me watch."

Her head fell back as she slid her middle finger inside herself and moaned. "Jax, mmm, baby."

He sighed in pleasure, rubbing his denim-covered cock, the view obstructed. "Yeah baby, fuck your little pussy. Imagine it's my cock inside you."

"Mmm, let me see it. I need to see it, baby, please?" Her desperation grew as her desire and pleasure increased. She withdrew her finger and shoved it in again, grinding the heel of her palm into the apex of her thighs as she did so. Then gasped as he stood and peeled his jeans down his hips, then his boxers, so slowly that her sex ached painfully. "Jax!" she whimpered and he chuckled.

"Such a bad girl. You need a spankin'."

The vision of his big palm slapping her ass made her sex clench, and she began pumping her fingers in harder as Jax sat back down.

"That a girl." He moaned and squeezed his now-visible cock in his hand. It looked so hard and thick and–

"Oh God, Jax. Oh God." She was so close as she watched his hand pump his erection, watched his hips arch up, imagined he was inside her, fucking her like there was no tomorrow.

"Come for me, sweet girl. Let me hear you let loose as I hit that little spot of yours over and over again."

Cass went wild on herself, writhing and grinding, even as she watched her lover's face, his eyes closing in satisfaction.

Her eyes stayed open, visually and audibly stimulated to no end by her sexy cowboy's gloriously naked body and deep moans, even as she cried out and climaxed. She came hard and shook violently, keeping the camera trained on herself so Jax could see her.

When her breathing returned, she noted Jax had stopped his stroking and now had both hands on the phone. He was giving her that sexy grin of his that made her want him more than she'd ever wanted anything in her whole life.

"That was so sexy, baby girl. I wish I had a video of it."

"Why– Why didn't you finish?" She suddenly felt unsure of herself.

"Because I'm saving this for you, sweetheart." He moved the camera to show her his erect shaft and he squeezed it once more. "And I don't really think meeting my new clients for the first time with cum all over my jeans is the best idea, do you?" He chuckled.

Surely he could have grabbed a towel or something. She wanted to see his face when he orgasmed. He was so sexy when he let go.

When she looked down, he said, "Cass, don't worry. You'll have me all to yourself tomorrow. I promise. And I'm gonna go hog wild on you...like you just did on yourself, so I hope you're ready." He winked.

She smiled and felt ribbons of desire course through her once more at the visual. She nodded. "I'm always ready for you, my sexy cowboy." She moved her fingers back to her lower half and watched his face as she touched herself again.

"Shit, Cass, you're a really bad girl, you know that?" he groaned.

She giggled. "You like me bad. Don't even pretend like you don't."

"I love you, hummingbird, every inch of you, and I can't wait to prove it. Now come for me again like a good girl."

"Bad, good–make up your mind, big boy."

But played a bold card, moving her slick fingers from inside her to her lips and tongue, licking her fingers and sucking them into her mouth.

"Fuck *me*, Cass. You're killin' me tonight, baby." He was practically whimpering.

"Then get yourself off. Let me see you come too, my love."

"Not a chance. It's so much better in person than with my own hand. I'm far too sick of my hand. I need *you*, angel."

She couldn't deny that fact. Tomorrow, the awkwardness of time spent apart for too long would come into play once more, like it always did when they were face to face. It was easy to do naughty things over the phone, miles apart. It made them brave. But even after years together, nothing could banish the momentarily discomfort distance always seemed to manifest; things were just different. They were getting older, their personalities changing...They weren't the same couple they were a month ago, a year ago, four years ago.

The thing was, what did she plan to do about that?

CHAPTER 11

*E*li held his breath as he called his folks for the first time in a year.

His father answered on the third ring, and Eli could tell it was on speaker phone when he said, "Dad. Mom. Hi. It's, uh... It's me."

"About time you called," his father said.

"Elias. It's...it's so good to hear your voice, son." Eli could envision the tears in his mother's eyes and hated himself a little more than he already did.

"I'm sorry," it was all he could think to say at the moment. He was sorry for being a sorry excuse for a son and a human being these last twelve months.

"Where are you?" his mother asked.

"In Lubbock, currently. Just got settled in yesterday. Thought I'd check in–"

"*Check* in?"

"Gavin," his mother scolded. "Eli, honey, how are you?"

Eli felt tears brim his eyes. Wishing his mother were there so he could embrace her, comfort her–as much as he'd *take* comfort from her. "I'm good, now. Better."

"Oh? What changed?" Damn, Gavin Kinsen was in a pissy mood, apparently.

"I found out... I-I'm a father."

Silence greeted him for a moment before his mother finally said. "Oh, Eli. Honey. I'm so happy for you."

"Who's the mother of this *bastard*?" Gavin asked gruffly.

Eli frowned. What was up with his dad? He'd never been so cold and callous. Had Eli's absence done more damage than he even imagined possible?

There was shuffling on the phone, and it was set down for a moment before Eli heard voices, then his mom said, "Gavin, go lie down. I'll wake you later for dinner."

Eli felt his heart tear. Was something wrong with his father? "Mom?"

"Just a moment, sweetie," she said into the phone, then cupped the receiver. "That's it. Lay down. I'll come check on you later. Get some rest."

A door closed, and Eli's heart pounded harder when he heard his mother's footsteps on the stairs and she sighed into the phone. "Alright. Now let's talk. So, you're a–"

"What the hell is wrong with *him*?" Eli demanded.

"Honey, he's just tired, he–"

"No, I know when Dad's tired. That wasn't it. What is going on?" A sense of dread filled Eli.

Veronica took a deep breath in. "It's... It's better if we talk in person, Elias."

Fuck. What the hell did that mean? "Well, I'd really like to see you guys. I was calling to see if you thought you could come this weekend to the rodeo or even meet up before then?"

"I–" she paused. "I'll fly to you. But I probably won't be able to get away until next week, is that ok?"

"Yeah, absolutely." He wondered why she couldn't "get away" until then but didn't press. He could feel something was off. "Next week we're just in Sweetwater, not too far. I can come pick you up at the airport."

"Ok, honey. I'll look at my planner and text you the best day. Then I'll book my flight if it doesn't interfere with your–"

"Mom, we don't rodeo 'til the weekends and practice during the week, so I'll *make* time."

"Ok, sweetie." She let out a big sigh, and her tight tone softened. "Now, tell me about meeting your son?"

"You...you knew I had a son?"

"Of course, Elias. We all did...everyone but you."

Eli inhaled sharply. That's right. Of course he'd be the last one to know since he'd gone MIA.

"I haven't seen him yet, though. Avery told us. She told us when she found you. Told us she was coming to find you."

Avery had still been in contact with Stella, too. So, Avery had been the one to tell them all about the baby then.

"He's beautiful, Mom. I can't wait for you to see him."

"Oh, honey. You don't know how good it is to hear from you, having you back." His mother's voice broke, and she began sobbing on the phone with him. He broke down too, unable to help himself.

Finding out he had a child had changed so much in such a short period of time. He'd realized how very much he loved his family, how much he'd missed them, and how precious they truly were to him. They were everything and always had been. Even if they hadn't all lived as close as he would've liked.

He pondered his father's gruffness after saying his goodbyes. It wasn't a moment or two before his mom texted him, making plans for next Wednesday. She'd fly into Sweetwater around 11 AM, and they'd have lunch before she flew back. He'd insisted she could stay overnight with them, but she said she "simply had to be back home." He puzzled as to why, and why it was only her flying in, but knew he would have more answers come next week.

Eli headed back to Stella's camper, but RV was a better word. It was far bigger and more luxurious than any "camper" he'd ever seen.

When he came through the door, Stella was feeding Toby, and

Gabe and Avery sat at the table. Jack and Natalie stood by the stove, cooking.

"Giving the young'uns a break," his Uncle Jack stated with a wink.

"They lost a bet," his Aunt Natalie crooned and smirked back at Gabe.

"I told you I wasn't good at remembering names of bands," Gabe defended.

"Wait, then shouldn't *he* be the one cookin' tonight?" Eli asked and sat down beside Stella, wrapping his arm around her. She grinned up at him before leaning in to kiss his puckered lips.

"Well, they tricked us," Avery said, blushing up at her aunt and uncle. "They make dinner tonight, we do the dishes. Then tomorrow night, we have to pay for *their* dinner—wherever they choose to go."

"Shouldn't make bets you can't win...clearly." Jack shrugged, and Eli burst into laughter.

"Sounds pretty smart to me. Y'all got ripped a new one."

Gabe nodded. "Indeed."

"D'you talk to Mom and Dad?" Avery asked, looking up at her brother.

Eli nodded. "Yeah, Mom's flyin' in next week after we get in to Sweetwater."

"And Dad?"

How aloof his mother had been regarding their father put a bad taste in Eli's mouth. He shook his head. "I don't know. I guess we'll know more next Wednesday. We'll go pick her up from the airport and take her to lunch." He looked to Stella, who smiled at him.

"She'll get to meet this sweet angel, then." Stella cooed to the baby, who almost looked like he grinned at her in turn.

"Holy shit, did he just smile? He just smiled!" Eli's heart burst in joy.

Gabe laughed. "Probably farted."

Avery narrowed her eyes at him.

"No, it was a smile. He's eager to meet his grandmother, aren't you, sweet boy?" Stella kissed Toby's cheek and brought him to her shoulder to burp him.

Eli smiled again and kissed the back of his son's head.

"Everything ok?" Jack asked, sensing Eli's mood.

He gulped but nodded to his uncle. Until he knew for sure, he wasn't going to say anything. He knew how private his parents were. Jack seemed to pick up on it and gave him a subtle nod.

Dinner was a delicious Mediterranean-style chicken with a salad, roasted veggies, and fingerling potatoes. Everyone scarfed it down like they were starving, but Eli knew what great cooks his aunt and uncle were.

"Damn, that was delicious," Gabe complimented them first and everyone else followed. "I say we lose more bets in the future, Ave– dishes be damned."

Avery laughed. "Right? I was thinking the same thing."

Natalie smiled at Jack knowingly. "Your uncle has always been good with grilling."

"That's after I burnt dinner a few times and learned the hard way." Jack shrugged.

"Well, I'll gladly do the dishes, myself," Eli said. "You guys pick anywhere you want, it'll be well deserved."

"Thanks, kids," Eli's Aunt Natalie said. "Date nights are not easy to come by nowadays. I'll take it."

Jack wrapped his arm around her shoulders and pulled her against his broad chest. "Well done, wifey."

Eli smiled when they kissed. They'd always been an affectionate couple, especially compared to his own parents, who weren't big on PDAs. Eli had never heard the girls complain, but Jax had always teased them about their romantic ways. Truth be told, he'd just been railing them because he had nothing else to complain about. Jack and Natalie were awesome parents whose home had always felt warm and welcoming. Eli had always loved being around them, in their home. If they wanted to make out in front of everyone, hell, he'd let it slide. His aunt was a beautiful woman, and beautiful women needed to know that they were loved and special.

Looking at his own beautiful woman, Eli smiled at her then his baby, who now lay in his Aunt Avery's arms.

"Think he likes me?" Avery asked.

"Of course he does. What's not to like?" Natalie asked, gripping Avery's forearm warmly.

Avery shrugged.

"He loves you, Aunt Ave," Gabe insisted. "And his Uncle Gabe too. And we're gonna spoil him rotten."

Eli smiled again.

"Well, I'm stuffed and ready to take my boots off and relax for a bit. Stella, babe, we got a hard morning, especially since you're running off by eleven to go pick up Veronica. I expect you up by dawn, cowgirl." Jack pointed his finger at her with conviction, but his eyes were warm and Eli knew how proud he was of Stella, as proud as Eli was of her.

"Yes, coach. I'll be ready." Stella nodded.

She was such a warrior. So strong, and determined...and sexy. It was humbling and turned Eli on like nothing else.

"Yeah, we'll take care of the dishes, then we'll get out of your hair so you guys can put the baby down." Gabe began gathering the dirty dishes and moved to the sink. Avery started to move out of the booth, but Gabe stopped her by clasping her shoulder. "Nah, I got this. Hold your nephew." He smiled at her, and she returned it, holding his gaze for a moment before he turned.

Natalie cleared her throat and took Jack's extended hand as he stood. "Well, good night, everyone. Sweet dreams, baby Toby." Nat kissed Toby's little head, then moved to embrace Eli as they stood. She whispered in his ear. "Welcome back, honey." Eli closed his eyes in reverie as she kissed his cheek.

He squeezed her tight and said, "Thanks for not giving up on me, Aunt Nat."

"I must admit, at times I wasn't so sure, but it was *she* who didn't give up on you." Natalie pointed to Stella, who grinned sweetly.

God, he loved his sweet little star with his whole heart.

Jack moved in then and patted Eli roughly on the back. "You got a second chance, kid. Don't ever squander it."

"I won't. Not ever again."

Jack tipped his hat at Eli. "Love you guys." He patted Avery's back and she blew them both a kiss before glancing down at Toby with a grin.

"Love you both. See y'all in the morning." Eli waved as they moved toward the door.

He'd always had such a good, loving relationship with his aunt and uncle. He'd probably told them he loved them more than he'd told his own parents, truth be told.

"You're cookin' breakfast in the morning, right, Gabe?" Eli's Aunt Natalie quipped as she stilled at the door.

"Shit," a soap-bubble covered Gabe grumbled and got a laugh out of them before they exited. "Man, your aunt and uncle really duped us."

"Well, you asked for it, going toe to toe with them on eighties bands, you knew we wouldn't know 'em," Avery countered.

"Pride. It's an evil thing," Gabe offered with a shrug, Stella and Avery laughed.

"I mean, I can't top that meal from tonight. You didn't tell me your aunt was a skinny, dark-headed version of Paula Deen." He looked at Eli with reproach.

"GrubHub Waffle House, then, you'd be better off." Eli shrugged. "Dude can't even boil water," he told Stella and his sister.

"I'll take breakfast since you're doing the dishes. It's only fair." Avery volunteered with a grin. "I can cook up a mean slice of bacon."

Stella moved into Eli's chest then, and he coiled his arms around her waist, loving the feel of her curvy frame against him. His palms splayed across her back and he inhaled her floral-smelling hair. She'd always smelled like an angel sent straight from Heaven.

"Here, take Toby. I'll help Gabe finish the dishes so we can get out of your hair." Avery offered the baby to Stella, who shooed her off.

"You sit down and hold your nephew, Ave. We aren't kickin' y'all out just for adult time." Damn, Stella's accent had thickened since living in Texas the past year. "Eli can be patient. Besides, I reckon I could volunteer to help Gabe out. I dirtied the dishes, too."

Eli smirked, "Ok there, country girl. If I didn't know any better, I'd think you'd been raised in Abundance, instead of L.A." He leaned in to kiss her before she huffed and pulled back.

"Well you know I was *born* in Abundance, cowboy." She poked his stomach. "So technically I'm just as much a Texan as you are."

He'd forgotten. Shit. He was apt to pay for that comment later if her narrowing eyes was a precursor.

"Eli here could also volunteer his services, as well." She propped her hands on her hips and motioned to Gabe, who was scrubbing a pan like his life depended on it.

"Nah, y'all go enjoy this lovely night. I'm fine. It's the least I can do, honestly," Gabe said.

Eli grinned victoriously at his girl. "Thanks, Gabe. You know we can have adult time *anywhere* so I think we shall, seeing as Stella's about to bust my balls in all the right ways."

Stella gaped at him in shock, and his sister groaned, "Gross, Eli," even as he leaned in to kiss his girl, grabbed her around the waist, and pulled her out of the RV with haste.

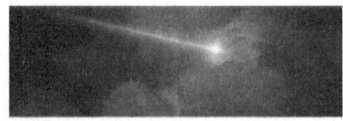

AVERY GIGGLED and tucked Toby to her shoulder, smiling down into his sweet face. "He's so darling, isn't he?"

"And tiny."

"Yeah, to a giant like you." Her eyes sought his, and he gave her the once over, making her body heat rise.

"Giant in more ways than one, little mermaid."

"My goodness, you're as bad as my brother."

"What? I do remember you saying that I was big," he defended, drying another dish before placing it into the cabinet.

Avery rolled her eyes but avoided his because she knew she was blushing at the memory of it all. She focused on her nephew, his breathing in and out, little rosebud mouth open, lashes resting on his tiny cheeks. She smiled and kissed his forehead for the dozenth time.

She remembered when Stella had told her she had her brother's baby and how excited she'd been for both herself and her brother. She knew her life would be even further enriched by this precious child, but she hadn't known exactly just how much until she'd held her nephew in her arms.

"He's perfect," she whispered as Gabe came to sit on the couch next to her.

"He's pretty spectacular. Like his aunt."

Avery's eyes held Gabe's and her lips parted.

"Do you want children, Avery?" he asked before she could say anything to his prior comment.

She looked back to Toby and grinned again. "Yes, maybe one day. Although I'm kinda ok if I don't have any. Does that sound selfish?"

"No, I understand."

They sat quietly for a moment, just watching the baby as he slept.

"He favors you, too, you know?" Gabe insisted, running a finger over the little swirl on top of Toby's head.

"You think so?"

"Yeah, those lips. So kissable." Gabe touched her lips, and she stifled a moan.

She swallowed hard before looking up at him. His eyes were dark, almost animalistic in their intention. He was the predator, she the prey, and he intended to devour her.

"So, what were you curious about?" he asked, his voice as deep and smooth.

"What?" Dammit, he had her all kinds of flustered.

"What things were you curious about, regarding sex? You said you were curious. You wanna do anal or–" His fingers moved to her bare arm, and she exhaled the breath she'd been holding.

"No. God, no! I mean, I..." She wasn't grossed out by the thoughts of anal so much as just uncomfortable. She'd like to feel at ease doing it the "regular way" first. "Just other places. Like *locations*, not on the body, just..."

"Wall. Shower. Table?" His eyes moved to the table they'd just eaten off of, and she pulled her lip in to keep from whimpering.

Before she said, "Yes, please," she found herself asking, "People can actually do it against a wall?"

Of course she'd seen people in movies do it against a wall, but that was the movies. They did all kinds of things that weren't exactly humanly possible.

Gabe grinned at her and twisted his finger around a strand of her hair that sat atop her breast, bringing her nipples to stiffening peaks that hurt. "Oh yeah. I'm fit enough to fuck you against a wall, Ave, for sure."

She had once despised the word fuck, now she basked in how wet it made her. It could just be because his deep voice had said it, though. He had the sexiest freaking voice. She looked his body over. He was fit, fit as all get out, strong as an ox. Strong and masculine...and she wanted him so much that she ached for it.

He grinned, realizing this. "Why don't you put that baby down in his crib and let me show you what *else* we can do?"

She immediately shook her head. "We can't–"

His finger came to her lips and his mouth followed. He kissed her softly, as if coaxing her hesitation from her. "Don't worry, darlin', I'm not going to fuck you. Not with my cock, anyway. Not in here."

That's right because they'd said they'd do it in a hotel room, where they wouldn't get caught. But this was too risky.

"Avery," Avery's eyelids fluttered closed at her name on Gabe's sexy lips, "they won't be back for a bit. They'll never know."

Taboo. So forbidden. The little sister. Her brother's best friend. It was so naughty. It was so wrong, but God did it feel *so* freaking good.

"Go. Put him down or I'm gonna do it while you hold him, then you'll really be blushing."

Holy shit! He wouldn't! Would he?

His Cheshire cat smile said otherwise. Her eyes widened when his hand slid between her jeaned thighs. She whimpered. Then moved away to go lay Toby in his bassinet.

Much to her relief Toby didn't utter one whimper of protest and simply grunted his sweet baby grunt and stretched his sweet baby stretch and was out like a light again. She moved the blanket over him, tucking it on either side before she turned and her nose hit Gabe's sternum.

She gulped and looked up at him. His hand returned to her hair, running his fingers through it. "Your hair is like honey."

It was bland, plain. She'd always wished it was another color instead, dark like her aunt Nat's or even cornsilk blonde like Dallie's.

"Your lips are like rose petals." He stroked his fingertip over her lips next and got a strangled moan from her.

"Your breasts are like the firmest, softest pillows." She gasped out as his hands cupped the breasts he'd just mentioned, his thumbs swirling around her nipples.

"And your tight little pussy is like a steaming hot tub that I can't stop wanting to dive right into."

He separated the distance between them and slid an arm around her waist, his other hand sliding between her legs. She moaned and closed her eyes as he stroked the seam of her jeans. His thumb tormented the apex there, the bundle of nerves that seemed to crave his touch more than any other part of her. She whimpered and covered her mouth.

He chuckled and moved his lips to her ear. "You gotta be quiet if this is gonna work, sweetheart." She nodded. He laughed again. "Good girl. We were in such a hurry last night that I didn't introduce

179

you to oral sex. It's almost as fun as the regular kind." He winked. "Let's get your jeans off."

His hand moved to the button of her jeans, and he unzipped them. "But, Gabe..."

"Trust me, ok?" His smile was playful. "Take your jeans off. I can't fuck you with my tongue if I can't get to you." He winked again and her face blanched in surprise. He slid his hands from her waist into her jeans and slid them down her legs, kneeling in front of her.

Her breathing and heart rate accelerated. Last night she'd been good and buzzed, drunk even, but tonight she was sober as a judge, and embarrassment painted her cheeks as his nose settled at the seam of her womanhood and sniffed.

"God, Avery, just the smell of you gets my cock so damn hard."

She'd never known men got aroused from smelling...

"I couldn't stop myself from the need to be inside you last night. I shouldn't have neglected your pleasure. I cheated you, angel, and now I'm going to make it up to you."

What was he saying? She was having a hard time concentrating as his finger sought the source of her wetness and he assisted her, one leg at a time, out of her jeans.

Once she was clad in only her lace panties, Gabe popped up and turned, his erection prominent as he moved to the fridge and pulled a full baby bottle from the door.

"Wh-what are you doing?"

"Finding an excuse for you to be bare-legged. In the event that they come in before I'm done." Gabe smiled and inverted the bottle onto the legs of her jeans. She frowned but he explained, "Toby spit up on you so you shucked your pants. If we hear them, you run to the bathroom, and I'll proceed to be looking for a pair of sweatpants to cover you."

Once he was done with the task, he moved back to the fridge and replaced the bottle, then returned to kneeling in front of her. He grinned up at her, and her heart stilled at his eagerness to pleasure her.

"Now, where were we?" His tongue licked at the seam of her through her panties and she whimpered. "Good girl. Way to keep it low."

He guided her down to the floor, since the couch was too awkward and he was too tall. His fingers played with her again as he positioned his chest between her lower legs, his face inches from her sex.

"How often do you touch yourself, Avery?"

She blushed. "I-I don't."

"Really? If you don't know how to pleasure yourself, how can you tell a man how to please you?"

She didn't have an answer for that question, so she just shrugged.

"Touch yourself, baby. Show me where it aches the most."

She hesitated but slowly spread her legs and pointed to her lace-clad center. He grinned.

"Anywhere else?"

"Here." She strummed her finger over her clit and whimpered.

"Ok, I'm gonna make this real easy, alright? I'm gonna touch you and kiss you, and I want you to tell me if it hurts or feels better in one spot than another." She thought she might die of mortification first as his finger snaked into the crotch of her undies and pulled it aside. He smiled deviously. "Your pussy is so pretty, darlin'."

She'd never imagined in a million years anyone describing the female anatomy with such open appreciation, but he seemed happy enough so she said nothing. His hot breath on that sensitive part of her brought another whimper to her lips, and she inhaled sharply as his tongue began exploring her folds.

"Oh my God," she whined as her sex throbbed and swirled at the pleasure his licking tongue was eliciting inside her body.

"Feel good?" he asked as a hand came up to squeeze her breast.

"God, yes."

His tongue moved ever so slowly from her clit to her center, which clenched when the tip of it probed there.

181

"Mmm, yeah." He fingered her aching bud and she mewed like a kitten. "That feel good, baby?"

He moved his tongue further inside her and his palm clutched her breast harder, his fingers pinching. She moaned aloud.

"Fuck, Gabe," she hissed.

"Too much?" he asked and pulled back.

"No! That was... Shit! Don't stop." Her hand moved to his head, pulling him back to her.

He chuckled even as he buried his face into her folds, and she swore as her eyes rolled back in her head at the sensations he was bringing to the surface. His tongue was wreaking havoc on her, time stood still, and her calves were cramping as her toes curled from the pleasure of his mouth on her. Just when she thought she couldn't take any more, his finger replaced his tongue and his mouth moved back to the little bud that when stroked, vibrated her insides like the chords on a guitar.

His hand slid into her bra and pushed the cup aside as he kneaded her breast like bread. He slid another finger inside her, and she moaned again.

"Too much?" he asked.

"No, it feels...Mmm, oh, God, it's s-so good."

He chuckled, his tongue battering her clit. "Tell me how this feels?" His mouth latched on and sucked hard. Avery arched her hips into his face. Her body might have levitated as she gripped his head and shoved herself into his bearded stubble, grinding herself against him. She swore as her body succumbed to his sucking and licking and stroking and bit into a nearby pillow to keep from screaming at the top of her lungs, her mind soaring above the clouds, into the stars and beyond.

She panted into the pillow as she came down from her sexual high, looking Gabe's wet, red face over in shock and awe and tenderness.

He smiled, a man pleased with his work. "I see you like having your pussy eaten out."

She'd always despised that word until it was uttered from his mouth and bashfully nodded.

"Good. Most men don't know how to do it well. Or so I've been told." He shrugged.

God only knew the amount of "pussy" this man had "eaten out" in order for him to know how to be good at it. She remembered that with time came experience and didn't feel vindicated to call him out for all his sexcapades. But now she wanted to know how to rock his world the way he'd done hers and looked him over as he stood.

"Can I, uh, return the favor?"

He shook his head. "Not here. Not now."

She was chewing a hole in her lip, wondering why he didn't want her to do so.

He grinned and leaned down to kiss her, the smell of her sex pungent in her nostrils. She wrinkled her nose when he pulled back to speak again. "What? You don't like it?"

"It's...just...strong, I guess."

"It's delicious." He licked his lips as if to prove his point.

She scowled. "If you say so."

He grinned again. "We'll see what you think when you're returning the favor, doll."

Her face went white, and he laughed again before he pulled her to him for a searing kiss.

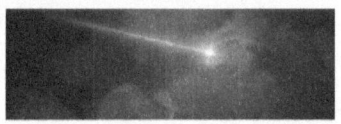

"But Eli," Stella protested as they walked into the dimly lit barn, bodies tight together, his lips on hers. "What if someone sees?"

"No one's gonna see, my sweet star. They're done for the day. Out at the bunkhouse."

They'd set up their campers at the grounds of a friend's ranch, to train and practice before the fairgrounds opened to them on Thursday afternoon.

Now they headed into the barn, away from his aunt, uncle, sister, and best friend so he could make his woman scream as he buried himself deep inside her.

"What about Toby? What if–mmm–what if Avery needs me?" Stella whimpered as his mouth sought her collarbone, licking at the soft skin there, while his hands undid the buttons of her shirt.

"Avery's fine. If she can handle a killer whale, she'll do with half an hour of babysittin'. Let her play aunt. Didn't you see she was lovin' it?"

Stella's smile made his heart ache and his cock throb. "You just want me all to yourself."

"Damn right, I do." He licked a trail up her neck and squeezed her breast, swearing when she grunted in equal parts pain and pleasure. "Shit, Stell, I'm sorry." But her head shake was reassuring enough that he continued his exploration of her body. He traced the swell of her breasts, restrained within her nursing bra, as his mouth sought hers again. He set her on a nearby hay bale, peeling her shirt over her head and tossing it to the side. A horse whinnied in the distance, and he chuckled.

"They can smell us," Stella established.

"Yup, but ask me if I care. I want you. I need you. I've missed you so, Stella Rose."

"Oh, Elias." Her arms went around his neck as he took her mouth again. She fumbled for the buckle of his jeans and succeeded in getting them undone, as he did the same with hers. He lifted her and slid his palms into her denim, cupping her bare ass and squeezing. He peeled the material down hastily, and her freed legs straddled his waist, pulling him even closer to her. His shaft hovered at the entrance of her body, the heat beckoning him like a roaring fire to a freezing man.

"Since when don't you wear panties, Ms. Jenkins?"

"Since you ripped the last pair off of me, Mr. Kinsen."

He chuckled even as he arched his hips up to join their sexes.

The kiss was sweeter than the last time–and the time before that–and he moaned as his hands moved from her waist to her face to kiss her. He leaned her back onto the hay bale, thrusting hard.

"Oww, shit." She hissed, grabbing for her back.

"What? What'd I do?" he asked, concern filling his face as he looked at their joined bodies and withdrew from her.

"That hay is rough stuff. It scratched me." Indeed when she pulled her hand from her lower back, there was red blood on her palm.

"Damn, I'm sorry. So much for sweeping you up in passion." Eli grimaced and pulled her upright and off the hay.

"It's ok, I'm not deterred." She gripped his face and kissed him. Her hands moved to his ass and grasped it in her palms. "Fuck me, Eli. Fuck me like I'm the only thing keeping you tethered on this earth."

"You are, my sweet star. You're everything. You always have been."

He guided his cock back inside her sweet heat and moaned at the pleasure that flooded his body and soul. She held on tight as he pistoned up into her, squatting to improve their center of gravity, his palms on her hips a death grip. Sweat beaded his forehead as he plunged and withdrew, letting the squeeze of her pull him closer and closer to oblivion. Soon, her body shook with fatigue and his own muscles and joints protested the stretch on them both, tired from their day of hard practice.

"Eli, I-I can't," Stella declared.

He ceased his pumping and rested his forehead on hers, sitting her back on the bale of hay.

"I'm cramping, too," he confessed.

"Cramps happen," she remedied with a grin and gripped his cock in her fist, working him to a rolling crescendo. She pushed him back, dropped to her knees, and took him deep into her throat.

"Shit, Stella," he gasped and closed his eyes briefly, loving how she always flicked her tongue over him and squeezed the base of him at just the right moment. "God, I always loved watching you do this to me. Almost as much as I love watching your face when I do it to you." That caused her fervor to increase, but just before he could finish in her mouth, he pulled her off her knees and turned her around. He bent her over and guided himself back to her center, thrusting in nice and slow to allow her body to stretch and accommodate him.

"Jesus, Stella, you feel so damn amazing." He gripped her hips and took his time plunging and withdrawing, feeling her body clench him as he coaxed her into submission.

She jutted her ass into his thrusts, causing him to grit his teeth in order to hold back his release. Each moan reverberated through him, breaking down every barrier, until Stella's hand moved between her legs. She groaned into the hay. His hand moved into her scalp and held her fast.

"Oh, shit...shit. Eli.... Oh baby," she whimpered her release, her pleasure cries echoing in the quiet barn. Finally, Eli let loose, hammering her as control left his body and he was soaring away into the abyss.

When he came back to earth, Stella pulled away, turned and sat, her gloriously half naked body flushed from their lovemaking.

"So much for impromptu apology sex," Eli offered in defeat.

"You have nothing to apologize for." Stella frowned.

"I have a *million* things to apologize for, but I'll start with this." He motioned to the hay.

"It'll make for a funny story when I'm in the nursing home one day and an orderly points out the scar on my back." Her genuine laugh of amusement made him smile.

"The Stella I used to know would have balked at any scar."

"Yeah well that was before the Stella *now* had a shit ton of stretch marks to go along with a hay injury."

When Eli tilted his head, she motioned down to her lower abdomen where the barely visible white marks were embedded deep in her skin. She rubbed wistfully at them. Eli wasn't sure if she were wishing she could wash them away or admiring them. Either way, he moved her hands and lowered his lips to them, gently kissing the proof of life she carried like a badge of honor.

"It makes you all the more beautiful to me. Proof of where our son slept, where he grew, where his mother's body fed and nourished him. Proof of my love for you."

Stella smiled, emotions alighting her eyes. "I remembered every word you said to me that day."

Elias ran a hand through his hair and took a deep breath. "I can't take back what I said–"

"I don't want you to. I needed to hear those words. And the stretch mark comment stuck with me. So when I started to get them, I honestly didn't mind. Because of you." She cupped his cheek in her palm and put a hand to his chest, where his heart was. "It takes a brave man to speak the truth."

"Yeah, it also takes a coward not to wait for a response, too. A coward to walk away from the woman he loved more than life itself."

"That was a learning experience for the both of us. Not to just assume things of the other before communicating. We're better for it."

"Better or not, despite having the rest of my life to make up the time I lost with you and Toby, it's still not going to be enough. Stella, I need to know you forgive me."

"Of course I forgive you, Elias. I love you so much. I've never thought ill of you. It was such a misunderstanding."

"*My* misunderstanding. One that almost cost me everything." For a year, it *had* cost him–so very much.

"Because of my lack of ownness, Eli. Tony always had me by the balls, and I didn't realize what a bad influence he was, until he was gone."

"You miss him?"

"Not that much, honestly."

Eli laughed, she followed.

187

"Nothing hurt as badly as missing you. Not knowing where you were. If you were safe. Hurt. Alone."

"I'm sorry," he repeated and took her hands.

"Me too. Do you forgive me for my selfishness?"

"A thousand times, yes. Let me make love to you?"

"Every day for the rest of our lives," she confirmed.

"That's a *given.*"

When he kissed her this time, it was more tender, less rushed, more fluid, as if their bodies, their souls, were finally back in sync once more.

"This time, let's find somewhere more comfortable."

"Oh?" she asked as he lifted her, and she straddled his hips again.

He grabbed a horse blanket from the hook on the barn wall, walked them out of the side door of the barn and toward the tall grass out in the dark pasture.

"Elias, you're gonna get us bit by a snake or somethin' out here."

"My little star, I could get used to that sexy twang, you know?" He chuckled and laid the blanket down before easing her to it. "How's your back?"

"Fine now," she cooed.

"Mmm, well then, let me work on another body part."

His mouth fell to her lower half and he had her quivering before he settled himself between her legs once again. He eased himself inside her slowly, letting her encompass him once more.

"I don't think every day is gonna be sufficient to quiet this thirst."

"No?" She gripped his shoulders, wrapping her legs around him as he grunted in pleasurable agony.

"No, I'm gonna need *hours* of every day for it."

Stella laughed, her sex clenching his, his eyes rolling back in his head. "I'll work it out with my new manager. See if he can share me."

"Sounds like a hard ass." He pulled out and thrust in again, looking into her eyes.

"He's young. Maybe he'll grow out of it."

"Doubtful," Eli groaned as his speed increased. "He'd be a fool to spare even one moment away from you."

"Oh Eli," she sighed and surrendered once more, her moans buried into his shoulder.

"I'll never take you for granted again, my little star, never. Ever. Again."

CHAPTER 12

*J*ax Kinsen glanced at his girlfriend, Cass, and took her hand, pulling it to his chest as he drove from the Lubbock International Airport to the fairgrounds about thirty minutes away. They were finally together, but weren't completely alone. His fellow ranch hand, Tate Banks, sat in the back on his phone. He'd looked away when Jax had deepened his kiss and his arms had wrapped tighter around her than was appropriate, but the younger man didn't seem to grasp the concept of love yet. He either hadn't known love or didn't want it, opting only for unbridled lust–unlike Jax, who'd been all consumed upon seeing Cassidy's face for the first time in over a month.

Jax had thought it would get easier over the years, their time apart, but the opposite had been true. Letting her go each and every time to travel somewhere further away was getting more and more difficult for his heart to bear. He'd never gotten used to it, the distance, the loneliness, his heart being carried so far away from his body that he couldn't breathe at times.

But now she was here. He couldn't get close enough, couldn't stop inhaling her hair, her skin, as if he could keep the essence of her in his nostrils forever. She grinned at his actions and rubbed his forearm with the hand he wasn't holding.

"You're tanner than the last time I saw you."

"It's getting warmer out. Been wearing short sleeves again."

He hated that, too. The weirdness of being apart so long. The small talk. Not knowing every inch of her body as intimately as he wanted to. Feeling like she had changed since the last time they'd talked. Some new hobbies, new personality traits, new habits she'd picked up that he wasn't aware of. It was like he was dating someone new each time he saw her, and he didn't get to see her as often as he wanted or needed.

He hated the distance with a burning fire that had begun to ignite in his soul. He wanted to beg her to stop doing it, to come home for good, to choose to stay with him. He'd never considered himself selfish and didn't want to do it. It might break him apart to walk away from her. He'd traveled with her on occasion here and there, but he wasn't passionate about it like she was. He loved being home, on his ranch. Problem was he wanted her there with him.

Tate had his headphones in and couldn't hear their conversation. Even still, Jax wasn't going to push it and risk him overhearing something inappropriate.

Cassidy's smile appeared playful, and he asked, "What?"

"You're broader. Been workin' out?"

"Not much else to do when my girlfriend's perpetually out of town," he tried to soften his tone, make it less accusatory.

But Cass looked down.

"You look like you've been working out too, baby," he stated, trying to ease her doubts.

"Ha. I've gained five pounds." She rubbed her belly, but she looked just as slender as always to him.

"Maybe you gained it in your butt." Jax bobbed his brows and got wide eyes from Cass.

"Jax, you better take that back." She shoved at him.

"Nope. I'm gonna inspect it real thoroughly when we get to

191

where we're going, too." He winked and watched her eye-fuck him, pulling her lips in. He gulped and adjusted his tightening jeans. She covered her giggle, and he put his other hand on the wheel. Last thing he needed was Tate to tattle on him to Wyatt and his dad.

Cass told him about her current assignment that would end next week. She'd be home for three weeks, then out again. She was finalizing the details, but she'd be heading to Anchorage, Alaska.

"*Alaska?*" Great...even further than California.

"Yeah, we've never been. Thought we could check out a few of the touristy places. It's cold, but I've heard Alaska is gorgeous."

"It's a seven to eight-hour flight, and soon it will be winter. Did you even think about that?" Alaska was cold in the summer months, Jax couldn't even fathom the winter ones.

"Oh Jax, you can just watch a movie and–"

"You know I hate flying, Cass. Why do you always choose such far places to go?" He was whining he knew, but dammit, all they did was fight about her destinations of choice. He hated flying with a passion. It made him sick to his stomach: the cramped seats, the screaming kids, the heights. He hated being out of control. And planes crashed. He knew cars and trucks did too, but still...

He hadn't meant to sound so harsh, scolding himself when her head fell and she fiddled with her fingers in her lap.

"You don't *have* to come visit me."

"Don't do that."

"What?"

"Reverse psychology me."

"Well, you don't."

"You know that's not what I meant..."

"Love is a compromise, Jax. We knew it would be like this."

"It doesn't *have* to be, Cassidy."

She looked him over, frowning.

He pulled into the lot of the grounds though just as she was about to respond. She put her face in her hand and propped her elbow on the window, turning away from him.

The security guard stopped him at the gate of the fairgrounds.

"Can I help you, son?"

"Yes, sir. I'm Jax Kinsen. Here to meet up with my cousin, Elias Kinsen."

The man flipped through the list then nodded. "ID please?" Once Jax pulled out his ID and the man verified his claim he said, "There in that group over there with the A&M flags. Here's your pass."

"Thank you."

"Yup. Y'all have a blessed day."

"You too."

Jax drove toward the grouping of large RVs, spotting Stella's trailer almost immediately due to its size alone, and parked. Cass got out, and he followed, retrieving their bags from the back seat.

"Well, well... Look at what the cat dragged in," came a familiar voice. Jax turned to see Eli in a cowboy hat, smiling brightly with baby Toby tucked into his arm.

"Could say the same about you, cuz. You look better than I expected." Jax took his hand and clasped it in his own.

"The joys of fatherhood will do that for you," Stella said from behind him, beaming. "Oh my goodness. Cass, you look amazing."

Stella pulled Cassidy in for a hug, even as Jax patted Eli's shoulder.

"It's damn good to see you, man," Jax said and grinned down at the baby. "He's a good-lookin' kid, ain't he?"

"Took after his mama, thank the Lord," Eli teased, knowing Toby could pass as his mini-me.

Jax was glad to see his cousin looking so well. It'd been far too long, and he'd spent far too many nights comforting Stella, his emotions ranging from angry to worried along with hers.

Jax had always looked up to his cousin Eli. They were just four years apart in age and had been raised like brothers, spending many hours and years of their lives working together on the ranch.

"Hey, Jackson," came a soft female voice, and Jax's eyes moved toward Eli's sister–his younger cousin, Avery–waving from the doorway of Stella's RV.

"Ave, holy shit! What are you doin' here?" He grinned and approached her as she came down the stairs.

He wrapped his arms around her and pulled back to look into her face. It'd been a while since last he'd seen her, since Christmas probably. She looked just as beautiful as he remembered.

"I had to come see my brother. After Stella told me where he was, I just had to see him with my own eyes." Her blue-green eyes shot to her brother's, and his head lowered in shame.

The hell Eli had put them all through clearly bothered him now. Jax could tell he was humbled. Good. He needed to know how much his family had suffered for his actions.

Jax's mom and dad rounded the corner then, followed by a tall auburn-haired cowboy. He greeted his mom and dad with hugs before Elias re-introduced his friend and heeler, Gabe Halloran.

"Gabe, you recall my little cuz, Jax, right?" Eli looked to Jackson then. "You remember this crazy ginger a-hole, right?"

"Nice to see you again, Gabe." Jax extended his hand. "I don't believe you've met my girlfriend, Cassidy."

Gabe shoved at Eli before shaking Jax's hand. "Jax, how are ya?" He then tipped his hat to Cassidy. "Ma'am."

Cassidy nodded to him and moved back to Jax's side, where he wrapped his arm around her, glad to have her here for the reunion.

"Y'all should all hang out tonight." Jack said, "Hell, it's been a minute since the Kinsen clan all got together."

That was the truth.

"Yeah, Jackson, too bad your sisters aren't here," Natalie stated.

Yeah, too bad. They would've enjoyed seeing and catching up with Avery and Elias.

"Well, we'll be in Dallas soon. Maybe we can all have dinner together or something?" Eli offered.

"They'd like that," Jax said. "I'll text 'em and see. What, week after next, right?"

Eli nodded, and Jax began texting his sisters in their sibling group text.

"They're both down for that." He grinned and looked up at his folks. Then he frowned when Cass gave him a sad smile. Of course she wouldn't be there. She'd be back in California, because she was never around long enough.

"Uncle Jack, you and Aunt Nat were supposed to have a date night tonight," Avery said with a frown.

"Oh, nonsense. There's always tomorrow, hon," Jax's mom said, brushing it off.

"And we'll keep Toby too. We'll just have a date night in." He winked, getting a laugh from Eli and an eye roll from Jackson.

Sheesh. His parents had never been shy in the intimacy department, he knew for a fact.

"That's really kind of you guys, but are you sure you don't mind?" Stella asked even as Toby began to fuss. She moved up next to Eli and patted the baby's bottom.

"Of course not, dear. Besides, how long's it been since Cassidy was around?" Natalie winked at Cass, who blushed, and pulled her in for a hug. "It's good to see you, honey."

"You too, Aunt Nat."

It was still weird having his girlfriend call his mom by the title of "aunt", but he knew that Cassidy had always seen her as her second mother. Just as Stella, too, called his mom and dad aunt and uncle. What could he say? He had the coolest parents ever. And he knew it too.

He'd taken lead at the ranch and was working more on the business side than usual, with his parents away assisting Stella. It had been good, but also bittersweet, despite knowing his dad still had years before retirement. Hell, Jax knew that even when his father was frail and on a walker, he'd still be down at the barn running Kinsen Ranch.

Thank goodness for Wyatt Montgomery, their foreman. He ran a smooth ship, and Jax hadn't had to worry too much being away for a little while.

"Well, girls, let's go get all dolled up." Stella beckoned and took Toby from Elias, giving him a kiss in the process. "I'll feed him, and we can go hang."

"That's fine. Don't worry. I'll put the horses away," Eli slammed his hand on his hips dramatically, getting a laugh from everyone.

"That's the least you can do, brother," Avery sassed back and puckered her lips as she pulled Cassidy with her toward Stella's RV.

Jax didn't miss the sorrow that filled Eli's face when he looked back at her and nodded.

"Ah, don't be so hard on him, Ave," Jack said and patted his back. "We all have to hit rock bottom before we can appreciate life's blessings."

Rock bottom, huh? Was that where Jax and Cass were? He looked longingly at Cass as she followed Avery and Stella into the large RV. Rock bottom. Because he wasn't sure his heart could fall any lower than it suddenly felt.

STELLA LAUGHED and brought the one cocktail she allowed herself up to her lips, slapping Jackson's arm.

"That is absolutely not true. I was *not.*"

"Were too," Jax retorted and pulled her against him, hugging her. "I love you so much, Stell Bell, but you were a damn hot mess, if ever there was one." He kissed her forehead, laughing even as she swatted at him again.

Stella felt her cheeks redden, she *had* been "a damn hot mess" without her beautiful Elias for the last year and remembered every excruciating second with clarity as her eyes moved to his. Eli gave her a tight smile and took a swig of his beer before pulling her to his chest and resting his head on top of hers in longing.

She didn't miss the cautious flash in Cassidy's eyes as she smiled at them. Jealousy. She knew that emotion well herself. It was what she felt for the gorgeous brunette now eyeing them from the corner of the bar. The sultry and stunning Cassia McCormick. The other woman. One of many Elias had slept within the last ten months. But she'd also been "more intimate" with him than the others had, Eli had told her, and Stella hated that her heart prickled at the thought.

Despite what had happened in their past, Cassidy knew where Stella and Jackson now stood. Before Eli had rescued Stella–in between Jax and Cassidy's break up–Stella and Jax had momentarily been an item, rounding pretty much every base but home plate. Nothing had ever happened afterward, though. He'd not touched her with anything more than the hugs of casual friendship since. Stella–nor Jackson–could deny that there'd been an obvious attraction between them. They couldn't. Perhaps it would always be there, skirting around the periphery of their consciousness. But their hearts remained tied to Eli and Cassidy respectively, and that's where they would stay.

She and Cass had many heart-to-hearts over the last several years about it. Stella could only apologize so much. She couldn't change the past. She couldn't change the fact that she knew Jackson's body almost as intimately as she knew his cousin, Elias's. She couldn't change the fact that Jax knew her body just as well. Or that her menstrual blood had covered him, ruining the moment, that night when she'd had every intention of going all the way with him. It had probably saved their friendship. God knew, it might never have recovered had she and Jackson taken it any further.

She could look back now on what had once been the most embarrassing moment of her life and laugh about it as Jax grinned at her again. She was grateful they hadn't had sex, even if there'd been times during her pregnancy when she hungered for intimacy. Jax had been just as needy for human touch at times, given Cassidy's distance. But neither had acted on that impulse, and she would remain ever grateful. They would have been combustible, she and

197

Jax—both too hot-headed, too spirited. As much as she loved Jackson, they weren't right for each other. Perhaps complimenting, but not compatible, like she and Eli were. Eli was Stella's soulmate, and Cassidy was Jax's.

Stella's gaze moved from Jax to Cassidy, who eyed Jackson lovingly when he took her hand. Then her eyes moved to Avery's, who was heatedly glancing over at Gabe. His eyes roved her frame, and Stella had a moment of startling clarity. *Holy shit!*

She cleared her throat and leaned up to quickly kiss Eli's puckered lips. "Girls, I need a bathroom break. Let's go!"

She moved to Cassidy and Avery, grabbing both their hands as she hauled them behind her. When they cleared the doors, Stella rounded on Avery. "You're *sleeping* with him, aren't you?"

Avery gaped, eyes flaring wide.

"Dammit, Avery, I knew it!" Stella laughed in triumph, only to frown. "Shit, Elias is gonna *kill* him. You know that, right?"

Stella covered her mouth. Damn, the liquor was hitting her hard right that moment. Perhaps she could no longer handle booze.

"*Please* don't tell him," Avery begged, looking from Stella to Cassidy.

"Pssh, of course I'm not gonna tell him, woman, but how darn long do you think you can keep it hidden before he figures it out? You guys are obvious AF!" Stella exclaimed, slamming her hands on her hips.

Cassidy was clueless and put her hands up. "Wait, we're talking about the good-looking red-headed cowboy, right? Gabriel? What's the problem? He seems nice enough?"

Cass's brows went up to her forehead, waiting for a reply, before Avery softly said, "He's Elias's best friend...and has been since grade school."

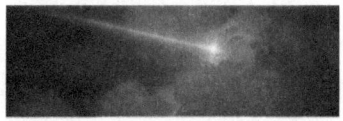

ELI CHECKED their horses that evening, watching Jax and Cass leave in his truck. They'd all had a good time together, hanging out and shooting the shit. It'd been good seeing his first cousin. Jax was like his little brother, and he was glad he'd be around to see more of him in the future.

Eli was eager to return to Abundance, where he'd fallen head over heels in love with Stella Jenkins and named a shooting star after her. It'd been on a whim, but he hadn't hesitated. He made a wish that she be his, unsure who exactly he was speaking to–be it the star, itself, or The Almighty. He'd watched that jet trail in awe, shimmering and bright, as mesmerizing as his sexy, perfect Stella Rose Jenkins. It was unthinkable. The stunning girl he'd seen in so many movies had been as strikingly gorgeous in person as she was on screen, and as wonderful as he could have ever hoped for or imagined. This woman was in his arms, looking at him like he was that amazing star, not her. He'd gotten lost in those sexy eyes of hers, in the feel of her velvet skin, and kissed her. He'd kissed her with all he had, knowing she was his future.

Elias turned when he heard footsteps behind him and was shocked to see Cassia McCormick approaching. He took a deep breath, prepared for almost anything, save the words that came out of her mouth next.

"You're happy, cowboy."

"Yeah, uh... Found out my girl had my baby. It was, apparently, a big mix-up on my part." He cleared his throat, not feeling the need to explain himself to someone he really didn't know that well, and turned to his stallion, Ricochet, who whinnied at him.

He stroked his throat latch and saw Cassia brace her forearms on the fence.

"It's a good look on you, Elias. Stella's a lucky woman."

"I'm the lucky one. That's for damn sure. I don't deserve a woman as amazing as her, yet here I am, calling her mine. It's incredible." He looked off, feeling his throat tighten as emotion overwhelmed him.

He'd cheated on his beautiful little star with the woman standing next to him. He'd been inside Cassia, whether he remembered much about it or not, slept in the same bed with her laying next to him, let her put her mouth on him... But he'd never felt anything with her, not like what he felt when he was in Stella's intimate embrace. That didn't change his spiteful actions though. He'd slept with a slew of women who weren't Stella while she was pregnant with his child and pining for him.

As if reading his thoughts, Cassia said, "If she's a good woman, she'll forgive you for your trespasses."

"She already has."

He looked Cassia hard in the eyes. Her eyes were deep brown pits of chocolate. She was a beautiful woman. Gorgeous, actually. Just as gorgeous as Stella was in her appearance alone. She could have any man she wanted and pretty much had. The way she looked at him, though... It was as if she wanted more. From him? Why? He'd been nothing but rude to her, despite that she'd given so much of herself to him. Was she broken too? Looking for love in the bed of strangers? Searching for something?

She snapped out of the inner reverie she'd pulled him into and smiled. "Well, I wish you the best, Elias. I'm glad you've found your happiness. Although, it would have been nice if it'd been *me* you'd found it with instead."

He frowned, surprised, but didn't have time to respond before she was leaning in to kiss him.

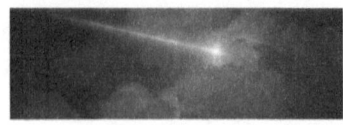

STELLA FROZE as she saw Cassia lean in and kiss Elias on the lips. Her heart tripped over itself as she watched the interaction. Eli was the first to pull back and shake his head, in shock—surprise, even? What had they said to one another?

Stella didn't wait to find out as she stormed up to them. Cassia moved back two steps. "That's right, homewrecker, back the hell up." Stella's hands came to her hips. "Don't you think you've done enough? Guess what? This cowboy's mine! What? You don't have enough *here* to choose from? So you gotta go after one who's already taken?" Stella opened her arms, gesturing to the trailers in the fairground.

Cassia looked taken off guard and put her hands up in defense.

"You know what happens to dumb sluts like you? You get exactly what you ask for. Flaunt your goods long enough, and one day, you're gonna attract the wrong kind of attention. I hope for your sake, you wise up before something bad happens to you. But you stay the hell away from my cowboy, or next time, you'll have a black eye to go with that black soul of yours—you hear, she-devil?" Stella balled her fist in promise, and Cassia simply gaped at her.

"Do. You. Hear. Me?"

Cassia nodded, looking briefly back at Eli then turned on her booted heel and stalked off.

Stella watched the bitch go, hoping like hell she'd slip on horse shit and fall on her overconfident ass, before she turned to Eli, whose eyes were burning into hers.

"Stella, I *swear to God*, I didn't–" He held his hands up in defense.

"I know. I saw." She crossed her arms over her chest.

He grinned at her. "Damn, baby, that was hot as fuck. I've got a semi right now. My feisty little star taking the bull by the horns." His eyes moved down her body, licking at her sensitive spots.

"And I'll take the stallion by the *balls* if you ever so much as consider cheating on me ever again, is that understood?" As if needing to drive her point home, her hand shot to his undercarriage, gripping said balls fiercely.

Eli gave a cry of discomfort before his hand fell to her wrist. "Whoa! Ease up, baby doll. I–"

"Is. That. Understood?" she emphasized with a little squeeze, getting another croak out of him.

He nodded. "Yes! Yes ma'am." He grunted before she let go. He exhaled a breath. "Damn, Stells. You are super fucking sexy when you're possessive."

"Good. Now fuck me. Right here and now. I'm drunk and horny, and I want every damn skank in this trailer park to know who the hell you belong to."

He gave her a crooked grin and nodded his head. "Yes, ma'am. Same goes for the cowboys. If they didn't know already, this little cowgirl is all mine."

He pulled her to him and kissed her breathless, weaving a hand through her long, thick mane.

"Show 'em, stud."

"With pleasure." He hauled her to the side of the building, fusing their mouths together, where he pushed her skirt up and slid his finger inside her panties. Her hands already had him unbuckled, unzipped, and working his erect cock before he lifted her and she straddled him. He pulled the crotch of her undies aside and with one thrust, his cock slid right in and all was right again. "I'm yours, Stella. Always and forever, my love."

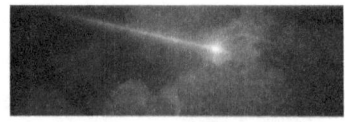

JAX COULDN'T SEEM to get to Cassidy fast enough, and the passion of it overwhelmed Cass's senses.

"Jackson David," she scolded as he grabbed her before she could even close the hotel door properly.

His mouth was on hers and his fists were gripping her clothes.

He backed them to the bed, and she fell to the mattress with an "Umph."

Jax grinned at her predatorially and threw his hat onto the table, then peeled his shirt over his head and tossed it at the armchair in the corner.

"You have seconds to get naked, or I'm ripping your dress off with my teeth," he warned and went at his belt buckle, the one she loved with a buffalo on it. His brows went up when she didn't move, and she gasped. He was dead serious.

He whipped his belt off with incredible speed and folded it in half, holding it up and shaking it at her.

"You've been a bad girl, Cass. You deserve a spankin'." His pecs and ab muscles bunched as he snapped the belt together with force. Her jaw dropped.

When had he become such a dominant alpha? Their phone sex had gone from shy and subtle, at first, to downright raunchy over the years. He'd always had a healthy sexual appetite for her, but this was more demanding than he'd ever been, and she felt her panties dampen in arousal.

"Fine, you wanna play coy. I'm down, darlin'."

He knelt and moved his hands to her waist, his nose teasing her hairline.

"I'm dying to see what's beneath this sexy little dress. Lace, thong, silk...nothing at all?"

She started to tell him it wasn't wise–or sanitary, really–to travel with no panties, even in a maxi dress that came to her ankles, but she refrained.

His mouth moved to her neck and licked. As one hand moved to cup her breast, the other gripped the fabric covering her hip. He settled atop her, pressing her into the mattress as he bit into the sensitive flesh of her throat. She whimpered, and he growled. She'd forgotten all about the belt as his hot mouth destroyed her sanity, licking, sucking, and biting until her nipples were achy. He could feel them hardened through her bra, on his bare chest, and stroked them with his fingertips, first one then the other.

"How wet are you for me, baby girl?"

She moaned in answer when he bit at the mound of her breast–even through the fabric she knew it would leave marks–but she was so aroused she felt drunk.

He chuckled deviously before taking her mouth again and fucking it with his tongue. Just as she was moving her arms up to wrap around his neck, his hands gripped hers. He pulled her arms above her head, toward the headboard, and she realized what he planned to do with the belt. He looped it through the wood headboard slat and restrained her wrists.

Cass's heart rate accelerated. Her sex clenched as he rose to his haunches and unbuttoned the fly of his jeans.

The sweet, gentle boy she'd fallen in love with all those years ago had turned into a sexy, hard-muscled stud. All she wanted in that moment was to be overtaken by him and his dominance.

He seemed to sense her desire and grinned down at her, his perfect mouth quirking up, his moss green eyes looking her over like she was a dessert he couldn't wait to indulge in.

"I'm gonna fuck you 'til you scream and management gets so many complaints we get kicked out."

Damn! That sounded amazing.

"Then do it, cowboy, and stop talking about it." She bent her knees and arched her hips in invitation.

His eyes narrowed and his hands moved up her legs, pulling the dress with him. He moved it all the way up to her chest, over her breasts and grinned again.

"Damn, you're beautiful, Cassidy."

Jax lowered his mouth to her chest, just below her collarbone, and began sucking, licking, and torturing her. Death by desire was fully real as she squirmed, whimpered, and whined before he finally unclasped her front-clasp bra and tortured her some more. His mouth fell to suckle her, leaving her arching her hips, yearning to have the insistent ache between her legs quenched.

"Jax, please?" she begged, watching as he eyed her from his perch at her breast. He pulled hard and nipped, getting another whimper from her.

"I love having you at my mercy. See how hard I am?" He motioned down to the bulge in his jeans, straining against the zipper.

"Show me, baby."

He grinned again. "Such a naughty girl."

Instead of shucking his jeans, he moved atop her once more, those full lips of his trailing kisses down her ribs, her lower belly, to the top of her lacy panties.

"These new?"

"Yes," she cried when his finger moved through the seam of her womanhood.

"Just for me?"

"Always, Jax." She felt he was talking about more than just the panties. He was talking about her wetness, and her sex clenched again in answer.

He moved the crotch of her undergarment aside. His mouth settled over her bare skin, tongue licking the wetness that pooled at her center before he sucked at the apex of her thighs. She felt his fingertip press into her and her head shot back. Her orgasm hit her hard as his finger thrust into her. She cried out in pleasure, wave after wave knocking her down. Tears gathered at the corner of her eyes as she came back to earth, and Jax chuckled at her tender flesh, jarring it enough to get another whimper from her.

"Missed me, I see."

"Please, Jackson?" she pleaded, her eyes searching his.

"You aren't the only one who's crazy with desire." He popped back up to his knees and unzipped himself, rewarding her with the view she'd been wanting. His long, thick shaft bobbed out his jeans as he peeled them down his hips.

He grabbed her ankles and jerked her down toward him. The leather of the belt bit into her wrists, but she didn't protest. She needed him, had to have him inside her or she was going to die.

The initial penetrating thrust was hard but satisfying. He settled his chest over hers and moved his hands into her hair, cradling her head.

"Damn, Cass," Jax grunted as his face moved into the crook of her neck. "It's been too long, too damn long." He withdrew, only to lunge harder, getting another gasp out of her. "Mmm, fuck… So sweet. So damn sweet."

He looked into her face as he withdrew again. He began pumping harder and faster into her, his breathing accelerating as his body loved hers with each velveteen thrust. Her arms burned, her heart pounded, but it was her center that was home again, filled with the one and only thing that could ever satisfy it. Home after being without its match. Home. Jax was her home, and she his. Always. He'd always be her home.

"Mine. You're mine. Say it?"

His eyes held hers even as his hands moved back to her breast, squeezing and kneading. His mouth took her nipple again, and she moaned.

"Say it, Cass. I need to hear it." His mouth came off her nipple with a loud "Pop", and her head flew back, her womanhood contracting around him.

"Yes, I'm yours. I'm all yours, Jackson."

And, together, they split apart at the seams, pleasure and love seeping into every open pore, filling it to the brim as they left earth in an orbit of stars.

Jackson emptied himself inside her, his hips still pumping as he rode out his climax. When the spasms eased, he stayed atop her and moved his hands over her arms, her face, into her hair.

His gorgeous eyes roved her face as if drinking in every detail and he said, "I can't do this anymore, Cassidy."

She frowned and gulped, feeling her heart ache at his words.

Hadn't he just said–?

"Do you know how crazy I've been? This time apart is killing me. I hate it. I hate you being gone. I hate FaceTime. And phone sex. And anything that keeps you from me. I hate your job."

"Jax," she whispered.

"No! Let me finish. I need to get this out."

Her arms protested, but she held onto every word, feeling her pulse pound in her neck.

"I want to wake up to you every morning. I want to hold you every night. I want to be with you. Not be with you intermittently. I can't live this way anymore. I've been patient. I've let you fly free, hummingbird, but each time you leave again, a piece of me is ripped away. I need all of you, all the time."

He looked down at their naked bodies, still joined. "This is how it should be, every day. Not once a month or two for a week. It isn't enough for me. Not over a damn video chat where I can't touch you, kiss you, smell you, *feel* you."

His eyes moved back to her wrists, still restrained. She had been forcibly shown what he was dealing with, unable to touch and explore. He'd punished her.

As pissed as that made her, it pulled at her rising emotions. He felt the same way she did. She'd needed him too–not just sexually, but physically. The time apart had killed her as much as it had him.

"I'm tired of worrying about needing a condom. I want to come inside you with no consequence or concern for conception. I want babies, Cass. I want you to be my wife. Be in Abundance with me. For us to build a home together."

"Let me loose," she whispered, tilting her head back to the belt her wrists were manacled to.

He ignored the request but withdrew from inside her. She watched him rise off the bed and shuck the condom he must have donned before taking her. He tossed it into the trash and crossed his arms over his sexy chest.

"I'm gonna do something I swore I would never do. Out of

desperation. Out of need. Out of selfishness." He looked down and a tear sparkled down his face. "It doesn't feel good, does it? Not being able to truly have what you want? Having your hands literally tied?"

Jax had always been such a straightforward yet emotional person. It tugged at her heartstrings. The metaphor hit her hard and tears clouded her vision.

"I'm proud of all you've done, and I respect you and your decisions, but I need more from you, from our relationship. I'm going to do something that I absolutely hate myself for...but I'm asking you to choose. It's me or the job."

He moved forward and came to her side, uncinching the belt. Her wrists burned as much from the release as the pressure that was holding them.

"You may think my methods extreme–cruel, even–but I needed to show you how much this has affected me. I love you with my whole heart, but I'm breaking, given only half of you. If I have to let you go, then I'll do what I must. If that's what you truly want." He turned his back to her. "I'll give you time to think it over, and I won't be angry if you don't choose me...but I really hope you do."

THE BEDSIDE PHONE RANG, but they both ignored it. Cass's insides felt torn apart.

Jax began putting his clothes on, the silence eating a hole inside her so wide that she finally moved from the bed to approach him, needing his warmth. He was buckling his belt back when she stilled him. He looked her over, dread piercing his soft green eyes. She saw the love he'd always freely given her and smiled softly. He didn't return it, just looked down. He took her hand in his, turning her wrist over.

"Damn," he sighed at the marks there, but Cass didn't care. His point had been well comprehended. Just as she was about to tell him her decision, the phone rang again and Jackson huffed. "What the hell?"

He moved to the phone hastily and picked it up.

"Hello!" he almost shouted into the receiver. "Kelsey? Calm down. What is it? Shit, yeah, hang on."

Cassidy's heart stopped in her chest as Jax's eyes turned dark with fear. He motioned to the phone. "It's Kels. She's crying. She says she needs to talk to you right this minute."

Cass gulped as she moved forward, taking the receiver from Jax and pulling it to her ear. She could hear her sister, sobbing softly, and other voices in the background. Jax's palm came to her lower back for support, and she rested her free hand on his adjacent forearm. She looked up into his handsome face as she said. "Kels? What's wrong?"

"Oh, Cass. It's Daddy. H-he... Oh God."

Cass felt her world spin and would have stumbled if Jackson hadn't held her tighter to him.

"Is he...?" she couldn't say the words.

"He's had a heart attack. It's bad, Cassidy. Really bad." Kels's voice trembled. "He's being Life-Flighted to Dallas. He needs bypass surgery."

CHAPTER 13

"Damn, that sucks," Avery said what the rest of them were thinking the next morning as they all sat in Eli's aunt and uncle's RV, eating breakfast.

Jack sighed heavily and Nat's hand interlaced in his. He gave her a tight smile, and Eli felt Stella's hand come to his back. He pulled her against him and kissed her softly on the lips.

Jackson and Cassidy had headed home last night. It was about a five-hour trip. Eli had slept through the text he'd received from him and hated it.

Jack and Natalie were planning to head out soon and wouldn't be back before the weekend was out, so Dallie and her girls were coming to watch baby Toby while Stella and Eli rodeoed.

It would be good to see them, but Eli hated the circumstances. Avery's friend, Scarlett, was heading in tonight too. She was meeting her at the airport mid-afternoon.

"He's gonna be ok," Natalie reassured. "Luther Boyd is stubborn as a mule."

Jack grinned at her. "Y'all just say a prayer for them." He looked back at Stella, who swiped at a tear on her cheeks, and Eli pulled her closer.

"I don't know what Cassidy will do if..." Stella trailed off and looked away.

Eli kissed her temple. He knew how close Stella and Cassidy had gotten over the years and how much she ached for her friend. Luther was family to her too.

He was also Jack's best friend, and he could see how badly this was affecting his uncle as he continued to look away and comfort his wife whose face looked moments from crumbling.

"I'm sorry," Jack told Stella.

She immediately shook her head. "No, UJ. Don't you dare be sorry. I'll be fine. You just go and be with them all and give them our love. I feel guilty that Eli and I aren't going." She looked into Eli's eyes and he shook his head.

Jack spoke first. "Nah, they'll understand completely. Don't you worry none. You go after that ribbon tonight, darlin'."

"And you don't be one bit deterred by that Cassia, either. You just keep ridin'. Your day will come." Natalie winked.

Stella gave her a reproachful grin. "I dunno. Until she's knocked out of competition, I highly doubt it, but thank you."

Stella had rode hard this week, in fact, they'd all been practicing hard and would be again soon after their breakfast was done.

They ate in muted silence, absorbed in their own emotions. When Avery volunteered to clean up and babysit, Eli and Stella hugged his aunt and uncle and saw them off.

They moved out to the pens where their horses were and began tacking them up. Gabe joined in too. Soon, Stella was riding off around the corral while they moved into a separate practice area for calf-roping. Gabe had never been so quiet and soon, Eli was needing his annoying voice to ground him.

"Say, you ain't staked out the newbies yet. What gives?" Eli pointed to a cute ginger brushing her gelding down at a nearby pen.

Gabe shrugged.

"What? Don't tell me your cock is suddenly broken or something. You ain't even flirted with Holly or Lily or what's her name?" Eli stuck his hands out from his chest, trying to remember the name of the busty one Gabe always talked about.

Gabe gave him a half smile and looked down, bashfully. Eli arched a brow.

"I dunno, man. I just... Hell, we're almost thirty. I think it's time I find a good woman to settle down with."

If Eli hadn't stopped his horse, he might've fallen off of him. "*What?*" he asked incredulously. "Says the perpetual bachelor? Since fuckin' when?"

"Since you reunited with Stella, and had a baby–and hell, your uncle's friend almost dying." Gabe pulled his hat off and ran a hand through his thick auburn hair, looking off again. "You start to see life come into perspective when things like that happen. It... reminds me of my military days, ya know?"

Gabe hadn't really spoken much about his time in the Marines. He'd served eight years, and Eli knew he'd been through some rough shit in Iraq.

"Well, just find a woman you can't function without is my only piece of advice. You'll know when you meet her. She'll invade your mind, body, *and* soul, and you won't feel whole when she ain't around."

His best friend gave him a knowing smile. "Love is a rare and wondrous thing, isn't it?"

"It is, buddy. It is." Damn, since when did their conversations get so damn serious? "Now let's stop talking and start working." He practically shoved at Gabe, almost forcing him off his horse before Gabe growled and righted himself, giving Eli the laugh he needed.

"Yes, sergeant." Gabe rolled his eyes.

"Now tell me about your dream girl, and we'll see if we can find 'er." Eli looked back at Stella, rounding her barrels with determination, even as he led Rich into a jog.

"I think I might have already met her," Gabe mumbled.

212

Eli grinned. "Even better. She probably doesn't even know you exist, though, being a ginger and all."

"Fuck you, asshole."

With that, Eli threw his head back and laughed, signaling his horse into a gallop.

"OH GOD, Gabe, yes, oooh, right there. Shit. I'm gonna..." Avery gasped as Gabe pistoned harder into her.

"Come for me, beautiful. I love it when your tight little pussy squeezes my big cock." Gabe groaned in sweet agony as he clutched her breast, tweaking her nipple with his thumb and index finger. His head fell to take the pebbled peak into his mouth, and when he suckled her, she climaxed.

Her cry of submission and thighs tightening around his waist drove him closer to the edge and he gripped her wrists, fastening them together above her head as he thrust in and out of her harder and faster. He watched her face. Her brows drew and mouth opened as her orgasm continued to assault her.

"Fuck... You're so gorgeous with your sexy O-face, darlin'. I must be hitting your G-spot, huh, love?" he coaxed, knowing he was as her eyes began to roll in the back of her head, and her moans sounded like someone possessed.

Her body spasmed, and her back arched, pushing her breasts in his face. He buried his head in the valley between, kissing, licking, and sucking as Avery's body became putty. He continued to pump into her like his life depended on it, his thighs screaming in protest and his cock begging for release.

Her scream of ecstasy echoed around them and he swiftly moved his mouth to cover hers, afraid they'd get kicked out of their hotel room.

"Oh shit, Ave, baby. You're gonna make me come." He growled when her body contracted harder around his. He had two seconds before the earth split and he roared, slamming his hips violently into hers. "Fuck, fuck, fuuucckkkk."

He shook with a force that rattled his soul. Never before had an orgasm made him feel so alive, so drained, so shattered–all at once. It tore through him. He kissed her lips, and face, and neck, loving everything about her, them, their joining while he came down off his sexual high.

He squeezed her breasts and moved his hands down her beautiful body then up to her face, cupping it and kissing her like she was the fuel that gave him life. She kissed him back, equally as blown away. He pulled back and grinned at her, his entire soul content, satiated, yet yearning to have her yet again.

This feeling wasn't going to stop anytime soon. He was straight up fucked, and he didn't know what to do. Dammit to Hell... Gabe was falling in love with his best friend's baby sister.

"Mmm... My God, Gabriel." Ave sighed and ran a hand down his chest. "What the hell was that? It's never felt quite like..." She blushed and the sight had his cock reigniting with desire.

Gabe's shaking legs moved them away from the wall he had her pressed against, down to the bed, where he laid her gently down and stayed atop her. He cupped her cheek.

"That was an internal orgasm. Not many women have those or even know what they are."

"Sucks for them."

Gabe chuckled, even as Avery ran a hand over his face and into his hair. "I didn't hurt you, did I, sweetheart?" he asked when he shifted, and she grimaced.

"No, just..." She reached for her back. "I think I pulled a muscle," she giggled.

"Me too." He reached for his thigh and massaged it. "But damn was it worth it." He kissed her nose, and her hand fell to his chest, pressing a hand over his heart.

214

They stayed quiet for a few moments, time suspended in her beautiful eyes, the color of the ocean he knew she loved so very much. He wanted to see her there. On the beach, like when they were younger. He wanted to see her giggling in glee again as the water lapped at her feet like she had when she was a child, see the sun setting and lighting her honey hair on fire. His heart felt so whole imagining her in his future. He wanted that. He wanted her. Only her.

At that recognition, his dick hardened. He wanted to cum inside her. See her holding his babies, like Stella held Eli's.

"Avery..." Her name was a breathy request, and he closed his eyes to kiss her again.

He felt her palm encircle his shaft and moaned in both content and desire equally.

"God, I swear you could go all night, couldn't you, stud?"

Fuck yes. With her he could.

"What's your record, Gabriel? How many times?" she asked, and his eyes popped open.

He frowned. He wasn't sure. He hadn't ever counted. But the shame that filled him stilled all thought.

Her hand continued to pump him, and he sighed, needing to be back inside her. He didn't want to answer. He was embarrassed by his experience, all the women he had been with.

"Let's count now. Today."

Avery giggled again. "We can't. I gotta head to the airport, and you got a rodeo to perform in, cowboy." She pushed at his shoulders, and he moved off her, to his side, propping on his elbow to look at her.

"I'd rather stay here, inside you," he answered honestly and cupped her cheek again.

She pulled her lips in and looked down at the cock she was caressing, running her fingertips over the tip of it as Gabriel hissed in pleasure.

Soon, he was a grunting and groaning mess as she tortured him

215

with her fingers and fist. She coaxed him to his back where she straddled his rock-solid member and began to love his flesh with fascination and determination, grinding herself on him as she rode him for all she was worth. She came hard and fast as he kneaded her breasts. He was swearing and sputtering before he pulled out to ejaculate onto her belly.

He watched as stream after stream hit her breasts and navel, and she stared down at his essence in awe.

"Jesus, aahhh..." Gabe growled his orgasm as his hips arched in release. "Fuck, I love that perfect little honey pot of yours, Avery Kinsen." He cupped her scalp, even as she giggled, and kissed her hard.

Translation: I love you, Avery Kinsen.

"DAMN GIRL, you look well sexed up!" Scarlett smirked and pulled Avery to her for a hug. Avery blushed, feeling confident and bashful all at once.

"Do I?"

"Is that beard burn on your neck?"

Avery grabbed for her neck only to get a cackle from Scarlett.

Scar took her arm, and they headed toward the fairground's arena.

Scarlett had flown in, and when Avery told her she might be late picking her up because she was still in at a hotel with Gabe, she'd offered to take an Uber to the fairgrounds.

Avery felt guilty about it, but Scarlett was far more independent than most women. Being from NYC, she was used to taking public transportation–and had, for most of her life. She'd traveled abroad frequently, alone too, so having a short drive from the airport to the fairgrounds wasn't a big deal.

Avery hadn't meant to abandon her bestie, but she couldn't shake how amazing and sexy Gabriel Halloran had made her feel. She was loving their taboo sex-capades and couldn't wait for their next rendezvous. It was more than the fact that she was off-limits to Gabe. It was the way he held her after he'd come inside her, the way he touched her, kissed her. The look in his eyes as he lost himself to her, only to pull her back to him and attempt to squelch that hunger over and over again and again. They couldn't get enough of one another, and Avery knew it would eventually run its course...but God, it was an incredible feeling.

"You got it bad, lady. I can see it. It's written all over your face."

"I haven't been able to talk about it with *anyone*. It's been amazing."

"I see..."

"No, seriously. Today, he gave me an internal orgasm. Do you know what that is?"

Scar pulled her lips to the side, hiding behind a laugh.

"Oh, shut up! I'm new to all this, I didn't know." Avery bumped her hip against Scarlett's, getting a giggle.

"Well, sexed-up Avery looks good on you. You deserve some happiness."

Avery smiled even as she pulled them up the bleachers to a front row seat where they could take in all the action.

Being from New York originally, Scarlett had never been to a rodeo. She hadn't been too keen on the idea until Avery explained that she needed to see it for herself. Despite Avery's support with PETA and animal cruelty, she too had become fascinated by the art of rodeo...and a pair of tight Wranglers.

As the rodeo began, Avery pointed out her brother, Stella, and Gabe, who tipped his hat upon seeing her in the crowd. Her heart sputtered, a million emotions filling it to bursting. The parade of cowboys and cowgirls went by, along with the American and rodeo company flags. The national anthem was sung, and the fun began.

They cheered, whooped, and hollered when the events started.

Soon Scar was just as drawn in as Avery was to the sport of competition. They cheered them all on, along with Dallie, who came with her girls and baby Toby in tow, whom Avery took into her arms.

Scarlett oohed and ahhed over his tiny cowboy attire.

When intermission came, they went down to talk to Stella, Eli, and Gabe. Eli and Stella had met Scarlett before when Avery had brought her home Christmas before last, but she'd not met Gabe.

Gabe greeted her with a tip of his hat. "Ma'am."

"Damn, I can see now why women swoon for all you cowboys." Scar said, getting an elbow from Avery. She shrugged. "What?"

Stella laughed. "Right? I don't know exactly what it is...but a man in Wranglers and a cowboy hat." Stella fanned herself and threw her arms around Eli, who kissed her soundly.

Scarlett laughed. "It's the Wranglers, for sure."

"I dunno, ladies, them Wranglers gotta come off...eventually." Gabe grinned over at Eli, who smirked knowingly. "The hat, well, it can stay on all night long." He winked over at Avery and her knees grew weak, remembering the time when Gabe had left his hat on while they'd made love, and damn, it'd been sexy.

Love. Made love. That's what they'd been doing, right? Making love. It hadn't been fucking. Well, they'd used that word sometimes, but it seemed wrong to claim that's what it was. It was more than that, wasn't it? It felt like more to her. Fucking was something one did with strangers. It was impersonal, just a means to an end. But what she and Gabe did was more. At least, that's what her heart kept telling her.

She gulped when Gabe leaned in, his nose swiping at her earlobe. He whispered, "I'm gonna win Best All Around this weekend... for you darlin'."

He winked and puckered his lips as he turned. Her heart slammed into her ribs. Was he trying to impress her? To show her he was worthy of her?

"Avery?"

Avery blinked and looked to her best friend.

"Damn girl, you seriously got it bad."

Avery was glad her brother and Stella had walked off because she knew she was giving herself away. She had to tell her brother soon because when he found out, he was gonna lose his shit on her and Gabe both.

"I do, don't I?" She shrugged and took Scar's elbow, steering them toward the concession stands. "Now to get *you* all laid and happy. Let's find you a hat, girlie. I think we need to introduce you to some cowboys tonight. And I got just the one in mind, too."

"Ha," Scarlett said. "It'll be a cold day in Hell before this city slicker gets all hot and bothered by a dirty cowboy, Wranglers or no."

Avery smirked, she knew Scarlett might eat her words before the night was over.

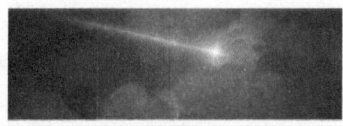

GABE CUT his eyes at Mac McCormick, whose gaze met his over the firepit in the center of the shindig. Cayden hadn't been happy with his run, but he wasn't much for groveling, Gabe knew. Still Gabe couldn't stop internally cheering for himself as he beat his time, and planned to continue that streak in the coming weeks–if only to have Avery see he was serious about his life and where he wanted it to go. He'd started this rodeo season out roughly, not taking it quite as seriously as even Eli had–hell, he had women to get to know and beer to drink–but things had swiftly changed. Now, it was time to show his grit and determination, become a ribbon winner.

Across the fire, Eli threw his chin up, tucking Stella against his chest and kissing her forehead. Gabe knew it was a heads up as Cassia came sashaying into view and stopped next to him. Did Eli seriously think Gabe was gonna go after her? Sure, he'd made some comments in the past in regards to doing just that. Cassia was all cowgirl, gorgeous in both face and body. She would no doubt be a sexy little filly in bed and had a confidence most envied–men and women alike. He couldn't and wouldn't deny that at one point in time, he would have tried real hard to hit that–Eli or no Eli–but all that had changed the night he'd taken Avery Kinsen into his bed.

Still, he was cordial as Cassia asked, "Who's the sexy brunette? My brother wants to know." Cassia nodded her hat to Avery's friend, Scarlett.

"Don't tell me Mac's being a sore loser *and* a pussy, too chicken to ask her hisself," Gabe drawled.

Cassia grinned. "He just doesn't want to step on any toes, not with Eli and Stella being all pissy with me still."

He crossed his arms over his chest and arched a brow at her. "Tell Asshole Extraordinaire that if he wants to talk to that 'sexy brunette,'" Gabe did air quotes, "he can do so, but to stay the hell away from Avery, or I'll beat his face in."

Cassia shook her head in amusement and walked off, only for Avery and Scarlett to head over.

"What was that?" Avery asked as Cassia spoke to her brother, just out of earshot.

"Territorial dispute." Gabe shrugged. "But I have a feeling we'll be talking again...very soon."

As if by invocation, Cayden McCormick–never one to back down from a challenge–ambled over, chest puffed out like a peacock. He eyed Scarlett like she was a feast and him a starving peasant.

"Gabe," Mac greeted Gabe with a nod, then looked to the girls. "Ladies." He smiled like a shit-eating possum. "It's a fine evenin', huh?"

Avery grinned and looked at Scarlett, who stared at the dark-headed cowboy as if he'd just appeared out of thin air. Avery cleared her throat and elbowed Scarlett, who shifted.

"Umm, yes, it is," Scarlett noted, looking up at the brilliant stars over their heads.

"First time at a rodeo, eh, darlin'?" he drawled, and Gabe almost rolled his eyes. Damn, he was layin' it on thick. Typical Mac, the schmoozer.

"It was. Very...entertaining, I have to say."

"Glad you enjoyed it. I'm Mac, by the way, winner of last year's Best All Around." He stuck his hand out for Scarlett to shake.

"Scarlett. Scarlett Ciminello."

The minute their hands connected, Cayden jolted slightly, appearing as if he'd just touched a live wire, and Gabe's brows rose in surprise. He'd never seen the man so shaken.

Avery appeared just as surprised as the two continued to clasp hands, far longer than a handshake usually lasted.

Not one to be put out, Cassia cleared her throat as she stepped in, looking at her brother harshly. "And *I'm* this cowboy's award-winning barrel-racing sister, Cassia." Her chin went up proudly.

Scarlett blinked in surprise but smiled over at Cassia. "Hi."

Mac hesitantly pulled his hand from Scarlett's and shifted his booted feet. "You two friends?"

"Yes, we're best friends. We met our freshman year in college," Avery elaborated with a knowing grin.

"Well, I certainly hope you'll be joining us for the entire weekend, Scarlett. I could use another fan against this guy." He smirked over at Gabe, who laughed.

"Hell yeah, you could, Mac."

"Oh, can it, you two," Eli said, "I'm gonna beat the pants off both of you, so you ain't got nothin' to worry about, McCormick."

Cayden laughed cynically. "That'll be the day, Kinsen. I could beat you with both hands tied behind my back."

"I don't know, Cayden, you might have your work cut out for you, looks like," Cassia said, her eyes moving from Gabe to Eli. "I sense new determination in these guys." Cassia boldly winked over at Stella, who simply observed wordlessly.

"Cayden?" Scarlett looked Mac over curiously.

"Oh, yeah. That's my real name." Mac's bronze cheeks flamed red. "Mac's my nickname, short for McCormick."

Gabe had never seen Mac look so flustered, but he understood. Avery tended to do him the same way. In fact, the way she was looking at him now made him remember every sinful second of their last copulation, and he wanted it again.

"Oh, that would make sense... I guess." Scar shrugged.

"You ain't from around these parts, huh?" Mac asked Scarlett, trying to place her accent.

"New York."

He whistled dramatically. "A city slicker, eh?"

"New York has farm land too, ya know? It's more than just The City." Scarlett sassed, crossing her arms over her chest defiantly, and the guys all answered with, "Ooh." *Shot down, McCormick.* City Slicker- 1. Cowboy- 0.

Undeterred, Mac tried again. "Say, you wouldn't want to go meet my horse, would you?"

Scarlett's face tightened, and her brow rose in defiance. "I know what that's code for, and thanks, but no. I'm not interested. I'm here to visit my bestie, and I don't have time for arrogant pricks like you. Now fuck off."

Scarlett jerked Avery away so fast, Gabe's head spun. Damn! What the hell was that?

Mac looked as if he'd been punched in the balls, his grimace deep and pained. His eyes followed her receding back as she faded out of sight.

Gabe even felt bad for the poor bastard.

Before he could say anything though, Cassia laughed humorlessly, "Well, brother, looks like you need to up your game."

She patted his back and bid the rest of them a goodnight, her eyes lingering ruefully on Stella, who continued to face forward. The tension wasn't as high as it had been, but there was still animosity between the two of them for obvious reasons.

Mac looked to the ground where his boot shuffled in the gravel.

"Well, Mac, better luck tomorrow, man," Eli said and patted his shoulder.

Mac pulled away. "Kiss my ass, Kinsen," he grumbled and ambled off.

Eli smirked and Stella yawned, clearly exhausted.

"Get your lady to bed, my friend. She needs to rest." Gabe grinned at Stella, who blushed in turn.

"I know. I've worn her out." Eli smiled at the woman who clearly owned his heart, and Gabe couldn't help but be happy for them. "Let's go rest up, my little star. Sorry you gotta go to bed alone, bro." He patted Gabe's shoulder, and Gabe scowled as they walked off together.

He hoped one day, and soon, he could explain to his best friend about him and Avery. That she now owned his heart.

He just didn't know where to even begin going about it.

JAX GAVE Cassidy a firm smile and took her hand in his as she led him into the CCU room to see her father. He'd stayed by her side the entire time, holding her tightly and letting her cry into his shoulder, being her rock while her world flipped upside down.

He was glad to be there, with her, experiencing this difficult time and able to support her. Most of all, he was glad Luther was going to be okay.

Triple coronary artery bypass graft surgery had been performed, which meant having his chest cracked open, and being put on a cardiopulmonary bypass machine while reestablishing blood flow to the damaged vessels of his heart. It had taken almost six hours. He'd had a massive heart attack and, apparently, his left anterior descending coronary artery was one hundred percent occluded, which meant emergency surgery. The "fixing it" involved taking healthy arteries from other parts of his body and using them as grafts to bypass the damaged vessel and restore blood to the heart muscle.

Jax felt like a damn whiz when it came to the heart now, as he'd heard the story over and over again from both Luther's cardiologist and the cardiothoracic surgeon–plus Cassidy had explained it to them all and his sister also helped translate when he'd called with questions. Vanna was a genius in engineering, so Jax was pretty sure she could have explained it too if given the need. To Jax, it meant being in bed for far too long, and he prayed he'd never have to worry about needing what the nurses kept calling cabbage–CABG–anytime in his future.

Now, he followed Cass, his dad and mom inside, as it was their turn to see Luther.

Morgan and Kels, LJ and Levi, Jax and Cass, and Bella had all spent the last couple days taking turns going home to rest and eat. It had been exhausting, but as Cass squealed in delight at seeing her father sitting upright in bed, it was all worth it to Jackson.

She gently fell into his arms and sobbed.

Luther grunted in pain, keeping his heart-shaped throw pillow between his chest and Cass, but chuckled lightly as he stroked his youngest daughter's hair. He was paler than his usual self and had a nasal cannula in his nostrils, tubes running out of his arms.

"There, there, darlin'. I'm alright."

Jackson stopped just behind Cassidy and kept his hand on her back. His father stepped up behind him and took his shoulders.

"Luth, what'd you mean scaring us all like that, brother?" Jack asked with a snort.

"Too much beef, the doc said. You believe that shit?" Luther's voice was a touch hoarse, but his conviction was there. Jax grinned at him.

Jax heard his dad stifle a laugh. "Hell Luth, it's too much beef, cheese, *and* beer. That doctor lied to you. Not to mention the extra pounds you've put on."

Luth snarled and looked down at his rounded belly. "Shit. I ain't too bad for a man 'a my age, Jack. Not all of us can be as committed to the gym as you are."

Jax looked back at his old man and smiled. Jack Kinsen had worked out almost every day of his life and it showed, even in his sixties. He'd instilled the importance of fitness into his children, and Jax was glad for it. He might hate cardio, personally, but he was grateful to have a strong core when it came to lifting those darn hay bales. Not to mention, chicks always dug a man with abs. Or so Austin told him, anyhow.

"Jax, thanks for taking care of my little girl here." Luth nodded, and Jax returned it and smiled at Cassidy who looked back at him briefly with a grateful grin.

"Oh, Daddy," Cass whimpered and kissed his cheek, "I was so scared."

"I know, baby, I'm sorry. You know, old men live forever, though, right?" Luth winked at her then looked to his wife, Bella, who was hugging Jackson's mom. "Gotta stick around for my woman a while longer."

"Now I know what *he* felt like all those years ago when I was the one in here," Bella said softly, then her face crumpled. She covered it with her hands. Jax's mom pulled her back in for an even tighter hug. Jax scowled. He knew the story and was grateful Bella had Luther to save her that day. He was also glad the doctors had been wrong about their ability to have children. He didn't know where he'd be without his sweet hummingbird.

Luth cooed to his daughter and stroked her cheek. She grinned at him and took his hand in hers, kissing the back of it and laughing when he gave her a big smile. Jax felt he was imposing on an intimate moment, but no one told him to leave. This was his extended family and had been all his life. Luth and Bella had been his second mom and dad. The Boyd children had been like his own siblings. He'd especially looked out for Cassidy, falling in love with her long before he'd ever known what love really was.

"I love you, Daddy," Cass murmured. "Don't you scare me like that again, promise?"

"I'll try..."

"No, you gotta promise." She looked back to Jax and took his hand. "You promise me this, right here and now. That you'll be alive and well to walk me down the aisle to this man. You promise us both." She gripped Jackson's hand firmly, and his heart leapt into his throat at the intent of her words. Never had she sounded so certain.

Luth was as taken aback as Jax was and glanced back up at him in surprise. "Cass–"

"Promise me, damn you," she commanded, and Luth smirked.

"My little gingersnap, so sassy... Fine, ok, I promise. But y'all gotta get married sometime this century. I ain't gettin' no younger, ya know?" He winked up at Jax, and Jackson gave him a smile. He knew that statement was as close to a blessing as he would get. Luther wasn't too keen on giving his girls away–what man was?

"Sing to me, my hummingbird. You don't know how much I longed to hear it as they were wheeling me back into that cold as hell operatin' room." Luth beseeched his daughter.

Cass grinned then giggled and began to sing, "Must Jesus Bear the Cross Alone." Jax's heart swelled with awe and pride at the sound of Cassidy's beautiful vocals.

He got goosebumps as his mother chimed in too. He smiled over at her, so beautiful and soft, yet so strong. She returned it, mouthing an, "I love you, baby."

He blew her a kiss, then reached down to take Cassidy's hand again. He squeezed it, feeling whole despite their family almost being torn apart.

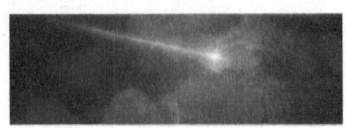

"I'VE LOVED your mother for so long that I don't remember who or what I was before I loved her," Jackson's father told him as they sipped coffee down in the cafeteria, just the two of them.

Jackson had loved Cassidy his entire life, for as long as he could remember. Even when they'd briefly broken it off for a short time before she headed off to Atlanta for college, his heart had not been completely whole again until they'd been reunited.

The short time he'd been with Stella now seemed like a distant dream. Although he and Stella had always had an attraction of sorts–and possibly always would–it wasn't like what he had with Cassidy. He knew it was the same for Elias and Stella too. She only had eyes for Eli now, just like Jax only had eyes for Cassidy. But if their eyes happened to wander, it was always to one another's. Perhaps God had originally chosen them to be soulmates, then changed his mind at the last minute? Fate was odd that way.

Now as he sipped his coffee and stared at nothing in particular, he knew, despite his ultimatum to her back at the hotel, he would never stop loving Cassidy Jane Boyd. If they parted ways, he would always carry her in his heart, until time's end. But he couldn't continue to give everything of himself, to only receive half in return. He had to have all of her or none of her. Having none would crush him, but he would accept the fact that he'd always loved her the most. Every couple had one member who loved the other more; that was him.

Since their frenzied departure, they'd not discussed what had happened in the hotel room, what he'd done to show her he meant business, as they wordlessly grabbed their things, headed back to the airport, and boarded the first plane home. He'd not pressed her for a decision, nor made her feel beholden to answer him before she was ready. Every doubt, every question, every hesitation between them, had ceased to exist until she'd known her father was okay.

Now that he knew Luther would live, albeit that he had a long road to recovery ahead, urgency suddenly pressed Jax's shoulders in a vise grip.

"Penny for your thoughts, son?" his dad asked and flicked at his coffee cup, directing his attention up.

Jax cleared his throat. "Just tired, Dad. Sorry. I... You were sayin'...about mom?"

"I don't need to tell you what I feel for your mother. You see it and have every day of your life." Jack grinned.

That statement was true. Jax had never questioned his parent's love, not for a second, his family's love for another, for him. It oozed from their pores and their actions. To this day, at twenty-four years old, his father still told him that he loved him. He said it back, without shame or reproach because it was the truest thing. Love surrounded them all in such a beautiful embrace.

"I can see you love Cassidy, Jax, and that she loves you. But as I've asked you before: Is that going to be enough?"

"Are you asking me if I love her enough to live without her?" Jax's brows drew.

"I'm asking if you can be happy loving her, even if that love doesn't give you all the other things you require to be happy?" His father's green eyes stared deeply into his soul, implanting a tiny seed of wisdom that only the wise and experienced possessed the capability to do. "I'm not saying I don't want y'all together, or that I don't think you will be. I just want to see you both happy. I've seen over the years that word means two different things to you both."

Jax knew his dad was right. Hell, he was *always* right.

Jax couldn't mention what he'd done at the hotel, if not only out of modesty. That had been cruel, despite his desperation, but he still felt it'd been necessary.

"Cassidy loves to travel. You don't," his dad continued. "I don't know when or if she plans to stop, and I've seen how it affects you, Jackson. Now, I've always been of the mind not to sweat the small stuff, but you have to if that small stuff starts turnin' into big stuff. You catch my drift?"

"Yes, sir, I do. Loud and clear." But the thoughts of being without her turned his stomach. He adored her, revered her, and losing her would break him in two. He knew he could probably eventually move on–hopefully, given time–and take a wife who didn't mind being a homebody, have a few children... but his heart would always be split in two, wondering what would have been had he only taken a chance and just fully compromised with Cassidy. He could compromise, couldn't he? But he wasn't happy with the current compromise and hadn't been, not for a while. He missed her like crazy when she was gone and didn't know if he could continue to abide it.

"Thanks, Dad," he said and nodded when Jack gave him a tight smile.

"I know you'll make the right decision in the end, kiddo. You're my son."

Jax just nodded, a knot forming painfully in his stomach as they rose to take the trays of coffee back to everyone else.

His heart had never led him astray before, and it wouldn't now. He just had to sync his heart and mind together somehow.

CASSIDY SMILED as Jax came forward with a large cup of coffee.

"God bless you, Jax."

He gave her that beautiful smile that made her go weak in the knees, and her eyes lingered on his sexy mouth.

Days had passed, and they'd not spoken of the awkward conversation and sexual tension at the hotel, but Cass hadn't forgotten the conviction in his eyes or his voice. He'd given her an ultimatum, him or her beloved job. As much as she wanted to hate him for making her choose, she understood his frustrations and was even relieved. She couldn't explain the why of it, but she was somehow.

When he yawned and planted an arm around her shoulder, she felt bad that she'd let him get so tuckered out. She looked to her older sister, Kelsey, and said, "I think we'll head on home. Y'all going home tonight, too?"

"Yeah. Mom's got the littles for the night, so I think we'll go on and get some rest, right, honey locks?" Morgan asked and ran a hand into Kels's hair. Her sister closed her eyes and leaned into him, and Cass looked away, wistfully. She didn't envy what her sister and Morgan had, their marriage, their children. She just wished she wasn't in such turmoil regarding her own future.

"Well, you ready?" she asked Jax.

He gave her a swift nod.

Cass hugged her sister, brother-in-law, both brothers, Jack and Natalie, and bid them all a goodnight before Jax took her hand and they silently walked down the hall toward the exit.

Nothing was said as they got into the truck and nothing was said on the long drive home, so many things whirling through Cassidy's head. Her job. Her love of travel, new sights, excitement. The man she loved. Her father. How fearful she'd been for his life. The surgery. The recovery. What she needed to do versus what she desired. What Jax needed from her versus what she'd limitedly given him.

It was clear now that her career was no longer top priority, nor her need to see the world. Perhaps this was fate's way of telling her she'd done her time abroad. Now with her father's new condition and long recovery ahead, she would need to be closer to help out, need to settle in back home, despite her rampant wanderlust. Jax had been needing her closer as well. But how did she really feel about being back home *permanently*? Would she be suffocating surrounded by four walls for too long? A caged bird, once again? And if so, what then? She'd be in the exact same predicament all over again.

She looked over at the handsome man she'd given her heart and virginity to so long ago. She'd never been with anyone but Jackson Kinsen. Never even kissed another set of lips. Well, save for Tommy Turner when she was in the fourth grade, and she didn't really count that.

And she hadn't needed to. She'd known he was meant to be hers almost from the beginning.

Jax, on the other hand, had kissed other girls–including Stella.

Speaking of Stella, she texted her a quick: *"Headed home. Dad is doing well. We're all exhausted. Call you tomorrow. Love you guys."*

Her and Stella's relationship had gotten better over the years, and they were as close now as they'd ever been, but that didn't stop Cassidy's wandering brain from focusing on what all had happened between Stella and Jax. Jackson and Stella both, on separate occasions, had told her everything–despite that she'd not really wanted to hear it, but they insisted. But surely there was more than they'd wanted to tell. Had they gone all the way but sworn one another to eternal secrecy?

She knew Jackson loved her. He'd always been good at showing it. It was Cass that had been slacking–well, in being *physically* there, anyway. She loved him too, with all her heart, and she had to finally face the music, the truth about how she really felt. Love was about putting someone else first, and she'd not really done that. Not in a long time, fear always crippling her, wanderlust pushing her to flight, afraid of commitment, abandonment, but she wasn't really sure why. Now, she had to clip her wings and who better to hand the scissors to than Jax Kinsen? The man who'd loved her so selflessly, allowing her to fly even as it destroyed him.

The abrupt stop of the truck jarred her senses, and she gasped, realizing they'd arrived at her home.

"You ok, hummingbird?" Jax asked and ran his thumb across her knuckles.

She nodded vigorously and reached for the door.

Jax grabbed their bags and took her hand as they walked toward the dark house. No one had left a light on the last time they were there, and Cass realized that it was probably her own fault since they'd been the last ones there.

She sighed heavily and dropped into a rocking chair on the front porch, spent–both emotionally and physically. Sensing her hesitation, Jax let the front screen door he'd just opened snap closed.

"You ok?" he asked again.

She shook her head vigorously, then realized he couldn't really see her well in the dark.

"No. No, Jackson I'm not. I'm not happy. I haven't been. I was given an ultimatum two days ago, and seconds after that, I was terrified my father was gonna die before I got to see him again."

Jax inhaled sharply and exhaled slowly. "I'm sorry, Cass, that was–"

"No, *I'm* sorry. I've been awful to you these past several years." When Jax knelt down and scoffed, reaching for her, she pushed him back, needing to continue. "No, it's true. After everything we've been through, I *left* you. I went off and chased my dreams and said the hell with yours. Who *does* that? I'm supposed to put you first, our love, but I've been so busy with me... Me. Me. Me."

She took a deep breath in and held it, seeking his eyes. There was just enough moonlight to light his gorgeous face, the curve of his square jaw, his long nose, and perfect lips.

"I love you, Jackson. I've always loved you. You know that, right?"

A smile tugged at the corner of his mouth. "I've always loved you too, hummingbird."

"Kiss me," she whispered, and he leaned forward and captured her lips. It was a soft brush at first, a feather-light flirting of his lips upon hers, then, spontaneously, he deepened it. His tongue delved in and he angled his head before reaching for her and bringing her up and into his arms as he stood. They were steel coils holding her to him, and between the rippling muscles and his kiss, she became heady with lust. She'd forgotten how good he tasted, how good he felt, his body so hard and masculine against her own.

Soon, she whimpered as she rubbed herself against his growing erection and held him tightly to her, for fear she might swoon and fall. She grappled for his jeans, and he chuckled lightly.

"Might wanna go inside. Nowhere for me to love you like I want to out here on the porch, darlin'."

She pulled her lips from his and looked around. It was a perfect starry night, and the rebel in her wanted to do it out in the open, like an exhibitionist, despite that they didn't have a neighbor for miles. No one was expected. They wouldn't be caught.

When she pursed her lips in thought, Jackson seemed to have the same idea. His nose nudged hers.

"Wait here. I'll go in and grab a blanket." He quickly fumbled with his phone for light and the key in his pocket.

Cassidy looked around into the darkness, feeling a newfound sense of unabashed wildness fill her veins. When Jax came back outside with a throw over his arm, she giggled in rampant excitement.

He led her out onto the grass of the front yard, just beneath the massive oak tree that had held the tire swing they'd once swung on as kids, and spread out the fleece blanket. Jax grabbed her and pulled her down, pouncing on her and pulling her hands above her head. He kissed her with all the pent-up passion they'd both been missing. She moaned as he thrust his clothed erection against the apex of her thighs.

"Mmm, Jax, please? Don't tease this time." His eyes flashed something that told her they should be talking instead of doing this, but she said, "Just make love to me. I need you, baby."

He said nothing as his mouth moved from hers down her neck to nibble and suck at her pulse point, making her desire spike from simmering to sweltering. She was panting as he gripped her shirt and literally tore it apart. She didn't have time to respond as he moved her bra down and his mouth sought her nipple. He suckled her hard, and her hips bucked up as she cried out.

"I'm gonna take you... just how I've been fantasizing, Cass."

Damn, his fantasies were as hot as hers were, but she had no time to say otherwise as his hands slid into her yoga pants and pulled

233

them down her hips. She'd barely had time to pull her legs out before he reached for his belt and undid it.

"Mmm, yes," she cooed and stroked him through his jeans. His eyes were dark with desire as he shoved his jeans and boxers down. He dug a prophylactic from his wallet and threaded it over his hard cock before he moved back between her legs. "You say you've been a bad girl, Cassidy?"

She giggled in anticipation. "Very bad, sir."

"Then you need a good tongue lashing, young lady."

Her giggle became strangled when his mouth moved back to her breast and assaulted first one nipple with a strong tongue and teeth before doing the same to the other. His finger slid through her folds and he moved lower down her body, planting little love bites that had her begging for more.

She gasped when his mouth hovered at the apex of her thighs before his finger disappeared inside her. The other hand moved to her breast to squeeze and twist at her nipple.

"Mmm, I see you like my methods of punishment. Dare I punish you further?" The smirk made her womanhood ooze with carnal need, and she nodded. His tongue grazed her aching bud and moved ever slowly to her throbbing center, where he worked her into a blissful stupor. He had her writhing and twisting, her eyes rolling heavenward where the twinkling stars winked to her nestled within the dark blanket of the sky. She was so close to a mind-blowing release when Jax's mouth left her sex.

There was no time to whine as he gripped her and flipped her over and onto her belly. Then his tortuous ways continued with his mouth moving ever slowly down her back and his teeth biting into her ass cheeks before giving them sound smacks that had her grunting in sexual frustration.

"Jax?"

When she moved to reach for his sex, he grasped her wrist and manacled both behind her back. She felt like a roped calf, ass in the air, limbs helplessly drawn. But she'd never felt more alive or free than when she felt Jackson's rock-hard shaft gliding into her.

"Oh God, yes," Jax said exactly what Cass was thinking.

It felt so good having him filling her, fucking her, giving her the pleasure she'd sought for weeks now. She bounced her bottom back against his thighs, the sounds of their connecting flesh filling the night along with the bugs.

"Mmm... Ooh, baby, don't stop. Please, don't stop."

Jax growled then chuckled. "I hold the leash here, hummingbird." As if needing to reestablish his dominance, he tugged at the wrists he'd captured behind her. She whimpered and felt her sex clench his. He moaned. "Fuck, yes, you love it. Tell me you do, Cassidy. I need to hear it."

She couldn't answer him because, just as a hard smack came to her butt cheek, she cried out in orgasm. Her world splintered in pleasurable agony. He didn't stop pounding into her, hard and fast, and as quickly as the first release had come, the second came barreling into her with an overwhelming swirl of ecstasy that shot down her back and caused her toes to curl.

"Shit, shit... Oh my God, Jax..." She whimpered and breathed through her orgasm.

She felt him pull out and was flipped back over on her back to face him. She brushed the hair off her face, then her hands were quickly pinned back above her head and his mouth was feasting on her breasts again. She bit into her lip to keep from crying out once again when he teased her opening with the tip of his manhood.

"Jax..."

"Want it, hummingbird?"

"Yes. Yes, please."

"Say it."

"I want your cock. Please, baby?"

"That's right. Whose cock makes you sing, little bird?" His eyes were playful even if his deep voice was serious.

He was so sexy when he held the reins. It made her pure putty.

"Yours, Jax."

"You gonna stop running from it? From me?"

Cassidy whined and whimpered when he began to push inside her, needing that glorious shaft of his buried deep and hard.

"Yes. Yes. I will. I swear."

He cupped the back of her head, lowering his body onto hers as his cock plunged deeper. She cried out in pleasure.

"Were you serious about what you told your dad tonight? About him walking you down the aisle to *me*?"

His eyes bounced back and forth in between hers, and she smiled at him. "Yes. I was. I want to marry you, Jax Kinsen. Will you marry me?"

Jax growled again and began pistoning into her without mercy. His cock battered her womanhood, hitting that incredible sweet spot over and over again as she pulled her legs over his hips and wrapped them tight, holding on for dear life.

Their mutual pleasure cries echoed into the night as their releases came simultaneously, synchronized as perfectly as they'd always been.

When the earth stopped spinning, Cass opened her eyes to see Jackson staring at her. The serious tone was still there when he said, "In order to marry me, you have to be here, in Abundance. Not off gallivanting where I can't be with you, take care of you, or protect you. Do you have any idea how much hell you've put me through? How much I worry about you? Constantly? It's fuckin' torture, Cassidy, and not the good kind."

Her eyes fell to his muscular shoulders and chest, barely visible where it met hers.

"Yes, I know." She inhaled then exhaled her revelation. "I'm gonna stop traveling. You need me here, and so do Mom and Dad."

Jax frowned. "You mean that? You'll stay. Are you sure you'll be–?"

"Happy? Yes. So long as I have you, Jax. That's what matters. I've missed this. Being with you. Making love with you. Holding you.

You're right, it's not the same for us to have the closeness for a couple weeks, then we're apart for far too long before being able to be together again."

Jax took a deep breath, his belly pressing into hers. "Well, I'd made a decision, and I didn't come to it lightly, you know?"

Cass's heart began to flutter, fearing what he was going to say.

"I'd planned to tell you that I'd travel with you for a time. If that's what you wanted me to do. In order for you to be truly happy."

"R-really?"

"Yeah. I'll set my dreams aside for you, Cass. 'Cause you said it, love is about putting the other person first, and you, my sweet hummingbird, are what I need more than anything else. I know I gave an ultimatum, and that wasn't fair, but I needed to know how much you really loved me. I thought that if you told me you'd sacrifice your job for me, that it meant you love me as much as I love you. It was selfish, though. I should never have done that to you. I'm not willing to let you go, not ever, because I can't be me without you, Cassidy Jane Boyd." He pulled her restrained hand to his lips and kissed it before taking her mouth once more.

Tears filled her eyes as she laughed in happy tears. "Oh, Jax... Do you know how long I've wanted to hear you say that?"

His jaw clenched before he gave her a tight smile.

"But everything happens for a reason...and with Daddy's condition now, I think it's time I settled down once and for all."

"For all? What about those itchy little wings of yours and that insatiable wanderlust?"

"My wanderlust might be curbed with quarterly vacations," she offered with a brow lift.

Jax scoffed, rolling them over where she was on top.

He ran a hand through her hair and grinned. "Vacations I can do, given the timing and all, and how long you wanna be gone for." When Cass narrowed her eyes, he rolled his. "Fine. We'll compromise." When she squealed, he full-out laughed. "Your family will be as thrilled about this as I am."

"I'm eager to tell them." She agreed as she sought out his shaft and began to pump it in her fist.

Jax groaned and put his hands behind his head to watch her stroke him. Soon, he was hard as a rock again, and she was guiding the head of him to her entrance.

"Mmm, shit... Cass, you own me, baby girl."

The fun part about having Jax Kinsen dominate her was that she got to return the favor and she did, riding him for all she was worth and running her hands over his sexy, broad chest as he did the same to hers. She had him swearing, spitting, and sputtering before they were both falling over the edge again together.

She sighed contentedly when she fell on him, spent and satiated. She lay across his chest, his big hands rubbing her back as her breathing returned to normal. She loved this part of their love-making almost as much as having their sexes fused, the feel of him holding her like he would never let her go, as if they would meld together and become one being.

"Do me a big favor though and don't tell your family about the other thing."

Her brows drew in consternation when she tilted her head up to look at him.

"You askin' me to marry you. You know men are supposed to be the ones doin' the askin'. I'll never hear the end of it if they find out it was *you* who proposed to *me*."

With that, Cassidy giggled, then squealed when Jax rolled her back over and began kissing her breathless.

CHAPTER 14

$\mathcal{E}$li grinned over at his baby boy yawning sleepily in his bassinet while his mother showered. His heart was so packed with love that it overflowed.

The weekend had gone by fast. He and Gabe were neck and neck with their standings, knocking poor Cayden for a loop. He hadn't seemed the same since Scarlett had insulted him or since her departure, to be honest.

Avery's visit with her best friend had gone well, and the two seemed to have a great time catching up before Avery took her back to the airport on Sunday evening.

Monday, they'd packed up, headed out to Sweetwater, and settled down in the campgrounds they were at now. Jack and Natalie had rejoined them last night, and he was glad to see them—especially given the news that Cassidy's dad was now doing well.

After passionate lovemaking to his sweet cowgirl this morning, Elias's heart was happy, his cock was satiated, and his life fulfilled. If he died that very moment, he'd couldn't be mad because he'd fully lived to know love in all its glory.

"You got it good, buddy, you know that?" he asked Toby, who just stared at him. "You know I'm your dad, don'tcha?" Wow, that seemed so surreal when said aloud. "I'm sorry I wasn't there when you first came into the world. I'm sorry I didn't get to feel you kicking inside Mommy's belly. I'm sorry I was such an idiot." Eli's head fell and he sighed heavily, only to look up as Toby cooed.

Elias grinned. "You understand me, don'tcha?" He moved forward and leaned his face down to kiss his son's tiny cheek. "I love you so much, baby boy. You know that, right? I was so happy when I found out your mama was pregnant with you." And so destroyed when he thought she'd aborted the pregnancy. "I promise to make it up to you every single day for the rest of your life. You'll never wonder how I feel about you. How deeply my love for you goes, Toby."

His own father had always made him feel loved, even if Gavin wasn't as vocal as the rest of his family was about it. The entire Kinsen clan had always been a loving and supportive family, but that hadn't been enough to keep Elias from isolating himself from them all.

His father had never been mean, unsupportive, or distant...which was why Eli was frustrated with their last conversation. His words lingered heavily on Eli's heart.

"I will never let you down again, son. Do you forgive me?" He held the infant's stare even as tears blurred his vision.

As if the baby understood, his teeny hand came up and rested on Eli's nose. He cooed again, and Eli laughed happily. "Toby, my boy."

"If that isn't the damn sexiest thing I've ever seen," came Stella's voice. "If you're trying to get me turned on and ready to have another baby, well, you're succeeding, cowboy."

Eli grinned as he looked up at his blonde bombshell, then she dropped the towel and he straightened.

He surveyed her sexy body. Plump breasts, flat belly, curvy hips... His cock rose in salute.

"God, you're gorgeous, my little star."

She hit her knees in front of him, and he sighed when her mouth took him in.

"Jesus, Stells... Mmm." He gasped in pleasure and gripped the hand on his thigh, the other hand sinking into her hair. "Our son is watching, you know?" He turned his head to see Toby's eyes close as he yawned again.

"Don't care. His daddy is about to get his world absolutely rocked," Stella said, doing as she promised with her lips, tongue, and hands.

After, they lay spent, in bed once again–his world thoroughly rocked. Eli ran his hands through Stella's hair and down her back.

"I love you, Stella Rose Jenkins."

"And I love you, my beautiful Elias." Her hand moved over his chest and abs, and he sighed happily.

He thought of the ring in the drawer beneath his bed and wondered when he'd ever feel worthy enough to give it to her, to ask her to be his bride for all eternity. He'd not earned her hand. Not earned her love. Yet she'd freely given it, time and again, despite all the awful things he'd done to her.

"We *have* to get ready and go get your mom at the airport." She checked her watch, bringing him out of his inner thoughts.

He nodded and motioned to the sleeping baby. "I'll get him ready while Mommy dresses."

She grinned and kissed him before popping up to dress. Eli followed, pulling his jeans over his hips and a clean shirt from the drawer next to the bed.

As he moved to his sleeping son and lifted him, he thought of his mother's words on the phone last week. He knew something bad was happening. Today, he would find out what.

241

"CANCER?" Avery's voice wavered, and Eli, seated across from her, took her hand, even as their mother nodded.

"Brain surgery?" Elias asked, feeling his heart drop into his stomach.

"It's like he's had a stroke. The tumor is pressing on the part of his brain that controls emotions and memory. That's why he was so short with you the other day, Eli. He gets confused and easily stressed, which just makes it all worse."

"Who's with him now?" Eli asked.

"Our neighbor, Becky. She helps when I need to go to the store and stuff."

"Mom!" Avery protested, grabbing her mother's arm. "Why didn't you say something? I could've stayed home..."

"We didn't want to worry you. Besides you're soon to head back to school and–"

"*Fuck* school!" Avery shot up. "I'm coming home with you, *today*."

Veronica shook her head. "No. I don't want you there. Your father doesn't want you there."

"*What*? Why?" Ave's brows drew and jerked away from her mother's side as if she'd just told her she was infected with anthrax or something.

"He doesn't want either of you to see him like this. He begged me when we found out he needed the surgery. You know your father and that Kinsen hard head." She eyed Eli then Stella and tilted her head. "Besides, he'll be getting a home-care nurse to help once he's back home. We go in on Friday."

"This Friday? As in two days from now?" Avery sighed. "Our father is having brain surgery in two days, and you expect us to...what, stay *here*? Eli rodeoin' and pretendin' like we aren't worried sick to death!" Avery's face was red as a tomato.

"Yes, that's what we want." Their mother cleared her throat in finality and looked to her hands, the ones now knotting in her lap.

"Who *are* you people?" The entire restaurant seemed to pause at Avery's screeching voice as she abruptly stood from the booth. "This is ridiculous. I can't believe you... I– I need some air." Avery stalked off, her booted heels clicking on the floor, everyone around them staring her down while Eli's eyes moved back to his mother's.

She gave him a weak smile. "I'm sorry, baby."

This was all a bad dream, and Eli was going to wake up at any moment.

He felt Stella's hand slide into his and looked over at her seated beside him, their baby tucked into the crook of her arm.

"Is your sister ok?" Stella asked and looked toward the front door. "Should I go and check on her?"

Eli nodded, and she handed the baby off to him, leaning down to kiss his cheek before walking away.

His mother sighed heavily, eyeing the baby. "Elias, I know this is hard. I don't necessarily agree with your father's take on the matter, but he just doesn't want to interfere with your lives." Eli lowered his head. He'd done this to himself. Alienated himself from his family. Made them feel inconsequential in his life. But he also understood that his father wouldn't want them seeing him so weak and vulnerable.

"What about you, Mom? Don't we need to be there for you, too?"

"I'm fine, truthfully. I would tell you if I wasn't. This has been a rough few months, and we just found out last week what was going on. I promise I wasn't trying to keep it a secret from either of you. With all the tests and preparations, I haven't had much time for anything else." She shrugged, looking ill at ease.

"Avery should come back and be with you, at least. I think she'd feel better if she was home," Eli reasoned.

"What? So she can just sit *there* and worry? No. Maybe in a couple weeks? Yeah. But right now, I'm fine. Honestly. She just found you, and she's needed you. Please try to help her understand."

"I don't, and I won't," Avery pouted as she slid back into the seat next to their mother, tears streaming down her cheeks. "I'm mad at both of you, dammit, and I want to hit a punching bag."

"Oh, Avery. My spunky little mermaid," her mother cooed and

pulled her into her arms. Avery hugged her back forcibly, and Eli had to look away to keep his emotions in check.

He felt awful, sick to his stomach, and not at all wanting the food that was suddenly set in front of them at the steak house they'd chosen for lunch.

Stella rubbed his back as she moved up to the table and he looked up at her, then down at their content son. As bad as surgery and cancer was, Eli couldn't imagine not wanting his family around to support him in such a dire time.

Even if it meant forfeiting the circuit, Eli would do what was necessary for his father.

"Listen to me, both of you." His mom pulled back and took Avery by the shoulders. "You know we love you so very much, but you're so happy here, together. Enjoy the time you have while you can. Your dad is gonna be fine. We're going to the best hospital in the state, and he's got the best surgeon for his condition. If I need you, *either* of you," she cupped Avery's cheek, "I will call you immediately. I promise."

"But... What if...what if he..." Avery's trembling lip caused Eli's gut to clench.

"He's gonna be fine. I know it. Ok? You're worrying for no reason."

He wanted to believe his mother's conviction, but they would both worry until the surgery was over and their father's condition was stable. The weekend was gonna suck major balls.

"Now, let's talk about happy things: give me my grandson, and tell me all about how you two reconciled." Veronica clapped her hands together and looked at Toby.

Eli smiled and handed him over to meet his grandmother.

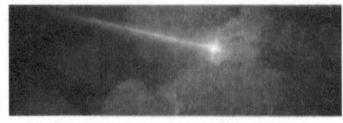

244

"JACK?" Natalie called to him. "Are you ok?"

His best friend had just had open heart surgery last week and now, his brother was soon to have brain surgery. Was he ok? Not at all.

He shook his head.

Her hand came to rest on his forearm and he felt her lips press to his stubbly cheek.

"Talk to me."

"I..." He gulped audibly. "I don't know what to say."

Gavin. His little brother. The thoughts of losing him were unfathomable. They'd grown closer than ever over the years as Eli and Jax had, before Eli had split. He didn't see Carson as much as he wanted to either, but they'd all still managed to get together for holidays and such.

Jack looked to Eli, who frowned with unshed tears in his eyes.

Luther had come through his surgery just fine, so perhaps Gavin would too, despite what Veronica had told him. When Jack insisted he and Nat come down to help, she'd explained that Gavin hadn't wanted anyone there, not yet. Jack understood, but he was still worried sick. Veronica promised to call if she needed anything.

Natalie's hand moved up Jack's arm and squeezed. Her head fell, and she rested her cheek on his bicep. He kissed her forehead and wrapped his arm around her, pulling her tighter and taking comfort in her presence as he always had.

"It's all gonna be ok," she whispered in his ear. He closed his eyes and prayed she was right.

Jack looked up to see Avery sniffle and wipe a tear from her cheek. He didn't miss how Gabe's arm moved around her, his eyes reflecting concern at her turmoil. She didn't curl into his embrace as Natalie did Jack's. Either Avery was resisting or didn't want anyone to see the intimacy that Jack did at that moment. Jack would put his money on the latter. He sensed something had changed between Gabe and Avery as the weeks had passed. Lord help when Eli found out, though, despite Avery's age.

Jack looked at Eli then and frowned. Eli's hands were cupped together, his elbows resting on the table. His head was bowed and his frame pitched forward. He was deeply troubled too. Stella's hand rubbed up and down his back as he inhaled and exhaled.

Jack couldn't help but grin at their reconciliation. Stella had finally been validated and was where she'd wanted to be all along. She'd won back her stubborn cowboy. Jack prayed Eli was grateful for every day he got to spend with a woman who loved him like Stella Jenkins did, that he appreciated her and all she'd done, how hard she'd fought to win back his heart.

Jack glanced at his wife whose sapphire eyes held his. She smiled, her gorgeous face lighting up and making his heart beat faster. He grinned back and squeezed the hand that moved into his. So small but capable. Capable of so much. Being a mother, creating fictional worlds in her writing, being an incredible wife, an incredible woman. He wanted her, needed her, and he was going to take her back to their RV and love her like there was no tomorrow because right now, he feared tomorrow might not come for his brother–and almost hadn't for his best friend.

As if Nat read his mind, she kissed his cheek and stood, pulling him with her.

Jack looked back to Eli, who didn't budge. He then nodded to Stella and Avery before heading out of Stella's camper.

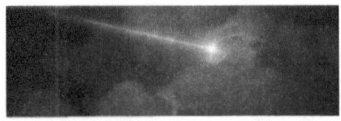

GABE WATCHED Jack and Natalie leave and looked back to Avery. His grip tightened on her waist, but she squeezed his hand hard and jerked it down. Rejection stabbed him in the heart, and he frowned. She warned him back with raised brows and wide eyes.

He tried not to take it personally, but it stung. He wanted to be able to comfort her, Eli or no Eli. But he also knew this wasn't the time nor place. He let his arm fall from around her and crossed his arms over his chest. The bereft feeling wasn't lost to him as her shoulder still lingered beside his.

Eli's shuddering breath had Avery moving forward. She gripped his arm, and, in a flash, Eli was up off the bench and pulling her tight against him. Avery broke then and the dam of emotions spilled from her. It rattled Gabe to his core, and he felt like his knees might buckle. Love for the beautiful girl he'd always revered filled every pore of his soul, and he found his own eyes tearing up. Stella covered her face and sobbed silently.

A pang of jealousy shot through Gabe as Avery clung to her older brother. Jealousy that she sought Eli's comfort instead of his, but he knew and understood that they needed this moment together.

He bowed his head and shuffled his feet when he heard Eli's sobbing in turn.

For a time, the cabin was filled with their combined grief before Eli said, "I can't even remember the last thing I said to him, Ave. The last time I spoke to him, when I last saw him. I hate myself right now."

"Shh, stop it, Eli. He knows you love him." Avery pulled back to look at her brother. "You can call him tomorrow and tell him."

"What if he can't understand, or doesn't remember because of the tumor. What if...? Dammit, Avery, I've been so stupid pushing everyone away. I don't deserve any of you." He looked from his sister back to Stella, who gazed at him with understanding. She stood and ran a hand up his back.

"You have us. All of us. And you *do* deserve us." Stella nodded her head vigorously.

"We weren't letting you go, brother. Not without a fight." Avery laid her head on his shoulder.

Gabe stood in awe of them. His family had never shown the amount of love the Kinsens did. He envied that love, craved it, and knew that's what he wanted from Avery, from Eli, from all of them. He wanted to be a part of them. Have Eli, who'd always been like a brother to him, *be* his brother. He had to tell Eli how he felt about Avery and soon, before he found out the hard way.

"Get in here, Gabe. You know you want to." Stella laughed to break up some tension, and Gabe grinned as she beckoned him forward. He was unable to stop his feet from moving and wrapped his arms around the three of them.

Eli sighed. "Family. That's what matters. I'm sorry it took me far too long to see that." He kissed Avery's head, then Stella's, then rubbed Gabe's head. "Even you too, asshole. I love you all."

Gabe chuckled. "Yeah, yeah, love you too, dickwad." He scrubbed his knuckles over Eli's head in a manly gesture of affection.

"Speaking of dicks, you mind getting yours off me?" Eli's elbow softly connected with Gabe's diaphragm, and Gabe grunted dramatically.

"Oww, way to show your love, man." Gabe grabbed at his belly.

"I'm about to show you a fist to the nose." Eli joshed and swatted at him. Gabe ducked away with another chuckle.

"Hey, don't be threatening this mug." Gabe straightened and touched his cheeks. "I'm a ginger. I got enough against me."

Everyone laughed then, and some of the heaviness seemed to lift from the cabin.

Eli pulled Gabe back in for a half-hug then shoved him away again with a laugh. "Fine. I guess you're right. Don't need to jack you up too much. What with you being my kid's godfather and all."

Gabe's brows shot up. "Wow! *Really?*" Gabe looked at Stella, who gave him a nod. "Dude, shit... I'm... I'm honored." He clapped his hand in Eli's. "That's awesome."

"Can't think of a better role model for this guy."

Everyone turned toward little Toby, sleeping so sweet and content in his bassinet. Warmth spread through Gabe's core. He felt emotions rise inside him and moved the back of his hand to his eye. "Damn. I... Shit... Y'all got *me* crying now. Fuck."

Eli pulled him in for another half-hug, and Gabe patted Eli's back vigorously.

He *had* to tell his best friend that he was in love with his baby sister, but he had no damn idea how to go about it.

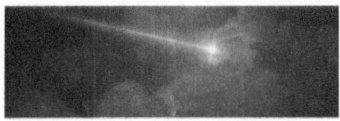

AVERY TOOK a deep breath and looked back to Gabe, whose eyes shifted to the floor.

"Well, I'm heading out," she said, "I'm exhausted. I love you guys. I'll see you in the morning."

Eli nodded and pulled her in for one more tight hug. She halted the tears that sprang forth once more, grateful to have her brother back in her life. He grinned at her as she pulled away and squeezed her hand.

"See y'all tomorrow." Eli said and turned back to Stella, who stepped into his outstretched arms.

Avery wished them a good night and went out first, followed by Gabe.

She ran her hands up and down her arms, the chill not from the night but from her own inner emotions. She heard Gabe's footfalls behind her as she moved to his RV and climbed the steps. She halted when she entered the darkness, feeling Gabe's hard frame hit her back with an "Umph."

"Sheesh, Ave, what gives?" he asked, nudging her forward as he gripped her shoulders. He turned on the lights then moved around her, searching her face.

Those deep eyes of his reached into her soul, and her heart fluttered. She couldn't stop the tears that came forth as he cupped her cheek.

"Hey, it's ok, sweetheart. C'mere." He pulled her into his arms, and her emotions spilled forth once more. She took comfort in his embrace, his solid build against hers. His big hands splayed over her back and rubbed, pulling the sorrow from her. He murmured sweet nothings as he comforted her and let her cry it out. "Shh, it's gonna be ok. It's all gonna be ok."

"I'm s-so mad at h-him."

"I know, baby girl, but it's his choice."

"How am I just gonna sit h-here and p-pretend like I'm not freaking the f-fuck out while he gets b-brain surgery?" Avery grumbled.

She wiped her nose on the back of her hand, and Gabe chuckled lightly.

"Let me get you some tissues."

He went to the bathroom, and she sat on the couch to rest her weary body and cover her face with her hands.

Gabe sat down and slid a hand down her back again. "Here."

She wiped her eyes with the tissues he handed her, then blew her nose. She inhaled deeply then exhaled slowly and looked at Gabe's face. "I know. You don't have to say it."

"Say what, Ave babe?"

"I'm a hot flippin' mess."

"No, you're just concerned. You have every right to be. It's not every day your mother flies in to tell you that your father has brain cancer and needs surgery."

She looked away. "I just want to be there. He's so damn stubborn."

"Can I say something without you getting mad at me?" When she shrugged, he continued, "It's hard for us guys to be weak. Everyone sees us as strong and hard and resistant to everything. We're supposed to be tough and not cry and not break and not feel. Except...we do. We're human, too. I can tell you without regret or remorse or shame that I cried many times in the military, seeing my brothers in arms fall in death. I was lucky to never get hurt too badly or shot where it couldn't heal back. The worst thing that ever happened was seeing my buddy's head blown off his shoulders right beside me. When I close my eyes at night, I can still see it, feel the blood splatter my face, smell the gun smoke and charred–"

Gabe looked down and fiddled with his hands. Then he leaned forward, bracing his elbows on his knees. "Let me tell you, I cried then. Hell, I think I even screamed. That's what wakes me sometimes is the screaming–*my* screaming–as it plays over and over again."

Avery felt her stomach drop, and she reached out to her to take his. "My God, Gabriel. I'm so sorry."

He seemed to come out of his self-induced trance then. "The point is, after that happened, I went through some shit. I was afraid of so much when I got back stateside. Loud noises. Crowds. Smoke. Firecrackers. Not only did I have my own war wounds to tend to, I was fucked up in the head. PTSD. Most soldiers experience it, but you don't really know what it is–the gravity of it–until you go through it yourself.

"Anyway, I was at my weakest point, and I didn't want anyone to see me that way. Not my friends, not my family. No one. I wasn't myself. I was weak, ashamed, depressed, even suicidal at times. I..." When Avery's hand squeezed his tighter, he grinned. "I digress... Your dad not wanting you to see him at his weakest is understandable, Avery. As a man, I get it. And you should honor his wishes. I know doing so is gonna be hard for you. But, keep in mind, this is hardest on him."

Avery's lip quivered, and she nodded. "I know, and I hate that. This fucking sucks. I'm sorry." She broke into sobs again, and Gabe pulled her back to him and held her tight. It took a little longer for her to expel her emotions, but when she did, she pulled back and looked him over before wiping her eyes and nose. "I'm sorry you went through all that. I didn't know."

"I could blame my self-isolation on all that I experienced in Iraq, but I know I just preferred the easier way out." Gabe shrugged. "Horses and rodeo always grounded me. I felt at home, at peace, in what I knew best. I like the spotlight, but I also like the quiet after. Knowing I can face my demons in my own way. The open road gives me space and time to get out of my own head, focus on a goal."

"You don't have to face it alone." She reached up and touched his face, running her thumb over his freckled cheek.

"I know. Being around you has made the nightmares wane, you know?"

"Really?" She pulled her bottom lip in, nibbling it with her teeth. "What makes me so special?"

"You don't know?"

She shook her head. He grinned deviously. "Well, you're smart and funny and pretty and...sexy." His hand moved to the half-opened button on her shirt, and he flicked at the top button, spreading the fabric widener, the button giving way. "Especially when you're not wearing clothes."

Her body heat rose, and she began to tingle as his fingertips coaxed the other buttons free. "Gabriel Halloran, are you taking advantage of me in my weakened state?"

"I'm just comforting a damsel in distress, ma'am." At that, Avery snickered, and Gabe gave her a crooked grin. "Seems you're in need of my services. What kind of man would I be if I didn't give in to all your needs?"

She moaned when his hand moved into her shirt and cupped her breast. His head leaned in and he began to sprinkle kisses over her neck. She gasped as he nibbled lightly at her pulse point. "Mmm, Gabe."

"God, baby, I love it when you say my name all breathy like that."

She wanted to giggle, but moaned instead as he began to reshape her breast. His mouth lowered to hers and she savored his kiss, her hands reaching for his shirt. He moved, pulling it off his head and grabbing for hers as her hands went to the button of his jeans.

"Yes, baby, I want your hands on me. Touch me." As her hand moved into his boxers, he hissed. "Fuck. I've never had a woman get me so hard so fast, Avery."

Avery grinned and pulled back. "Really?"

"Really. Your touch drives me wild."

She ran a fingertip down the underside of his shaft, and he shivered. "Mmm, curious things, cocks..."

"*Cock*. Singular. I only got the one. And that'll be the last one you touch, Ms. Kinsen."

Avery froze and looked his face over. He was serious. Dead serious, that sexy scowl taking his face.

"Gabe, I..." She exhaled with a smirk, but he cupped her face and kissed her softly, stilling her words.

"I know. Just..." He sighed and rested his forehead against hers. "I know it's unexpected. I know I've moved too fast, and this is very poor timing. But, dammit, Avery, the thoughts of anyone else touching you, kissing you... It fills me with absolute rage."

Avery had no words as his hands moved over her body like they owned her.

"I can't explain this attraction, this feeling I have with you. I just know I don't want it to stop. I want it to keep going. I want you, Avery. I want every single inch of you, baby girl."

Avery's heart leapt into her throat as Gabe's mouth fell on hers again. She soared with wonder at his words, soared with desire, need, bliss. She pushed his shoulders back as she let the feeling overtake her, his back hitting the back of the couch. He reached for her as she pulled back, scowling.

She giggled. "Just a sec, stud. I wanna try somethin'."

His brows perked up as she grabbed for the waistband of his jeans and began tugging. He helped her, amusement covering his face. "Oooh, new position, eh?"

"Well, I..." She blushed. "I want to return the favor now."

"That isn't necessary. You..."

"Please, Gabe?" She pouted, and he grinned.

"Hell, angel, I'm never gonna tell you no when it comes to having your mouth on my cock."

She giggled and moved her finger down the length of him, admiring the thickness and hardness, the way it jerked in response to her touch.

He moaned as she moved to her knees. "Take your top off. I wanna see those sexy tits of yours."

She blushed once more and pulled her top over her head and unbuttoned her front clasp bra, letting them pop out for his view.

"Mmm, yeah… These are a sight for sore eyes." He gripped them and pinched her nipples with his thumb and index fingers.

She pulled her bottom lip in with her teeth, unsure where to start, the length and size of him intimidating. She feared gagging or even puking on him. Most girls said they gagged and tears came to their eyes when they performed oral on a man.

"Ave? You ok, baby?" His hand moved up to her face and into her hair. "You don't have to do this if you don't want to, you know?"

"I want to. I just… I don't know how or where to start."

"Kiss the head of him."

Why was it that men always referred to their penis as a different entity altogether? It baffled her.

She leaned down, her eyes staying on his, as she puckered her lips and kissed the tip of his cock gently. It was velvety soft and flared as her hand fisted him and moved down to the base. Gabe's breath hissed through his teeth as she licked at the bead of precum there and curled her tongue over the opening. Her mouth opened and encompassed the head of him.

"Fuucckkk, Avery." His coaxing increased her bravery, and she relaxed her jaw, taking him further into her mouth. She went down a bit more than halfway then pulled back. She sucked a bit harder the next pass as she moved back down. "Mmm, just–just like that, baby girl. Just. Like. That." His head fell back, and he groaned.

She dared go further and challenged herself to take more of him down her throat, encouraged by his words and actions.

"Shit, girl, yesss. You don't even need me to… *Fuck*, that feels so good." She began a slow rhythm, sucking him down then moving back up. Up and down, up and down, letting her saliva coat him and her fist work him. "Shit, baby, shit." He grunted, moving his hand into her hair and pulling it atop her head so he could watch her. Her eyes moved to his. They were focused on her mouth. "Watching you suck my cock is the hottest fucking thing ever, I swear to God."

Victory danced in her veins, and she began to move faster as one of his hands moved to her breast, squeezing along with her rhythm. His pants and grunts got louder and his hips bucked easily as she went down.

"Fuck, you gotta stop. Ave, baby, stop." He gripped her face and pulled her mouth from his member. She gaped as she came upright.

"Did I do something wrong?" She continued to stroke his rock-hard shaft, unsure where she went wrong.

"N-no. I just... Fuck, I was so close." He smirked. "But I got an idea if you're feeling adventurous."

"You don't want me t-to swallow you down?" Wasn't that what guys wanted?

"Oh, I do. You have no idea how much I do, but... I want to pleasure you too. It isn't just about me." He stroked her cheek with one thumb, her nipple with the other. "What I *do* want is to know what it feels like to have my cock nestled between your boobs."

Avery blushed but complied as he scooted forward and moved his cock between the valley of her breasts. He had her plant her elbows on his knees and press them together, effectively squeezing his hard shaft between the curvy mounds. Then he began to move his hips.

"Mmm, yeah, shit. This view is just as hot as the last one was. Fuck me." He bit into his lip as he continued to pump and soon, he was panting and arching as stream after stream of cum began to spew from the tip of him onto her breasts and face. "Oh, shit. Fuck. Shit... I'm sorry." He groaned as his release overcame him, and Avery's mouth moved to take him within, curiosity getting the best of her. The salty taste of him spurred her on. His head flew back as he swore, her sucking furious as her arousal dampened her panties.

Gabe finally took her face in his hands again, attempting to pull her mouth off him, as he quaked between her sucking lips. "Jesus Christ, Avery. That was so damn sexy, my little mermaid."

She blushed and bit back into her lip. "Did I do ok?"

"Are you serious? What do *you* think?" He scoffed and released her. It took him a moment to catch his breath and he leaned back onto the couch, looking exhausted. "That was... Damn, girl."

She giggled and moved to search for her bra. Gabe's hand grabbed for hers, stopping her.

"What are you doing?"

"Putting my clothes back on."

"Why?"

She motioned to his lap where his cock lay, deflating.

He gave a loud, sharp laugh. "You ever known me not to rise to the occasion?" His grin was self-assured. "C'mere, sexy lady." He pulled her to standing and began to unbutton her jeans. She felt sheepishly bashful but complied as he guided her out of them, one leg at a time.

When she stood naked before him, his dark eyes fell over her. He grinned like the cat that ate the canary for a snack and was now wanting his full meal. He leaned forward and his nose brushed her pubic hair, she gasped feeling her cheeks flame.

"God, I love the smell of you." His tongue lapped at her seam, and she spread her legs instinctively. His finger moved in between her lips and sought the damp center that yearned to have him inside her. She moaned. "That's my girl. Always ready for me, aren't you?"

She nodded as his eyes returned to hers. He leaned back and smiled when her eyes fell to his growing erection. "See, I told you. Just the hint of your pussy wrapped around me has me wild with want for it." He moaned and his fist gripped his shaft and pumped, once, twice, three times. "Mmm, touch yourself, baby girl. I want you good and soaked for me."

God, the way he talked... It was so dirty, but so yummy. It had her sex clenching, awaiting to have him inside her.

Without hesitation, she moved her fingers to the apex of her thighs and rubbed, moaning when he did.

He smiled again and beckoned her forward with his free hand. "Straddle my knees, but keep stroking yourself."

She awkwardly climbed across his knees and sat her bottom down on them, awaiting further instruction as she continued to stroke her fingers over herself. Shame painted her cheeks as Gabe watched and pumped his cock, gasping when she did, and groaning as her body yearned for release.

"That feel good, angel?"

"It'd feel better if you were inside me."

"Yeah?"

She nodded.

His free hand moved to her breast and brought the nipple to his lips. He flicked it a few times with his tongue before suckling. She moaned.

"Come for me, little mermaid, then I'll reward you with my big cock. How bad do you want it?"

Her eyes drifted down to the erect shaft he was fisting easily, as if he had all the time in the world.

Avery moaned, feeling so wanton, as she murmured, "I want it. I want it so bad, Gabe."

"Show me how bad. Come for me." He chuckled when she whimpered, his mouth tightening over her nipple again. He sucked hard and bit lightly, making her jump. "Come baby, I can't wait much longer. I wanna see you make yourself come."

When he pushed her hips back so he could watch her, the head of his cock fell between her legs and she reached for it. She placed the tip at her clit and began flicking it against her, whimpering as her sex clenched hard, needing, wanting. She moved her hips, shoving it to the aching little bud.

"Fuck, baby… You're such a bad girl. Bad, bad girl." He growled, and his mouth moved back to her nipple.

"I-I can't. Gabe, I want it." She began to move his stiff shaft toward her aching center.

Gabe's dark eyes moved to hers and his lips murmured against her breast. "Then take it, angel."

As soon as she felt the velvet-steel rod pierce her opening, she was crying out in orgasm. She began to ride him with all her might, rocking her hips and chasing the release that assaulted her.

The gentle Gabe was gone then and a fierceness took hold of him that stunned her. He moaned deeply, his brows tightening across his handsome face. He gripped her hips and assisted her as she cried his name, the pounding of his cock inside her a punishing rhythm.

She whined and whimpered and groaned while he pumped inside her and her hips rose and fell on him, helpless to the call and need of her body. Gabe's hand moved into her hair and held her as his hips rose to meet hers, the slap of flesh loud to her ears.

She'd barely broken free of her orgasm when another followed closely behind.

"Yeah? You gonna come again, baby girl?" he huffed out a groan.

"Oh, Gabe... Oh God." She whimpered as she gripped his shoulders hard, anchoring herself to him.

"Feel good?"

The high-pitched voice and scream that answered him was foreign to her as his eyes held hers, and he grinned the grin of victory.

"Fuck yeah, baby," he said with a chuckle.

When the last of her contractions eased, he moved her off him and gave two more hard tugs of his cock, shooting his seed onto her belly.

He fell back against the couch, one hand on his dick, the other on her breast and sighed heavily. "Dear God, Avery. I don't know that I've ever had this much fun until you."

She looked his tall, muscled frame over, her hands falling to stroke his chiseled abs. He shivered and delight filled her stomach.

"Here. Let me get you a towel." He picked her up and set her back down on the couch, running off to the bathroom.

Avery didn't miss the scar on the back of his large thigh and wondered if that was one of the wounds he'd endured while serving in the Marines.

She didn't have long to contemplate before he was returning and wiping her stomach.

He gave her a grin and leaned in to kiss her.

Soon, the towel was dropped and he was pulling her up and into his arms as he stood. His hand cupped her cheek and he kissed her like there was no tomorrow, like he was going off to war.

Avery grunted when her back hit his bed and his big body fell atop hers, moving between her legs. She didn't protest, only sighed in contentment, when his thick sex was being thrust inside her once more.

There was nothing to protest because she, too, didn't want this incredible hunger to stop. She didn't want anything but Gabriel. Gabe's lips, Gabe's mouth, Gabe's hands, Gabe's cock. Gabe. Gabe. Gabe. She felt like she hadn't lived until he'd opened her body and her emotions. Like Pandora's box, they'd unlocked some secret, magical taboo chest that had taken over them both.

She moved with him, letting her hands roam and memorize him, while his mouth took hers in devouring kisses that left her breathless. She lost herself to his feel, his touch, his lovemaking.

All the while, praying that they'd not released an indelible curse upon both their houses.

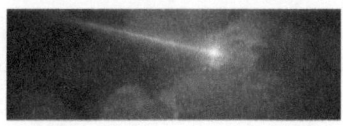

GABRIEL AWOKE to pounding on his trailer door and grunted.

Fuck, what time is it? he thought.

He squinted at the brightness streaming in through the open window blinds. Damn, he'd forgotten to close them. He grabbed for his phone, stroking the small arm draped across his chest and getting a little mew from Avery. He grinned. God, last night had been incredible, despite the awful news they'd received from both Gavin and Jack's best friend, Luther.

Gabe looked at the time. Well past ten.

"Fucking open the door, Gabe. Avery? Gabe! What the fuck, guys!"

Eli's loud voice had Gabe sitting up as the knob began to turn. Shit! He'd even forgotten to lock the door... Not good.

Terror filled him, knowing what was coming. He barely had time to come upright and pull his boxers on before the door was wrenched open and Elias's red face moved inside.

Gabe looked from Eli to Avery, who'd bolted upright in the bed, hair askew, sheet drawn across her naked breasts. Her eyes were wide as she looked back at her brother in horror.

Gabe's eyes went back to Eli, who took in the entire scene all at once. Gabe in only his boxers standing beside the bed, Avery in bed, clothes haphazardly strewn across the floor.

Elias growled. "What the *fuck* is this?"

"Uh, hey man, it's...uh… It's not what it seems..." Gabe began.

"You could've fucking fooled me. I think it's *exactly* what it seems." Eli took a menacing step forward. "Avery, get your damn clothes on. Gabe, put some fucking pants on and meet me outside. This entire fucking camp is about to see me beat the absolute hell out of you."

"Eli. Stop. He didn't–"

"Can it, little sis. This is between me and my *former* best friend. You're the biggest dick I've ever known." Eli gnashed his teeth. "Get the fuck outside. NOW!" Eli shouted and turned on his heel, his boots pounding the floor of the RV.

Gabe didn't flinch as he moved toward his jeans, pulling them up his legs. He deserved this. He was a traitor. He'd known he hadn't deserved Avery. He hadn't deserved her virginity. She was too sweet for him, too good. Now he would incur the wrath he'd brought upon himself.

She took his hand as she shucked the covers and stood. "Gabe, this isn't just your fight. I'm to blame too."

Gabe shook his head and cupped her beautiful face. "I knew what was at stake the minute I took you. But the punishment is gonna be well worth the crime, sweet Avery." He grinned and kissed her softly.

He didn't wait for her to dress but began putting his boots on and moving toward the door Eli had left wide open.

He could hear Avery scrambling in the background as he saw Eli pacing back and forth, looking ready to murder him.

As he came down the stairs and his feet touched the ground, Elias lunged. A fist connected with Gabe's jaw and he braced himself to go down as pain ran through his face. He didn't, though. Eli's hands clasped his shoulders before he whaled on him again. And again. And again. Eli moved back a step and shook his fist while Gabe spit blood and wiped at his broken lip.

"Can I explain?" Gabe held out a hand.

"Explain *what*? That you're a fuckin' back-stabbin' sonova–" Eli growled and came at him again.

Gabe held up his hands. "C'mon dude. I–" His protest was cut short as Eli's hard fist connected with his kidney. Gabe went down then, coughing and gasping for breath.

"How fuckin' dare you go after my sister! You piece of shit." Eli spit at him, even as Gabe attempted to catch his breath, feeling like he might pass out. Fuck, he should have been prepared for that hit. "You fuck everything with a set of tits. Why am I not surprised? But *Avery*? My little sister! You are the lowest of low, you prick." A boot came at Gabe's face, and he grabbed it and twisted.

Eli fell with a loud thud and crawled back at him, anger seething from him.

"I fucking hate you. You were my best friend. How could you betray me like this?" Fist and spit flew as Eli pummeled at him, and Gabe pulled his arms over his head, protecting himself.

Eli was roaring, yelling, and flailing so that Gabe feared the end would come before he had a chance to tell Avery how deeply he felt for her.

Suddenly the weight was lifted and Gabe looked up to see Jack and Avery pulling Eli from him. He grinned as he saw her despite that he was pained and bleeding; it was all ok now that she was there.

He reached for her and she took his hand, cupping his jaw. "Oh my God, Gabe. Dammit, Eli. Stop it! This is *none* of your business!" She rounded on her big brother, pushing at his chest.

"None of my b— Are you out of your fuckin' mind? He's a walking hard-on. Ask him how many chicks he's slept with? Ask him, Ave? Want to know the truth? I'll bet you really don't! And you wanna know why? 'Cause *he* don't even know. Do you, Halloran?" Eli fought to get free of the bulky arms that held him back.

Avery gave Gabriel a reproachful smile even as she moved back to his side and cupped his bruised and battered jaw once again, looking into his eyes. He felt nothing aside from sheer bliss in her presence.

It didn't matter how many women he'd been with. He knew it. She knew it. Maybe it had once before, but not anymore. With her reassuring smile, he felt his love for her take over every cell in his body, and he would be quieted no longer. He stood and pulled her into his chest, looking her over with sheer joy.

"Eli," he said and looked back to his oldest friend. "I love her."

"Wh— What the fuck did he just say?" Eli cocked his head and his uncle Jack let him go.

By then half the camp was out of their trailers, including Stella and Natalie who closed in around them.

Gabe grinned and took in Avery's surprised and beautiful face. "I *said*, I love her," he stated louder. Avery pulled a breath in and smiled, looking at him as if he'd just lost his mind. "And yes, she's your little sister, Elias, but I don't care. I watched her grow into a fine, beautiful woman. I protected her then, and I'll continue to do so now. If she'll allow me to."

Avery's hand came to her mouth.

"It's sudden, I know. I didn't expect it, and I know you didn't either, but it's true, little mermaid. I love you. You're it for me. I knew the moment..." he trailed off, realizing his audience could hear everything, including a pin drop at how quiet it had become.

He looked back over to Elias, who scoffed, appearing as if he might keel over at any second.

"I'm sorry, man, but I don't need your permission to fall in love. Neither does your sister. It's Avery's choice. Not yours," Gabe stated with confidence.

Eli frowned and planted his hands on his hips, looking Gabe over in disgust before his eyes came back to his sister. "And what do *you* have to say about that?"

Avery's head tilted back to look Gabe over and said, "I say, I'm not one to stand in the way of love." She grinned before glancing back at Elias. "And neither should you, brother."

Avery's eyes went to Stella, who giggled beneath her palm, baby at her shoulder.

Eli scoffed and threw his hands up in incredulity. "Fine. You know what? Fuck this. I don't fuckin' care. You... you just stay the hell away from me, you traitor." He pointed to Gabe. "I got nothin' else to say to you. You can go fuck off. You *and* the horse you rode in on."

Eli spun around and stormed off.

Gabe's eyes came back to Avery's and he grasped the wayward strand of honey brown hair that drifted in the breeze. Time stood still as her eyes held his, and he got lost in their hazel depths. The sun made them lighter, brighter, breathtaking and he leaned in to savor her lips, before pulling back as he responded to a chuckle from behind them.

Jack approached then, shirtless. For an old man Gabe was surprised at the sheer muscle tone he still had.

"Well, can't say as I miss that kinda excitement, kids."

Avery blushed, and Gabe scowled. "Sorry about that, sir."

"Don't worry, son." Jack looked at his niece and grinned. "This guy bothering ya, darlin?"

She shook her head. "No, Uncle Jack. I kinda like him. I think I'll keep him around a bit longer."

Jack laughed again. "Good deal. Gabe, welcome to the family." He shook Gabe's hand as if meeting him for the first time, and Gabe gave him a crooked grin. Jack's grip tightened though as he pulled back. "Just know that should you hurt my niece, the next fist to your face will be mine. And I don't plan on you gettin' up when I hit you, if you catch my drift."

"Loud and clear, sir. Loud and clear." Gabe gulped because the conviction in the older man's eyes was, indeed, crystal clear. Gabe had only seen that determined look one other time. When he was staring down the barrel of a gun with eyes aimed at him.

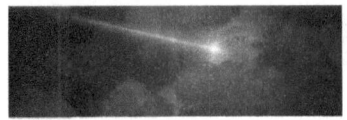

ELI TAPPED his fingers against the table that night, still fuming at his best friend's deceit. He'd spent most the day out, away from everyone—even Stella. His emotions were too much to withstand. He'd gone to the gym and pounded the hell out of a punching bag. It got some of his frustrations out, but not many. He was pissed at his old man, pissed at his sorry excuse for a best friend, and pissed at himself. He was also worried and hadn't eaten all day.

Stella came in all dusty and sweaty, grinning at him. "Welcome back, cowboy."

He couldn't continue the scowl as he glanced up into her beautiful face. He shook his head. "I'm sorry, Stell–"

"It's ok. I practiced most the day, me and UJ."

"UJ?"

"Yeah, ya know... Uncle Jack," she giggled as she opened the fridge and pulled a big bottle of water out, chugging it. His eyes roved her jeans, tight over her plump rear end. He almost groaned aloud in need.

"Where's my son?"

"You mean *our* son?" A brow went up as she turned and planted a manicured hand on her slender hip. Damn, she was hot. Dirty, sweaty, dusty...all cowgirl and still sporting curly ribbons and makeup. A cowboy's dream. *His* dream.

"C'mere, gorgeous. I want to taste you."

He didn't give her time to protest before he grabbed her and planted a long, deep kiss on her lips, tasting the sand and salt and reveling in it.

After a moment, she pulled back for a breath and laughed. "I see someone missed me."

"Damn right I did."

"Welcome back... I think. You still upse-"

"I don't want to talk about it. I don't want to talk about nothin'. All I want is you, Stells. Naked. In the shower, with me inside you." His mouth moved to her neck as he brushed her hair aside and peppered kisses over her damp skin.

"Is that a request or a demand, cowboy?"

The corner of his mouth ticked up, "What'd you want it to be, my sexy little star?"

She grinned again. "Well, we ain't got nothing but time, baby. Our son is with your aunt-who's the baby whisperer, at the moment-and she told me to take my time, so..."

Eli grinned and pulled her back to him, loving her mouth and moving his hands over her frame as if she might disappear if he didn't. She was the pillar that kept him grounded, the strength that kept him going, everything he'd ever wanted and needed... and he needed her now more than he ever had before.

She helped him strip her as they clumsily moved into the bedroom and toward the shower. Next, they removed his clothes, kissing and groping each other all the while. Elias turned the shower on as Stella's hands worked him into mindless stupor. Soon, she was pulling him beneath the hot spray. His hands moved over her wet frame, and he admired her tan skin beneath the water, fingering the curves of her glorious body.

"God, you're stunning."

His fingertips ran the length of her stretch marks, the ones that meant she'd carried his child safe within her. She was strong and capable.

"I want to give you another child, Stells. This time I'll be there to experience every kick, every doctor's visit, see your belly grow round with life." Eli's lips quivered, regret filling his very soul.

"I know you will, Eli. And I'll gladly carry as many children as you desire to give me, my love."

Her wide smile did him in, and he kissed her like there was no tomorrow. She kissed him back with equal fervor, moaning as he caressed her breasts and teased her nipple with one hand and moved the other between her legs to stroke her. Her back arched up like a kitten being stroked, and she practically purred with wanton need. Eli picked her up, and her hips wrapped around his. His cock was fully erect and ready to rock as he entered her with an easy thrust, her head falling back.

"Oh yes, Eli," she moaned as he withdrew and thrust again.

"God, Stella... It's like the first time every time with you, my sweet, *sweet* star." He took her lips as he pumped inside her, holding her like she was his lifeline because she was. Everything. She was his everything, and he'd been a damn fool to think he could exist without her.

Too soon, his release hurdled toward him. He couldn't hold back any longer.

"Come inside me, Eli. Let go, my beautiful cowboy. Come." She knew how close he was and didn't protest, didn't fault him for not letting her go first. She was being selfless.

He exploded with a roar that echoed through the shower, the surge of pleasure coming from his toes and spiraling outward, wracking his body.

He groaned even as he spilled every ounce he could inside the most precious honey pot he'd ever had. He shook violently as his orgasm faded, then gazed at her face. He was suddenly filled with immense disappointment in himself. He pulled out and stepped back. Then he crumbled to the shower floor, sobbing like a baby.

"Oh God, Stella. I'm so sorry. I'm such a horrible person."

"Elias..."

He clasped her hands and kissed them profusely then laid his head in them.

"The guilt of what I've done to you is crushing me. Abandoning you, our son. I know you forgive me, but I can't forgive myself." His head fell to her lower belly and he nuzzled her there, where his infant had slept all those months without his knowledge or concern. "I'm so angry at what my dad is doing to me and Avery. Jesus, what Gabe did behind my back. *Fuck!*"

Stella moved his head back and knelt with him. "C'mere, my love." She cradled his head to her shoulder, held him tightly against her, and let him break down. It felt good to get all his pain and anger out, to let it go beneath the spray of the shower, to ease the demons haunting him.

The shower beat a cadence of comfort against his back, for a time, but it was her hands that washed him clean of his transgressions—small, but beautiful, and capable hands that washed his sins away. As he looked into her eyes, he knew what he planned to do next.

CHAPTER 15

Stella took Eli's hand as they walked back to Jack and Natalie's RV later that evening. She could hear the baby crying before they closed in, and her milk let down, momentarily startling her. The human body was fascinating, and her own body had amazed her by growing and birthing a baby and being able to sustain him. It was a miracle, truly.

Stella cooed to her son as she came through the door, and he quieted as soon as he heard her voice. When she grabbed him up and pecked his cheek, he took a shuddering breath in relief. Stella giggled. "Better now, little cowboy?"

Toby blinked at her, and she grinned into his dark blue eyes.

"Momma just needed to get clean. Is my baby hungry?" When he whimpered as if understanding her, she sat in a nearby chair, pulled a blanket over herself, and began pulling at her shirt to feed him.

"Tell you what, I'm mesmerized by that sweet voice too. Kid don't know just how good he has it," Eli said to everyone present.

Jack sighed and leaned back in his recliner. "Ain't that the gospel."

The women laughed, and Nat offered to make drinks for Stella and Eli. Eli took a Coke, while Stella asked for coffee. She needed it. Otherwise she was liable to fall asleep.

Toby latched on greedily and began to feed. His need reminded her of his father earlier in the shower. Eli had always been passionate and eager to have her, even if this last time was more emotional and desperate than their usual unions. It'd been a tough day, and Eli's nerves had been frayed bare, reeling from the news of his father's upcoming brain surgery and the fact that Gabriel had been hooking up with his sister for Lord knew how long. Plus, he was still beating himself up about leaving her. Stella knew he would always regret their time apart, but it would seem everyone had a cross to bear. He'd have to forgive himself in due time.

Stella recalled his shouting that morning. She'd grabbed the baby up and moved out the RV just in time to realize what had happened. Eli had finally found out that Gabe and Avery were an item—the hard way.

Nat sat down across from Stella then, watching Toby eat. "Sometimes they just need their mamas." She reached for Toby's little arm and ran her finger up and down it, causing his eyes to close in contentment.

"I'm sorry, Aunt Nat. I hope he didn't cry too long."

"No, no, he'd just started to fuss. He's been perfectly comfortable."

"He's probably feeling all our emotions today, I'm sure." Stella frowned.

"I don't doubt it." Natalie looked off into space, and Stella took her hand.

"Have you heard from Bella?"

Nat nodded and grinned. "Yes, Luther's out of the hospital and home now. He's got a long recovery ahead of him."

Stella nodded. Sure. He'd had his sternum split in two and his heart replumbed; that couldn't be an easy surgery or recovery.

"Your dad called, and, I quote, wondered where the hell you are." Nat's brow's lifted.

Stella grimaced back at her aunt. That was yet another bomb to be dropped. Her dad was going to go bat-shit crazy on Elias Kinsen, not unlike Eli did on Gabe–only worse, *much* worse.

Stella gulped. "Don't say anything yet, please?"

"I won't, honey, but you know what your dad is gonna say. The sooner you rip that Band-Aid off, the better. It's been months. You *have* to tell him and soon."

"I know." She took a deep breath in, and Toby's eyes widened as he woke. "I'm sorry, sweet boy," she murmured to him and stroked a finger down his tiny cheek. "I was just hoping to have a little more time with Eli before..."

"Before your dad kills me?" Eli joked and propped himself across from them, against the kitchen island.

"Before I talk to him one-on-one first," Stella corrected.

Eli frowned. "But–"

"Just," Stella held up her hand, "before you say anything, and before he sees you, I need to fill him in on some stuff he doesn't know about." When Elias continued to frown, she continued, "He doesn't know about this, Eli...*any* of this." She twirled her finger around to indicate the RV, Jack and Natalie, the rodeo.

"Wait..." Eli took a step forward. "*What?*"

"Yeah," Jack interceded. "Ya see, Buck Jenkins told Stella months ago that he didn't want to hear your name ever again, and he damn well meant it. Buck is the most easy-going SOB I know, but not when it comes to his one and only daughter. He sees y'all together, and he's liable to lose his mind. I ain't seen Buck mad at much over the last thirty years, but he ain't one you wanna tangle with when he is." Jack shook his head.

"We didn't tell him the plan," Natalie said, "so in his eyes, we've betrayed him as much as Stella has. In all honesty, she needed our support. What other choice did we have but to help her? She wanted this so much and believed she could win you back, if only given the chance. But Buck isn't likely to see it that way. He's gonna be angry with all of us because we kept this secret for so long. His *best* friends..."

Eli inhaled sharply and looked at Stella. "Damn, baby, I'm so sorry. I messed up so bad." He covered his hands over his face, and Jack stepped up and put an arm over his shoulder.

"Eli, we all mess up, son. None of us are perfect. You've paved the way to make things right, so that's what we're gonna do. We're making things right."

Eli uncovered his face and gave his uncle a tight smile. "Yes. *I* am. It needs to be me to go talk to him."

"What?" Stella gasped, and Toby startled in her arms. She bounced him and shushed him as he whimpered. She cradled his head. "Eli, that's a terrible idea." She shook her head at him.

"I'm the one who wronged you, my little star. *Me*. It's my job now to set things right. I need to beg for his forgiveness now too. I'm the reason you kept this secret. I'm the reason you did all this. I'm the reason y'all are even here. It has to be me." He fell to his knees before her and cupped his son's head, he kissed it before leaning in to kiss her lips. "I know what I've done. What I almost lost. And if that means getting my ass kicked by your dad, then so be it. Maybe I deserve it—hell, I *know* I do." He ran a hand through his hair. "But I love you, Stella, and in order to move forward, I need your father's blessing as much as you do."

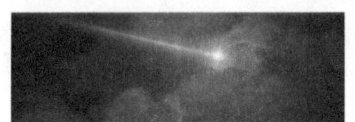

BUCK JENKINS WAS in a foul mood. One of his best friends in the world just had triple bypass, and Jack had just told him that his brother, Gavin, was having brain surgery today for a tumor and had a fifty-fifty shot at making it. Stella still wasn't home from the cameo she was doing down south, and he was worried that she hadn't spoken to him much. He felt in his bones that she was keeping something from him.

To top that off, they'd had a bad storm last night and a large tree had fallen into his media room, leaving one hell of a mess in its wake. Now, he was looking at both the inconvenience and cost of having to chop the massive tree down and have the entire room fully stripped, treated, and renovated.

The day was just damn peachy.

But to add insult to injury, when his doorbell rang and he opened the door to Elias Kinsen on his doorstep, he was ready to throw down.

Eli took his cowboy hat off and stood to his full height.

Buck's first instinct was to step out swinging, but then Eli produced a box in his hand and opened it, taking Buck off guard.

"The fuck is that, Kinsen?" He frowned.

"An engagement ring, sir."

Buck scoffed as he looked it over. "Say what now?"

"I said–"

"I *heard* what you said, idiot. Why the hell are you even here?" Buck opened his arms wide in surprise, but then his temper got the best of him. "You know what? I don't give a shit why you're here. You got two seconds to get off my property, or I'm calling the cops to escort you off it."

"Please, sir, don't–" Eli grabbed for the door Buck had begun to close in his face.

"Don't make me beat you senseless, Elias. I swear to God! Just give me one good reason to pound out my frustrations," Buck growled.

Elias shoved against the door with one mighty push, and Buck stumbled backward, surprised by both the younger man's strength and audacity. "Mr. Jenkins, I've come to talk, and I ain't leavin' here until I do."

"You must be achin' for an ass-whoopin', boy." Buck grinned viciously, cracking his knuckles, then clenched his fists at his sides.

"BUCK," came his wife's voice from the landing. "Stop it!" Vivian hissed and held a hand to her chest, looking Elias over as if she were seeing a ghost. "Elias, what on earth..."

"Ma'am." Eli nodded to Viv. "I'm sorry to come here unannounced, uninvited, and clearly not welcome." Eli looked back to Buck, expectantly. "But I got to get some stuff off my chest."

"Ha," Buck snorted. "Me too, sonny boy. Come on in. Let's have a chat!"

Anger bubbled in every vessel in Buck's body, and he yearned to feel the bastard's blood on his fists. He'd not hit anyone in years upon years, had never been quick to violence unlike some of his friends, despite his size, but with Elias Kinsen, the man who jilted his baby girl and grandbaby, he'd make an exception.

"Of course, Eli. Come in and sit, won't you?" Vivian approached and ushered Eli into the sitting room. Propriety always won over emotions for her. She'd been bred that way, even if she wasn't as stuck up as her counterparts. Their differences had always been the allure. Elegant, regal, Vivian Alexander Jenkins had always shone bright, his starlet, just like his darling Stella, his precious little star. The precious little star whose light had been snuffed out by the presumptuous cowboy now ambling into Buck's parlor.

The lion within wanted to pounce on the man who'd hurt his only child, shred him to pieces, and feast on his carcass, but for his wife's sake—and Stella and Toby's—Buck would at least give the father of his grandchild his last words before killing him slowly.

"Thank you, Mrs. Jenkins." Eli grinned as she sat next to him on the couch opposite the one Buck did.

"Oh, Eli. There's no sense in all the formality. You can call me Vivian, like always." Her smile had to be forced, for as much as Buck hated Eli, she wasn't too fond of him either at the moment.

"You got two minutes, kid." Buck checked his watch then narrowed his eyes at Eli. "Make it count."

Eli took a deep breath and exhaled slowly. He looked back to the small blue box with a sparkling diamond ring, showing it to Buck and Viv. "This ring right here is the one I plan to give your daughter."

Buck and Vivian were once more taken off guard. Buck shook his head in frustration. "I ain't followin', kid."

"I've done Stella very wrong, sir. I'll have to spend the rest of my life making it up to her...and to my son."

Vivian was the smirking one this time. "Eli, you... You know about Toby?"

"Yes," Eli smiled brightly. "He's as beautiful as Stella is. He's amazing."

"How did you...?"

"Stella found me. She's been training to be a barrel-racer and entered the rodeo circuit I've been following."

Buck's stomach dropped to his balls. "E-excuse me?"

"She..."

"Wait," Vivian snapped, all decorum gone. "You mean to tell me, she's *lied* to us about where she's been for months now."

"She didn't want y'all worrying is all."

"Wait just a fuckin' minute here." Buck pinched his nose, trying to calm his anger. "You said she's *been* training, as in, she didn't just start training... Who trained her to be a barrel racer?" Buck snarled.

He knew damn well who as his eyes flickered to Eli's before the younger man said, "My aunt and uncle."

Vivian looked like she might be sick as she inhaled sharply. Buck's anger flared, only to cease when Vivian laughed. The laughter echoed across the marble floors of their home and rattled Buck's last nerve.

"Dammit, Viv, what the hell is so fuckin' funny about this?" Buck stood and crossed his arms over his chest.

"Oh, my love, I'm sorry." Her cackling grew louder, and Buck tapped his foot impatiently before Vivian composed herself and cleared her throat. "You've always said it, Buck. Our daughter is so much like me, but *God*, she's so much like you, too." The beautiful smile on her face didn't break his frustration, not one bit. "Buck!"

274

She put her hand out in explanation. "She went after him. Of course she did. She's always gone after anything she wants, come Hell or high water. We raised her to reach for the stars. Did you honestly expect anything else?"

Buck realized that was the damn truth, if ever it had been spoken. He sighed heavily, took his wife's hand, and plopped back down onto the couch beside her.

"So, y'all made up, huh?" he asked Elias. "Apparently. Now you come here seeking my blessin' to marry her? And what am I supposed to do? Be the bad guy and say no?" Buck smarted.

"I've come to tell you how much I love Stella. That I never stopped." When Buck rolled his eyes and waved the statement off, Eli sighed. "She never meant to betray you. Neither did Uncle Jack or Aunt Nat."

"Oh, your *Uncle Jack* and *Aunt Nat* are gettin' a talking to as well, just you wait. Then Stella... But go on, speak your piece."

"Sir," Eli sighed heavily and ran a hand through his hair, sitting the box down and the hat with it onto the table. "There are no words to tell you how very sorry I am for what I've done. No matter how many times I apologize to Stella, it won't ever be enough. I know that. I messed up. I was wrong. I was..." He looked back up, eyes filled with conviction. Buck held still. "She's everything to me. When I thought she killed our baby, a part of me died that day. I didn't give her a chance to talk, to explain that she hadn't done what I thought she had, and I have to live with the repercussions for the rest of my life. Trust me. That's punishment enough. But I will always put her first, her and Toby, from now on.

"I need you to know that I deserve whatever you got planned for me. If you beat the shit out of me, Buck, I know I deserve it. If you throw me out, I understand. If you call the cops, then I'll gladly be arrested tryin' to plead my case... Point is, sir, I'll be back. Every day, if that's what it takes. Until I prove to you that I mean what I say. However long that takes.

"I love your daughter with all I have. I want to marry her, give her more children. Stand by her, like she's stuck by me, even when I don't deserve it and *didn't*, but she..." Eli swiped at the tears on his cheeks. "She never stopped trying. And dammit, sir, I won't either. So, do what you must, but I'm putting that ring on Stella's finger and making her mine once and for all. With or without your blessing, if I must."

Buck grinned at the young man's moxie–and at the fact that he'd had the balls to come and pour his heart out to him.

"*Hellfire*, Eli..." Buck sighed heavily and looked over at his wife, who had tears sparkling on her cheeks. He chuckled in exasperation. "Well then, I reckon, welcome back is in order."

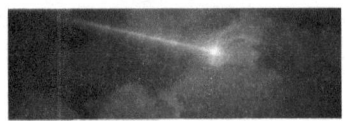

WITH ONE MESS taken care of, when Eli got back from ironing things out with his future in-laws, he had another situation to confront–Gabe and his sister.

Gabe took Avery's hand in his, even as Eli's mouth tightened and he looked away.

"You can stop looking at my boyfriend like you want to murder him, Jeffrey Dahmer," Avery smarted at her brother.

Gabe was still bruised from Eli's fists, looking worse for wear.

"I'm still mad at you, by the way, and waiting..."

Eli inhaled and exhaled sharply. "I'm sorry."

"For?"

"For beating up your *boyfriend*," he growled.

"Your best friend," Avery retorted.

"My *best* friend," Eli's eyes narrowed.

"Elias," Stella's soft voice called. Her hand smoothed his, the one that was balled into a fist on the table. "They love each other. Like you and I do."

Eli snorted. "Love, right? That's what it is, huh?" His eyes raked

276

Gabe's frame, remembering all the women he'd dragged into his camper and screwed like they meant nothing to him, because they hadn't. Eli didn't want his sister in that crowd. Not now or ever. The thought twisted his stomach even worse, knowing many of those women had been in his own trailer too.

Hypocrite, he thought to himself.

"You know what, I don't have to sit here and take your bullshit, brother. I am a grown woman, and I can–" Avery shot up out of her seat and pointed to him.

"Sit down!" Eli commanded and stood too.

Gabe's arm went at Eli's, then, clasping hard. Eli had never seen Gabe's eyes so dark. "Don't! Don't talk to her like that, Elias."

Eli froze, reading the anger all over Gabriel's suddenly very serious face.

"Brother, best friend–hell, *whoever* you may be–I won't stand for you shouting at her. I don't give a fuck how mad you are at me, us, whoever. You can take your anger out on me, but leave Avery out of it."

Gabe's face flared red, and Eli almost recoiled in shock. Could it really be that Gabe was in love with his sister? *Bless my day!* Eli's brows rose.

Avery looked at Gabe and grinned. Finally, the anger dissipated from him as she touched his shoulder then his face. He leaned in to kiss her, softly, sweetly. As annoyed as Eli was with them both, he couldn't deny that he saw something more in their embrace than lust.

Stella smiled at him, and he returned it weakly. He sat down and pulled in a deep breath. He looked at his baby, all nestled in his mother's arms, and calmed down.

When Gabe and Avery sat back down, Eli told them, "I guess I have no right to tell either of you how to live or what to do. I've been absent and have a lot to make up for, myself. I'm glad y'all are happy, and truthfully," he admitted, "if Buck Jenkins can find it in his heart to allow me to be with his daughter, I can be content to see you two together."

Avery was the first to break eye contact. "Really?" she asked.

"Yeah, really. Just do right by her, will ya, asshole?" Eli pointed at his best friend.

"I plan to treat her like a princess, ya dickwad," Gabe retorted and kicked at Eli's boot, getting a laugh at him. He then looked at Avery with nothing but tenderness.

"For your sake, you damn well better," Eli threatened, knowing he had nothing to worry about at that point as Gabe squeezed Avery's hand.

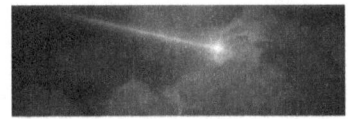

ELI HELD his breath as his father's eyes opened. The gauze draping his head and paleness of his face was like a kick to the gut. He'd never seen his dad looking so helpless and feeble. But he wasn't there to judge, only for moral support.

Gavin Kinsen inhaled deeply and smiled at him. "Hey, son." His voice was strained but held acknowledgement. That was all Elias needed.

Emotion seized him, and tears stung his eyes. "Hey, Dad." He wanted to launch himself at his father and hug him but feared pulling the tubing from his arm or hurting him. Instead, he simply sat in the chair next to him and held a sleeping Toby.

"You're looking well, Elias." Gavin's eyes fell to the baby. "Who you got there?"

"This is your grandson, Tobias. My son."

Gavin grinned. "He looks like you."

"No, he looks like Stella," Elias contested but grinned despite himself. He knew Toby had the Kinsen lips.

"You did good, kid." Gavin reached his hand out, and Eli took it and brought it to his face.

"I'm glad to see you, Dad. You had us worried there for a little while."

When his mother called to tell them the surgery had been a success, Eli had fallen to his knees in relief, sobbing. He'd needed to make amends with his old man, and the Lord must have known it. He'd gone on to win event after event that weekend, feeling as if fate was on his side for a change.

That following Thursday, once his dad had been released home, Eli, Stella, Toby, Jack, Natalie, Avery, and Gabe flew down to Corpus Christi to see their father—with or without his knowledge, and despite his wishes.

His mother had been glad to see them all and welcomed them with open arms.

"You got a rodeo to be in, don't you?" his dad asked.

For a man who'd had brain surgery recently, surprisingly, he was still with it.

"Tomorrow night. We're in San Anton. Not too far a drive." Jack had hired some folks to drive their trailers while they visited.

"You win a lot?" his dad asked, and Elias laughed.

"I do. I'm pretty good, and so is my girl."

"I'll have to come watch one soon, hopefully," Gavin said with all seriousness.

"Nothing would make me happier, Dad."

"I'm sorry, Eli."

"For what?"

Gavin shrugged, looking away, his emotions catching up to him.

"If anyone should be sorry, it's me. I shouldn't have shut y'all out like I did. I promise, I won't ever do it again. Knowing I'm a father has changed a lot for me."

"You'll never love anyone or anything like you do your children."

"I know." He squeezed his father's hand. "I'd do anything for this little guy. He has me wrapped around that little finger. That one there."

When Eli pointed to Toby's extended index finger, his dad laughed.

"It's good to see you, Elias. I've missed you, son."

"You too, Dad."

He held his dad's hand for a time, letting silent tears fall as the rift he'd felt for too long ebbed away as if it'd never been there.

His dad closed his eyes, and Eli figured he'd drifted off to sleep.

"I'm gonna ask Stella to marry me." Eli told him, asleep or not. "I think we'll wait 'til rodeo season is over. Maybe get married down here, on the beach somewhere. I know she wants to finish out the circuit. December, maybe. It'll be cool but hopefully not cold."

Gavin's eyes opened, and he smiled. "Cherish her. Love is a blessing."

"It is, isn't it?" Eli asked. "I expect you to be good and healed up by then. Maybe you won't still be bald, though." He teased, and his dad laughed lightly.

"I'm just as sexy bald as I am with hair." Gavin attempted a wink.

"Not what mom says," Eli joked.

"Do me one favor, son," his dad requested.

"Anything!"

"Please don't wear a cowboy hat to your wedding."

With that, Eli roared in laughter.

"AND NOW I present to you, the barrel-racing queens of the IPRA circuit and Lovington rodeo company. First up is our very own reigning rodeo queen, Ms. Stella Rose Jenkins. Yes, you heard me right, Ms. Stella–" Cooper cleared his throat into the mic. "Umm, hold up here just a moment. Our rodeo clown, Cash, seems to be confused about what the barrels are intended to do. Cash, what in the ever lovin'...?" Cooper trailed off.

Cash cued up his mic. "Seems we have a cowboy here who's lost his way, Coop."

The crowd laughed and cheered, looking at Elias, who shrugged as rehearsed. "Elias, what in tarnation are you doin' down there? Don't you know the calf-roping event is over?" Coop huffed in mock exasperation, getting another round of chuckles from the audience.

"Well, you see, Coop, I ain't lookin' to rope any more calves tonight," Eli confessed, "I aim to rope the rodeo queen, though."

"Goodness gracious, these cowboys," Cooper planted a smack to his forehead. "Ms. Jenkins, darlin', do you mind coming out here real quick and seein' what on earth this cowboy is 'a talkin' about?"

Stella urged her mare into the arena, nose wrinkling at Eli and looking around curiously.

"Look at our lovely queen tonight, isn't she gorgeous? She can really dazzle a crowd, can't she?" It was Elias's voice over the loud-speaker now.

Stella looked from him to the crowd in question and ate up that spotlight she was so good in. Love swelled in Eli's heart so fiercely he could have cried.

"She's the mother of my son, you know? Tobias Edward Kinsen. We made one fine-looking little cowboy, didn't we, darlin'?" When Stella blushed back at him, he sighed. "Oh, my beautiful little star, you don't know how happy you make me, do you? I love you, angel." He looked from Stella to the crowd, splaying his arms wide. "I love this woman, San Antonio!"

The crowd cheered vibrantly. Who didn't love a romantic story, after all?

Eli waited until they'd quieted down before continuing, "You know we met as children. Her dad and my aunt and uncle are best friends. I always thought she lit up a room, but it was the night of one of my many rodeos almost four years ago when she stopped me dead in my tracks. Not long after, I got the pleasure of taking her home. Together, we wished upon a shooting star together that I happened to name Stella, and...well, folks, I got my wish." The long sounds of, "Awww" echoed through the crowd.

Stella's hand came to her mouth, and she covered her smile.

"My sweet star, this past year has been literal Hell without you. Having you back in my arms is all I've been dreaming of. So now, I ask you in the sight of our Lord and these good Texas folk...will you make me the happiest rodeo cowboy in all of San Antonio and marry me?"

Cheers erupted around the arena as Eli fell to one knee beside Stella's restless mare and presented her the ring he pulled from his pocket.

"Quiet, folks, quiet," Cooper shushed the audience. "I need to hear her answer."

Eli's eyes held Stella's as her chest rose and fell in unshed emotion. She looked around at the crowd, then back down at him before dismounting.

She stood before him and nodded vigorously.

"Yes?" Cooper gasped. "Did she say yes?"

Stella laughed and covered her mouth again, nodding.

Eli popped up and pulled her into his arms, kissing her with all the passion he could muster and still manage to keep it PG-13. When he pulled back, he grinned into her tear-stricken face and motioned to the ring.

"For my little shooting star, the one I'll always follow, no matter how far." He motioned to the inscription inside the ring, the one he'd had engraved years ago.

"Oh Eli," she sighed as he placed the ring on her left ring finger and brought it to his lips.

"I love you, Stella."

"I love *you*, Elias."

He hugged her to him again and kissed her once more before he motioned to the crowd.

She giggled and spoke into Elias's mic. "Well, San Anton... I reckon I got a little more riding on this event now, don't I?"

Cheers and applause rained all around them.

"Either way, win or lose, I roped a cowboy's heart tonight." She winked and got even more cheers from the crowd.

Eli grinned along with her and pulled her back into his embrace.

He patted her back and motioned for her to mount her ride.

"Alright, cowgirl, I expect a good race, now," he told her.

She scoffed and shook her head as she got back up onto her mare with ease.

She was headed back out of the arena as Eli said, "Win big, baby. I want a nice honeymoon."

Stella gave him a thumbs up even as Cooper said, "Alright, cowboy, you can scram now." He feigned a grumble at Eli. "Let's congratulate the couple on their engagement and everyone put your hands together for Ms. Jenkins, soon-to-be Mrs. Kinsen."

EPILOGUE

"And so we felt it only proper to have our reception here in Abundance," Eli announced at their wedding reception, tucking Stella to his side. "Our friends and family have meant so much to us, to both of us," he looked into his bride's beautiful face, "and we're damn glad to have y'all here. So thank you for coming. We love you all."

Their friends and family applauded. Gabe, his best man, patted him on the back, and Eli pulled him in for an embrace, wiping the tears that fell unabashedly down his cheeks.

Eli pulled back and hugged his father next, who had fully recovered from brain surgery, then his mother, sister, father-in-law, then mother-in-law. He then grinned at his baby boy, clad in a cowboy hat and jeans, sitting in his Aunt Natalie's lap.

An oversized tent had been set up in the one of pastures on Kinsen/Butler property overlooking the creek. All their family and closest friends had been invited to celebrate their recent nuptials. His aunt Natalie and his cousins, as well as Cassidy Boyd, had a field day decorating, sparing no expense on the food, décor, photography, or music. A gorgeous three-tiered cake sat on a pedestal adorned with stars, horseshoes, and cowboy hats–and both he and Stella loved it.

"Dada," Toby clapped in glee as Eli came forward. He reached for his proud papa. Eli picked him up and held him high, getting sweet baby cackles from his six-month old son.

They hadn't been able to wait until December to wed. They'd gotten married exactly six months from Toby's birth. It was early November, rodeo season was still in full swing, but they'd taken a much-needed weekend off.

Eli grinned at his cousin, Savannah, and her husband, Austin, as they came forward. Dallie and Cole, Jax and Cassidy, and Jack and Natalie also stepped in, forming a large circle. "Thanks, y'all."

"No need to thank us, Eli. We wanted to do it," Vanna said and bumped her hip against his.

"It was high time y'all got married, anyway," Jax teased, getting a playful swat from Cassidy.

"Plus, you know we love having reasons to celebrate, especially love," Dallie shrugged, getting a grin from Cole.

"What I wanna know is where's the honeymoon gonna be? We all know that's the best part of weddings," Austin teased and winked at Eli. Savannah shot him a look, even as his hand smoothed over her rounded belly. She clasped her hand in his.

"Well, we've been thinking long and hard about that," Stella said and looped her arm through Eli's.

"And?" Natalie asked.

"And we're going to Disney World," Eli exclaimed and lifted Toby again who squealed. Lily, Gracie, and Rowan giggled and clapped their hands in glee. When his uncle Jack looked at him as if he'd lost his mind, he laughed. "Just kidding. We still don't know." Eli shrugged. "He's too little for Disney–and flying, to be honest. We've been to exotic places before, so we're at a loss."

Stella tilted her head thoughtfully. "Not like it matters, anyway."

"Of course it matters," came Avery's voice, and Gabe wrapped his arms around her.

"Not really," Stella shot her eyes to Vanna knowingly.

"What's she talkin' about?" Gabe asked Eli, and Stella giggled.

"I guess now's a good enough time to tell 'em, huh, wifey?" Eli asked.

Stella's mom and dad had come closer by then, too, along with Eli's uncle Carson, aunt Olivia, cousins Ethan and Alex and their wives and children, forming a very large group of Kinsens.

Stella smiled, even as Elias kissed her. She then cried, "We're goin' to the finals!"

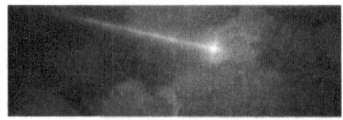

FOLLOWING THE RECEPTION, Eli called for a meeting in the barn. His uncles: Jack and Carson, and his first cousins: Alex, Ethan, Jax, Dallie, and Savannah, extended family: Nate and Morgan Butler, ranch foreman: Austin and Wyatt Montgomery, and Eli's wife, Stella, were all in attendance, crammed into Jack's office.

As patriarch of Kinsen Ranch, Jack began, "Eli here has called for a meeting with the land and stockholders of our respective businesses and requested we, in attendance, hear his proposal. Eli, you have the floor, son."

Eli grinned at his uncle, his family, and his wife then began, "As you all own stock in Kinsen ranch and personally have ties to the family's companies, I wanted to propose a business deal for you all. Stella and I are planning to settle down–not right away, but eventually." He sighed dreamily, and took Stella's hand. "And we know there's no better place than here, in Abundance, the place where we met. Uncle Jack, Dallie, Jax, and Savannah have all been gracious enough to offer us a piece of land here, and it truly warms our hearts to be given such an incredibly selfless gift."

Elias placed his hand over his heart and attempted to hold his emotions in. "This ranch has always been home to us. I don't know if you guys even know what you all mean to us, what Kinsen Ranch means to us." Eli wiped at a tear and watched Dallie, Stella, and Savannah all do the same. "We love you. All of you. Which is why we'd eventually like to have a home here, and not *just* a home, but a place where we can also carry on our passion for rodeo. This ranch has bred and trained horses for over half a century. Dallie's veterinary services have cared for them for many years now too. Uncle Carson, you've had a polled Hereford cattle ranch for over thirty years. You know cattle well and could easily add in a herd of Brahmas bred and trained for PBR, no problem. Nate, your horses have been used and trained for commercials, movies, and various other entertainments. But not rodeo. Not yet."

Eli's grin deepened as he looked around to Austin, Alex, Ethan, Jax, Nathan, and Morgan. "Me and Stella, personally, feel the businesses should incorporate a rodeo company. Think of the possibilities. Like Stella and I, Uncle Jack and Nate have also participated in extreme sporting events and their input is highly valuable. Uncle Carson's new herd of Brahmas, and the Kinsen and Butler horses, will supply our livestock for the rodeo. We can set up a rodeo school, and then have the company itself running circuits. It can be a fully self-functional rodeo company."

Everyone looked around at one another in delighted surprise.

Austin elbowed Savannah and muttered loudly, "Shit, Savvy, maybe we should tell 'em how good you are at ridin' bulls then."

Vanna's jaw dropped and her cheeks reddened. They apparently were sharing a private moment before his uncle Jack cleared his throat. "My son-in-law thinks he's funny, but he ain't." Jack cut his eyes at Austin, who shrugged, nonplussed as usual. Wyatt shoved at his younger brother and rolled his eyes. "Either way, kids, I think it's a brilliant idea."

"Who's plannin' on runnin' this rodeo company?" Jax asked and crossed his arms over his chest. "You, cuz?"

"Well, no, not me personally. See, I'm not asking for y'all to be investors–or well, not *just* investors I should say. I'm asking if you'll make me and Stella partners, make this an expansion of three very lucrative and successful ranches. Stella and I would like to eventually work at the rodeo school when we're not in the circuit. Be here to train and teach, if you guys all agree."

Nathan and Morgan both shrugged and nodded eagerly, along with Carson, Alex, and Ethan.

"I like this idea," Dallie told Eli and Stella with a bright smile. "I think it has great potential, guys."

Nate nodded to Dallie. "Expands our marketing with even more connections, takes the ranches to new heights, more outreach."

"That's what we thought too," Stella added. "Starlight Valley, CK Ranch, and Kinsen Ranch all working in tandem with the rodeo company, incorporations of all three. With all the combined money of our families and some outside investors, we'll have no problem starting this up."

"I like it," Carson told Eli, who nodded to his uncle and thanked him. Ethan and Alex agreed. "I'm in."

"A good way to finally connect the two separate ranches, for sure," Alex said. "You got my vote, Elias, Stella." Alex tipped his hat to Stella and Eli, who smiled at his cousin in turn.

"Good," Jack said, "Any opposed?" Jack looked around, and Eli searched for any hesitation within the group.

"Are you kidding?" Austin piped in. "Have the ranches associated with the famous Stella Jenkins-Kinsen. Yes siree, Bob." He winked.

Jack smiled. "Alright then, the motion passes. We're starting a rodeo company, people!"

Stella squealed and hugged Eli. Eli shook his uncle Jack's hand and Stella began moving around the room, hugging everyone, giddy as a school girl.

"Thanks a lot, Uncle Jack," Eli told his uncle.

"My pleasure, son. Glad to have you back where you belong."

"It's good to be here."

Nathan Butler came up then and shushed the crowd of loud

voices. "Hey, wait just a minute y'all. We didn't discuss the name of this rodeo company." His dark brows drew mischievously.

Jack smirked. "I think that's kinda obvious. Don't you, Nate?"

"Hell, I figured!" Nathan teased. "I've been overrun with Kinsens for a long damn time now." He winked as Dallie came forward and playfully punched at his arm.

"Oh, Uncle Nate." She hugged him, and he kissed her cheek. "You love us Kinsens and darn well know it too."

"Hey, what about Mom and Aunt Jordan, don't they get a vote?" Jackson asked.

"They already knew," Stella stated, "I told them both this morning, and they were all for it."

"Thank God," Nate feigned relief. "That redhead of mine would never let me live that down."

Eli grinned. "So, it's settled then. We're naming it Kinsen Rodeo Company?"

Savannah's husband came up then, Austin Montgomery, along with his older brother, Wyatt.Austin patted Eli's back and joshed, "Just you remember who runs these *very lucrative* ranches, Kinsen. Couldn't have such success without the Montgomery brothers."

Morgan rolled his eyes heavenward. "These Montgomerys and their overinflated egos."

"*His* overinflated ego," Wyatt pointed to Austin. "Leave me out of this, please?"

Eli knew Wyatt and Austin made great foremen for both Kinsen Ranch and Starlight Valley. "Hey, I'm just glad y'all said yes and are gonna give us a chance. Thanks everyone. We really appreciate this."

"Why not, kid?" Eli's Uncle Carson approached then, patting his back. "We all deserve a chance at our dreams, don't we?"

Eli pulled his other uncle in for a hug and grinned at him as he pulled back. He looked to Stella, who was talking to Ethan, Jax, and Morgan.

"We do, Uncle Cars. We certainly do."

None of them knew just how much he'd dreamed of coming

home to Abundance. Home to Stella. Mrs. Stella Kinsen. His little star. The shooting star he'd also given her name to after he wished upon it, wished to make her his. And it had.

He now had all he'd ever dreamed of.

Love, happiness, family. He'd never take any of it for granted again.

THE END

EXTENDED EPILOGUE

"A rodeo company, huh?" Buck asked Jack as they sat some distance away from the festivities of the wedding. They'd taken up residence on the couch across from the firepit and with a view of the barn. "I mean... I guess I understand but... hmm."

"What?" Jack asked and sipped on his beer.

"Well, who's gonna own it? All of you?"

"Elias and Stella, essentially, of course, with over a dozen investors backing them from the get go, including the three ranches."

"And will Eli run the thing?"

Jack shook his head. "He doesn't want the responsibility, but I'd bet he wouldn't mind running the school." He rubbed his chin in thought.

"Think he'd be good at runnin' a business?"

"Sure. He might prefer teaching calf roping, though. Heck, he's been a cowboy almost from the get-go—much to Gavin's dismay," Jack smirked ruefully, recalling the day he'd informed his brother that his only son was destined for the western lifestyle.

Elias and Jackson were solid dust from playing with the horses all day, donning hats and boots bigger than they were. Gavin corralled his young son inside the barn, practically cringing as he gingerly touched his shoulders, fearing he might soil his own clothing with all the dust and hay.

"Daddy, oh, I want to ride the horsey again. Please let me ride him again," a very young Elias grabbed for his father's hand and pleaded so precociously.

Jack laughed, and Gavin gave him a look of frightful apprehension.

"I'm afraid your boy doesn't take much after his father," Jack told his baby brother.

"Lord...not you too, Jack." He gave a heavy sigh. "Veronica's already freaking me out, saying he's gonna be a cowboy, just like his uncles."

"And what's so darn bad about that, huh?" Anger took him then, knowing their own father and mother both were impressive equestrians to their core. They had been humble people but proud to be surrounded by love. "You so afraid of germs that you're gonna let it stop you from living a little? Lighten up, would you?" Jack gave his brother a shove.

Gavin rolled his eyes. "I'm not afraid of germs. I just...well, I don't like to be dirty. Is that really such a bad thing? To want to be clean? Dirt makes me itchy and..." He cringed.

Jack rolled his eyes. "Oh, BS. Dirt is a rite of passage. It's our duty as men to be one with the earth."

Gavin's brow rose. "And it is also my rite of passage to have some sense of refinement and propriety."

"I am both of those things, along with gracious, fair, not to mention good-looking... thanks so much. Playing in the dirt doesn't make you dirty." Jack felt a bit judged.

Gavin's hands went to his hips, and he huffed loudly. Jack realized he was about to get something big off his chest. "You know... I have always loved you, dear brother. You and Carson both. But I didn't always like you. Both of you ganged up on me, made me feel inferior...and different."

Jack literally recoiled. Although, he remembered quite well the hell he and his older brother put their baby brother through. They picked on him relentlessly, bullied him, and blamed everything on him. But it was because they were so jealous of him, it was ridiculous. They knew he shared a special bond with their mother that they never would. But he figured now that they were grown men, Gavin had forgotten all about it, letting bygones be bygones.

To affirm Jack's internal reverie, Gavin said, "I envied and despised you both, but I felt the need to prove myself to you and would never do anything to let you down. But try as I might, I couldn't live up to either of you, and y'all made me never forget that fact."

Regret swamped Jack's heart. "Gavin, I never—"

"It's fine. I don't blame you. You were kids. Despite how mean you were to me, I knew you loved me as much as I loved you, especially when others would bully me only for one or both of you to come to my rescue, every time. No matter how mad at me you might be at that moment in time. We fought, sure, but all brothers do, don't they? I knew it was tough love, just as you knew I loved you in return. I was always trying to be what y'all wanted me to be, but I didn't like the horses as much as you did. I enjoyed other hobbies and business wear because it was different. I realized early on that I couldn't fit into that lifestyle, so I found my own." Gavin shrugged. "I'm not upset. It helped me grow into the man I am. I'm proud to be a Kinsen. I'm just the one who decided to venture out of the mold."

Carson would say Gavin had been rejected by the mold, only because he'd always been harder on Gavin than anyone else had been, given he was the oldest Kinsen sibling. Cars still ragged on him, but Jack knew he did it for Gavin's own good. They'd both been intimidated by their youngest brother's keen intelligence.

Jack gave him a grin. "And that makes you brave as hell, little brother."

"I am who I am, take it or leave it. Mom always told me in secret when I'd come running to her crying that it was because I took more after her side of the family. Though, we never knew much about them, did we?"

Jack looked at the ground. No, they didn't. His maternal grandparents, The Suttons, had disowned his mother, Lillian, after she'd chosen a "dirty cowboy" instead of who they'd picked for her. She rarely talked about them. Jack figured it was too painful.

"I am sorry, though, that we bedeviled you so much, Gavin. I'm sure life wasn't easy."

"Nothing worth having is easy," Gavin smirked. "Didn't Dad always tell us that? It's true. Life isn't easy, Jackson, and that makes it something to cherish—the good times."

Jack nodded, grinning that Gavin still called him Jackson on occasion. He'd not shortened his name to Jack until he'd gotten to high school.

"So... Eli likely being a cowboy?" Jack coaxed, still wondering what he'd meant by his original comment.

"Right, sorry, I got off on a tangent." Typical Gavin. "I just... I guess I'd hoped Elias might take after me, instead. After all, yours and Carson's sons are all big into the family businesses, and I wanted Eli to be something other than a cowboy. Maybe go into finance or numbers, like I did. I know, it sounds petty when I say it out loud. I shouldn't care, and I truly don't, it's just... it was wishful thinking, I guess." Gavin shrugged, his face falling in disappointment.

"The Kinsen genes are strong, you know. But I do see you in him too, Gavin. He might be business savvy one day, if given the chance. He's good with Jax, watches after him, and directs him easily. He's patient and giving. He's a good kid, and he'll make a fine cowboy."

"Well, if anyone knows horses, brother, it's you. I'd not settle for anyone else to train him, should this hobby of his become serious. But I'm hoping he'll grow out of this phase. There's still time yet."

Jack laughed when Gavin grinned mischievously and rubbed his hands together.

"I'd be honored to train my nephew. And I, personally, hope it's not a phase. Now, get over here and give me a hug...before I give you a nudgy."

Jack laughed now, wiping at his eyes, as he recalled the story to Buck.

"Ya see, when it was just Gavin and I—or even Gavin and Carson, without me—we were good to him, doted on him, made him feel loved. But together, we were hard on him, pushing him to be better—and even beatin' up on him on occasion. As shitty as that was, I think it might have been a good thing too. It built his personality.

"But he always was more Sutton than Kinsen. He and Dad got along well enough, too, but I think, deep down, Gavin felt he'd disappointed our old man by not following in his footsteps like Cars and I did. He was still at home when they passed, you know."

Buck's lips pursed, and he patted Jack's bicep. "I'm sorry, man."

"No, I am. This conversation went sideways." Jack laughed and tried to shake off his emotions. He sighed and leaned back on the love seat, looking around at the crowd, drinking, laughing, dancing, and talking. "It's good to have our families connected by blood, don't you think?"

Buck's brow lifted but then he laughed. "Tell ya what, I'd rather it have been Jax, personally, but if Elias makes my little star happy, then who am I to say otherwise."

"Jax, huh?" came Stella's voice at that moment. "Playing favorites?" She planted her hands on her hips and glared at her father.

"Now, Stella, angel..."

"Daddy, you take that back, right now." She stomped her white cowboy boots, the bedazzled ones beneath her long, white, lace wedding dress. "It's my weddin' day, for God's sake."

Buck had amusement lighting his face even as he tried to appear humbled. "Oh darlin', I didn't care who you ended up marrying. You gotta know that. It's just..." Buck looked back to Jack who shook his head and held his hands up in surrender, rending himself neutral. Buck sighed and extended his hand.

Puckered lips and sass aside, Stella reached for it and moved to sit between her father and Jack. Jack started to leave, to give them their moment, but Buck jerked his arm, stopping him.

"Thing is, baby girl, I don't dislike your...husband."

"Could've fooled me." The venom in her tone was unmistakable. "Daddy, that man isn't *only* my husband. He's the father of your grandson, and the love of my life. I adore Jax, but Jax and I..."

295

"I know, Stell Bell, I know," Buck reassured her and pulled her into his side. "It's only... Jax is just...well, *Jax*."

"And Eli is Eli. What's your point?" Stella hissed and got a snort from both men.

Buck looked at Jack once more before he said, "Jax is as solid as his old man, here: stone of the earth, as genuine as it gets. Eli is a bit...harder to figure out, I guess."

"As am I. Look, I love Jackson. He's wonderful, but he's not Elias."

Buck inhaled and nodded. "I understand. More than you know." Buck brought his daughter's chin up with his thumb and index finger. "I'm happy that you're happy, darlin', but trust me, the first time someone hurts your child, you'll want to rip their heart out. Thing is, Stella, I will love Eli, too, because you do and because he *is* my grandson's father. But...he still has to prove himself, to me and to you. And that's gonna take time. Doesn't mean I'm gonna hold it over his head. Doesn't mean I'm still angry, but...unfortunately, you'll better understand one day."

Stella looked from her father to Jack. "You forgave UJ and Aunt Nat for their deception. What's so different?"

"It was done to *me*, not to you. *That's* the difference." Buck's brow rose. "Besides, sometimes people do things for their own good, even if it feels like the opposite at the time. I understand why Jack and Nat didn't tell us what they were up to. They were protecting and supporting you. But that doesn't mean I wasn't mad as hell about the deception."

Buck looked to Jack then, eyes narrowing. "Friends..."

"Family," Jack corrected with a smirk.

"*Family* takes care of each other. And, in this family, we do. Always."

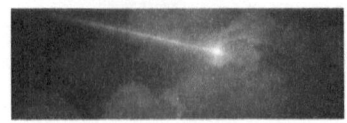

Stella grinned over at her husband as he pulled her hand to his lips, kissing her knuckles.

"I love you."

"I love you," she told him.

"You smell incredible."

She giggled as he leaned in and kissed her neck and collarbone, working toward her bosom.

"When do I get your breasts back? My son is now six months old, you know?"

She cocked a brow. "Don't rush it, *Daddy*. Besides, I thought we were gonna start trying for another one?"

"So... I won't get your boobs to myself for another year?" His puppy-dog eyes did her in.

"*I* will get my boobs back to myself soon. Besides, I only feed him at night now, and I don't want to rush him into weaning too early."

"Fine," Elias whined and nuzzled her breasts. "You're missin' out, my star."

She giggled again and pulled his face to hers for a sultry kiss. He embraced her, pulling her tightly against him as the limo drove them to the bed and breakfast they were to be staying in.

"Say, what are Avery and Gabe plannin' on doing now?" she asked randomly.

"Hell if I know," Eli dismissed. "I don't wanna think about them while I'm making out with my wife."

He continued to make out with his wife, and she enjoyed the sound of that word on his lips, but then she pulled back, thinking. "I just meant... Avery said he's planning on going back to Corpus Christi with her."

Eli sighed. "Way to ruin the mood," he grumbled then shrugged as Stella's eyes narrowed. "Yeah, he said he was. Why?"

"You'll need another heeler, if that be the case."

"Yeah. So?"

"Yeah, so..."

"I'll find one, darlin'. Or I won't and continue solo. Is that a bad thing?"

"No. I just... I want you to be happy, Eli." Stella took his hand in her own and admired those long fingers, palms calloused as they were.

"Stella, my wife," he smiled again, "I *am* happy. For the first time in a really long time. Because you now share my name as well as my life."

Emotions erupted inside her belly, spreading outward like a blast.

"Whatever Gabe does has no bearing on my happiness. So long as he treats my sister well, we're good. But I'll find a heeler, or I won't. Either way, we'll continue to rodeo until you tell me you're ready to settle down."

"No regrets?"

"I've never regretted a single moment with you, Stella Rose. When I wished upon that star, I knew everything would work out so long as I had you by my side. You're here now, and that's where you'll stay. As long as we're together, that's all that matters. Now, kiss me, and let's not talk about Gabe anymore tonight. Please?"

Stella laughed heartily and leaned in to kiss her husband as requested. "Deal."

SNEAK PEEK AT BOOK 1: THE STOIC COWBOY(KRC COWBOYS)

AVERY AND GABE'S STORY

Gabe had told Avery that having sex for the first time would open a can of worms, and he'd been completely correct because sex was all she thought about now, even as she doodled on the paper she was taking notes on in class on at the moment. A mating manatee couple. *Lord help*!

Falling for Gabe had been easy. As easy as slipping into bed that first time with him had been. Their one-time sexual experience had turned into a steaming hot fling, and next thing she knew her brother was beating the ever-living shit out of him and Gabe was confessing his love for her.

It had been fast—and also romantic and fun—but Avery had never felt more alive than she did and grinned as a text came in from Gabe.

Gabe: Thai for dinner, you for dessert? (smirk emoji)

Avery: Um, yes, please, but I want YOU for dessert. (kissy face emoji)

Gabe: Sounds like we're gonna (Cancer zodiac emoji) then (tongue emoji)(kiss emoji)(fire emoji)(cowboy emoji)

Avery: First off, that's the zodiac sign for Cancer, not a 69. Second, emojis—

"...Ms. Kinsen, and what is your take on the matter?"

Shit, shit, shit.

Avery looked up to her professor, Mr. Harris, who crossed his arms over his chest in annoyance. She grimaced, hating that she wasn't paying attention in her favorite class with her favorite instructor.

Lo and behold, the bell rang, and Avery felt the heavens align. *Praise, Jesus!* Saved by the bell. She blushed and looked down to her bag, collecting her things, as her professor assigned homework and she stood.

The sounds of feet shuffling and talking didn't deter him as he said, "Ms. Kinsen, a word please?"

Great white shark!

Avery nodded and headed down the stairs to his desk, where he was propped against the corner. He sat his tall frame down. He was dressed in a black UA polo and khaki trousers. His dark hair came mid-neck, brown eyes were hard, and his jaw was scruffy. He reminded her of a darker, older Austin—her cousin Savannah's husband, who reigned from Alabama.

Mr. Harris waited until the others had left before he spoke. His eyes focused on hers, and she knew a scolding was coming.

"You're back."

She blushed. "I am." She ran a hand through her hair and squeezed her book tighter to her chest.

"It's been a year, Avery."

"I, uh, had family issues. But everything is settled now."

"Is it?" He tilted his head.

She'd not returned after Elias had gone missing, staying only long enough to finish out the semester. Mr. Harris had been the head of the Marine Biology lab then, and she'd sent him an email explaining that she needed to take some time off for family matters and wasn't sure when she'd return to finish out her final year of study. He'd been very understanding then and had been just as understanding when she'd emailed him last month and said she was ready to come back.

It hadn't been an easy decision, but Eli and Stella were back together and happy. They needed time together, without Avery tagging along. She knew she needed to finish college, before she got so far away from it that she didn't. Avery had always been a go-getter and loved learning, but her world had been rattled when she couldn't find her only brother; he'd broken up with Stella following a grave misunderstanding and had gone back into the rodeo circuit. Then her father needing brain surgery had been the clencher to push her back to Corpus Christi. She needed to be home and available for her parents. And she needed school to help ground her again.

"You seem distracted still. I don't know what you've been through and I won't ask. It's none of my business, but just know, I'm here to talk anytime you need to. Ok?" His large hand rested on her forearm.

She gave him a soft smile. "Thank you, Mr. Harris. I appreciate your concern."

Mr. Harris had always had an open-door policy, and she loved that about him. He was a passionate instructor, passionate about taking care of the eco-systems and teaching conservation, plus he was easy to talk to. And it helped that he was kind—and handsome.

"I just need to know you're on board."

"Oh, I am. I promise." She didn't want him thinking she wasn't, so she ignored the buzzing of her phone in her back pocket.

"Good, because I got some big opportunities coming up for you and as one of my best students, I wanted you to get first dibs."

"Wow, really?" Avery perked up, and her professor grinned.

His eyes warmed and he nodded. "You have a passion in you that

I recognize." He winked. "Your thesis on the bottle-nosed dolphin last year was both eye-opening and spot on. I even pushed to have it published in the Journal of Marine Biology and they're discussing it as we speak."

"No way!" Her jaw dropped.

"Yes, way. Girl, you can go all the way to the top. But you have to want it bad enough."

Oh she wanted it! She wanted it so bad she could taste it. She fought the urge to jump up and down. "I do, sir. I swear."

"Good." He nodded, removing his hand from her forearm. "It's good to have you back in class, Avery."

"Thank you. It's good to be back." Excitement blossomed in her belly, and she took a deep breath in.

"Well, I expect an exceptional essay on sea turtles then." He winked again and gave her a broad grin. "And if so, then guess who gets to be lead on our next observation."

"Y—yes sir," she answered, her mind rolling a mile a minute.

"Call me Mick, Avery. *Sir* is my old man." He laughed, and she nodded.

"Thank you. Thank you so much."

"You're welcome. I'll see you on Wednesday. Bright-eyed and bushy-tailed."

"Absolutely!"

***

Mick Harris, associate professor and director of the Marine Biology Program at Texas A&M University Corpus Christi campus, watched the beautiful honey-blonde haired student of his leave his class. She was a great student, or had been last year before abruptly leaving for personal reasons. It'd been a while since he'd had a student so in love with her studies. Avery Kinsen claimed to "be back" and have her head in the game, but Mick knew that wasn't entirely true. She was distracted, and if he had to chance a guess, he'd say it was a boy doing so.

He'd watched too many girls fall hard and fast in college—their first time getting out from under the protective wings of their families and obtaining the freedom they'd been missing out on—only to destroy their dreams when they ended up pregnant, borderline alcoholics, or heartbroken. Avery seemed to be an innocent, naïve girl with high hopes. She was super smart and had what it took to succeed, but she needed to be rid of this distraction before it destroyed her future career.

She was a senior, and her dedication this year would determine so much about where she ended up in her field. It was going to be tough on her. She would be tested and her grades and decisions would be imperative for her placement. He wondered if she was dedicated enough. She said she wanted it, but he knew actions spoke more than words did.

And so far, her actions this first week hadn't said much. He would continue to encourage her, continue to mentor, and guide her in the direction she needed to go. He wanted her to succeed. It was also a **reflection** on him too. But mostly, he sensed her desire to flourish in the field. She was young, she was eager, and she would go far.

She was also stunningly gorgeous. Her eyes were the color of the gulf and she had the most exquisite set of lips he'd ever seen on a woman. He wasn't a pervert, just observant, plus he admired beauty in all forms from chlorophyta (sea algae) to the hide of a killer whale. And Avery Kinsen was beauty personified with hair the color of honey and skin a soft tan, perfectly sun-kissed.

Mick knew she was off-limits to him as a student, but there wasn't a strict policy against it either. Conflict of interest. Didn't mean he couldn't look.

He sat down at his desk and opened his laptop to grade the papers sitting on his desk, noting Avery's handwriting and smiled. Even her handwriting was unique. He traced the S of her name with his finger and began to daydream. He realized he might have a slight crush and scowled.

He'd been single most his life, his career always coming first, but he preferred it that way. Relationships could be destructive, like his parents had been.

For now, he could admire a student for her brains and beauty. For now, his crush was innocent and would remain as such.

To be continued…

***

Book 1: The Stoic Cowboy
A brother's best friend/cowboy romance

Coming soon!

ABOUT SHANNA SWENSON

Shanna Swenson is a cardiac sonographer by day and a weaver of various fictional tales by night.

She's an Amazon bestselling author for her book *Until Kingston*. Shanna's been an avid reader all her life and started writing at the age of fourteen. She finally published her first novel, *Abundance*, after it sat patiently on her laptop for well over fifteen years and she hasn't stopped writing since.

Shanna fits her zodiac sign of Cancer with a capital C and enjoys life's simplest things—sunsets, rain, and coffee—to name a few.

When Shanna's not supporting her fellow indies with her face buried in a book or writing her next novel/novella, she enjoys action and horror movies, pro football, hiking, working out, and traveling with her own "knight in shining armor".

You can find her on the following social media platforms.

Her website is www.shannaswenson.com

facebook.com/shannaswen
twitter.com/shanna_swenson
instagram.com/shannaswen_author
goodreads.com/Shannaswen
amazon.com/author/shannaswenson
pinterest.com/shannaswen
bookbub.com/profile/shanna-swenson
tiktok.com/@shannaswenauthor

ALSO BY SHANNA SWENSON

~THE ABUNDANCE SERIES~

Abundance

Return to Abundance

Escape from Abundance

Stars over Abundance

Abundance Legacy

Starlight Valley: The prequel to Abundance (FREE ebook)

~THE GODS OF THE GRIDIRON SERIES~

UNSPORTSMANLIKE CONDUCT

FALSE START

PASS INTERFERENCE

ILLEGAL FORMATION

PERSONAL FOUL: Prequel novella (FREE ebook)

—

~Aurora Rose Reynold's HEA WORLD~
Until Kingston

~Sin and Secrets Collection~

RISE

Marked by Sin

LEARN MORE AT WWW.SHANNASWENSON.COM